Warlord

ALSO BY ANGUS DONALD

Outlaw
Holy Warrior
King's Man

Warlord

Angus Donald

St. Martin's Press
New York

This is a work of fiction. All of the characters, organizations, and events portrayed in this novel are either products of the author's imagination or are used fictitiously.

www.stmartins.com

Design by Phil Mazzone

The Library of Congress Cataloging-in-Publication Data is available upon request

ISBN 978-1-250-04081-7 (hardcover)
ISBN 978-1-4668-3660-0 (e-book)

St. Martin's Press books may be purchased for educational, business, or promotional use. For information on bulk purchases, please contact Macmillan Corporate and Premium Sales Department at 1-800-221-7945, extension 5442, or write specialmarkets@macmillan.com.

First published in Great Britain by Sphere, an imprint of Little, Brown Book Group, an Hachette UK Company

First U.S. Edition: November 2013

10 9 8 7 6 5 4 3 2 1

For my son, Robert David Hilary Donald,
the real Robin in my life

France, 1194–99
London
ENGLAND
N
Boulogne
St. Omer
County of Flanders
0 100 200 miles
0 100 200 300 km
St. Valéry
Aumale
Barfleur
Rouen
Lisieux
Évreux
Mantes
Paris
NORMANDY
County of the Perche
Seine
BRITTANY
FRANCE
Le Mans
Châteaudun
Fréteval
Vendôme
Loire
Tours
Loches
Atlantic Ocean
AQUITAINE
TOULOUSE
Toulouse
Milly
Gournay
Beauvais
Rouen
Sérifontaine
Seine
Gamaches
Gisors
Suzay
Dangu
Courcelles
Boury
Vaudrail
Château-Gaillard
Gaillon
Epte
Vernon
Eure
Évreux
Mantes
Verneuil
Tillières
Avre
The Vexin

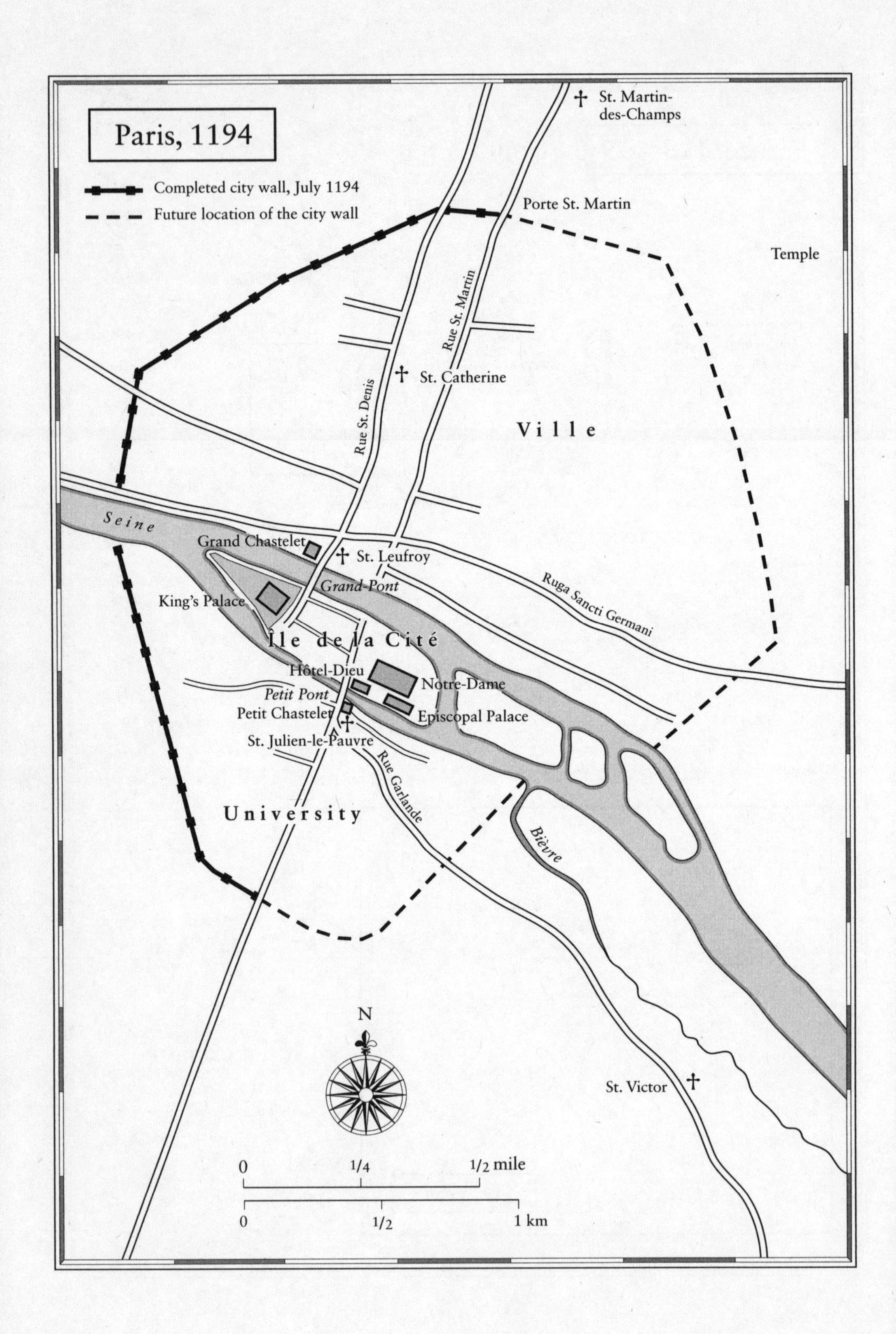
Paris, 1194
Completed city wall, July 1194
Future location of the city wall
St. Martin-des-Champs
Porte St. Martin
Temple
Rue St. Martin
Rue St. Denis
St. Catherine
Ville
Seine
Grand Chastelet
St. Leufroy
Grand-Pont
Ruga Sancti Germani
King's Palace
Île de la Cité
Hôtel-Dieu
Notre-Dame
Petit Pont
Petit Chastelet
Episcopal Palace
St. Julien-le-Pauvre
Rue Garlande
University
Bièvre
N
St. Victor
0
1/4
1/2 mile
0
1/2
1 km

Part One

1

I have been thinking much upon Death of late; my own demise mostly, but also that of beloved comrades. I do not fear the Reaper—I like to think that I never have—and yet I can sense his presence just over the next rise. Death is not the enemy; no, he is an old, old friend coming as promised to collect me and take me on a strange journey. And perhaps when he raps at my chamber door with his bony knuckles I shall even be pleased to see him, weary as I am: for he will take me to a place where I shall see the face of God and, I earnestly pray, be reunited at last with those whom I have loved and who went on before me.

Friend or enemy, he is coming, and soon. I can feel it in my old and creaking bones; I feel it in my bladder that now needs to be emptied almost hourly in the long nighttime, or so it seems. I feel Death in my aching kidneys, in my shortness of breath and my constant, grinding weariness. But I have a task to complete before his shadow stains my threshold: I must set down another tale of my young days as a bold warrior, another tale of my friend Robert Odo, Earl of Locksley; a lord of war, a master thief, King Richard the Lionheart's loyal lieutenant, and the man the people remember best as the outlaw Robin Hood.

I have not recalled this part of my life for a long time; it has been five years since I last took up the quill to write about my strong, youthful self. My daughter-in-law Marie, who, with her husband Osric, runs this manor of Westbury on my behalf, had convinced me that it was not good for me to be dwelling on ancient battles and fruitless quests. She told me with uncommon firmness—it was indeed little short of a command—that I must pay attention to the present, that I must accept the life of the man I am today, white-haired, stooped, and well past sixty winters, and not pine for the man I was and for all my glorious yesterdays. And I think she may be right; for a while, for a year or more, I spent my days at Westbury inside the hall at my writing stand, setting down the old stories of Robin and myself. It was not a healthy life: my eyes grew blurred and tinged with blood, my hands ached from the long hours of scribbling, and my legs protested at their forced stillness, for I stirred little beyond the courtyard for months on end. The unbalanced humors in my torpid body made me irritable, even angry; worse, my mind became clouded and confused. In these past five years, with the writing stand dismantled and packed away and my quills curling, moth-chewed and dusty in an old wooden mug, I have rediscovered the joy of fresh breezes and bright sunlight, and of riding, if only on a gentle ambling mare, and I have joined my hunt servants in flying noble falcons and running the eager hounds over my lands.

However, a visit to Westbury this week by my only grandson, Alan, has changed my mind, and decided me that I must grind black ink, cut a fresh goose feather or two, and pore over parchment once again. That and the fact that Marie has gone to visit her sick cousin Alice in Lincoln, and will not return for a week or more. So here I stand in the hall of the manor of Westbury, in the fair county of Nottinghamshire, casting my mind back forty years, scratching out these lines as quickly as I may and rekindling my old, half-forgotten skills.

He is a delightful lad, Alan; strong-limbed, cheerful, clean and obedient, with a fine seat on a horse and an ear for a pretty tune—though he cannot sing a true note. He serves as a squire to the Earl of Locksley, not my old friend Robin, who has long been in his grave, alas, but his vigorous son, the new earl. Alan is being trained in warfare and gentility at Kirkton Castle, and seemingly has a respectable amount of talent with a blade; and I have received good reports of his courtly conduct, too. But my grandson has almost no notion of events that took place before his birth, fourteen short summers ago. He knows nothing and is oddly incurious about his grandmother Goody, my beloved but blazing-tempered wife, and about his own father Robert, our son. Alan seems to believe that our good Henry of Winchester has been on the throne of England for an eternity, since time began, when it has been no more than four and twenty years. And, while he has heard garbled tales of the noble sovereign King Richard and his long wars in France, he once asked me, I believe quite seriously, if it was true that he had a lion's head. So it is for young Alan, in order that he might learn the truth of these long-ago struggles and the men and women who took part in them, that I set down this tale, this tragic tale of cruel wars and savage devastation, of ugly, unnecessary deaths and the inevitable search for bloody vengeance.

Prince John was on his knees. The youngest son of old King Henry, second monarch of that name, and brother of Lionhearted Richard, now cowered on the greasy, fishy-smelling rushes on the floor of a run-down manor house in Normandy. Tears streamed from reddened eyes down his pale cheeks and he clutched at the right hand of his elder brother, who was standing over him. John's thick shoulder-length reddish hair brushing the back of Richard's hand, his oily teardrops anointing the King's knuckles as he babbled of mercy and forgiveness, swearing before Almighty God and all the saints that he would be a loyal man, a true subject from this moment forth and forever, if only his generous brother could find it in his heart to forgive him. Richard remained silent, looking down coldly at his disheveled sibling. But he did not pull his hand away.

I was watching this strange performance in the solar of the old manor house of Lisieux, in northern Normandy, some thirty miles east of Caen. I was in the small, crowded room off the main hall, standing with a score of knights a pace or two behind King Richard, and I must admit that I was thoroughly enjoying the spectacle. Prince John, once titled Lord of Ireland and Count of Mortain, who had until recently enjoyed the enormous revenues of the plump English counties of Gloucestershire, Nottinghamshire, Somerset, Devon and Cornwall, was once again John Lackland, a man without a clod of earth to his name. Yet his fall was richly deserved, for John had a list of black crimes to his credit as long as my lance: when King Richard had been captured and imprisoned in Germany the year before, this sniveling prince had made an attempt to snatch the throne of England—and he had very nearly succeeded. He had schemed with Richard's enemy, King Philip Augustus of France, to keep the Lionheart imprisoned, hampering the collection of the enormous sum in silver that Richard's captor, the Holy Roman Emperor, had demanded—and even going so far as to join the French King in making a counter-offer to the Emperor if he would hold his brother in chains for another year. But he had failed, God be praised: the ransom had been painfully gathered from an already tax-racked English populace and paid over, and Richard had been freed.

On his release, the Lionheart had crushed the rebellion in England in a matter of weeks. Then, just a few days prior to this painful scene, he had crossed to Normandy with a large, well-provisioned army of seasoned fighting men. His avowed aim was to push King Philip and his French troops out of the eastern part of his duchy, which they had annexed during his long imprisonment, and contain them in the Île de France, the traditional land-locked fief of the French kings. And Prince John, who had so treacherously sided with Philip, was now on his knees before his brother, weeping and begging for forgiveness.

Truly, John had been a bad brother; disloyal, duplicitous and treasonous, and all of this despite Richard's great kindness to him before his departure for the Holy Land. I despised the man—and not only for his underhand actions against my King; I hated him on my own account, too. The previous year I had found myself, unwillingly, in John's service—and I had seen, at close quarters, his evil deeds, his callousness toward the people of England and his unholy delight in wanton cruelty. He had, in fact, ordered my death on two occasions, and it was only by the grace of God and the help of my friend and comrade, my lord Robert, Earl of Locksley, that I had escaped with my life.

I found that I was actually grinning while watching John's kneeling discomfort. King Richard was quite capable of inflicting a terrible vengeance: in the Holy Land, victorious after the fall of Acre, he had ordered the public beheading of thousands of helpless Muslim captives; and while he was retaking the fortress of Nottingham on his return to England, he had casually hanged half a dozen English prisoners of war, just to make a point to the occupants of the castle about his very serious intent. So there was no doubt that Richard was equal to the task of punishing his brother in a fitting manner; but I also knew deep in my heart that he would not. Richard would forgive John, and almost every man in that small overcrowded chamber knew it. For the King loved to show mercy, whenever and wherever he could; it pleased him to display a magnificent clemency as much as to demonstrate his wrathful vengeance. More to the point, he had a very strong sense of family duty. Whatever his crimes, the fellow now snuffling wetly on the floor before him was his own flesh and blood. How could he tell his mother, the venerable Queen Eleanor, that he had executed her youngest son?

John continued to babble and sob at the feet of the King—who remained stern and silent—when a voice from the far side of the chamber, a dry, cold voice, with a hint of the nasal twang of Gascony, called out: "Sire, give him to me, I beseech you. Give him into my hands and I will strip every inch of skin from his living body and leave him in raw, screaming agony, begging for the sweet mercy of death."

Prince John's whimpering stopped as if his mouth had been plugged; his bowed red head whipped round to the right and he stared into the gloom on the far side of the chamber from whence the voice had come, seeking its owner. I knew that voice. It belonged to Mercadier, King Richard's longtime captain of mercenaries, a grim and merciless man. Mercadier had been fighting on Richard's behalf in Normandy longer than any of us and, as a warrior and leader of several hundred battle-hardened paid fighters, he was worthy of respect—yet he had the most unsavory reputation of any man in Richard's army. His men, while fanatically loyal to the King, were, when unleashed to ravage an enemy's territory, capable of a savagery that was certainly bestial and very nearly demonic. There were tales of nuns raped and crucified, churches looted and burned to their foundations, of babies tossed into the air and caught on his laughing men's spearpoints; the streets of towns captured by these men quite literally ran with hot, fresh blood. A ghastly foretaste of the Hell they would doubtless one day inhabit followed these soldiers of fortune, these *routiers*, as they were sometimes called, wherever they plied their ungodly trade.

Mercadier stared boldly at the King from the far side of the chamber, awaiting a response to his bloodthirsty offer—which I had not the smallest doubt was entirely genuine. He was not a handsome man, I reflected, although his looks were certainly striking. Beneath a mop of jet black, longish hair, which looked as if it had been cut with a sword, and probably had been, the mercenary captain's dead brown eyes stared out of a swarthy, sun-darkened face that was bisected by a long, jagged scar that ran from his left temple, across his broad nose, to the bottom right-hand corner of his mouth. In the slanting afternoon light of the chamber that long yellow-white cicatrice gave him an almost monstrous appearance, like some misshapen creature from one of the Devil's uglier realms. Mercadier's offer to flay the royal traitor hung in the air: the silence thickened, clotted, until John gave a little coughing sob and dropped his red head into his two cupped hands.

Then I heard a deep voice, growling like a bear, half under its breath: "Oh, for God's sake, Sire, have we not had enough of this tomfoolery?" and looked to my left where William the Marshal, Earl of Striguil, Lord of Pembroke, Usk, Longueville, Orbec and Meuller, and dozens of other castles and manors in England and Normandy, was scowling over the King's shoulder. This veteran warrior—perhaps the finest in the army, and a man of unimpeachable courage and chivalry, a knight *sans peur et sans reproche*, as the *trouvères* put it—was looking disgustedly at the tableau before him, impatient for this pantomime of contrition and forgiveness to come to an end.

Finally, the King spoke, with an edge of grumpiness in his voice, the tone of a man whose private pleasure has been curtailed. "Oh, all right. Get up now, John, will you? And let us put an end to all this nonsense."

"Do you forgive me then, Sire?" asked Prince John, his white-and-red blotched face staring up piteously at his elder brother, looking very much like a well-whipped lapdog.

Richard nodded. "Let us put it behind us. You are no more than a child who has been badly advised by your friends. Come, brother, on your feet."

As John rose, I caught his eye and he gave me a glare of such ferocity and hatred that for a moment I was taken aback. I managed to suppress my broad grin and adopt a stern expression while our eyes were engaged. But I understood that look. Quite apart from our past involvements—and the fact that, as he saw it, I had tricked and betrayed him—he was a proud man in his late twenties, the son of a king, who had been forced to humble himself in front of a room full of his brother's knights—and, to boot, he had been called a stupid child to his face. His humiliation was complete.

Richard gave no sign of having seen the spark of fury in John's eye. He raised him up and kissed his younger sibling, clapped an arm around his shoulders and said: "Come on, let us all go and have a bite of dinner together. What have you got for us today, Alençon?" The King addressed his question to a gloomy young Norman knight standing by the doorway, who owned the hall in which we were gathered. The knight sighed lugubriously; housing and feeding a royal household full of active hungry men put a heavy strain on the purse of even the richest lord: "We have two pair of salmon, Sire; caught fresh from the Touques this morning. And there is cold venison, left over from yesterday. Some boiled ham. Rabbit pie, too, I think. We have a milk pudding . . ."

"Excellent!" Richard clapped his hands together, cutting short his host's doleful speech. "Then let us eat at last."

As we all trooped into the hall, the knights joking quietly with each other as they filed through the door, I heard one say a mite too loudly: "He's no more than a naughty little boy!" His companion half-laughed, then frowned and said: "Have a care, Simon, he's still royalty; he might even be King one day and, if so, I doubt he'll be as forgiving as his brother to those who have crossed him."

At first light the next morning, well fed and rested, I rode out of Lisieux at the head of a column of a hundred armed men. At my left shoulder, on a quiet brown rouncey, rode Thomas ap Lloyd, my squire, a serious dark-haired youth on the lip of manhood, who cared for my weapons and kit, spare lances and shields, cooking and camping equipment and so on, with a zeal and efficiency that verged on the miraculous. At my right shoulder rode Hanno, a tough, shaven-headed Bavarian man-at-arms, who had attached himself to me on the long road back to England from the Holy Land, and who treated me with the friendly disrespect warranted by an oak-hard killer who had taught me so much of the arts of war, ambush and bloody slaughter.

Behind Hanno and Thomas rode Owain the Bowman, a short and deep-chested captain of archers—my second in command. Owain carried a banner on a tall pole: an image of a snarling wolf's head in gray and black on a field of white. It was the standard of my lord and master the Earl of Locksley, whom I had left behind in Yorkshire to recover from a javelin wound to his left thigh, taken at the siege of Nottingham in March.

It was now May, in the Year of the Incarnation eleven hundred and ninety-four, the fifth year of the reign of King Richard, and a magnificent spring morning. The fruit trees were still adorned with the remains of their delicate lacy blossom, the grass on the verges glowed vivid green, birds called and swooped about the column, men smiled for no particular reason, the sky was a deep, innocent blue, with a scattering of plump clouds. The world seemed fresh and new and filled with possibilities; and I was on a mission of great import and no little danger for my beloved King.

Because Robin had been wounded, as had his huge right-hand man "Little" John Nailor, I had been given the honor of leading a company of a hundred of Robin's men to Normandy as part of King Richard's army. I had never had sole command of such a force before, and I have to admit that the feeling was intoxicating: I felt like a mighty warlord of old; the leader of a band of brave men riding forth in search of honor and glory.

The bold Locksley men of my war-band were a mixed force of roughly equal numbers of men-at-arms and archers—all of them well mounted. The men-at-arms were lightly armored but each was the master of a deadly lance twice as long as a man. In addition to his lance, each cavalryman had been issued with a protective padded jacket, known as an aketon or gambeson, a steel helmet and sword, and a thick cloak of dark green that marked them out as Robin's men. Many of the men had additional pieces of armor that they had provided themselves: old-fashioned kite-shaped or even archaic round shields, iron-reinforced leather gauntlets, mail coifs and leggings and the like, scraps of iron, steel and leather, strapped here and there to protect their bodies in the mêlée; and many had armed themselves with extra weapons that ranged from long knives and short-handled axes to war hammers and nail-studded cudgels.

The mounted archers were mostly Welshmen who boasted that they could shoot the eye out of a starling on the wing. The bowmen had each been issued with a short sword, gambeson, helmet and green cloak, as well as a six-foot-long yew bow, and had two full arrow bags, each containing two dozen arrows, close at hand.

Under a billowing red linen surcoat emblazoned over the chest with a wild boar in black, I was clad in a full suit of mail armor—an extremely costly gift from Robin. The mail, made of interlocking links of finely drawn iron, covered me from toe to fingertip, saddle seat to skull, in a layer that was very nearly impenetrable to a blade. I had a long, beautifully made sword, worth almost as much as the armor, hanging on my left-hand side, and a very serviceable, long triangular-bladed stabbing dagger, known as a misericorde, on the right of my belt. A short, flat-topped wood-and-leather shield that tapered to a point at the bottom was slung from my back, painted red—or gules, as the heralds would have it—and decorated in black with the same image of a walking or *passant* wild boar as adorned my chest, an animal I had long admired for its ferocity in battle and its enduring courage when faced with overwhelming odds. I was proud of my new device, which, since I had been knighted—by no lesser personage than King Richard himself—I was now entitled to bear, and which I had formally registered with the heralds. A conical steel cap with a heavy nose-guard and a long ash lance with a leaf-shaped blade completed my panoply.

We had sailed from Portsmouth in the middle of May, after a delay of several days due to bad weather, and landed at Barfleur to tremendous celebration from the Norman folk, overjoyed at the return of their rightful Duke. On that fine spring day, a week later, trotting southeast out of Lisieux on my tar-black stallion Shaitan, I felt the familiar lapping of excitement in my belly—I would soon be going into battle for the first time on Norman soil and taking my sword to the enemy. The King had charged me with reinforcing the garrison of the castle of Verneuil-sur-Avre, forty miles to the southeast, which was now besieged by King Philip. In truth, I had volunteered for the task:

I had a very good reason for wanting to preserve one of the occupants of Verneuil from the wrath of our King's enemies. The plan was to use surprise and speed to break through the French king's lines to the north of the fortress. Once inside, we were ordered to bring hope and good cheer to the besieged, stiffen their defense, and to reassure them that Richard and his whole army of some three thousand men were only a matter of days behind us.

Apart from my private reasons for wanting to succeed in this task, I was very conscious of the fact that, as captain of the Locksley contingent, I was representing Robin. While I knew that King Richard had confidence in me as a soldier, I wanted to do well in this task for Robin, my liege lord, and for all the men of the Locksley lands. But I was more than a little concerned about being able to fulfill Richard's instructions. He had spoken breezily of our galloping through King Philip's battle lines, as if they were merely a cobweb to be brushed aside. I didn't think it would be so easy. So, when we stopped at noon to rest the horses and snatch a bite to eat, I detailed Hanno and two mounted archers to ride several miles forward as scouts and bring back a report on the French dispositions.

As we approached the vicinity of Verneuil the mood in the column changed significantly. I put out more scouts to the east and south and we all rode in our full armor, with lances at the ready, swords loose in their scabbards and our eyes constantly searching the copses, woods and hedgerows for signs of horsemen. The flat land we rode through that afternoon, once so rich and well cultivated, now bore the harsh imprint of war. King Philip's Frenchmen had been ravaging the farms and villages hereabouts with all the usual savagery of soldiers let loose to plunder and burn at will. It was a common tactic that allowed the occupying army to provision itself at no cost to its commanders and at the same time destroyed enemy lands and deprived the local lord of the bounty of his wheat and barley fields, his root crops, animals and orchards.

We rode through a battered, scorched landscape, the crops burned down to charred stubble, the hamlets black and reeking, the bodies of slaughtered peasants—men, women and even children—lying unburied at the roadside, with the crows pecking greedily at their singed corpses. We did not stop to bury the dead like Christians, not wishing to delay our advance, though we could all feel the presence of unquiet spirits as we rode more or less in silence through those cinder-dusted, desecrated lands.

I was, however, sorely tempted to have the men stop and dig a decent grave for a young fair-haired peasant that we passed hanging by his neck from a walnut tree. There was something horribly familiar about the canted angle of his neck and the awful vulnerability of his dangling bare feet. I realized as I rode past that gently swaying corpse that it put me in mind of my father's death, ten years before, in the little hamlet just outside Nottingham where I was born. My father Henry, my mother Ellen and my two younger sisters Aelfgifu and Coelwyn and I all scratched a living from a few strips of land in the fields on the edge of the village. Despite long days of hard labor, we were barely able to feed ourselves; but there had been an abundance of laughter and happiness in our small cottage, and much music and singing. My father had a wonderful voice, slow-rolling and sweet like a river of honey, and my fondest memories of that simple household were of my mother and father singing together, their voices intertwining, their melody lines looping and folding over each other in the smoky air of the low, one-room cottage like gold and silver threads in a fine castle tapestry. My father was the one who taught me to sing—and it was thanks to that skill that I first came to the attention of my master Robin Hood. Six years later, I was his personal *trouvère*—a "finder" or composer of songs—and also his trusted lieutenant. In a way, I owed my extraordinary advancement from dirt-poor laborer to lord of war to my father's love of music.

He had been a strange man, my father. I had been told that he was the second son of an obscure French knight, the Seigneur d'Alle, and, as such, he had been destined for the Church. He had duly become a monk, a singer at the great cathedral of Notre-Dame in Paris. But somehow he had been disgraced and forced to flee to England. Robin, who had known him then, had told me that some valuable objects had gone missing from the cathedral and my father had been accused of their theft—accusations that my father had strenuously denied. Nevertheless, he had been cast out of the Church and had had to make a living with his voice. As a masterless *trouvère*, he had traveled to England and wandered the country singing for his supper and a place to lay his head at the castles across the land, but tidings of his expulsion from Paris ran ahead of him and he could find no secure position; no lord was willing to take a thief into his household. Eventually, during his long wanderings he met my mother, Ellen—a lovely woman in her youth—and married her and submitted to the dull but stable life of a common man working the land. I remember him cheerfully saying to me once, when I was no more than five or six years old: "None of us knows what God has in store for him, Alan; we may not have fine-milled bread on the board or fur-trimmed silk on our backs, but we can wrap ourselves in love, and we can always fill our mouths with song."

My family was a contented one, happy even; I might well have inherited the strips of land my father worked and been trudging behind a pair of plow oxen on them to this day, had it not been for his untimely death. Before dawn one morning, as we slept—my mother, father, myself and my two sisters, all snugged up together on the big straw-stuffed mattress in our tiny hovel—half a dozen armed men burst through the door and dragged my father outside. There was no pretense of a trial; the sergeant in charge of the squad of men-at-arms merely announced that the Sheriff of Nottinghamshire had declared that my father was a thief and an outlaw. Then his men wrestled a rope around my father's neck and summarily hanged him from the nearest oak tree.

I watched them do it, at the raw age of nine; restrained by a burly man-at-arms and trying not to cry as my father kicked and soiled himself and choked out his life before my terrified eyes. Perhaps I am weak, but I've never been able to watch a hanging since—even when the punishment is well deserved—without a sense of horror.

That act of unexpected violence destroyed our family. My mother lost the land that my father had plowed and, to stave off destitution, she was forced to gather firewood each day and barter it to her neighbors for food or sell it to any that would buy; and few would. Why hand over a precious silver penny for sticks of timber when there was plenty of kindling to be had for free in the woodlands not three miles away? We slowly began to starve: my two sisters died of the bloody flux two years after my father's death, a lack of nourishment making them too feeble to fight off the sickness when it struck. Faced with a stark choice, I became a thief; cutting the leather straps that secured the purses of rich men to their belts and making away with their money into the thick crowds of Nottingham market. I like to think that I was good at it—I have always been lucky, all my long life. But, of course, one cannot rely on luck alone. I was thirteen when I was caught in the act of stealing a beef pie; the Sheriff would surely have lopped off my right hand if I hadn't managed to escape. That was when I went to join Robin Hood's band of men in the trackless depths of Sherwood Forest.

I never forgot that it was the Sheriff of Nottinghamshire—a black-hearted bastard named Sir Ralph Murdac—who had sent his men to hang my father. Even as a child I swore to be revenged on him. Years passed and I learned to fight like gentlefolk, a-horse with sword and lance, and joined King Richard on the Great Pilgrimage to the Holy Land. At the siege of Nottingham, on our return, I had the good fortune to capture the same Ralph Murdac, who was defying the King, and deliver him bound hand and foot to my royal master. I had meant to kill him, to cut his head off in the name of my father—and I would have done so gladly, but for one thing. As he knelt before me, bound, helpless, his neck stretched for my sword, he told me that if I killed him I would never discover the name of the man who was truly responsible for my father's death. In the face of Death, Murdac claimed that he had been acting on the instructions of a very powerful man, a "man you cannot refuse." If I spared him, he said, he would reveal the man's name.

And so I spared him. But, as God willed it, he never told me the name of the man who had ordered Henry d'Alle to be destroyed. King Richard had hanged Murdac the next day, as a warning to the rebellious defenders of Nottingham Castle, before I could thoroughly question him.

I felt the weight of my father's death—and the need to find the man who had ordered it—like a lead cope around my shoulders. But I was a blindfolded man groping in the dark: I had no idea who this powerful man—this "man you cannot refuse"—could be, nor how I might discover his identity and, almost as important to me, find out *why* he had reached out his long arm to extinguish my father's existence. So, although I was in France on behalf of Robin, commanding his troops, I had chosen to be here because it brought me closer to the place of my father's birth, and perhaps closer to solving the riddle of his death.

For the moment I pushed these thoughts of vengeance and powerful, shadowy enemies away, to concentrate on the task at hand. A scout rode up on a sweat-lathered horse and reported that the enemy lines were no more than three miles away. The sun was sinking low in the sky and we made our camp, quiet and fireless in a small copse in a fold of a shallow valley. Sentries set, and gnawing on a stick of dried mutton, I conferred with Hanno, Owain and the returned scouts.

"The castle of Verneuil still defies Philip," began Hanno. "I see Richard's lions flying above the tower."

I nodded and swallowed a lump of roughly chewed mutton with difficulty. I found that my mouth was dry. "Earthworks?" I said. "Siege engines?"

"They dig earthworks, yes," said Hanno, scratching at his round shaven head. "But one, two trenches and a little wall to protect the diggers; they are not very far along. But I see four big siege engines, three trebuchets, I think, and a mangonel; also small stuff, balistes and onagers. The walls have taken some hurt, and the tower, too, but they are holding." Hanno paused and frowned. "But the siege does not feel very . . . lively, very quick. The Frenchmen are not working so hard, just waiting for the castle to fall. There is no discipline, no proper order. The men are taking their ease around their fires—drinking, gambling, sleeping. I do not think it will be difficult for us to break through."

"How many are they?" I asked the Bavarian warrior.

"King Philip is there; his fleur-de-lys flies over a big gold tent to the east of the castle. And many of his barons are with him, too, I think. So, perhaps two thousand knights and men-at-arms; crossbowmen, too—yes, two thousand men in all, maybe more."

I blinked at him. "Two thousand?"

"I think so," said Hanno. "But they will never expect us. We can get into the castle without much difficulty, if they will open the gate to us. After that . . ." He shrugged.

I had been told that the besieged garrison of Verneuil numbered just over a hundred men, and I looked at my own little command, my puny war-band, wrapping themselves in their thick green cloaks and bedding down for the night around me, and thought to myself—*ten to one. Not good.* But I said nothing, trying to appear as if I had absolute confidence in the success of our mission.

"Then we'd better kill as many Frenchmen as possible on the way in," I said, achieving a shaky nonchalance. "I think we will play this one straight as an arrow; we'll go in early tomorrow morning, kill the pickets, ride hard, cut through the enemy lines and proceed directly up to the castle's front gate. Hard and fast. Understood?"

There were murmurs of agreement.

"Fine. Now, let's sleep. But might I have a word with you, Owain? I need your bow to get a message into the castle. I need to make damn sure they open the gates to us."

The French sentry was alert: from his position on a small rise perhaps half a mile outside Verneuil he saw our column approaching slowly from the southwest. Though he had been reclining on the grassy ridge, taking his ease, he leaped to his feet the moment he spotted us emerging from a small wood a mile away and shouted something inaudible over his shoulder. As we walked our horses up the slight slope, affecting the tired boredom of men at the end of a long and uneventful journey, two horsemen in bright mail, with gaudy pennants on their lances, cantered down the slope to meet us.

With Hanno at my side, I spurred forward to greet the two knights, leaving the column behind me with strict instructions to continue their pose as exhausted travelers until I gave the signal. When we were twenty yards from the two strangers, the foremost one called loudly, angrily in French for us to halt. And Hanno and I reined in and sat obediently staring at the two heavily armed men.

"Who are you?" shouted the first knight in French. "What is your name and what business have you here?"

"I am the Chevalier Henri d'Alle," I said in the same language. For some reason the only false name I could think of was my father's; but then he had been much on my mind of late. "I serve Geoffrey, Count of the Perche," I continued, "and my men and I are riding to join my master's liege lord, King Philip of France, at Verneuil."

My answer seemed to calm the knight. He glanced at my boar-shield and nodded to himself; it was common knowledge that Count Geoffrey had revoked his proper allegiance to King Richard and come over to King Philip's side. It was also known that, despite pleas from King Philip for him to join the fight in Normandy, Geoffrey had refused his blandishments and had stubbornly remained in his fortress of Chateâudun fifty miles to the south of Verneuil. It was a plausible enough story, although it would not bear too close a questioning. The knight nodded and beckoned us to approach. "We will escort you to the King," he said in a more friendly tone.

Signaling to the company to come forward, I walked my horse over to the two knights. The four of us began to climb the gentle slope up to the ridgeline together. The knight beside me, who had politely introduced himself as Raymond de St. Geneviève, started to question me about recent events in the Perche, which I answered only in monosyllabic grunts—I knew almost nothing of the county, bar that it was famous for its horses and reputed to be full of hills and valleys and dark haunted forests. As we reached the top of the rise, the knight was frowning at my surly answers to his friendly questions and beginning to look at me curiously. I changed the subject.

"What news of the King of England?" I asked my companion. "Will he attack here?"

"Oh, he is still in Barfleur, we are told, marshaling his forces. His rabble of an army, many of them no more than filthy paid men, *routiers* and the like, is far away . . . ," said St. Geneviève with a dismissive roll of his shoulders.

I could hear the company coming up onto the ridge behind me, and out of the corner of my eye I could see Hanno fiddling with something out of sight, apparently a loose strap on the far side of his saddle. My own right hand went to the belt at my waist. Before me, spread out in a wide semicircle, was the encampment of the soldiers of King Philip—all two thousand of them—a great swath of drab blue tents and brightly colored pavilions and browny-green brushwood and turf shacks, a spill of campfires, a smear of gray smoke, the mounds of fresh earth from the siege workings, neat lines of tethered horses, stacks of fodder, weapons, shields and spears, and piles of baggage. Beyond the army, I could see the fortress of Verneuil, a gray, stone-walled block crouched on the north bank of the River Avre, with four square towers, one at each corner, and a large wooden gate in the center of the front wall. A gaudy red-and-gold flag fluttered from a squat stone keep in the middle of the castle, and I knew that Hanno had spoken true: the little garrison was still bravely defying the King of France and all his legions.

"What was that you said?" I cupped my left hand to my ear and leaned forward from the back of Shaitan toward the knight. "What did you say just then about the English?"

The knight looked perplexed. He leaned toward me in the saddle and enunciated loudly and clearly as if I were an imbecile. "I said: King Richard is in Barfleur—those cowardly English rascals are still many leagues away."

"Let me tell you a secret," I said quietly, leaning even further toward him and placing my left hand in a companionable fashion on his right shoulder. Obligingly, he bent his head to me until it was only inches from mine.

"They are not." And I swung my right hand up, hard, and slammed the point of my misericorde, my long killing dagger, through the soft skin under his chin and on, up through the root of his tongue and the roof of his mouth and deep into his skull. His whole body jerked wildly upward with the force of my sudden blow, but I kept him firmly in the saddle with my left hand on his shoulder. His eyes, massive with shock and pain, stared into mine as he took leave of his life. He coughed once, expelling a great scarlet gobbet of blood, and his hands scrabbled briefly at my right fist on the handle of the long blade still embedded under his chin, then he very slowly slid over backward out of the saddle and away from me, hitting the earth like a loose sack of turnips, his tumbling fall tearing my dagger free from his throat.

"Perfect," said Hanno, grinning at me savagely from his saddle and displaying his awful rotting teeth. He wrenched his own small hand axe from where it was embedded in the top of the second knight's spine and callously kicked the unstrung, speechless, dying man out of the saddle. "A perfect kill, Alan!" Hanno it seemed was very pleased with my performance. "A soldier should be very happy to die from such a perfect strike. I teach you well."

Neither of our victims had made more than a moan of complaint before we sent them to God. My mounted company was coming up the slope at a fast canter and we barely paused once they reached the top of the low hill. "Now," I shouted to the oncoming horsemen, their young faces rosy with the light of imminent battle, "now, we ride for our lives—ride for the castle gate, don't stop for anything. Ride as if the Devil himself were on your heels!"

2

WE CHARGED DOWN THAT SLIGHT SLOPE in two loose packs: the light cavalry—the mounted men-at-arms with their long lances—in the first group, the horse archers and our few pack animals, led by Thomas my squire, behind them. The plan, if our crude maneuver could be described as such, was for us to sweep down the slope, gallop across the trampled fields of wheat before the castle and ride directly up to its gates, which were about eight hundred paces ahead of our horses' noses. The fifty lancers in the vanguard of our company were a hammer blow designed to smash the enemy out of our way and clear the path for the mounted archers and baggage animals, and then it would be down to speed and brutal sword-work as we all tried to cut our way through the entire French army. Trying not to remember that there were two thousand enemy soldiers between us and safety, I gripped my well-trained destrier Shaitan hard with my knees, couched my lance, shouted my war cry: "Westbury!" and spurred down the slope at the head of the first wave of our men. The cavalrymen immediately behind me were screaming and whooping too; and with the pounding of the horses' hooves, we made a spectacular and noisy entrance to the battlefield as we charged down onto the flat land before the castle—and yet the enemy were initially very slow to react. The murders of the two knights on the ridge had gone unnoticed, it seemed, and the first that the French soldiery knew of our attack was the sight of fifty spear-wielding, screaming men on fast horses thundering down the gentle slope into their midst.

A man-at-arms in a knee-length hauberk was stirring the contents of a huge cooking pot hung over a fire as we charged into the camp. He gawped at me as I galloped straight at him: he was unarmed, apart from an eating knife at his belt, and I lifted my lance point above his head deliberately to miss as Shaitan and I charged toward him, nudging my horse with my left knee in a battle signal to my huge mount that I'd practiced hundreds of times in the three months that I had had him. Shaitan responded immediately, changing his line of gallop smoothly and smashing his black glossy shoulder into the man as we passed, the fellow reeling away and stumbling into the dust. Another fellow ran into my path, a brave man, unarmored, dressed only in a dirty chemise, braies and torn, muddy hose, who pointed a crossbow at me and pulled the lever to send a foot-long bolt of hissing death at my face. My boar-device shield came up instinctively, the moment I saw him on my quarter, and I felt the impact reverberate in the bone of my left forearm as the quarrel thwocked into the center of my stout shield. I turned my head to glare at him as I galloped past, and saw one of the horsemen in my wake, behind me and to my left, punch his lance deep in the man's chest and leave him writhing in his death agony on the ground.

It must be conceded that, once they had realized that they were under attack, the French reacted well: a ripple of sound and movement traveled out through the huge camp from our point of impact. The whole surface of the encampment seemed to shiver like the skin of a horse that is troubled by stinging flies. Men-at-arms were running hither and yon, calling their comrades to arms. Horsemen were swinging up into the saddle, whether they were in armor or not—I even saw one knight leap astride his charger bare-chested, helmetless, shouting at his squire to throw him shield and lance. From my bounding saddle, I could see the walls of the castle clearly, six hundred paces away, the battlements dotted with the black heads of the defenders—and something most curious struck my eye: on the dark wood of the tightly shut doors of the main gate some crude hand had drawn a giant image of a man wearing a large crown in thick white chalk lines. The man was pictured standing sideways, and his right arm reached between his legs to where a round-headed, spiked battle mace was depicted as springing from his loins. Underneath the chalk drawing the words "Philip Augustus" had been scrawled.

I pulled my attention back to the situation at hand. A crowd of knights, perhaps twenty men, armed and armored any old how in their haste to join battle, but mainly in hauberks and helms, lance and sword, were forming up directly to my front, barring the way to the castle. I shouted: "On me, on me. Westbury! Westbury!" and guided Shaitan to head straight for the foremost knight, a big man on a bay horse, with a flat-topped tubular helmet and a bright gold-and-white device, a stag, on his shield.

He leveled his lance and spurred forward to meet me and I had only a heartbeat to raise my shield and aim my own spear at his lower belly before we collided with an ear-numbing crash of metal and splintering wood. A gigantic blow smashed my shield painfully against my left shoulder. The long ash lance in my right hand snapped in two, and though I didn't have a moment to glance down at his midsection as we passed each other, I saw by the look of shock in his eyes through the slits of his helmet that I had found my target.

To my left I watched Hanno dip his spear and neatly skewer a half-armored man on a frightened gray horse. But other enemy horsemen surged forward, swords and spear-points glinting in the sharp air. One man cut at me with a sword as he rode past, and missed, and I stopped a glancing axe blow from another with my quarrel-impaled shield. The rest of my cavalrymen were all around me now, protecting me, fighting like men possessed and steadily hacking, pushing, grinding their way forward. Pulling out my own side arm—a beautiful sword, with a long, slim but strong blade and the word "Fidelity" engraved in golden letters on it, and a great jewel set in the pommel—I looked to the castle. It was a scant four hundred paces away and I could clearly see the marks the French trebuchets had made on the walls. One section of the battlements east of the gate had been badly smashed, although it appeared the defenders had rebuilt that part with the rubble, and barrels and planks of green wood.

There were French troops coming from both sides, and from behind us; the enemy was fully alerted. An enemy knight charged out of nowhere and jabbed his lance at me and I flicked it out of the way with my sword, and cut savagely at his neck as he rode past me, my blade crunching against his mail. More of the foe were swarming toward us on foot, hundreds of them; the whole camp, it seemed, was flooding toward us like a great incoming tide of men. The archers had caught up with the vanguard and were now fighting alongside my lancers; hacking with their short swords and axes, stabbing with long knives. The back of a horse is no place to use a war bow. But I could see that my men were dying, as well as killing the enemy; their horses were crushed against the mounts of our foes, their blades ringing against helm and shield; though some were surrounded merely by a seething press of footmen. Somehow we had lost the momentum of our charge and become embroiled in a mêlée—a vicious slogging, hacking, shoving match against an enemy with twenty times our numbers.

It was a battle we could only lose.

To my right I could see Owain at the center of a swarm of enemy knights, and men on foot, too, stabbing up with long lethal pole arms from a distance. They were attracted like wasps to wine by the black-and-white wolf's head banner that he bore: Robin's banner. Though the powerful bowman was laying about mightily with his short sword, and knocking men back with each stroke, they were too many. Before I could get close I saw him take a deep spear thrust to the small of the back from a French pikeman, and watched helplessly as a knight rode in and sliced deeply into the meat of his shoulder with a backhand blow from his long sword. The air was thick with the screams of dying men, the crack of metal on wood, the wild shouts and oaths of the combatants, and flying clods kicked up by the circling horses' hooves. A stench of fresh blood, horse dung and spilled guts filled my nose.

I shouted: "Men of Locksley! To me, to me!" I swung my blade hard at a mounted foeman but he jerked his horse aside just in time. My path cleared for one instant and I dug my spurs in Shaitan's side and launched myself through the gap toward Owain and the battle standard. Shaitan knocked a footman flying and I chopped into the arm of a passing half-armored knight, and he reeled away, swaying in his seat, fountaining blood and screaming the Blessed Virgin's name. Then I was knee to knee with Owain; my friend was sliding from me, his body limp in the saddle, and I reached out a hand and hauled him back into his place—but I could see life ebbing fast. His eyes were fluttering and his face was as white as a field of fresh snow. But he had the strength to rise, reach over and push the staff of the wolf's head flag into my shield hand before slumping back in the saddle.

I let the shield hang loose by its loops on my left forearm, lifted the standard high in the air, and screamed: "A Locksley! A Locksley—to the gates. To the gates!" I looked round and was relieved to see that a score or so of my men were forcing their way through the murderous crush toward me. When I glanced back at Owain I saw that his saddle was empty. There was no time to gather his body or even to mourn: I gave a signal to Shaitan, putting a mailed toe hard into his flank behind the off-side foreleg. My huge stallion reared up on his haunches, the forelegs windmilling in front of his long black nose, cracking an enemy footman's skull and clearing a small space immediately in front of us. I spurred my mount into that space, swung Fidelity at the helmet of an enemy knight, drove the spiked butt-end of the standard into another man's face, and urged Shaitan forward once more. I bellowed: "Come on, come on. A Locksley—to the gates! Follow me to the gates!" And my men were coming toward me, pushing their horses through the struggling crowds of enemy. With the battle standard in my left hand and my sword in my right, I charged straight into a milling knot of enemy horsemen, guiding Shaitan with only my knees and killing with a desperate ferocity; dropping one man with a blow to the back of the neck, hacking deep into another's face, ducking a sword stroke that whistled over my helmet, and cutting down another man-at-arms with a savage backhand across the spine as I passed him—but with Shaitan's weight and a pack of yelling Locksley men pressing close behind me, we burst through the cloud of enemy cavalry and suddenly we were free and clear, with only two hundred yards to go before the castle gates, which were black and forbidding and closed tight ahead of us. The scurrilous chalk-drawn image of King Philip seemed to beckon us on with his phallic mace as we all barreled forward at a frantic, pounding, heart-in-mouth gallop toward the castle gates.

An evil thought struck me: what if the defenders refused to open for us? Had they received our message: a note tied to an arrow and shot into the castle the night before by Owain? Did they know that we were friends and this was not some lunatic cavalry assault on their unbroken walls?

We were clear of the French horsemen now, with only a hundred yards to go, the rattling drumbeat of hundreds of hooves filling my ears, and looking behind I could see at least a good sixty or perhaps seventy so of our men, mostly archers but some lancers, too—including little Thomas, galloping on his brown mount, half-crouched in the saddle and still leading the packhorses, his mouth a grim line of determination. Hanno was on my left shoulder, urging his horse to greater speed with smacks from the flat of his sword. We thundered forward—and the gates remained firmly shut before us. The French were regrouping; I could hear shrill trumpets sounding above the thunder of our pounding steeds. I called upon St. Michael, the warrior archangel—"Oh holy one, let them open the gates! I beg you, let them open the gates!" But I knew in my heart that the defenders had not received our message: we'd be pinned between the stout portal of the castle and the might of King Philip's whole army and be crushed like a beetle under a workman's boot.

Fifty paces to go: I opened my mouth to give the order for us to veer right to attempt to make some kind of escape to the west. And stopped just before I gave tongue. Was it true? Could it be? Oh praise be to God Almighty: for the great gate of Verneuil was opening, men were clustered around the two huge wooden doors that were slowly swinging inward under their combined efforts.

My heart soared like a lark in summer; I lifted Robin's wolf's head banner high in the air and shouted: "Westbury!" at the top of my aching lungs, and what seemed like only a dozen heartbeats later Shaitan and I were pounding through the open gates, and reining in puffing and panting before the bulk of the old stone keep, my wonderful black stallion rearing up and dancing momentarily on his hindquarters with the excitement of the day. My men poured in behind me and, in moments, the central courtyard of Verneuil was filled with red-faced, shouting, laughing, sweating folk on horseback. And as the tail end of my little company—those who had survived the desperate charge and the short but murderous mêlée—cantered into the open space, the defenders swung the great doors closed, just in time, and barred them tight against the enemy with a welcome crash of heavy timber.

We were safe.

We had lost twenty-three men in that mad gallop through the enemy ranks—nearly a quarter of my force. And while the survivors, many with light wounds, grinned at each other, swapped jests and slapped backs, I could not help feeling that I should have handled things better. So much for Alan the great warlord: I had lost one fourth of my men and my second in command in the first clash of arms, and we still had to hold this castle for several days until King Richard arrived with the relieving army. So, while I was surely happy to be alive and unwounded, I was not in the least proud of myself. And I was already missing Owain—his kindly face and reliable strength. I offered up a prayer for his soul and begged God's forgiveness for not reaching him in time to save him.

This was not the moment for self-recrimination, however. The angry French horsemen had followed us down toward the gates and I speedily sent as many archers as I could to the battlements to take some revenge for their fallen comrades. After a dozen French knights and men-at-arms had been pierced with the bowmen's pin-accurate shafts, the enemy withdrew out of bow-shot and contented themselves with shaking their fists at us and bawling inaudible threats.

The castellan, a tall, spare, leathery Norman knight, came over to greet me as I was checking Shaitan's glossy black hide for injuries. He named himself as Sir Aubrey de Chambois and welcomed me to his command. I thanked him for his timely opening of the gates and he merely shrugged: "It is I who should thank you, Sir Alan. You have saved us; in another day we would have had to render ourselves to Philip. Our walls could not have borne much more battering and the next full-scale assault would have swamped us."

And he gestured with his hand around the courtyard and walls of his stronghold. I saw then, clearly for the first time, what a desperate situation the defenders were in.

The castle of Verneuil, which had been built in King Richard's grandfather's day to protect the southern flank of his duchy of Normandy, was square in shape, covered roughly an acre and sat on the north bank of the River Avre. It was rather small by the standards of some of the castles I had known; in truth it was not much bigger than a fortified manor. On three sides, north, east and west, it was protected by a three-foot-thick wall, made of the gray local stone, about fifteen feet high, with a walkway all the way round it on the inside that allowed a man to stand and fight with only his helmeted head exposed between the crenellations. At each of the four corners of the castle was a strong square tower. In the center of the northern wall was the gatehouse and the gate we had just tumbled through in such scrambling haste—a stout wooden construction, I was pleased to see, reinforced with heavy oak crossbeams on the inside. To the south, the wide slow brown Avre and its boggy, reed-covered banks formed a formidable barrier against metal-clad attackers—and the stone exterior of a mill, a brewhouse and several storehouses built of brick created the castle's defensive wall on that side. I did not believe the enemy could come at us successfully from that quarter; the south, at least, was safe.

The northern wall on the eastern side of the gatehouse, however, had been severely pounded by the French siege engines—a gap the height of a man and wide enough for three men abreast had been smashed clear through the stonework at the top of the wall. It had been patched by Sir Aubrey's men using the rubble from the breach itself and an assortment of old sheep hurdles, wine barrels and a dozen lengths of freshly cut wooden planking. The repairs looked a little rough and untidy, but I reckoned the patched section still presented a difficult obstacle for an attacking infantry force to overcome. However, it was a sign of what terrible destruction the boulders hurled by the trebuchets could wreak on the old masonry of the castle. Several of the wooden buildings in the courtyard had been reduced to loose piles of timber and kindling, smashed by barrel-sized stone missiles that had overshot the walls. While the small hall at the rear of the courtyard was still intact, in other buildings fires had plainly broken out, probably caused in the chaos of the trebuchet bombardment.

An old stable block against the eastern wall had been converted into an infirmary and I could see through its open doors that the straw-strewn floor was covered with wounded men. A priest was kneeling beside one and giving him the last rites. My eye lingered on the priest for a moment, then I continued to survey the interior of the castle. Over on the western side was an old chapel and in the graveyard outside it I could see row upon row of newly dug graves. The sour scent of charred wood, fear-sweat and human and animal waste hung in the air, overlaid with a strong whiff of pus and rotting flesh—it was a particular combination of foul odors that I had smelled before.

It was the smell of defeat.

I had been expecting a garrison of a hundred men, or maybe more, but I could see only a score of local men-at-arms on their feet who were not wearing one of the dark green cloaks that marked out Robin's fellows. As it turned out, the full, unwounded strength of Verneuil, including our newly arrived troops, now numbered little more than a hundred and twenty men in total. Given the vast numerical superiority of the French, any determined attack might overwhelm us. I looked around at the courtyard, my heart in my boots, and asked Sir Aubrey what he planned to do if Philip's men got over the walls. He gave a grimace but no reply, merely inclining his head toward the biggest structure in the courtyard.

In the center of the castle was a square stone tower—the keep, the dungeon, the final redoubt. It stood on a slight rise, though not much of one, and climbed about thirty feet into the air. I had very little confidence in the tower as a refuge of last resort. It was not high enough, for a start, and it had already been considerably battered by Philip's artillery. Chunks of elderly, crumbling masonry seemed to have been ripped out of the northeastern corner leaving semicircular indentations in the line of the walls—as if a stone-eating giant had taken a couple of large bites out of the corner of the building. Even the untouched walls looked shaky, the big square stones loose in powdery mortar. I could easily imagine that a good kick from a horse, or a single wrench from a crowbar, would tumble them out of their settings. And I wondered if the tower could survive even one more full trebuchet strike without collapsing in on itself.

We had no alternative: we would have to hold the outer walls against the foe; if they fell, we were doomed. It was as simple as that. Had I been Duke of Normandy, I'd have seen to it that a much higher round stone tower was built as the core of this castle—the rounded walls allowing the missiles of an enemy to slide off more easily like water from a duck's back. I'd have built a keep, a stronghold that would stand for a thousand years.

Nonetheless, as Sir Aubrey and I climbed the rickety wooden stairs inside the building that led to the flat roof of the tower, I realized that, for all its obvious shortcomings, in the flat country around Verneuil it did give a commander an excellent vantage point from which to watch the enemy. As we stood there enjoying the cool breath of a spring breeze, I saw that my squire Thomas had caused Robin's wolf's head standard to be raised next to King Richard's golden lions. I smiled at the sight and then frowned as I looked out over the enemy dispositions. Our bloody charge through the French camp had stirred up a storm of activity among our foes; servants were bustling, knights were riding to and fro along the edges of the camp with a purposeful air. The center of this tempest was the big white gilded royal tent, where the fleur-de-lys fluttered proudly. Men in armor dashed in and out of the tent, leaping on horses as they emerged and galloping off to deliver orders. I could see that companies of men-at-arms were being formed up and horsemen and their grooms were preparing their mounts for battle. The area around the trebuchets was like a hive of bees in high summer. My heart was sinking as I turned my eyes heavenward: the sun shone merrily down on us mortal men from the very top of the sky.

"They are going to come at us this afternoon with everything they can readily muster," I said quietly to my companion.

"I know it. Can we hold them off?" Sir Aubrey looked at me, and I noticed how tired the man was; he had been defending this position, against impossible odds, for more than a week now. I doubted he had shut his eyes once in that entire time.

I smiled confidently and clapped him on the shoulder: "I believe we can, Sir Aubrey, I believe we can—and if God wills otherwise, we shall make such a good bloody fight of it that our courage and defiance shall live forever in the memories of brave men."

I divided the bowmen into two groups of about twenty men under a vintenar, an experienced archer who would act as their commander, and posted them at the towers in the northeastern and northwestern corners of the castle on either side of the gatehouse. Mercifully, the packhorses had made it through the French lines without mishap, and we had plenty of spare arrows. From the archers' enfilade positions they could rain lethal shafts down on anyone approaching the front gate, and also each group could defend against attack on the side walls to the east and west.

Sir Aubrey's remaining crossbowmen, reinforced with a score of my best men-at-arms, stood over the patched section of the wall. I was fairly sure that the enemy's attack, spawned out of rage at our insolent violation of their camp, would come directly at us and surge up against the front gate. But in case I was wrong, I posted the rest of the men at regular intervals along the east and west walls and in the top story of the mill at the south side of the castle to ward against an attack across the river—and to two handpicked men, heavily muscled but not especially bright, I allocated a very special duty, and gave their command into my little squire Thomas's thirteen-year-old hands.

As I was directing the dispositions of the castle—Sir Aubrey had agreed to a joint command as I had the greater number of living men-at-arms—my squire came to me and in his quiet, steady way, said: "Sir Alan, I think I have found something that will be of interest to you." And he stood there waiting for my attention.

I was extremely busy, overseeing the distribution of the castle's remaining bundles of light javelins to the men on the walls, and it had been on the tip of my tongue to rebuke him, but one glance at his solemn face and I bit back my retort. He led me to a storeroom by the river on the southern side of the castle and wordlessly indicated a tun, a very large wooden barrel that stood at the rear of the space. I walked over and examined it closely, detecting a familiar scent even through the thick oak staves.

"Is it full?" I asked my squire.

"To the brim, sir," he replied.

I looked into his deep brown eyes and grinned. "Well done, Thomas, very well done. I will give you two men and you shall prepare it for us. Yes?"

Thomas nodded gravely. And I left him in the storehouse, shouting for carpenter's tools, kitchen implements and firewood, and ordering two big Locksley men-at-arms around, a little shrilly in his unbroken voice, but with the ease of a born captain.

I made my rounds of three sides of the stone perimeter—ignoring the south wall: trying to put heart into the men for the coming contest. And I was pleased that I could detect little fear among the men-at-arms and bowmen on that sunny afternoon. The archers strung their tall yew bows and examined their shafts individually for tiny flaws, and tightened their bracers, the leather sleeves that protected the soft skin on the inside of the left forearm from the lash of the bowstring. The men-at-arms sharpened their spearheads and swords and adjusted the straps on their shields. I was not alone in making my rounds: the castle's only priest accompanied me as I moved along the walkway and, as I made manly, warlike comments to the men and trotted out age-old jokes, the priest intoned words of prayer over their weapons, blessing the soldiers and assuring them that God was with them this day, and would humble the French King for breaking the sacred truce between himself and our divinely ordained lord King Richard.

As we moved along the narrow walkway behind the stone wall, stopping at each little knot of men, I kept shooting glances at the priest. I could not help myself—the trepidation I felt at the onset of such a one-sided battle was far outweighed by my curiosity about this man. His name was Jean de Puy; he was in his middle forties, with a kindly well-worn face and thinning light brown hair cut in a tonsure, and he spoke good, educated French and better Latin when he uttered the sacred words of prayer for the men. He seemed to be a genuinely good and holy man—not venal and corrupt, or lazy and cynical, as some small-town priests so easily become. At one point, standing with a group of our men-at-arms on the eastern rampart, I completely lost myself in contemplation of him, pondering the kind of man he must have been in his youth. I had to be jerked back to reality by a crude jest from one of the men, a huge, powerful warrior called Sam. I returned the jest with an even cruder suggestion concerning his mother and a selection of farmyard animals, then walked down the steps back into the courtyard, side by side with Father Jean. At the bottom of the steps, the priest turned and looked me square in the face.

"My son, your countenance seems to me to have a very familiar aspect. May I make so bold as to ask, have we met before?"

"No, Father," I said. "We have not met before this day. But I heard much about you from an old priest in Lisieux who told me that twenty years ago you used to be a chorister at the cathedral of Notre-Dame in Paris—as my father was. Indeed, you are the true reason I am here in Verneuil."

3

I WOULD HAVE SPOKEN FURTHER WITH FATHER Jean but I was interrupted by a fanfare of trumpets. "I must go, Father, but I would speak with you again when I have more leisure."

"I shall be in the infirmary with the wounded," said Father Jean, indicating the stable block on the eastern wall I had noted before. "I think I understand what you wish to speak to me about and, when you are next at liberty, you will find me there." And with that he nodded, turned on his heel and strode away to the western side of the courtyard.

I hurried to the gate, bounding up the wooden steps to the walkway to the right of the castle's main entrance. I peered over the parapet and saw, as I had expected, two horsemen in gorgeous surcoats of blue and gold, each holding a French royal standard and mounted on a superb horse, white as a lily. They were enemy heralds-at-arms.

I waved merrily at them, and grinned, and they stared up from their saddles in surprise: it was hardly appropriate behavior in the circumstances, but I had no herald of my own, not even a trumpeter. And a strange feeling of reckless cheer had come over me, as if I were drunk on strong wine. Nothing seemed important, least of all chivalric conventions and proper knightly etiquette—given the odds that we faced against these teeming French hordes, in a few hours I'd likely be dead.

"Hello there!" I called. "Beautiful day, isn't it."

The left-hand herald coughed into his slim, pale hand and began intoning in a solemn carrying voice: "His Royal Highness Philip Augustus, King of France, by the grace of God Almighty rightful overlord of the rebellious Duke of Normandy, sovereign lord of the territories of—"

"Sorry, didn't catch that—who did you say?" I shouted down to the herald. I had an almost overwhelming urge to giggle like a naughty schoolboy.

The herald was completely thrown by my flippancy. He looked up at me in bafflement and said in a slightly questioning, uncertain tone: "Ah, His Royal Highness, um, Philip, the King of France, by the grace of God rightful overlord of the rebellious Duke of Normandy, sovereign lord—"

I cut him off again, saying cheerfully, "Oh, *him*—you mean Old Mace-Dick. And what does *he* want?"

The second herald, who had been studying the rude chalk drawing on the outside gate, had gone red in the face. He was clearly furious and it was he who answered the question for his now-speechless colleague.

"His Royal Highness instructs and commands you to leave this castle forthwith, to come forth in the garb of penitents and to surrender your persons to his royal justice, trusting in his mercy—"

"I don't think so. Not today, thank you. We are rather busy. Perhaps some other time," I said. There were a few guffaws from along the battlements: our men were enjoying my cheeky performance even if the heralds were not. I continued: "God be with you both—but we have far more important matters to attend to. So I must ask you to go now and leave us in peace."

"His Royal Highness Philip Augustus, by the grace of God, the King of France, instructs and commands you, on pain of death—"

"I said 'Go.'" My voice hardened. "Get ye hence. Quit this place. Be gone. Go."

"But the King of France—"

"If you are not away from this gate by the time I count to five, I will order the bowmen to shoot you down."

The heralds gawped at me. Their mouths working like land-drowning carp. To offer injury to a herald during a parley was a grave crime of war, and a terrible sin to boot.

"One," I said.

The angry left-hand herald said: "So then, you formally defy King Philip's rightful demand—"

I said: "Two." And his fellow herald cut him off with a gentling hand on the arm. They both shot me a glare of deep hatred, but when I said: "Three," they turned their horses smartly and cantered away.

The men on the battlements cheered as the two heralds rode back to the French encampment, their refined spines as straight as the poles that carried the royal standards, and it felt as if we had won a victory, even if it had been won in such an absurdly childish fashion. I was pleased that my tomfoolery had put some heart into the men—although I knew that we could expect no quarter if the enemy breached the walls.

"Men of Verneuil," I shouted, and I was glad that the castle was small enough so that every man could make out my words. "Men of Verneuil, you may take comfort in the knowledge that your true liege lord is very close at hand. King Richard is no more than one or two days' ride away, and if we can only hold here for a little while we will earn his undying gratitude. Any man who fights valiantly here today with all his heart and soul, and lives to tell the tale, can expect a rich reward from our royal master."

I could hear noises of approval all along the battlements—not exactly cheers, but a pleasing mumble of approbation.

"My friends, a storm is coming, the bitter storm of battle. Those high and mighty Frenchmen think that they can run over us, and stamp us into the dust. But they are wrong. I swear to you, on my honor as a knight, that we can hold them; and we can beat them—but only if you will fight like lions. So, I ask you: Will you fight?"

There was a muted rumble of assent. I repeated myself, louder this time. "Will you fight?"

A shout came back at me, and I believe every man on those battlements replied in the affirmative.

Once again I asked: "Will you fight?"

And the answer was a deep roar flung back at me from more than a hundred lusty throats. It sounded like a mountain being torn up by the roots: "*We. Will. Fight!*"

The enemy host formed up just out of bow-shot, about five hundred men in four divisions—or battles, as these formations are called. On the left and right flanks stood great blocks of enemy foot soldiers, perhaps a hundred and fifty men in each, dismounted knights and men-at-arms. Even at three hundred yards' distance I could see that they carried long ladders, and it was plain that they meant to scale the walls both to the right and left of the gatehouse at the same time. In the center, I saw with a sinking heart a huge black shape, at least thirty feet long, with a swarm of men fussing around it with ropes and pulleys attaching it to an enormous wheeled cradle. It was a felled tree-trunk, a battering ram, its hammer end sheathed in beaten iron. Nearby, carpenters were constructing a pointed roof with steeply sloping sides, tiled with wooden shingles—this was known as a penthouse—and its role was to shield from our arrows the men who would swing the heavy ram against the front gate. Clearly the central battle intended to come straight through the front door, smashing it to kindling in the process. And with that great ram, they might easily do it. Behind the battering ram was a battle of knights on horseback, a hundred men strong, beautifully arrayed, helmet plumes nodding, spear pennants flying, the trappers of the big horses bright splashes against the drab trampled field. When the gates of Verneuil had been smashed open and our brave men on the battlements overrun, these gaudy horse-borne killers would ride into the castle and complete the slaughter with lance and sword.

However, my mood of reckless cheerfulness had not deserted me. I was fairly certain that we were doomed, but there was still a chance of survival—and, as I had said to Sir Aubrey, if God willed that we die, we would make a fight of it that would live on in song and legend forever. And two things were in our favor: as far as I could tell, King Philip was not attempting any subtle maneuvers—he was not bothering with any further artillery bombardment; he was just coming straight at us in overwhelming strength; and the second and more important point was, we had an ample supply of arrows.

I stripped all the men from the rear of the castle, leaving one single man to watch in case of an attack over the River Avre. I posted ten men-at-arms on the western wall, ten on the eastern, and kept the archers on the two northern corners of the castle. The rest of the fit men, about sixty in total, I divided between myself and Sir Aubrey and we took up our positions on either side of the main gate; myself on the left, Aubrey on the right.

I had not expected subtlety from King Philip, and I did not receive it. I had barely organized my handful of men, and made sure they had two or three javelins apiece, when the trumpets and drums started up and the two massive squares of men on the left and the right of the French lines started moving forward. At two hundred yards, when you could clearly hear the chink and stamp of three hundred marching men, I nodded to the vintenar of the archers of the northwestern corner of the castle, a steady young man named Peter, and watched with pride as, with a great creaking of wood, these twenty men drew back their massive yew bows until the flights of their arrows tickled their right ears, and loosed a small gray cloud of shafts into the clear spring air.

The arrows punched down onto the enemy like deadly hail, rattling off shields and helms but sinking deeply into flesh wherever they found a gap in the armor. The French began to die. Men dropped by the killing shafts were trampled by their fellows; others, screaming in pain from an embedded missile, staggered out of the ranks, bleeding and clutching at the feathered shafts that sprouted from their bodies.

But after the first barrage, the French held their shields above their heads and crowded tightly together, and my archers had time for only one more volley before the attacking French were given the signal to charge. Suddenly the enemy were running at us as fast as their legs would carry them, ladders to the fore, straight at the castle walls. My archers loosed once more, and I saw another handful of men falling, dying, skewered by the yard-long shafts, but nothing could stop their momentum now. In what seemed like a few brief moments the French men-at-arms were crowding under the very walls of the castle and staring up at us with pale, furiously frightened faces, as I shouted for javelins to supplement the arrow storm and we rained down death from above into the jostling, heaving mass of yelling foemen below.

Bows creaked and twanged as our archers poured their killing skill down upon the enemy surging below us. Our men flung down javelins, spears, cut-down lances, even lumps of jagged masonry to crush the seething mass of Frenchmen—but a dozen ladders were rising, swinging up and banging against the stone wall of the castle, and the bravest enemy knights were already swarming up the frail wooden rungs with terrifying speed.

Wherever we could, we hurled the ladders away from the walls, pushing them clear with wooden pitchforks or long poles cut and tied in the shape of a cross, tumbling the brave men who climbed them with oaths and shouts and the thump of flesh and crack of bone onto the earth below; but there were too many of them. Hanno and I had grabbed the end of a ladder, and were twisting the top of it with our combined strength, left and right, spilling the climbers, when I looked to my left and saw a Frenchman come screaming over the wall. He parried a sword thrust from one of Robin's men-at-arms and struck the man's head clean off with his riposte. Another knight crested the stone battlements two yards away and landed neat as a cat on the wooden walkway behind it. I took two fast steps toward him and lunged for his throat, but he was a swordsman of no little skill and he deflected my sword and counterattacked with a lightning stab at my heart, followed by a hard cut at my shoulder. I twisted to avoid his blade and went down on one knee; he swung at my head and I blocked his blow with my shield, but from the corner of my eye I could see another Frenchman rolling over the wall into the gap the first man had created, and another. I had to plug this hole in our defenses—and fast—or we were all dead men! I came up from my crouching position and lunged; a low, vicious blow that slid through the front slits of his mail coat and sliced up through his braies into the meat of his soft inner thigh. He screamed like a soul in torment and clutched at the fork of his legs, scarlet blood gushing from the wound, and he dropped. I left him to his fate and smashed my shield at the head of a man who was just appearing above the castle wall, cutting deep into his face with the edge; he fell straight backward out of view. But there were enemies all around me now. I whirled and hacked with my long sword into the back of the neck of another Frenchman who was dueling with a green-cloaked man-at-arms; he fell away inside the castle walls, yelling in pain. I saw Hanno, wielding an axe, cave in the skull of a man in the act of climbing over the wall. I killed a man on the walkway to my right—my sword Fidelity spearing into his throat. I blocked a wild sword swing and cut deep into the thigh of a Frenchman to my left. Another head poked above the wall nearer to me and I darted forward, slicing into an eye and causing the head to disappear as if by some conjurer's trick. A burly archer and I both grabbed the ladder top at the same time, and we heaved it away bodily, causing three climbing Frenchmen to spin off and crash to the hard ground in a cloud of flying dust and foul curses.

And suddenly there were no more ladder tops and the wall to the west of the gatehouse was clear of the enemy. I peered over the battlements, and jerked away just in time as a crossbow quarrel clattered against the stone inches to the right of my face. But I could see that the French were pulling back on our side, taking their wounded, but leaving a score of their dead in a bloody heap below our walls.

I shouted: "Archers, archers . . ." But there was no need. Robin's well-trained bowmen, under young Peter's direction, were already harassing the retreating French with deadly accuracy, their shafts easily punching through the mail coats that covered the running men's backs, and dropping their victims in their tracks. I looked across at Sir Aubrey's command and he too seemed to have fought off the first onslaught, though he was leaning on his sword, holding his side with his left hand, and I saw with deep regret that there was a dark quarrel shaft sticking from his waist, and a wet stain was spreading beneath his hand. He was not the only man to have received a grievous wound from among our ranks: more than a dozen of our archers and men-at-arms had been wounded or killed during the attack on both sides of the gatehouse. But we had held them off.

Yet that day's bloody work was only just beginning. The two enemy battles on the flanks had moved out of range of the deadly war bows of Robin's men, but they had not dispersed into the camp. They waited, loosely formed, mauled but still menacing. And in the center, trumpets rang out once again, and with dread I saw that the great ram was being hoisted onto its huge wooden cradle under the penthouse, surrounded by hundreds of men-at-arms bearing the five-foot-high, flat-topped, flat-bottomed, light wickerwork shields that were sometimes used to protect crossbowmen on the field of battle.

The trumpets blared, the drums sounded and the three foot-divisions began to advance. They were coming at us again. I looked to the west to the sun, which hung low in the blue vault of heaven. I judged that we had at most two hours of daylight left. I sent runners to the eastern and western walls and called the men I had posted there to me; I even sent a man down to the infirmary to summon any lightly wounded. I wanted every man who could stand on two feet and wield a sword on the castle's front wall.

The battering ram under its sloping shingle roof crept forward at the pace of a crippled old man. But it came on steadily, pushed by men-at-arms inside the housing and by a line of steel-helmeted, mail-coated shield-men on the outside. Once they were within range of our bowmen, we began to take our toll of these outside men, though four arrows out of five thumped and lodged into the long wickerwork shields that they bore on their outer arms, or skittered harmlessly from the shingle roof of the penthouse.

At fifty yards, we had dropped only half a dozen shield-men and, at a shout of command from inside the penthouse, the pace was quickened and the entire contraption began to trundle toward the gate at increasing speed. At the same time, the two infantry battles on the left and right, howling like mad dogs, charged into the fray seeking revenge and I realized that we simply did not have enough archers even to slow their furious charge.

"This is it, lads," I shouted. "This is it. If we hold them now, we're safe. Hold them, and we've won the day."

The foe was surging below us once more, the ladders were swinging up against the walls and banging against the crenellations. And we hurled the last of our javelins down upon the sea of taut white faces and red shouting mouths below us, following those missiles with rocks, earthenware jugs, even iron cooking pots. Anything and everything we had that could cause harm was hurled into the boiling sea of humanity below—but it seemed that nothing could stop the fear-spurred French from flying up the ladders and flooding over the wall in vast numbers.

Boom! The battering ram was at the gate and its first blow seemed to shake the very foundations of the earth.

A roaring bearded face appeared before me, framed by the rungs of a ladder, and I hacked with Fidelity, crunching deep through gristle and bone laterally across his broad nose; the man was hurled backward in a spray of gore, but almost immediately another head appeared, and an arm waving a sword, too. I cut down hard, all but severing the arm at the elbow, and the man dropped away.

Boom! The ram struck again, accompanied by a hideous splintering sound, and I realized that the castle gate was not going to last long under this ferocious assault. I placed my mailed hand on the empty ladder rung and pushed with all the strength of my left arm; it lifted an inch or two from the face of the castle wall, skidded to the right and slipped away. But to my right, from another ladder—one of dozens now against the wall—a well-armed French knight, his face protected by a flat-topped tubular helmet, was leaping over the crenellations, then slicing down savagely into a man-at-arms a few yards from me. His blade bit deep, through the poor man's green cloak and padded aketon, cutting into his chest cavity, and the man dropped with a panting, gurgling moan.

I quickly turned my head and shouted: "Thomas, Thomas. Now's your time! Come now."

And was rewarded by a high, clear voice from the castle courtyard, shouting: "Yes, sir; coming, sir."

The French knight, armed with sword and mace, stepped nonchalantly over the green-cloaked body of my dying comrade and came directly toward me, a challenge on his lips. His sword hissed at my head, and I parried. He swung the mace in his left hand hard at my body. I caught the blow on my shield, unbalancing myself, and momentarily blocking my line of sight, but recovered and swept low with my sword, smashing the blade into the back of the knight's left knee. And while my blade did not penetrate the tough steel links of his leg mail, it swept him off his feet and, as he floundered on his back in front of me on the walkway, I leaped forward. My sword tip found the eye slit in his helmet and I put my weight above it and crunched the blade down hard. The whole walkway was a mass of struggling men by then, scores of Frenchmen hacking, clawing, biting and butting; locked in life-and-death combat with our surviving green-cloaked men. The air seemed to be misted with blood. The noise was appalling: screams and shrieks and the clang and clash of metal. And more Frenchmen were coming over the walls with every passing moment. Wrenching Fidelity free of the dead man's helmet, I paused to take a fast breath and looked beyond him and espied Thomas, clutching two burning pinewood torches, incongruous on that golden afternoon, skipping up the steps that led from the courtyard to the right of the gatehouse. Behind him, lumbering with difficulty up the wooden steps, came the two burly men-at-arms I had allocated to him. In their hands, clasped between two long, pole-like wooden holders to protect them from the heat, was a huge cooking pot, a great cauldron of smoking walnut oil that had been heated to boiling on a fire in the courtyard below.

Boom! The battering ram struck once more, and I felt the wooden walkway shiver beneath my feet. A squat French man-at-arms hopped over the wall right in front of me—an axe in one hand and a round shield in the other. He swung at me, and I ducked and counterattacked purely by instinct, chopping my sword into his outstretched arm, then knocking him back with a punch from my boar-shield.

"This way! This way. Bring it here," a shrill voice was shouting. And I quickly turned to see Thomas's cauldron-carrying men levering the smoking pot up to the edge of the battlement at the very center of the gate—tipping the sizzling oil, perhaps half a dozen gallons of it, straight down onto the penthouse roof below.

Even above the dreadful clamor of battle, I could hear the agonized screams of a dozen shield-men below who were splashed by boiling oil: an unholy cacophony of white-hot pain. As I glanced over the edge of the wall, I saw the oil slicked across the wooden shingles of the penthouse below in a yellow, glistening, smoking sheet, and dripping through the cracks to scald the unfortunate men in the space below. Then Thomas hurled the two burning torches onto the sloping roof and with a huge, crackling roar the entire wooden structure of the penthouse burst into bright flame.

Almost immediately the men began to run from inside the burning ram-housing, discarding shields, ripping off burning surcoats, some shrieking wildly and beating at flames on their arms and chests where the dripping oil had ignited. These human torches ran, oil-soaked aketons doggedly ablaze, flesh scorching and blackening, hair exploding in a puff of flame to leave raw pink oozing scalps. Some fled heedlessly to their encampment as if trying to escape their own burning skin, while the wise ones dropped and rolled on the ground to extinguish the flames.

I had no time to watch the agonized antics of my enemies below—

the battle for the walls was very nearly lost. "Throw them back, throw them back, kill them, kill them all," I shouted, and charged a few steps along the walkway to my left, sword whirling, hacking into the struggling mass of men there. Feeling the familiar black fury of combat rise from the pit of my stomach, I screamed a war cry that blasted from my lungs like a trumpet and plunged into the battle on a wave of soaring, joyful madness. I sliced and cleaved and battered. I was snarling, spitting, barging, shoving, hacking and stabbing like a man possessed. My sword swung in great glittering arcs, crunching into flesh and bone with every cut, and the enemy quailed before me. I thrust the living enemy off the walkway with my shield, or cut them down without mercy. I felt all-powerful, invincible, imbued with the power of God and the saints. I know that I received blows in turn—I saw the brutal patchwork of purple bruises later on my arms and legs—but my costly mail suit kept the blades from my flesh, and in my battle-rage I scarcely felt them. Then Hanno was beside me and we were tramping grimly forward, shoulder to shoulder, unstoppable, blocking the width of the walkway with our bodies and chopping down Frenchmen with axe and sword like a pair of country scythemen reaping the corn. Some of the enemy ran back to their ladders, some leaped down to the courtyard floor and surrendered to our men down there; others hung from the outside of the wall and dropped the fifteen feet to the hard ground, stumbling away on jarred and twisted joints. But many of them died, chopped into meat beneath our swinging blades.

Suddenly I found myself face-to-face with Peter the vintenar, a battle snarl on his lips, a bloody sword in his fist—and the red fog in my mind slowly began to clear; I realized that the walkway was now clear of living enemies. Taking a huge gulp of air, I looked over the wall and saw that the whole attacking force was in full retreat. The surviving men beside me atop the gatehouse wall jeered them as they ran, our faces ruddy, and streaming with sweat from the heat of the conflagration below the front gate. My mail was thickly clotted with blood, my sword felt as heavy as a bar of lead, and my beloved boar-adorned shield had been battered and hacked out of shape and was now mangled almost beyond recognition.

But we had won.

With the sun low in the west, a mere two fingers above the horizon, I knew the enemy would not come again that day. But our victory had come at a heavy price. On my side of the gate, there were fewer than a score of our men still standing, and many of them were sorely gashed and bleeding. And below us, in the center of the wall, the big wooden gate, our bulwark, our main defense, was beginning to char and blister and burn. Unless we acted swiftly, the fire that was consuming the ram and its penthouse would take the gate with it and leave our entrance open to attack the next day.

I organized the whole and only lightly wounded men—and there were not fifty of them among the entire castle's garrison—into a bucket chain and we relayed water from the River Avre to men at the top of the gatehouse, which they used to sluice down the outside of the front gate to keep it from burning all the way through. It was hot, dirty, sopping work, and I took my place in the chain, too. The men could only stand at the top of the gatehouse for a few moments before being driven back by the heat—but the water kept coming, bucketful by bucketful, and gradually the blaze was defeated. It was well after dark when the oily fire was finally doused, and the ram was left a charred, smoldering spine among the blackened ribs of its housing. Even then I did not let the men rest: we built a ramshackle inner gate behind the scorched outer portal, not much more than a breastwork of boxes, tables, chairs, empty barrels, bales of straw . . . anything that a man could stand behind and fight. Hanno bullied the men with urgent energy and no little cruelty to keep them at their tasks, but even he was haggard and drawn when at last we agreed that there was nothing more that could be accomplished that night. After organizing a skeleton sentry roster, we went in search of food and water and somewhere to curl up and sleep.

In the morning, we would fight again—and I was certain that we would not be able to keep them out this time.

In the morning, the French knights, hungry for their vengeance, would easily smash through the charred gate, leap their great destriers over the chest-high tangle of barrels and chairs and stable-yard detritus, and the final slaughter inside the castle would begin.

In the morning, we would all die.

4

IN THE MORNING, WHEN I AWOKE—stiff, my whole body bruised and aching, my blond hair and eyebrows singed—King Philip and the bulk of his army were gone.

It seemed a miracle, and I gave thanks on my knees to God and St. Michael, the warrior archangel, whom I felt certain had preserved us. We were still besieged, of course, but the great royal tent with the fluttering fleur-de-lys was nowhere to be seen, and more than half the enemy's strength had departed. The siege engines were still there, the trebuchets and the mangonel; companies of men-at-arms still marched about the camp; French breakfasts were still being cooked over hundreds of small fires; and scores of horses were still tethered in their neat lines—but, astoundingly, our doom had been lifted. I watched the enemy encampment with Sir Aubrey from the roof of the tower, and though I tried very hard, it was impossible not to believe that we were saved.

Sir Aubrey was pale—he had had the crossbow quarrel removed the night before and he was walking only with great difficulty—but he managed the climb to the top of the tower without a word of complaint. He was clearly a man with steel in his spine.

"Where do you think they have gone?" I asked him.

He shrugged—then tried to disguise a wince. "I think they must have overestimated our strength. They cannot know how weak we are or, as we speak, they would be tearing down the gate and bursting into the courtyard."

"We must not relax our vigilance," I said, trying to appear the stern warrior, quite unmoved by our unexpected reprieve from certain death.

"Indeed," said Sir Aubrey. "They would still have more than enough men to take this castle if they had the strength of will to see it through."

"Indeed," I said, but I found that I was beaming at the older man, and I saw that a relieved smile had wreathed his leathery, pain-marked features as well.

The enemy, it seemed, were not of a mind to try conclusions with us again that day; and having seen that wakeful sentries were posted, and all the men had food and watered wine, and our horses were as comfortable as we could make them, I set off for the makeshift infirmary to check on the wounded and visit Father Jean.

I took Thomas with me, and found the priest cradling a dying man, giving him the comfort of absolution. The fellow was one of my men-at-arms, a former farmhand from the Locksley valley who had sought adventure in the ranks of Robin's men and become a good, steady cavalryman. He had been eviscerated by an axe blow in the last attack against the right-hand side of the wall, Sir Aubrey's section, the evening before. With that gaping wound, and the pink-white ropes of his guts plainly visible, I was surprised that he had lasted this long. He was in agony but gripped my hand hard and died almost silently, weeping few tears and only crying out once—"Oh Lord Christ Jesus, save me"—as Father Jean made the sign of the cross on his forehead. I found I was much moved by his courage, and felt my own eyes begin to moisten. I thought grimly that one day it would be me lying on a mound of dirty, bloody straw, in a drafty stable somewhere far from home, surrounded by other stricken men, riding into the next life on a wave of white-hot pain. I shuddered; I hoped I'd make as brave a death as he did when my time came. As I looked away from his corpse, I saw that Thomas was standing by the side of the open stable door and sobbing openly and without the slightest sense of shame.

I stood and went over to him and put my arm around his shoulders. "Do not weep, Thomas," I said. "He was a good man, a good soldier and a good Christian, and he is at peace in Heaven with God and his angels now."

Thomas stared up at me with his deep, oak-brown eyes. "It is not him, so much as all of them. All those dead men; and the ones I killed, especially."

I tried to think of some soothing piece of wisdom that would comfort him: I knew that Robin would have had one ready to hand. But I could not. "We are all in God's keeping" was the best I had to offer. "All we can do is our duty to God in Heaven and our liege lord here on Earth."

"I saw them last night," Thomas continued, mindless of me, "the burning men; the men I burned: running, burning and screaming, trying to escape a fiery death that I inflicted on them. It was truly awful; and I did it to them . . ."

I had to jolt him from this path of thought, and so I straightened up and cuffed him none too gently on the shoulder: "War is cruel, Thomas. It is monstrously cruel. But you played your part well, like a man, like a soldier. Think of your fate if those Frenchmen you singed yesterday had got inside the castle. What then?" My voice sounded unnecessarily loud and harsh, but I could not help myself. "That would be you lying there right now." And I pointed over at the blood-drenched cavalryman, just as Father Jean closed his eyes for the last time. The boy said nothing.

"Now, Thomas, I want you to go and find Peter the vintenar and tell him I shall be making an inspection of the castle defenses at noon. And his men had better be ready—or I'll have the hide off somebody's back. Run along now."

The obedient fellow sniffed, wiped a snail's trail from his nose with his sleeve, and trotted away.

Father Jean would not leave the wounded, even for half an hour to talk on a matter of great importance to me—and so I stayed with him as he made his rounds, helping the wounded men to drink cool river water from earthenware cups, and mopping the fresh blood and pain-sweat from the men's ripped and ruined bodies. It meant that our conversation was broken by screams and moans and appeals to the Almighty. But I was intent on hearing his tale, and longed so much to learn all he knew, that the awful sufferings of my men only remain in my memory as a blur. I wiped brows and helped to set broken limbs, and cleaned the filthy voidings from between their legs as Father Jean and I spoke, yet, God forgive me, I recall none of their heartbreaking travails in detail, while I remember his story with perfect clarity.

"As I think you already have guessed," Jean de Puy began, "I knew your father in Paris. I first met Henri d'Alle in the autumn of the thirty-sixth year of the reign of King Louis, the year of Our Lord Jesus Christ eleven hundred and seventy two. I was twenty-two years old, of an age with your father, and our meeting occurred in unforgettable circumstances. We were both young monks attached to the cathedral of Notre-Dame as choristers; it was our duty, indeed our honor, to sing the Mass inside the small portion of the new cathedral that had been completed—as well as in the old Merovingian cathedral, which was still standing then. We sang joyfully, for the glory of God and for the edification of our fellow men.

"Even in its uncompleted state, the new cathedral was a beautiful space and the sound of our voices echoing up through that huge space must surely have been a God-pleasing sound. I did not know Henri—there were fifty or so monks who gave their voices to God there under the energetic and much-loved Bishop of Paris, Maurice de Sully. As I was new to the choir myself, I did not yet know all the monks who belonged to it. But, as I say, I met your father in a fashion that it would be impossible to forget. In fact, I remember our meeting with a good deal of pleasure.

"I was hurrying toward the cathedral from the chapter house where I had been receiving extra tuition in Latin grammar from the master; it was mid-morning and I was late for the office of Nones when I came upon a crowd of young monks and novices beside a pile of masonry next to the half-built outside wall of the choir—they were mostly choristers, but also some visiting monks too; from Cluny, I believe. They were laughing and shouting—it was quite unsuitable behavior for men of the cloth just outside a House of God and, worse, they were taunting a young novice, whom they called Trois Pouces. He was a thin boy from somewhere in the far south, I believe—younger than us and very good-looking, and I think some of the older monks had been sorely tempted by his beauty—but he did have one defect that gave rise to his unusual name. On his left hand he had an extra thumb, which was why they called him Three Thumbs. The two duplicated digits were small but well formed with a complete nail on each one and both growing out of a central root. It was as if someone had taken a knife and split his true thumb about halfway down the center and the two halves had healed themselves as two perfect new digits. Some said it must be the sign of the Devil, others said that, having given him immense physical beauty, God had decided that there must be one tiny flaw in Trois Pouces to keep him from the sin of pride. But either for his looks or his extra thumb, or for whatever reason, the other young monks did not like him. And they made his life a living Hell, tormenting him night and day, making up little hurtful rhymes about his deformity and calling him Trois Pouces—or sometimes, casually, just Pouces.

"The young monks were at their sport when I came hurrying around the corner, late for the service in the cathedral. A gang of them had surrounded Pouces and were chanting something hurtful that had made the boy cry. The ringleader, a big, brawny fellow named Fulk, had Pouces by his left wrist and was holding up his arm to display the wretched boy's misfortune for his friends' ridicule. And then your father arrived."

At this point, Father Jean took a deep swig from the water jug, washed the stable dust out of his throat and spat into the straw.

"Now, Sir Alan, while I understand that you are one of those who fights, a knight, I must tell you that I do not approve of violence. I believe that Christ taught us to turn the other cheek, and we must listen to his message and obey if we wish to call ourselves Christians and assure ourselves of Salvation. Violence, to me, is distasteful. It leads to . . . well, to this." And he waved a hand around that blood-splashed stable, strewn with mangled, dying men.

"But on this occasion," he said, "I think that God was acting through your father to punish those unruly monks in a swift and necessary fashion. Your father did not hesitate for a heartbeat—there must have been a dozen monks around Pouces, but Henri charged in like a madman, his fists swinging like great bony hammers. He was a strong man and he laid about him left and right, boxing ears and crushing noses and doubling up his brothers with swift hard blows to their midriffs. He set about Fulk in a particularly alarming fashion, hammering him again and again in the face with his left fist, then breaking his jaw with a tremendous cross blow from his right. The monks scattered in the face of his righteous fury, hauling away the half-unconscious Fulk with them—and I was somewhat alarmed too, but I saw that your father's anger had been inspired by a desire to thwart evil, and I was reminded of Christ clearing the money-changers from the steps of the Temple. So I plucked up my courage and went over to him when the others had fled to tell him of my admiration for his actions.

"Well, the long and the short of it is, we became friends—the three of us, Henri, myself, and poor little Pouces. And for the next six months we were inseparable."

I found I was smiling to myself. It pleased me to think of my father as a fighter protecting the weak from bullies. And Father Jean noticed my expression.

"You know, you are extraordinarily like him, Sir Alan. Not just in your build and features, but also in the way you move. I saw you yesterday on the wall, repelling those dogs of King Philip, and you reminded me of your father attacking a crowd of unruly monks single-handed."

I could not speak for pride and dropped my eyes. After a moment, Father Jean continued.

"So Henri, Pouces and I were fast friends, and we spent every spare moment we had together. Henri had the best voice; he sang like a bird, and he was fearless and strong. But he also had a weakness for women. He loved them, he loved them all, and I am certain he made the cheeks of his confessor glow red on more than one occasion when he related his carnal sins with the girls of the Parisian taverns. Even if the calamity that occurred the next spring had not taken place, I do not think that Henri was made by God for a life in the Church. He had a warrior's soul, I fear. He brawled several times in the streets with common men who offended him in some way, and he went with women—may God have mercy on him. But though he was probably a bad monk, he was also undoubtedly a good man, and my good friend, and I pray for his soul."

In my mind's eye, I pictured this bully-punishing, brawling, womanizing monk, and I thought to myself—*this is very far from the gentle, musical man I knew growing up; but I would have loved this side of him, too.*

Father Jean continued: "Pouces was the cleverest of the three of us; and he was forever coming up with tricks and japes and little adventures that he devised to amuse us in our leisure time. He encouraged us to creep out of the cloisters at night and get a boatman to take us across the Seine and into the Ville de Paris, even though it was strictly forbidden by the order of Bishop de Sully himself and we ran the risk of being arrested by the provosts of the city, who maintained a curfew. But we felt that it was a great adventure, and we reveled in our disobedience. Once, Pouces stole Brother Cellarer's keys and the three of us crept into his cellar and swapped the contents of a barrel of his very best Rhone wine for some cheap vinegary muck that was so full of debris, bits of twig and grape skins and such that you had to drink it with your teeth closed to sieve out the detritus. The cellarer was a lazy man and, without tasting it, served this wine at a tremendous feast for the arrival of Heribert, the Bishop of Roda. The Bishop's face when he tasted the wine—what a picture! He thought he was being poisoned." Jean was chuckling. "We served the best wine out to the beggars of Paris, for free—just gave it away! Pouces said we were teaching the Bishop and the cellarer a lesson in Christian humility. Oh, that was a wonderful day.

"We were punished severely, of course—a whipping apiece and confined to our cells on bread and water for a week—but, God forgive me, it was worth it."

For the moment, all was quiet in the stable, save for a moan or two. We had been kneeling beside a man with a flesh wound on his leg, a Welsh archer named Gerry, and Jean had been cleaning and rebandaging the deep cut as we talked. "You had a high old time in your youth, Father, really kicked up your heels, didn't you?" said Gerry to the priest, with a smirk. "Let's hear a bit more about all the tavern sluts this young fellow Henry tumbled, then."

"You hold your tongue, Gerald ap Morgan." I glared at the man. "If you are truly so badly wounded, you would do well to lie still and keep silent. But if you are feeling lively I can easily have you on the wall doing sentry duty!"

Father Jean stood up and stretched his back. "Let us enjoy a little sunshine," he said, and he went over to the door of the stable and looked out at the courtyard, where the castle was drowsing in a bright, warm spring morning. All was quiet, it seemed, and for a moment it was difficult to believe that there was a hostile army outside the gates. I quickly checked that the sentries were all in their places and alert, and then gave my attention back to the priest.

"It was Bishop Heribert's visit that was your father's downfall, of course. He was a great man, very rich, well born and well connected—he had rather grand relatives in England, if I recall. The Murdacs—do you know them?"

I clenched my teeth and shook my head.

"Well, at that time Heribert was only bishop of a minor diocese far to the south in the Pyrenees, but he was ambitious. And he was surprisingly rich for a man with such a small see. He had an enormous retinue, more than a hundred servants—we had the devil of a job accommodating all his people; monks thrown out of their cells to allow his servants a proper bed, all sorts of chaos. He was planning to stay with Bishop de Sully for several months to learn about the construction process of the cathedral, and because he was very fond of the new music we were making in the choir—and it was something quite special, may God forgive me my pride. In fact, Heribert became so enamored of our voices that after a while he was attending every Mass and every service at which we sang: Matins, in the dead of night, in freezing January, in that drafty half-built church—he was there. The monks who had been allocated the duty of singing that office may have been sore with cold and slightly hoarse and longing for their warm beds, but Heribert was there. Praying on his knees, beaming at us, sometimes singing along—and not completely out of tune either. He even began to think of himself as one of us, but of grander rank, obviously, as our chanter, our choirmaster, in fact. He began to think that he was responsible for the music we were making, that we could not make it without him. This annoyed us no end, but Heribert, who was a little mad, I think, was connected to some of the best families in France and our own Bishop de Sully asked us to indulge him in his harmless fancies. But, as God willed it, Heribert had to cut his visit short. He was robbed. Right inside the Bishop's palace, if you can believe it. One of his store chests was broken into by a thief and several costly items were taken. And, as I'm sure you have been told, your father was blamed for the crime."

"Can you tell me what was stolen?" I asked.

"There was a strange air of vagueness over the theft. Bishop Heribert was reluctant to say exactly what had been stolen. But in order to aid in their recovery, he finally admitted that a pair of elaborate golden candlesticks and a silver carving platter and some other valuable objects had been removed." Father Jean rubbed his careworn face, his eyes distant as he recalled the painful past.

"The candlesticks were quickly recovered," the priest continued. "A goldsmith with a shop on the Right Bank reported that a cowled monk, his face hidden in shadow, had tried to sell him the candlesticks the night after they were stolen. When the artisan, a little suspicious, asked for the monk's name, he was told that it was Brother Henri; and when he was asked to reveal his face, the monk had refused and fled, taking the two candlesticks with him.

"The next day Henri d'Alle's cell was duly searched by Maurice de Sully's men-at-arms and—what a strange surprise!—the candlesticks and the silver carving platter were found among his meager personal possessions."

"You don't believe he stole them," I said.

"I didn't believe it then, and I don't now. Your father was not a very holy monk, but he was no dirty thief!"

I winced a little, remembering my own shameful days as a skulking cutpurse.

"So who was the culprit?" I asked.

Father Jean sighed: "I do not know. But I am certain that it was not your father. That, however, was not how our noble bishops Heribert and Maurice de Sully saw matters. The candlesticks and the platter had been found in your father's cell and therefore he must have been guilty . . ."

Again I looked at my own past actions and felt another twinge: I had once thrown guilt onto a boy by hiding a jewel that I had stolen among his spare clothing. He too had been driven from his home as a result. I wondered if God was reminding me of my own sins, through the words of this honest priest.

Father Jean, unaware of my guilty thoughts, carried on with his tale. "There was a huge scandal, of course, and although Henri protested his innocence in the strongest possible terms, he was expelled from the cathedral, and he had to leave Paris. He had no choice in reality: Bishop Heribert wanted Henri to be interrogated by the

King's provosts, which would have meant torture, to reveal the whereabouts of the other items stolen, and then for him to be tried and severely punished. De Sully demurred. As a monk, he insisted, Henri was protected by benefit of the clergy; he could not be handed over to the lay authorities for torture, trial and punishment. But had your father remained in Paris, the Bishop might have had to bow to pressure from Heribert's powerful family. It would be better for everybody concerned, de Sully said, if Henri were to be banished. I wept when he left us, still dressed in his monk's robe, and with one small sack of food and clothing over his shoulder. Pouces and I said goodbye to him on the big bridge that spans the Seine, the Grand-Pont—and he told me he was heading north to England."

"What happened to Trois Pouces?" I asked.

"He died, God rest him. I left Paris later that year to make a pilgrimage to Rome, and I heard that Pouces had succumbed to the smallpox—there was an outbreak in Paris after I left the city, thousands died, the bodies piled up in the streets, and a friend told me that Pouces had been called to God."

"And what became of the music-mad Bishop Heribert?"

"Oh, he thrived. He did not hold his Pyrenean post for long; his family made arrangements for him to join the Holy Trinity Abbey in Vendôme, and he is there to this day—he is now a cardinal, no less! And I hear that he is as enthusiastic about music as ever."

"So the last time you saw or heard from my father was twenty-odd years ago, at your leave-taking on the Grand-Pont?"

"Sadly, I never saw him again. I pray that we shall be reunited in Heaven."

"But what about his family: the seigneurs d'Alle? Surely Henri could have gone to them?"

"His father—your grandfather—was dead by then, and his elder brother Thibault had inherited the lands of Alle, and, well, I got the feeling that they were not as close as brothers should be. In fact, I asked Henri if he would go to Thibault for help and he told me that he would sooner starve in a ditch than be in the same house as him and his family. There was not much love lost between them, it seems. I believe the new seigneur was concerned about the consequences of the scandal and considered that Henri had disgraced the family name by his crimes. Henri was a proud man: he would never beg for succor from anyone."

"And so he went to England," I said, letting out a long breath. Strong emotions had been stirred by Father Jean's tale—it occurred to me that I'd like to meet my uncle Thibault, the meanspirited Seigneur d'Alle, and express my feelings about his abandonment of my father to him fully and frankly down the length of my sword blade.

I left Father Jean in the infirmary and completed a tour of inspection of the defenses of the castle. When it was done, I took a long look out over the wall at the enemy camp; I could only detect a sense of peaceful indolence among the depleted enemy, and it was hard to believe that these were the same men who had assailed us so ferociously the day before. The camp had the air of a holy day—indeed, it was Whitsun Eve if I recall correctly—and I guessed that with the departure of the King a good deal of the besiegers' determination had gone with him. I was almost certain that they did not intend to attack us that day, and ordered half the men to stand down and eat and rest.

I shared a loaf of bread and a lump of cheese with my squire Thomas, washed down with a jug of the local wine. Thomas had cleaned the blood and filth from my sword Fidelity, and was carefully sharpening it with a stone. It seemed the lad had recovered from his fit of remorse and I decided not to mention it in case it stirred up another bout of tears. Instead, I told him what Father Jean had said about my father. Thomas listened gravely and said: "I think we should pay a visit to Cardinal Heribert in Vendôme. That is, assuming the King comes soon to relieve us and we survive this siege."

My thoughts had been tending in another direction, toward Paris. I was wondering what the much-loved Bishop de Sully might have to say about the matter of my father's departure some twenty years ago and whether he might be able to throw any light on the identity of this most powerful person, this "man you cannot refuse," who, like a coward, had ordered my father's death from the shadows. But I could not for the life of me see how in time of war I might safely get across fifty miles of territory infested with hundreds of enemy knights and into the French capital.

Thomas was right, I concluded. While Vendôme, too, was presently in enemy hands, it had traditionally been one of Richard's towns and its loyalty was like a leaf in the wind. If the Lionheart's campaign went well, we were more than likely to retake it. And even if it could not be recaptured, Vendôme might be easier to enter than the seat of the King of France himself. If I survived this siege, I decided, then I would beg leave of Richard to go to Vendôme and seek out the music-loving Cardinal.

I spent the rest of the day in relative peace. I further reduced the number of sentries and allowed more of the men to rest. I talked a little longer with Father Jean, but it was clear that he had told me everything he knew, and he had no idea who the man might be who had ordered my father's death. At dusk, after watching the French make their preparations for the night, I felt confident enough to strip off my blood-crusted suit of mail and give it over to Thomas for cleaning.

That night, sitting on the ground floor of the tower, dressed only in linen braies, thin woolen hose and a rather grubby chemise that I had been wearing for a week by then, I composed a rude little satirical ditty, what the jongleurs call a *fabliau*, which I named "King Philip's Folly." It told of the haughty monarch's attempt to take Verneuil, his great mace swinging between his legs as he assailed the gates, but how the valiant men of the castle cut the mace from his body and sent him packing with a sore and gaping wound.

It was greeted with much merriment and many a cheer when I sang it that night, accompanied only by my vielle, a cherished five-stringed instrument that I played with a horsehair bow, which I was very glad to see had survived among the baggage during the giddy charge into the castle. The men liked my *fabliau*, and indeed, we all seemed to sense that our hour of peril had passed. And so it had, for, after a good night's sleep and a morning practicing basic sword maneuvers, cuts and blocks, in the castle courtyard with Thomas, Hanno came to me shortly after the noon meal, as I was taking stock of the castle's few remaining provisions, and said flatly: "The French are going."

Once on the battlements I saw that Hanno had spoken truly. The remainder of the enemy forces were packing up their encampment; tents, weapons, food, fodder, horses, siege engines—the lot. By mid-afternoon, the first of their units were disappearing down a track that ran parallel to the river and led through a wooded region to the east toward the French-held castle of Tillières.

There was much rejoicing on our walls at this sight, and I allowed a small cask of wine to be broached and served out to the men. The reason for the Frenchmen's departure soon became apparent, for by the time half the enemy forces had entered the wood and been lost from view, we saw the first outriders of King Richard's huge army arriving on the ridge where Hanno and I had murdered the knights two days before. At first it was just a single horseman, silhouetted boldly, almost heroically, on the skyline, then the low ridge bloomed into a forest of flagstaffs and spears. The colors of a hundred bright standards caught the slanting golden light of the afternoon sun, and the ridge seemed to swell and darken with the moving bodies of thousands of men and horses.

Although they must have known of its imminent arrival, the swift appearance of Richard's army sowed panic among the departing French troops. At the tail end of the enemy column was the slow lumbering siege train: three trebuchets, a mangonel and some smaller fry, all being pulled on their own wheeled bases or hauled laboriously on heavy carts by teams of lumbering oxen.

The siege train was protected by a meager handful of mounted spearmen; and when a single *conroi*—a cavalry unit of perhaps a score of knights—from Richard's army began to trot down the gentle slope toward the creeping siege train, the mounted guards did not wait to make a fight of it but spurred their horses' flanks and galloped away and into the little wood to the east. The ox-drivers did not wait to be captured either: from my lookout on the roof of the castle's crumbling tower, I could see the little figures of men, clutching long ox-goads, vaulting down from their positions behind the big beasts and running as fast as their legs would carry them into the safety of the trees. As the English *conroi* trotted up to it, the entire French siege train came to a complete stop, deserted both by guards and drivers, the oxen dropping their block-like heads and beginning to crop placidly at the grass between their feet.

King Richard had come to Verneuil in all his power and might. And King Philip had lost his siege train.

5

THE KING, DELIGHTED BY OUR SUCCESSFUL defense of Verneuil, was so overcome with happiness that he embraced Sir Aubrey and myself in turn, and kissed us both the minute he stepped off his horse in the center of the battered castle courtyard. He promised a pouch of bright silver for each of the men-at-arms who had fought there so valiantly, and lands and honors for Sir Aubrey and myself.

"I knew you would not fail me, Sir Alan," Richard said when he had embraced me, holding me by the elbows like an old friend. "You are clearly a man who can be trusted with a castle. Some of my counselors suggested that you were too inexperienced a knight to hold this place against Philip's might"—he shot a stern glance at Mercadier, who looked levelly back at him, his dark, scarred face unreadable, his brown eyes devoid of any expression—"but I knew you had the right stuff in you for this task."

I wallowed in King Richard's praise; it seemed to warm the very corners of my soul, and somehow it made all the slaughter and suffering of the past few days seem worthwhile. But while I was happy to see my King again, and receive his gratitude, there were two other men in his company who doubled my joy at the royal arrival.

As the sun began to sink, we had lit the courtyard with many torches to welcome the King. And as Richard clapped me on the shoulder and strode away across the open space toward the small hall, shouting for his steward and ordering the servants to prepare a victory feast as swiftly as possible, in the flickering torchlight I gazed up at my lord, Robert, Earl of Locksley, as he looked down at me fondly from the back of a huge red bay horse. My friend, the erstwhile outlaw, the reluctant pilgrim, the man the common people still called Robin Hood, said: "Well, Alan, I see you've been bathing in glory once again."

"Just humbly doing my duty, sir," I said, grinning up at him. My heart was full at the sight of him, though I noticed that he was paler and thinner than I recalled. Nevertheless, he was here in Verneuil in the flesh and I felt the weight of command, the warlord's responsibility for the lives of his men, float from my young shoulders and pass to his infinitely broader ones. And for that, and for the sight of him alive and well, I gave thanks to God.

"I've never much cared for humility," said my lord, with his familiar mocking smile. "And duty is merely the name we give to an unpleasant task that is unlikely to be rewarded. But I will say this: well done, Alan. You've done a man's work here. And I am proud of you."

I held his horse's bridle while Robin swung down from the saddle; he was moving a little stiffly and he winced when his boots hit the beaten earth of the courtyard.

"How is the leg?" I asked. The wound he had taken at Nottingham was the second to that same limb in two years.

"Almost mended. The muscles are still weak and I could have done with more rest; but the King summoned me and so I had to obey—obedience to one's lord is one virtue that I do hold with." My own lord gave me a quick smile, to show that he was half-jesting, and his strange silver-gray eyes twinkled at me in the torchlight.

A massive blow, like a kick from an angry mule, exploded in the center of my back, knocking me a pace forward. I turned fast, dropping the reins of Robin's horse, my hand going to the hilt of my sword and half-drawing the blade. A huge figure loomed over me, a human tower only half-visible in the leaping light of the pine torches. A thatch of blond hair crowned a vast lumpy red face that would have terrified an ogre—if it wasn't for its broad, friendly and very familiar grin. It was my old friend John Nailor, known by all as Little John. I released the handle of my weapon, allowing the long blade to slide into its scabbard, and clasped the extended meaty hand that had slapped me so hard on the back.

"God's bulging ball-bag, young Alan, you are as jumpy as a lady rabbit in a fox lord's bedchamber," said Little John, shaking his head in mock sorrow. "It must be a bad conscience. Feeling guilty about something, are you? Been indulging in one of your legendary bouts of onanism again, eh? Have you, lad? You can tell your old uncle John. Bit too much of the old hand-to-cock combat, eh? You've got to leave it alone sometimes, you know, Alan. You can't go on threshing the barley stalk all day and night. It weakens your nerve, rots your brains, can make you go blind, too."

"You do talk some rare horseshit, John Nailor. My nerves are absolutely fine. Nothing wrong with them at all."

I was blushing and I could see Robin trying hard not to laugh, covering his mouth with his hand and making as if to scratch his chin.

I summoned my wits: "I must say, John, it's very good of you to finally turn up. We might have had a use for you a couple of days ago, before the battle—there was a good deal of heavy lifting to be done: boxes, bales, cauldrons of hot oil . . . Donkey work, of course, but it would have suited you perfectly. And I say 'before the battle'; I doubt an idle fellow like you would have been much use during it."

"Aye, I can see you've had a bit of a scrap here," John said, looking around the battered castle, his eye fixing on the half-burnt front gate. "But I worry about you, Alan, I truly do. I'm not sure that you've got a firm grasp of proper tactics yet. It is generally not considered a sound idea to burn down your *own* defenses. You know, I think it's rather frowned upon by real soldiers. I can see I still have a lot to teach you." He shook his massive head sorrowfully, and made an infuriating tsk-tsk noise behind his big teeth.

I glared at John and opened my mouth to reply, but Robin interrupted our familiar bickering by handing me a heavy package, wrapped in sheepskin and tied with twine.

"It's a gift from Godifa," said Robin. "And it comes with all her love. Marie-Anne and Tuck send theirs, too."

"Is all well in Yorkshire?" I asked my lord. He nodded. "Marie-Anne and Tuck have moved down to Westbury to be with Goody. And Marie-Anne is with child again." I looked at him and I could tell that he was much pleased by his wife's condition.

"I heartily congratulate you, my lord," I said formally, but with a happy smile.

"Yes, it is good news," said Robin modestly. "I'll tell you all the rest later. Are you not going to open your gift?"

"I expect it's a dozen pairs of fresh, clean braies," said John with an evil smirk. "She will know that, with all these nasty Frenchmen about, you'll have been shitting yourself in fear like a stomach-sick goose . . ."

I weighed the package in my hands. Godifa, known as Goody, was my betrothed—a girl of startling beauty and immense courage, with an alarmingly violent temper, who had been raised by rough outlaws in Sherwood, and who was now attempting to learn to be a fine lady under the tutelage of Robin's wife, Marie-Anne, Countess of Locksley.

I fumbled open the sheepskin and discovered inside a mace—a beautiful flanged mace: two feet long with an iron-hard oak shaft and half a pound of wrought steel on the end. I had used one on the Great Pilgrimage, but lost it in battle in Cyprus. Goody knew that I prized it as a weapon, and that I missed the one I had lost. In the right hands, a mace was a fearsome killing tool. The head of the mace was covered with flat triangular pieces of steel welded in a circle around the head, the points facing outward. It was brutally effective in battle, designed to smash bones and crush organs through a knight's mail, but it was somehow an object of great beauty, too. I turned it over in my hands, thinking: *How typical of Goody! How useful and how ungirlishly practical a gift this is.* There was a scrap of parchment inside the package, and in a shaky, childish hand that I could barely make out in the gloom of the courtyard, these words were written in splotched Latin: *God keep you safe, my love.*

I felt a tremendous surge of emotion at those words; and I realized how much I was missing my beloved girl, my wonderful wife-to-be. I longed to be near her again, to kiss her perfect red lips, to stare into her lovely violet-blue eyes, to wrap her tightly in my arms . . .

"You are probably puzzling over what it is," said John, crudely breaking in on my thoughts. "Let me enlighten you. It's called a *mace*"—he spoke the last word deliberately, as if I was a simpleton—"it's a big club for hitting Frenchmen. If you are a very good boy, Uncle John will show you how to use it one day—"

"Be quiet now, John," Robin said with absolute authority. He could see that I was struggling to keep my composure under the storm of emotions that were besieging my heart.

"Owain is dead," I said, my throat swollen and clogged.

"Yes, I know," said Robin. "He was the best of men."

"I miss him already," I said.

"It's all right, lad. We all miss him," said Little John.

"Shall we go into the hall?" said Robin, after a moment's silence, and all I could manage was a snuffling grunt by way of an affirmative.

I performed "King Philip's Folly" for the French monarch's royal cousin Richard the Lionheart that evening. In the castle's small and rather shabby hall, now made as regal as possible with golden firelight and many beeswax candles, our knightly company enlivened with good wine, good meat and good cheer, I mocked the French King and made my own sovereign laugh until he wept, his white teeth flashing in the candlelight, his red-gold hair seeming to dance and sparkle with his immoderate joy.

The King had come to Verneuil with most of his strength, and among the faces that I glimpsed through the smoky hall were some of the noblest and most powerful men in Europe: William the Marshal was there, his battered soldier's face split with a huge grin at my impudence to French royalty, while Sir Aymeric de St. Maur, representing the English Knights Templar, and Robert, Earl of Leicester, both seemed a little shocked at the crudity of my *fabliau*. Scar-faced Mercadier, Richard's fearsome mercenary captain, stared at me steadily and soullessly. Gloomy John of Alençon seemed to be almost cheerful for once, and Sir Nicholas de Scras, an old friend and former Knight Hospitaler, who now served the Marshal, applauded my music vigorously whenever I paused, while Sir Aubrey de Chambois looked on, pale but contented, sipping his wine slowly and savoring his continued existence. A couple of Anglo-Norman barons whose names I did not know peered at me quizzically through the smoky gloom as I sang and played my vielle for Richard's traveling court, but they laughed in all the right places—while the Earl of Locksley watched me perform with the air of a proud older brother.

I had recovered my composure during the course of the feast, and I followed my raucous performance of "King Philip's Folly" with a tender *canso* directed at my lovely Goody. King Richard was especially kind to me when I had finished, uprooting several barons from their places and seating me beside him, sharing his golden goblet of wine with me and asking me to recount the tale of the siege and my part in it. He was treating me as a hero, and I must confess that I did not find it a distasteful experience.

I took the circumstance of my King's good favor to ask his permission to travel to Vendôme and seek an audience with Cardinal Heribert at the earliest opportunity. I told him of my desire to discover my father's killer, but the King, to my surprise, was guarded in his response. "We will see, Alan, we will see," he said. "I am going to need every fighting man I have to push Philip and his allies back in Normandy and in my lands to the south as well. So, I regret that I cannot allow you at this moment to go galloping off on a private quest—however important it might seem to you. But we will see how things turn out. It may well be that I shall be heading in that direction myself in the next few days, and perhaps I shall be able to grant you the freedom to follow your heart then."

And I had to be content with that.

The next morning Richard summoned all his knights and barons for a council of war in the castle courtyard. It was another bright spring day, and I stood beside Robin in glorious sunshine to hear what our sovereign had planned out for the coming campaign.

The King was in a buoyant mood, seemingly glowing from within, as if lit by the inner torch of his own enthusiasm. Without the slightest formality, without even a prayer from one of his priests, the King began: "Many of you already know this, but I think it is worth repeating so that we are all clear about the situation as it stands. For the past two years, King Philip has been pushing westward into Normandy, taking my castles, either by treachery or force, and extending his rule into my dominions. He has taken Gisors, perhaps the most important castle on the border, the key to the whole of eastern Normandy, and has fortified and reinforced it so that it is virtually impregnable. He also now holds a tongue of land thirty miles deep inside Normandy to the northeast of here from Tillières on the Avre, north to Beaumont-le-Roger and Le Neubourg, and east to Vaudrail—but for the moment his advance has been stopped here at Verneuil by the gallant actions of Sir Aubrey de Chambois and Sir Alan Dale. And I salute them both for their exemplary valor!"

There was a murmur of congratulation from the assembled knights; I could feel my cheeks flushing with embarrassed pleasure. I was aware that it was a rare honor to be praised by the greatest monarch in Christendom in front of the cream of its knighthood.

King Richard continued: "This is the turning point. While I have been indisposed, Philip has advanced. That stops now. From now on, we go on the attack. From now on, he is on the defensive. From now on, we start to win."

The King said these words casually, without any special emphasis, but I found that I believed him utterly. He had that quality, a quality that made you enormously confident of success just because he was with you. It was absurd, of course, but it worked. Richard's presence on the battlefield, it was truly said, was worth a hundred knights.

The King was still speaking: "The heart of the French enclave of conquered land is the castle of Evreux, which until recently was held by my brother John, for Philip."

There were a few murmurs, grumbles and muttered oaths, but Richard's face was a picture of seriousness. "For those of you who do not know this already, my brother has seen the error of his ways and has renewed his allegiance to me. I have forgiven him. I have absolved him of his crimes. He has since returned to Evreux with a strong force of our knights and that fortress is now back in our hands."

Once again a restrained babbling broke out, but as Richard raised a hand to quiet the crowd of barons and knights around him, a strong voice cut through the general murmuring. "Is it true that Prince John slaughtered all the French inhabitants of the town of Evreux? Cut down all of them—peasants, merchants, artisans, monks, nuns, priests—men, women and children . . ." I recognized the familiar growling tones of William the Marshal, and sensed a hum of righteous anger behind his question.

"Why would he do that?" I said, without taking time to think. "What would be the point of such savagery?"

For the tiniest part of a moment, Richard looked uncertain; he opened his mouth to speak but he was superseded before he could utter a word.

A cold, lapidary voice spoke instead. "It is true. He killed them all. Slaughtered every one of them. And I helped him do it," said Mercadier, who was standing at the King's elbow. "They were traitors, they were scum who served Philip and they all deserved to die."

The scarred man seemed to be speaking directly at me. I was drawing a deep breath, ready to condemn his brutality, when King Richard spoke: "Yes, my brother and Mercadier killed many in Evreux—and God may well judge them for it in the next world. But you should consider this, Sir Alan: in doing so, Mercadier and John saved your life."

I was completely wrong-footed, baffled, and it must have shown. How could a massacre of townspeople thirty miles away have saved my life?

Richard smiled sadly at me: "Why do you think King Philip disappeared so quickly with most of his army? Did you think your handful of men had frightened him away?"

"No," I said, a little nettled, "I thought that you had."

"It was neither of us, I am afraid," Richard replied. "It was John. When King Philip heard what my brother had done in Evreux, he hurried there with all possible speed to avenge his people. And while we still hold the castle there, Philip is now furiously besieging our loyal men inside it.

"But not for long. I will come back to that in a few moments, if I may. For now, let us continue." Richard cleared his throat. "There are three main areas of operation in this war against Philip. The first theater is here in Normandy; the second is south around Touraine and the Loire Valley; and the third is in the far south in Aquitaine, my mother's homeland. In all three areas, Philip will seek to cause mischief, either in person or through his allies; he will bribe and buy support from my vassals where he can, and intimidate others. He will be up to his knavish tricks from Rouen to Toulouse, and I must show my vassals, wherever they are, that I will not forgive treachery and I will put down any rebellion with speed and determination, and I will smash Philip's armies wherever and whenever they can be brought to battle. And so, we must be prepared to tackle him on all three fronts—simultaneously, if necessary." The King took a deep breath. "Accordingly, I've decided to split the army into three parts."

There was another outbreak of muttering among the assembled knights. Dividing an army weakened it and if the entire enemy force was able to concentrate against any one part, it could prove disastrous.

"I have no choice," Richard said, answering a rumble of half-asked questions. "I must act immediately in several regions hundreds of miles apart, and I cannot be in all places at the same time. Anyway, I have made my decision. This is how it will go: firstly, Prince John and the earls of Leicester and Arundel will hold Normandy for me. They will protect Rouen from Philip's depredations, and attempt to take back as much territory as they can without endangering their own ability to operate effectively in the northern theater. Secondly, in the center, Alençon, I want you to go down to Maine and link up there with my knights from Anjou, who are presently at Le Mans. Your task is to take Montmirail and destroy it and, if he ventures out of his bolt-hole at Chateâudun, I want you to give Geoffrey of the Perche a bloody nose. Thirdly, the earls of Striguil and Locksley, Mercadier and myself, and the bulk of the army will push on further south. We will join my ally and friend Sancho of Navarre and retake the castle of Loches."

It was a good plan, clear and simple, and despite their reservations about splitting the army, the barons recognized it as such. Sancho, the heir to the King of Navarre, a small country on the far side of the Pyrenees, was King Richard's brother-in-law. He had been a staunch supporter of Richard since his marriage to Sancho's sister Berengaria in Cyprus three years ago. While the Lionheart was imprisoned, the Spanish warlord had guarded the southern flank of Richard's huge dukedom of Aquitaine, battling restless local barons who had been encouraged to revolt by King Philip.

Loches was a powerful fortress with a massive keep, the stone walls of which were reputed to be twelve feet thick. It had been held time out of mind by the counts of Anjou, Richard's forefathers, and was the key to the County of Touraine, guarding the frontier with the King of France's territory in the center. Quite apart from the issue of family pride—which had been badly dented by its loss—our King could not ride south to reconquer the rebellious parts of Aquitaine so long as Loches remained garrisoned by scores of enemy knights, like a dagger at his back. He had to take it as the first step in subduing the south—pride and practicality, for once, marching perfectly in step.

So, in the sunny courtyard of Verneuil, the barons reluctantly accepted Richard's plan to split the army and began to confer with him individually on various points of detail—such as which castles should be reduced first, which could be safely ignored, which territories should be ravaged, known areas of enemy weakness, the numbers of men and horses, quantities of fodder and supplies, spare weapons, siege engines and the like that they might take with them—and all the crucial minutiae of warfare. Meanwhile, Robin dispatched Little John and myself to prepare the Locksley men for travel.

For in the morning we would march south. To Loches.

There was a final episode to my time at Verneuil, a strange and chilling event that set my mind racing. On the evening before our departure for the south, I called into the makeshift infirmary to bid farewell to Father Jean de Puy and to thank him for being so generous with his memories.

I walked into the stable block and scanned the lines of wounded men on the straw-strewn floor, some asleep, others gently moving and moaning—cursing their injuries, or calling for their wives or mothers. There was no sign of Father Jean. I brought water to a few of the men who requested it, talked quietly to a pair of injured men-at-arms who were awake and in only moderate pain, and waited a full hour for Father Jean to return. It was most unlike him, I thought, to neglect his charges for so long.

After turning over and over in my mind the mystery of the priest's absence, I determined that I would search the castle to see if I could discover his whereabouts. And it did not take long to find him—or what remained of him.

I found Father Jean lying behind the stable block, huddled in a narrow space between the rear of the infirmary and the dirty-gray stone wall of the castle. His face was bone white, his eyes were half-open, yet he looked strangely peaceful. He was dead, of course, and, as I reckoned it, he had been so for several hours. He had been stabbed in the chest; there was a deep puncture wound a little to the left of the sternum, caused by a single thrust directly into the heart. Jean de Puy had been murdered; killed quickly and quietly by what I judged to be an expert hand.

6

IT TOOK UNTIL MID-MORNING BEFORE KING Richard's column was ready to march. We were about three thousand souls—proud knights and their harassed squires, scarred men-at-arms, broad-backed archers and gaudily dressed crossbowmen; rough-tongued *routiers* and refined priests, long-nosed chaplains and pungent friars, raw-fingered washerwomen and saucy, giggling whores—butchers, bakers and candle-sellers, pardoners, fortune-tellers, beggars, blacksmiths and jongleurs . . . men and women of all ranks and every calling. And at the apex of this heaving, seething mass of jostling humanity stood the King and his senior barons and his household knights. Inevitably the column would be a slow-moving one: King Philip's captured trebuchets, mangonels and onagers swelled Richard's already far more impressive siege train of a dozen heavy pieces of stone-throwing artillery. Thirty feet high and constructed of foot-thick oak beams, these machines were affectionately known as the "castle-breakers" and were attended by a swarm of experts as well as the sappers, miners, carters and common ox-herdsmen of the siege train. The main column would only move as fast as the slowest trebuchet ox-team, pulling the heaviest piece of artillery, and even then a wagon might be stuck in a morass of mud or lose one of its massive solid oak wheels and the entire column must wait for it to be repaired or rescued before the march could resume.

I was happy, therefore, that Robin's men formed their own column in the vanguard of the King's army. My Lord of Locksley had orders to send men on ahead to scout out the land and report intelligence back to the main column. He knew this land, as did I, having traveled through it four years ago on our way to the Holy Land.

Robin had brought reinforcements with him from Yorkshire: another hundred and fifty men, once again mixed archers and light cavalry, and all well mounted. And when my advance troop, those who had survived the siege of Verneuil or who had been only lightly wounded, was rejoined to Robin's command we numbered more than two hundred fighting men. Robin had banished the hangers-on from our column, and the baggage and better-quality horses—including my beloved gelding Ghost and Shaitan my destrier—remained with the supply train of the main army. I rode a fast courser belonging to Robin, a horse better suited to rough riding and scouting work than my two more valuable warhorses. We were to be an exploring column, a light, fast-moving unit whose task it was to see what was beyond the next hill, report back to the King and his advisers, relay messages, and warn them of any trouble.

We were heading southwest, along the line of the River Avre, and we would soon cross that natural barrier and enter the realm of Count Geoffrey of the Perche, a vassal who had renounced his allegiance to King Richard and sided with Philip. Geoffrey was now our enemy and the troops had the royal license, as long as they did not stray far from the slow-moving column, to raid farms, empty barns, and collect domestic beasts—in short, to steal anything that they wanted while we traveled through his territory. We did not expect to meet the count and his forces; they were holed up down in the south at Chateâudun and Richard did not want to waste time in reducing the minor castles of the county. His thinking, Robin told me that morning, was that Geoffrey was a trimmer who would always go with the prevailing wind. If Richard were in the ascendant, then

Geoffrey would come back to our side. There was no need to squander men, resources and valuable time in reducing his fortresses when, if we triumphed in the south, he would come meekly back into the fold anyway. And Richard harbored no personal grudge against the man—Geoffrey was Philip's cousin, after all, and while Richard was his lawful lord, his lands bordered on those of the French King. A victory in the south was what we needed, Robin said, not petty vindictiveness against a man who, anyway, would have had little chance of resisting the might of King Philip's armies.

The sun shone brightly as we rode, but a keen wind prevented the day from becoming oppressively hot, clad as we were for battle in heavy mail and helmets. I had spoken to Robin about Father Jean's death before we left Verneuil, and he had informed the King, but there was no time to make a proper inquiry. So the great column had departed, lumbering its slow way southwest, leaving Sir Aubrey de Chambois to recover from his crossbow wound with a fresh garrison of men-at-arms and two experienced masons whose task it was to repair the castle's walls. Sir Aubrey had been shocked by Father Jean's death—and he had vowed that he would make all the necessary inquiries and discover whatever he could about the murder. But I had no high hopes that he would uncover the man who had killed my father's old friend, and I said as much to Robin as we crossed the River Avre by a mossy wooden bridge and rode into the foothills of the County of the Perche.

"I think you are right, Alan," said my lord. He seemed distracted that bright morning, almost fidgety. "I fear we shall never know who killed the man. And perhaps it would be best to put the matter from our minds." And then he fell silent, shading his eyes to scan the forested country ahead.

I was puzzled by his answer. "Surely we should seek justice for the poor fellow?" I said. "He was a good man, a fine priest, and he did not deserve such an ignoble end."

"He was a priest, yes—so surely you believe that he is in the Kingdom of Heaven now. So he's happy, isn't he?"

I was a little taken aback by Robin's words; I had long known, and indeed it was an open secret among his friends, that Robin was no Christian—indeed, he often mocked the Church—but I did not expect him to be so offhand about murder. I bit my lip, and Robin, sensing my discomfort, glanced over at me.

"I have no objection to justice as a general principle," he said, giving me a half-smile, "so long as it does not greatly inconvenience me. But he was not one of our men, nor kin to any of us, and so I see no reason why we should be concerned about punishing his murderer."

I opened my mouth to protest, and then closed it again. Robin and I had had this conversation many times before and I knew well his position. His philosophy was as brutal as a butcher's cleaver. He entertained no notions of a fair and just commonwealth of mankind; he considered such a notion a childish fantasy. Robin's view was that a man had a duty only to protect those around him: his family and the men and women who served him or whom he served. He called this small group of souls his "circle" or his *familia*—anyone inside it was to be protected with all his strength and resources, and I knew that he would readily give his life for anyone in that charmed ring. But anyone outside that circle—strangers, enemies, even fellow countrymen with whom he had no connection—meant nothing to him. It was a point we had differed on in the past: I felt that Christ's teachings, indeed the whole essence of the idea of Christendom, of civilization itself, was that all men were members of a whole, beloved by God, and all deserved mercy, justice and the chance of Salvation.

"Well, *I* should like to see Father Jean's killer caught and punished," I said, somewhat lamely.

"Perhaps he will be, perhaps he won't. We do not gain or lose from it, so far as I can tell."

I found Robin's disinterest irksome, and for some reason I could not stop myself adding: "I wonder whether there might have been anything more he could have told me about my father's death." Although in my heart I was certain that he had had nothing further to divulge.

Robin looked at me sharply—he knew all about the shadowy "man you cannot refuse" and my quest to find him. "Alan," he said, "I understand why this is of interest to you, but I must urgently counsel you not to pursue this matter. Your father is dead, he has been dead for ten years; Sir Ralph Murdac killed him; and Murdac is dead—you *must* let this go. I promise you that no good will come of raking over the past. You will achieve nothing—and you may well disturb something evil that is better left in peace. Now, be a good fellow, take a dozen men and sweep that covey yonder: it's a likely spot for an ambush." He handed me a small polished cow's horn with a silver lippiece. "Give three blasts on that if you get into any trouble, and we'll come running to save you."

He gave me a not-altogether pleasant smile as I looped the thong attached to the horn over the pommel of my saddle, but I had the sense to keep silent. And for the next two hours, accompanied by a band of mounted archers, I thrashed through the dense undergrowth of a small wood, scratching my face and hands, and my poor horse's hide, on brambles and branches, fruitlessly searching for foes that Robin and I both knew were not there.

The next day, Robin, it seemed, was in a better mood. As we rode along through the hilly, green and surprisingly tranquil countryside of the Perche, he gave me the news from home. Marie-Anne was as delighted as he was to be pregnant again: "She's glowing, Alan—I mean absolutely radiant—and already becoming plump. I think it will be a boy; a fine tall son for me to leave behind when I'm cold in my grave."

Robin already had one son—a sturdy four-year-old called Hugh, but there was a secret about his birth that was never mentioned in my lord's presence. Hugh was the true child of Sir Ralph Murdac. This erstwhile sheriff of Nottinghamshire had raped Marie-Anne and got her with child, yet Robin had publicly acknowledged Hugh as his own son—indeed, he made it clear that he would instantly kill anyone who suggested otherwise. And I admired him deeply for this act of compassion. It was a measure of his love for Marie-Anne that he took her to wife despite the fact that she had been despoiled by Murdac's touch, and that her son Hugh was not truly his. Even so, it was clear that he was elated to have another child that was his own blood beyond a shadow of doubt.

"And I have had a letter from our old friend Reuben," Robin continued. "He has left the Holy Land and settled in Montpellier to study medicine. He writes that he has a fine big house with a large herb garden, and hints that he has formed an attachment to a local widow. He's trading a little too, he says, with the Moors of Spain."

"Not frankincense?" I asked. Reuben, a tough, dried brown stick of a man, was a Jew who until recently had managed Robin's lucrative frankincense concerns in Gaza.

"No, not frankincense," said Robin. "Leather, spice, precious metals . . . Reuben is now a wealthy man, you know. Somehow, I can't see him settling down and growing fat just yet; he has a restless spirit that will not take its ease. But I may be wrong."

"Tell me about Goody—was she well and in good spirits when you last saw her?"

Robin smiled at me. "She is a fine lass, Alan, and you are a lucky man. Yes, she is healthy, and all is well at Westbury. It seems that she and your steward Baldwin have made an alliance and are turning Westbury into an orderly, productive and well-run place. She wants to please you, Alan, she wants you to be proud of her. So take a note of what she has achieved at Westbury, when you return, and make sure you praise her for it. But there is one thing that troubles me . . ."

"What? What is it?"

"It may be nothing, Alan, but . . . I still have many friends in Nottingham and in Sherwood from the old days who tell me things from time to time. And I have heard rumors, evil rumors of black magic and witchcraft . . ."

"It's Nur, isn't it?"

"It is. It may all be overblown, Alan. And it may well come to nothing. But they say she has been gathering followers—the mad, the deformed, the ugly, and some unhappy women who have run from their menfolk. And I have heard she has sworn vengeance on you and Goody."

Nur. I felt a shiver run down my spine at the mention of her name. Nur, once the most beautiful, exquisite girl I had ever seen, had been my lover on the Great Pilgrimage to Outremer. I had sworn to protect her, but had failed. My enemies had taken her and destroyed her beauty, cutting away her nose and lips and ears, and leaving her alive, a monstrous mockery of her once-lovely self. I had not protected her, neither had I continued to love her after her awful mutilation. And her love for me had turned to hate: she had followed me, alone, on foot, all the way home from the Holy Land, becoming wild and mad and richer in malice with every step, and she had burst into my betrothal feast and cursed Goody and myself in front of hundreds of guests. And yet Goody, my fiery, passionate Goody, had rebutted her curse and had beaten her to within an inch of her life before expelling her from the hall. And now Nur wanted revenge for all the humiliations inflicted on her. Suddenly the breeze seemed to blow cold.

"Alan! Listen to me," said my lord. "I have sent a dozen good men to Westbury as a garrison, and Marie-Anne and Tuck to keep Goody company there. She is safe, among good friends, surrounded by guards, and that poor, mad, bedraggled creature can do nothing to hurt her. Alan—trust me on this. Goody is perfectly safe!"

I prayed that Robin was right.

It took us more than a week to travel down to Tours, and while we encountered no enemies of any significance, it was still a busy time for me. One evening, bone-weary and lying in my blankets in camp, I reckoned that I must have traveled ten times the distance of a knight riding with the King's household, for I was constantly galloping back and forward, ferrying messages between Richard and the Earl of Locksley. I had come to the conclusion that Robin was right about Goody. She had proven herself more than a match for Nur at my betrothal feast; and Tuck, a man of God, would easily be able to counter any magical nonsense the deformed madwoman might concoct. She was safe, spiritually and physically. And I was comforted.

I was riding Ghost, my gray gelding, one day, to allow the courser to rest, and had a message from Robin for the King in my saddlebag, when I heard the sound of screaming on the still June air. Hanno and I reined up simultaneously, and Thomas, who had been riding some twenty yards behind us, clattered up and stopped his mount to my right. We were passing through a wide, shallow valley, a sheep pasture with a stream trickling down from a spring to the east and heading away south. The rutted earth road we were on ran straight through the center of the valley. The three of us sat in silence for a moment, and then a hideous wail of agony split the morning once again. It seemed to be coming from a small shrine—a one-roomed wooden-framed building no bigger than a cottage but with a tall cross on the roof ridge—built beside the spring, halfway up the side of the valley. I had ridden past this place the day before and had assumed that it was deserted. Now I could see a thread of smoke coming from behind the building and four horses tethered to a rail at the front of it.

Another scream wrenched at our ears. And I thought, *A wise man, knowing he had an important message to deliver to his King, would just ride on by . . .*

Hanno and I approached the shrine cautiously, having told Thomas to stay back on the road and if we got into trouble to ride for the safety of the main column, which we knew to be only half a dozen miles to the north. Our blades loose in their sheaths, all senses extended, and Hanno cradling a powerful crossbow that had been spanned and loaded with a foot-long steel-tipped oak quarrel, we walked our horses around the back of the wooden building. There we came across a knot of about a dozen rough-looking men gathered around a campfire. My eyes took in many things at the same time: something of a party or feast seemed to be in progress, the men were red-faced, glowing and some had hunks of bread and meat and what appeared to be cheese in their hands, and I could see a couple of half-empty skins of wine lying on the grass. One man was asleep in the lee of the wall of the shrine, cuddling a half-eaten joint of meat.

But this was no celebration; in the center of the group of revelers was a tight knot of men subduing a struggling bundle in brown wool—a man, and by his robe I could tell he was a monk. His feet were bare and red and blistered, and I knew with a lurch to my stomach what had been taking place here. Only one man of that company was still a-horse, gazing down on the proceedings with a crooked little smile on his lips—a mop of shaggy black hair and a deep scar diagonally across his dark face; it was Mercadier.

He looked over at me, incuriously, and slightly inclined his black head. "Sir Alan," he said in his deep, stony voice. "Good morning to you."

I said nothing, staring at the writhing scrum around the struggling brown-clad monk. One of the *routiers* had a firm grip on the monk's bare ankle, and as I watched with horror he and his fellows wrestled the limb toward the fire and, with a heave, plunged the bare sole of the foot into a heap of orange-glowing embers at the edge of the blaze. There was a sizzle and a puff of grayish smoke and a stench like rancid roasting pork was released into the air.

The monk let out a long, high scream of agony. I felt sick—my mind went back to a damp dungeon in Winchester some years ago, and the pain of a red-hot iron being applied to my soft underparts.

"His cries have a somewhat musical quality, do you not think so, Sir Alan?" said the mounted mercenary captain. "Perhaps you might compose something from his noise."

"What is his crime, that you should torment him so?" I asked Mercadier, feeling my anger rise and wishing to Christ that the poor man, clearly the guardian of the shrine, would stop his terrible yowling.

"Crime?" said the scarred captain. "His crime is that he has failed to render unto Caesar those things that are rightfully Caesar's."

"What?" I was taken aback. I had not expected Mercadier to quote the scriptures.

He sighed. "He will not tell us where he keeps his silver, his coin, his valuables—the rich offerings from pilgrims who come to pray at this holy little shit-hole."

"Perhaps he has none," I said.

"That is what we intend to find out," was the flat reply.

But I was slipping off my horse by then, all sense of caution flown to the winds. I marched over to the knot of men around the monk and roughly pulled one of them away by the shoulder.

"Put him down," I said, quietly and firmly to the rest of them. Hanno was still in the saddle, but I could see that the loaded crossbow just happened to be resting on the pommel of his saddle and pointing unwaveringly in our direction.

The *routiers* around the monk were confused; some glanced over at Mercadier for orders, others glared at me for interrupting their sport. They still grasped the monk by his legs, shoulders and arms, but the man was no longer struggling nor, thank God, screaming. I saw his face for the first time: he was old, perhaps sixty, very gaunt, twig-thin, with watery blue eyes and only wisps of white hair on the papery skin of his scalp.

"Put him down," I said again, this time louder and with a little more iron in the tone. "Put him down, gently!"

"Why don't you fuck off, Sir Knight, and find your own church mouse to play with," said a squat red-bearded man who was holding one of the monk's twig-thin arms. "This one is ours!"

Without pausing even for an instant to think of the consequences of my actions, I swayed my shoulders and powered my head down and across in a short hard arc, smashing my forehead with massive force into the bridge of his nose. The redhead staggered back and fell to one knee, blood spurting from his flattened nose. He should have counted himself lucky that it had been too hot that day for me to wear my steel helm. The rest of the men holding the monk dropped their load as if it was a bar of red-hot iron, stepped back and began fumbling for their weapons. My hand went to my sword hilt and I half-drew the blade.

"Leave him be," said a cold, dead voice with a slight Gascon accent, and every man around that fire froze. I ignored the men and their half-pulled weapons and reached down and tried to help the monk to his feet, but halfway through my action I realized that he would not be able to stand, so I picked him up bodily and slung him over my shoulder. He weighed no more than a ten-year-old.

I straightened up and looked round the circle of statue-like *routiers*, a hard challenge in my stare. And I caught Mercadier's eye as I began to move away, the monk balanced on my left shoulder, heading back toward Ghost. He was smiling sardonically down at me from his horse. A blur of movement to my right: the redhead I had knocked down was on his feet, an axe in his hand, and he was coming for me. My sword hilt was entangled in the priest's skinny legs. My heart banged once. The world slowed. I saw the red man, bloodied face snarling, draw back his axe to chop at my undefended head—then there was a twang, a thump and he was swept backward, off his feet. And I found myself looking down at his writhing body, a black quarrel jutting from the center of his chest.

Turning my head I saw that Hanno had already slung the crossbow from his saddle and drawn his sword. I moved quickly back toward Ghost, heaved the monk onto the gray's haunches behind the high wooden saddle, and climbed into the seat as swiftly as I could. The men on the far side of the fire were still frozen, watching me, and making the air heavy with their silent hatred.

Then Mercadier spoke: "You have saved one worthless old monk, and killed one of my prime men-at-arms." His voice had no emotion in it whatsoever—neither sorrow at his man's death nor anger at my interference in his actions. "I do not think it is a fair exchange."

"It is not," I said. I was angry then, and I let it show. I jerked my left thumb behind me. "This is a man of God, a decent fellow who does no harm but merely prays for all our souls; your man was a cowardly brute, of no more worth than a wild animal. It is certainly not a fair exchange, it is a great bargain for mankind."

Mercadier said nothing, just stared at me with his cold, brown eyes. I shrugged and, having nothing else to say on the matter myself, nodded to Hanno and turned Ghost around and trotted down the gentle slope to rejoin Thomas and the road north.

The monk's name was Dominic and he was a deeply pious individual, I soon discovered, even for a man of the cloth. When I tried to question him as to which religious order he belonged to, he mumbled something about the Holy Trinity. I couldn't make out whether he was praying or trying to tell me something. The poor man's feet were both very badly burned—indeed, he was almost out of his mind with pain—and I half-expected him to die as we bounced down the rough track away from that quiet valley and Mercadier's wolfish men. I had no wish to add to his pains by trying to force information out of him while he was so grievously injured.

When we arrived at the King's column an hour later, I left him in the charge of some of the half-fit Locksley men who were responsible for our baggage train, spare horses and personal possessions. A strange wise woman named Elise, who had followed Robin from Normandy to the Holy Land and now back to France, undertook to treat his wounds and make sure that he was comfortably ensconced on a baggage wagon as the column trundled along.

Having rescued him, I did not know what to do with Dominic. His shrine had been burned to ruins shortly after I had ridden away from that valley. I saw the still-smoking charred remains as I rode past it again the next day, delivering yet another message between the King and the Earl of Locksley, and presumed that Mercadier's men had done it as some sort of revenge for the loss of their redheaded *routier.* I would not have cared, were it not for the fact that I now had an aged monk on my hands, one who could not walk and had no way of fending for himself. I did not know which high churchman, which prior or abbot, was his lord, nor which monastery he belonged to, and had not had time to visit him and ask him. For the moment, I thought, he could stay under Elise's care and if necessary, we could find a position for him somewhere in the army; as a chaplain's assistant, perhaps.

I shoved that thought aside. We were approaching Tours: Robin's men had been given the task of reconnoitering the city and preparing it for a visit from their rightful liege lord, King Richard. The townsmen must now be very worried, Robin confided in me, as they had been a leaf's thickness away, on several occasions, from siding with King Philip. The flirting between the merchants of the town and the envoys from Paris had been as falsely coy as the relations between a willing milkmaid and a lusty plow boy, the way Robin explained it.

In truth, Tours was not one town, but two. To the east was the older settlement, containing the castle of Tours, the cathedral and the archbishop's palace—this was on the north bank of the River Cher, a tributary of the Loire. On the Loire river itself, to the west, further north and clustered around the Abbey of St. Martin, was the new town of Tours, known as Châteauneuf. Made wealthy by the lucrative trade down the Loire to the sea, Châteauneuf was walled, neat, opulent and filled with tall timber-framed houses. It was a distinct settlement. The two towns of Tours were separated by fields of green wheat and neatly ordered vineyards. Having crossed the Loire by an impressive stone bridge, it was here that Robin and his men made their camp, directly between the two halves of the city, in a position to threaten either one with siege or assault.

"The townsfolk are wonderfully nervous, Alan, I can smell it," said Robin, after he had summoned me to his newly pitched green woolen tent in the middle of a flattened wheat field. Robin rarely used the tent on campaign, preferring whenever possible to sleep under the night sky, but it was an impressive rig, embroidered with scarlet and gold thread at the seams and constructed of thick, soft woolen cloth of the finest quality. Robin himself was dressed in his grandest clothes—black silk hose embroidered with gold, ending in elegant kidskin slippers and an emerald silk calf-length tunic over the top. His head bore a fine black hat with a jaunty peacock's feather on the side; a golden chain adorned his neck and his fingers displayed half a dozen rings of silver and gold, studded with fine jewels. He was unarmed except for a dainty pearl-handled eating knife next to the pouch at his waist. He rarely dressed this way—and never on campaign. And I realized that he was dressing to play the part of the great magnate, the noble earl. I also had the feeling that he was intending to use the tent for a small piece of theater. The sides of the tent had been raised and buttoned back to allow cool breezes to temper the warm June day and, from my stool at the campaign table in the center of the space, I could, with a slight turn of my head, clearly see both parts of the town of Tours.

Robin seemed to read the unasked question in my mind. "The Tourangeaux are frightened of us, Alan, and they are right to be. And I intend to make them even more uncomfortable. They should be here any moment."

"What have you in mind for them?" I asked.

"You are the man who is so keen on justice: I think they should pay for their wavering loyalty to the King. In the name of justice." Robin grinned at me; I did not particularly care for his expression.

At that moment, Little John came into the tent. He was dressed in an old-fashioned, short-sleeved knee-length mail coat, freshly burnished, that seemed too snug for his massive chest; he had a round shield slung across his back, his blond hair was neatly plaited into two fat ropes that framed his battered face, and he was gripping his double-bladed axe, which I noticed had been polished to a bright sheen. He was accompanied by two of Robin's biggest and ugliest bowmen, all scars and scowls and knotted muscles, who after acknowledging me cheerfully, pulled up their hoods to shade their faces and stood like statues at the back of the tent emitting menace like heat from a brazier.

"Is this really necessary, Robin? All this . . . thunder and lightning? The Tourangeaux are not the enemy. They have declared for Richard, you know." I had divined what my master was up to, and while I knew it would amuse him, I also recognized that it was not the sort of behavior the King would have condoned. But sometimes, in his lordly pomp, when he played the great earl, I forgot that in his heart of hearts Robin was still an outlaw thief, his love of easy money and mischief embedded deep into the bone.

"Just trust me, Alan, and follow my lead—we will all profit handsomely by this. You'll see."

We did not have to wait long. Robin told his new squire, a big oafish lad called Gilbert, who was the son of a Yorkshire neighbor, to serve John, himself and myself with golden cups of wine, but not to offer anything to our guests when they arrived. If they were so bold as to complain of thirst, they were to be given earthenware beakers of water, he said. Poor Gilbert looked utterly confused by this breach of etiquette, and so I sent him to summon Thomas, and Robin repeated his instructions to my squire. Thomas said nothing but merely nodded his head in his steady, intelligent way, and went immediately to see to the arrangements.

The delegation of Tourangeaux arrived at dusk. It was headed by the Archbishop of Tours, a sharp-eyed old stick named Barthélemy de Vendôme, and he was accompanied by the castellan of Tours Castle, a mutton-headed knight of middle years called Sir Roger. The bulk of the delegation consisted of merchants from Châteauneuf—I remember them only vaguely as plump, greasy, balding men, nervously wringing their velvet caps in sweaty hands—wearing as many jewels as Robin, but somehow making them seem like cheap, tawdry copies. The Archbishop was calm, almost regal; the knight Roger was scowling, but the merchants of Tours did, as my lord had prophesied, seem extremely frightened.

They stood in a slightly forlorn huddle in the southern entrance to Robin's tent, while my master observed them coldly from a thronelike chair at the back. Fine beeswax candles had been lit, and their yellow light danced across the planes of Robin's handsome, impassive face. To the right of Robin's throne, Little John and the two ugly bowmen glowered and glittered at the delegation full of martial spirit and apparent bloodlust. To Robin's left, Thomas and I stood in silence, trying to look stern.

For a long, long while nobody spoke. Finally, one of the merchants cleared his throat, but before he could say a word, Robin roared: "Silence, you traitorous dog!" It was shockingly loud and jolted every man in the tent. And then Robin returned to a brooding silence for another seemingly endless length of time.

Finally my master began, in a voice as cold as a crypt: "King Richard is coming here," he said. "He is coming in fury, with all his might—a thousand noble knights of England and Normandy. He will arrive at this wretched place on the day after tomorrow."

Archbishop Barthélemy was smiling crookedly, apparently enjoying some private source of amusement. The head merchant licked his lips. Sir Roger looked deeply puzzled: "We are all, of course, Richard's loyal men, entirely at the King's command," the knight said hesitantly.

"Loyal? Faugh!" said Robin, and once again silence fell over our gathering. He raised his right hand and pointed his index finger accusingly at the group of bewildered laymen clustered around the knowing bishop, moving it slowly left and right, like a crossbowman taking aim.

"King Richard . . . is . . . coming," my master intoned slowly, jabbing with his finger at the foremost merchant, a fat man in a red robe trimmed with fox fur, "and when he is here, his wrath will know no bounds. The torments of Hell will be unleashed upon your miserable, turd-hoarding, flea-breeding, rat-feasting excuse for a town." He paused for a moment, and said: "He knows everything. He has learned the full extent of your perfidious dealings with King Philip."

"He has? How could he possibly . . . ," stammered the head merchant before his hand flew to his mouth. Then, realizing what he had revealed, he plucked wretchedly at his tawny fur collar in confusion. "What I mean is, we have had no such dealings with the French. We have remained steadfast, utterly loyal. We are King Richard's faithful subjects. Faithful unto . . ."

"Death?" said Robin, lifting one eyebrow.

Nobody spoke for several moments. Then Robin continued: "The Lionheart is coming with all his legions . . . and he knows that you have connived with King Philip to deprive him of his rightful revenues! And he is wrathful."

Sir Roger spoke; he sounded a little fretful. "We shall welcome him, open our gates and honor him as our true lord when he arrives here," he said. "We are all agreed . . ."

"Oh yes," said the merchant. "We are all agreed. We will prepare a great feast for all his knights, and have maidens strew his path with rose petals. Our monks will sing hosannas at his arrival. Our hospitality will be the most lavish ever offered a monarch . . . absolutely no expense will be spared . . ."

The head merchant tailed off in the face of my master's glower. Robin remained silent, dominating the delegation with his odd, silver eyes. I could see pearls of sweat breaking out on the brows of the merchants.

The Archbishop cleared his throat delicately, his faint superior smile remained in place. "Perhaps there is some way in which we can assuage the righteous anger of the King?" he suggested, with a tiny flourish of his hand.

"Perhaps," said Robin.

"Perhaps if we were to make some solid gesture of our loyalty to His Highness . . ." The Archbishop cocked his head to one side, and raised an eyebrow at Robin.

"Yes, yes," said Sir Roger, now absurdly, puppyishly eager. "But what? What does he want?"

The Archbishop's eyes flicked up to the ceiling of the tent and back down again, as if he were seeking the gift of patience from the Almighty. He murmured: "Perhaps some small contribution to ease the pain of the Lionheart's heavy expenditure in this war, a small emolument . . ."

"Perhaps not a *small* contribution," said Robin.

"Oh," said the head merchant, and his fur-covered shoulders sagged under the weight of comprehension.

I was not present when the merchant and Robin thrashed out the details of the *douceur* that the city of Tours would offer up to cool King Richard's temper. Robin usually preferred to have as few witnesses as possible for his shady money dealings, and when the Archbishop and Sir Roger had left, John, Thomas, the bowmen and I quit the tent, leaving my lord and the miserable-looking head merchant to haggle for almost an hour until a price had been fixed.

The next day, at noon, when the money had been delivered, however, Robin could not keep his delight to himself. "Two thousand pounds, Alan! Two thousand pounds of silver. That is what I wrangled from the guilty bastards. I had no idea Tours was so rich. Perhaps I should have persuaded Richard to sack the place and we could have filled a dozen wagon trains with our plunder!"

I found this side of Robin's character disheartening: I wanted him to live up to the noble behavior that I knew he was capable of and which I had witnessed so many times—yet I also recognized that he harbored a hunger for silver, almost like a drunkard's lust for wine, that could cause him to do the most unspeakable things solely for personal gain.

"How much of that will our good King Richard see?" I said, perhaps a little too sourly.

Robin looked at me hard, a glint of steel in his gray eyes. We were once again in his tent, alone but for a clerk who was seated in the corner, making notes on a parchment roll. In the center of the floor was a waist-high mound of small, lumpy linen bags that chinked whenever they were moved by the clerk's counting hand.

"Most of it, Alan. Almost all of it," Robin said coldly. "I'm sending Richard two-thirds of the money—a full two thousand marks this very afternoon."

"That is *very* generous of you." I could not keep the vinegar out of my voice.

Robin stared at me for a long moment. "Earlier this year, you will remember, Alan, I was forced to give up a very lucrative trade in the East, at King Richard's demand. I think I have the right to compensate myself fully for this loss. Do you not agree?"

"The King gave you half a dozen new manors to compensate you for that loss, as I recall." In spite of myself, and my great regard for my lord, I was becoming angry at Robin's unabashed greed. "Is that not enough for you?"

"He gave me a few manors, yes, and *you* the rich manor of Clermont-sur-Andelle, as I recall." Robin's tone was icy. "But your Clermont and the Norman manors that Richard has given over to me are presently occupied by the enemy; all of them are in the eastern part of the duchy and are now under the control of Philip's men. Nary a penny will either of us see from those *gifts* until the French are beaten. Richard gave us both rewards that we must fight in his cause to claim. That is largesse with rather large strings attached to it, don't you agree? So I believe that I am entitled to a little taste of honey when I secure some trifling payment from a pack of shifty merchants who have been thoroughly disloyal to their rightful lord."

Robin was genuinely angry now, but I could only tell by the cool, reasonableness of his tone—and the dangerous glitter in his eyes. I had no wish to argue further with my lord over this matter, and so I bowed and bade him a good day. As I turned to leave the tent, I caught a glimpse of an object moving very fast out of the corner of my eye. I whirled to face Robin, and something large, hard and round smashed into my chest. I only just managed to grasp it, rocking back on my heels in surprise.

"That is your share, by the way," said Robin dryly, and I looked down into my hands and saw that I held a heavy, bulging linen sack, the round outline of silver coins clearly visible through the thin material.

You may call me a hypocrite—and I shall surely have to answer for it on the Day of Judgment—but I kept that money: five pounds of mint-bright silver pennies. It was half what the manor of Westbury yielded in a whole year! I could make excuses, such as I needed it to pay for new weapons, saddlery and tack, or that my clothes had been worn by hard travel and needed replacing. But the truth is I wanted to have it: like Robin, I was not immune to the lure of Mammon. I shared a little of it with Hanno and gave a few shillings to Thomas—but the rest I wrapped in an old sheepskin and stuffed guiltily into my saddlebag.

7

KING RICHARD WAS DELIGHTED WITH THE "gift" that Robin had squeezed from the Tourangeaux—and no royal notice was taken of the fact that my lord had appropriated a fat slice of it. So the King was well pleased with us, and as a mark of his approval he made the Locksley men his honor guard and reserve force in the engagement two days later, when he assaulted the formidable castle of Loches. He stayed only one night at Tours, lodging with the mutton-headed Roger and, as promised, there were celebrations, rose-petals strewn and monks singing hosannas at his arrival. The very next day, Richard rose long before dawn and marched his army the thirty-odd miles southeast to Loches.

The castle, which stood on the borders of the counties of Berry, Touraine and Poitou, was the eastern gateway to Richard's continental lands. It barred the path along the Loire Valley, denying that route to the King of France and his vassals who held the lands to the east. Loches was famous for its massive, thick-walled keep, and had the reputation for being almost impossible to take by force. It was only occupied now by the French troops because Prince John had cravenly given it away to Philip as part of a secret deal they had made together when they were united against Richard. Sancho of Navarre's men—a strong force of a hundred knights and a hundred and fifty crossbowmen—had been besieging the castle for more than a week, but Lord Sancho himself had been suddenly called away to the south, across the Pyrenees, to his father's deathbed. His remaining men had neither the will nor necessary heavy equipment to capture Loches in his absence. The Spanish troops had surrounded the castle and prevented anyone from entering or leaving it—but there had been little else they could do. With King Richard's arrival, all that was about to change.

To my mind, Loches was the very opposite of the castle of Verneuil, with its weak, stubby, crumbling keep and strong outer walls, which I had defended so successfully only ten days before. Loches had a huge, oblong, immensely strong stone keep about eighty feet long and forty feet wide, and soaring up more than a hundred feet into the air with a slight taper toward the top. It loomed over the rest of the castle, completely dwarfing it—the rest consisting of a twenty-foot-high stone curtain wall, only two feet thick but studded with half a dozen round towers and surrounding the usual timber buildings: stables, a forge, bakeries, cook-shacks, barracks and so on. There was a large stone church in one corner of the castle bailey, and a chapter house—for this mighty fortress had been built around an ancient monastery. To the east of the castle flowed the slow River Indre, which through time immemorial had protected its flank from attacks coming out of the territory of the kings of France.

In many ways, Richard's attack was a classic of its kind and amply demonstrated my King's mastery of all the arts of war. After one very hard day's travel, with all the men-at-arms and servants ordered to assist in pushing the great siege engines along the dusty road that ran for a goodly way beside the Indre directly from Tours to Loches, and knights galloping up and down the column urging on the sluggards, Richard had his entire force of more than a thousand men encamped outside the walls, a little to the north of the castle, by dusk.

The French garrison continued to defy us, of course. And the next day, in the weak pink light of early morning, when the heralds had reported to the King the castle's bold refusal to surrender, the bombardment by the massive "castle-breakers" began.

Robin and I were with the King on a slight rise about a quarter of a mile to the north of the castle. Robin had not yet forgiven me for questioning his ruthless mulcting of the merchants of Tours, and he barely spoke to me as the sun climbed into the sky to herald a glorious June day. I sat astride Shaitan, stroking his glossy black neck, and a tiny, cowardly part of me was grateful that I would not, unless something went badly wrong, be engaging in the brutal, slogging fight that the day promised. On the far side of the King, on a huge white stallion, sat William the Marshal. That well-seasoned warrior had begged leave to storm the first breach in the curtain wall, claiming that it was his right—but the King had merely thanked him for his zeal and said calmly: "This is work for Mercadier's men. They know their business well and today they shall demonstrate that they are worthy of their hire."

"I must insist, Sire, that you give me and my men the honor of making the first assault," the Marshal had growled, glaring at the King like a hungry mastiff that had had a juicy bone stolen from between its jaws.

"No, William, I said no." Richard seemed a little irritated that his orders were being questioned. "It will be very hot, hard, bloody work, and I want Mercadier's ruffians to bear the brunt of it. Once they have taken the outer wall, your men can tackle the keep. Will that satisfy you, you old gore-guzzler?"

The Marshal had merely grunted his assent.

Beyond the bellicose Earl of Striguil sat the Navarrese captain in earnest discussion with Sir Aymeric de St. Maur, a Templar knight, who with another of his Order, Sir Eustace de la Falaise, commanded half a dozen black-clad Templar sergeants. Sir Aymeric was an old adversary of mine and Robin's, with whom we were now publicly reconciled. He was a pious man and a renowned warrior, a serious, impressive fellow, and yet I could not respect him—this knight had tried to have Robin burned as a heretic the year before, and had threatened me with dire torture. We had both evaded his malice and Robin had made an arrangement with the Templars—conceding his lucrative frankincense business to them to keep the peace. And so we were reconciled, although it could not be said that we were bosom friends. The Templars would not be taking part in any fighting during this campaign—it was contrary to their vows to fight their fellow Christians without a direct order from their Grand Master or the Pope himself. They were here as observers, to report the events back to the Master of their Order in London, and ostensibly to urge Richard to make peace with his fellow Christian monarch, Philip Augustus.

As I looked along the line of knights that flanked the King, I was struck by the noble profiles of the men as they gazed out over the castle, and I noticed a curious thing: every man had had himself shaved that morning in preparation for the battle—apart from the Templars, of course, who as was their custom sported neatly trimmed beards. I felt my own lightly stubbled chin, and silently cursed myself for not thinking of having Thomas do the same for me. I felt untidy, and so a little angry with myself. As I had been so recently dubbed, I did not want to stand out from the other knights, or to look foolish or unkempt or peasant-like in any way. But my stubble was light and fair, and I persuaded myself that nobody would notice.

Richard had divided his heavy artillery in two unequal halves: the weaker company—six big siege engines, mangonels and trebuchets, and half a dozen smaller onagers and balistes, manned by engineers and experts in this type of weapon—was on the left of our position, east of the main road and near the banks of the River Indre. Their objective was to reduce the outer wall, to knock a gap at least twenty feet wide between the main gate and the first strong tower on the east of the castle wall. The second, stronger artillery company—consisting of ten thirty-foot-tall "castle-breakers"—was placed on the right of the main road, to the west, and they had the more difficult task of pitching their missiles in a long arc over the outer wall to batter at the northwestern corner of the massive keep.

As I watched, with the sun only a finger's width above the eastern horizon, even at that hour an impossibly bright yellow stain that promised a furnace-like day to come, the first trebuchet on the eastern side of the road prepared its missile. The twenty-five-foot-long solid oak arm was winched back by the muscle-power of a dozen men-at-arms, the massive D-shaped iron counterweight rising into the warming air. The arm was then firmly secured by stout ropes, and pegs driven deep into the ground. A boulder the size of a fully grown sheep was carefully rolled into the broad reinforced leather sling attached to the end of the long arm. A shout of command; the ropes were loosed; the lumpen counterweight swung ponderously down; the arm flashed up, dragging the sling and its missile behind it; at the top of its arc, the throwing arm crashed into a padded wooden bar, stopping its path dead; the sling whistled over the top and the boulder was catapulted toward the outer wall. With a shattering crash, the quarter-ton missile struck the top of the target close to a small tower, exploding in a storm of flying masonry.

I winced, imagining the fate of the men on the wall in that deadly maelstrom of scything stone chips—the faces ripped and gashed, limbs crushed, bodies pulped by airborne lumps of razor-like rock. Agonized screams floated to us on the still morning air. And after only one strike I could see a dent in the smooth line of the top of the wall. And then a second trebuchet arm swung up, loosed its load, and a second missile crashed into the wall with a spectacular cracking boom and shower of shards. And a third. And a fourth.

And all the fury of Hell was unleashed on the defiant castle of Loches.

Even from our positions a good quarter of a mile away from the point of impact, the noise was deafening. The creak and thump as the arm pounded into the padded bar, the crash of stone against stone, the shouts of the trebuchet captains, the cheers of their men, the pain-soaked yells, cries and curses of men defending the walls, crushed, ripped and sliced by flying slivers of rock.

Then the second, yet more powerful artillery company on the right of the road began its own deadly tattoo, looping their missiles at a higher trajectory over the walls to dash against the corner of the massive keep.

The engineers and their well-trained sergeants knew their work. I watched one team around a thirty-foot-tall trebuchet, known by its crew as the "Wall Eater," and counted my heartbeats with a hand on my wrist—and I saw that they were able to loose a fresh boulder at the castle almost every fifteen beats. It was a staggering pace, and I wondered how long they could keep it up. But their diligent work meant that, with almost every one of my heartbeats, a missile from one of the sixteen engines on either side of the road crashed into the castle—crack, crack, crack, crack. It felt almost like sitting before a giant's forge with a mad blacksmith hammering determinedly at a stone anvil without pause. The horses were a little frightened by the noise at first, but after a half-hour they became calmer, and accepted the hellish banging as a natural part of the sounds of the day.

The pounding went on and on. The artillery men on the left smashed boulder after boulder into the outer wall with surprising precision. A few missiles missed their mark and sailed over the wall or went wide, but eight stones out of ten crashed and splintered into the same twenty-foot stretch of outer wall. The more powerful company on the right were less accurate—theirs was a difficult, vertical target—but, by my count, at least six out of every ten of their missiles smashed into the corner of the tall keep.

After an hour's solid battery from both sides of the main road, I heard a huge cheer from the artillery company on the left, and looked up to see a great crack appearing in the outer defenses just to the left of the main gate. An hour after that, and whole chunks of masonry began to fall, almost slowly, from the crumbling outer wall.

The King was in high spirits; he smiled and joked with the men around him, the sunlight reflecting from his red-gold hair and the simple gold band he wore to keep it from his eyes. He leaned over to Robin and, punctuated by the crash of stone missiles on masonry, he shouted: "I think, Locksley, that we shall see this matter concluded today!"

"Indeed, Sire," replied Robin in his battle-voice. "That outer wall will be practicable by noon at the latest, I'd say."

"Aye," said the King. "I agree. Noon, if not earlier. Pass the word to Mercadier to be ready to attack by noon."

Robin looked at me. "Would you be so kind, Alan?" he said, with much more formality than I was used to from an old friend. Clearly he had still not forgiven me.

I guided Shaitan down the slight hill to a hollow on the left of the road where Mercadier and his men were encamped. As my destrier picked his way through a sea of low grubby tents, campfires and lounging *routiers*—an evil-visaged crew if ever I saw one, who stared at me with varying expressions of sullen contempt and indifference—I heard another cheer, this time coming from the far side of the road, and turned round in time to see a great eye-tooth-shaped chunk of stone slide from the northwestern corner of the enormous keep.

As I rode up to his tent, Mercadier was shaving himself, dipping a long dagger in a bucket of muddy water between strokes, glaring into a polished steel helm at his dark reflection, and carefully guiding the blade, which must have been extraordinarily keen, around his Adam's apple.

My hand went unthinkingly to my own bristled chin. I did not wish to fall out with Mercadier on this day, a day when he would be facing mortal danger and I would very likely be safe from the fighting, and so I said in my most civil tone: "The King requests that you have your men ready to attack the outer wall at noon."

"Yes, fine, noon it is," he said, his Gascon accent particularly nasal.

I waited a moment for any further communication, and when he said nothing but merely continued to scrape away carefully at his jawline, I turned Shaitan and began to make my way toward the King.

While my back was turned, and I was a dozen yards away, I heard him speak: "Not with your precious priest today, Sir Knight?"

Scenting mockery, I turned in the saddle and saw that he was smiling crookedly at me, the bright sunlight making even more of a contrast between the long, puckered off-white scar and his half-shaven face. After weeks of campaigning, I noticed, his complexion was almost as dark as a Moor's.

"Not today," I said.

"Well, you keep him safe, Sir Knight. Wouldn't want anything to happen to such a saintly old man. That would be a terrible tragedy." And he laughed; a horrible dry sound.

I paused for a moment, groping for some rejoinder, but nothing came to me; and so I turned Shaitan's head and rode on, a wave of grating laughter lapping in my wake.

Mercadier's parting taunt turned my thoughts in the direction of Brother Dominic. We had been reunited at Tours and he seemed to be recovering from his ordeal, his feet healing steadily thanks to Elise's charms and unguents. I discovered that he belonged to the Abbey of the Holy Trinity in Vendôme—the abbey in which the current abbot, who also had the dignity of the title cardinal, was . . . the erstwhile Bishop Heribert, author of my father's expulsion from Notre-Dame.

"Oh yes, the Cardinal is still in very good health for his years, praise God," quavered Dominic when I questioned him about his spiritual lord. This information lifted my heart—the Almighty had put this doddery old monk in my path, I was quite certain, for a reason, and I felt that the mystery surrounding my father's death might not prove so impenetrable after all. It caused me to alter my plans for Dominic. When he was fit to travel, I hoped to send him back to Cardinal Heribert with a letter humbly requesting an audience. I had asked King Richard at Tours if I might be permitted to leave the army and pay a visit to the Cardinal myself, but I chose the wrong moment, it would seem. The King was in conference with a gaggle of his senior knights and barons, and was displeased to be interrupted with a petition such as mine. He had gruffly refused my request for leave and repeated what he had told me in Verneuil: that he could not spare me, he needed every sword, but that I might be permitted to pursue my quest at a later date.

As I headed back toward the ridge where Robin and the King were positioned, I saw that the outer wall of Loches Castle now had a gaping hole beside the main gate, which the defenders were making heroic efforts to plug with barrels and boxes and pieces of broken masonry. Before the wall, a loose and rocky ramp had been formed by tumbled stones and rubble from the defenses. It was a rough and treacherous stair, but one that would make it possible for Mercadier's nimble *routiers* to climb up and attack the breach. The enemy, however, had by no means given up: it was heartbreaking to watch those scurrying ant-like men hopelessly trying to patch the breach in their defenses, for every few moments another huge stone missile would crash into the hastily repaired section, smashing the new wooden barricades to splinters and crushing the heroic men struggling to close the gap.

The massive keep, too, had been severely knocked about. The northwestern corner had been gnawed away by the Wall Eater and the other engines on the right-hand side of the road and a large section of the corner was missing, while the rest was pocked and scraped where the boulders had struck the masonry.

As I walked Shaitan up the slope toward the royal party, there was a flurry of activity in the eastern artillery company. Four of the big siege engines ceased their pounding, and four teams of oxen were led to the massive wooden frames and yoked up to them. The company was changing its point of attack. Whips cracked, sharp goads stabbed, the oxen leaned into their wooden yokes and the four machines rumbled fifty yards closer to the castle—though still well out of bow-shot. There was much shouting, and a scrum of men heaved at the engines as they were re-situated, but by the time I had rejoined the King and Robin, they had been secured in their new positions. And the pounding began anew—but this time joining their efforts to those of the big machines on the right of the road. Now fourteen "castle-breakers" were concentrating their fury on the northwestern corner of the keep.

In the diminished left-hand company, two smaller mangonels continued their ravaging of the open breach on the outer wall, pulverizing any man who dared to show his face for too long, and they were reinforced by a pair of onagers—simple spoon-like catapults that used the power of twisted leather to hurl rocks the size of a man's head—and four balistes, gigantic crossbows mounted on a wooden frame that shot four-foot iron bolts at the enemy.

The sun was high above and it must have been noon, or nearly so. I saw that Mercadier had formed up his men, perhaps four hundred of them, and they were waiting patiently in three long lines, sweating in their leather and mail armor under Mercadier's black banners, each dark as pitch but adorned with three bright golden coins. These waves of frail men would soon hurl themselves at the breach in the outer wall and try to force an entrance.

It must be time to go, I thought, *it must be time.* The breach could now easily be scaled by an able-bodied man, even one encumbered by shield and sword or spear. I wondered what the delay was—what was Richard waiting for?—and then I realized what it must be. The King was waiting for a similar breach to the one on the outer wall to be made in the great keep. He wanted to take the castle in a single bloody surging attack, his men sweeping through the outer walls, across the courtyard and into the keep in one long screaming rush.

Sensible, I realized. At the siege of Nottingham earlier in the year, Richard had taken the outer defenses of the castle but failed to batter a hole in the stone core of the keep before the initial assault. As a result, his soldiers, once in the courtyard below the keep, had been easy victims to crossbowmen in the heart of the castle, defenders who were secured from the attackers' anger by unbroken high stone walls.

Richard was not prepared to risk making the same mistake again. Crack . . . crack-crack . . . crack . . . the battering continued, missiles smashing relentlessly into the corner of the keep of Loches. My head was throbbing from the din of the bombardment and the heat of the day. I realized I was terribly, desperately thirsty, but before I could slake my desire, at that very moment, with a roaring, tearing, thunderous rumble, a noise that seemed to shake the foundations of the world, a whole section of the northwestern corner of the keep crashed to earth. Through the clouds of stone dust I could actually glimpse the interior of the castle—a hall of some kind with flapping tapestries and a long trestle table and benches.

"That will do," said Richard, nodding to William the Marshal. "Send word to Mercadier, and get your own men in position. You are to follow his lads in there only *after* they have cleared the breach in the outer wall. You will go in when the outer wall has been taken. Is that clear, William?"

"As a mountain stream," said the Marshal, somewhat grumpily, and without another word he spurred his huge warhorse down the slope to the east.

To watch a battle is to take part in it only in spirit—and yet, when it was over, I felt almost as exhausted as if I had single-handedly fought the entire French garrison myself.

Mercadier's lines of footmen moved forward almost casually, covering the three hundred or so yards to the wall at a brisk trot. As they reached the first loose stones before the breach they were met with a withering hail of crossbow fire, and I saw a score of men in the front ranks fall. The sole weakness of Richard's plan was that the garrison knew full well where the attack would come, and when our punch would be delivered, and I could see hundreds of defenders gathered at the breach—nearly the whole garrison I guessed—crowding together, their arms glinting in the hot sun, light bouncing from polished helms as they prepared to defend to the death their walls. A last giant quarrel from a baliste on the eastern side of the road smashed into the jostling crowd of foemen in the breach, smashing two of them away—and yet more men eagerly filled the ranks, their steel points glittering as they awaited our assault. A shout of rage erupted from hundreds of throats as Mercadier's men, now less than thirty yards away, began scrambling up the loose piles of rock and stone, shields on their backs, helmeted heads tucked low, clambering up the treacherous rubble using hands and feet like a swarming herd of human beetles—launching themselves into the maw of Hell.

They were rascals, bandits, priest-murderers and gutter-born thieves—but Mercadier's men did not lack for raw courage. They swarmed up the loose rubble toward the breach in the outer wall of the castle—and were met with a devastating volley of crossbow bolts, spears, and loose rocks hurled down upon them. Many men fell under this onslaught, crushed by hurled boulders, spitted by quarrels, and those who reached the top of the stone stairway were swiftly cut down by the well-trained knights and men-at-arms at the top, their swinging swords spilling light and spraying blood as they hacked into the desperate, yelling horde of men surging toward them. Mercadier's men boiled up the rocky slope—and died in their scores at the top, and yet more men came on behind them, trampling their dead and wounded comrades, mashing their bodies into the uneven stony incline as they forged upward, screaming taunts and lunging madly at their enemies.

The men of Loches were stalwart in defense; a score of knights in full iron mail, supported by crossbows and spearmen, held that breach, cutting down the leather-jacketed *routiers* who hurled themselves at them with swinging blows of sword and axe. The second wave of mercenaries attacked. And a hundred more of Mercadier's men were fed into that cauldron of pain, rage and death, into the riot of scything steel and spurting blood.

Yet the breach held.

Now I could see that the mercenaries of the third wave were beginning to hang back a little on the rocky slope, and were milling around beneath the walls, rather than rushing to their deaths in that terrible blood-splashed bottle-neck. They were still dying in great numbers, plucked from this life by a hissing crossbow quarrel, an arrow or a hurled spear. Sergeants were screaming at the men, striking them, urging them onward—but the impetus of the initial attack had been lost. Here and there a brave man, or perhaps a pair of friends, even a small group, would rush up the slope, stumbling on the loose stones, which were now red and slippery, screaming their battle cries and waving weapons—and would die, chopped down by the long blood-slick swords and jabbing spears of the defenders.

Still the breach held.

I heard a trumpet, loud and strong from my left; two long blasts. Turning my head away from the appalling spectacle of bloody heroism and death at the breach, I saw a massive formation of unhorsed but fully armored men start forward from our lines, thirty or so knights on foot, each clad from head to foot in protective iron links, and a couple of score men-at-arms and squires behind them. A standard fluttered above the foremost rank: it was William, Earl of Striguil, and his knightly followers; the Marshal blatantly disobeying the King's orders and ramming his men into the battle, just at the moment when they were needed most.

"The old fool! The disobedient glory-hunting fool," I heard the King mutter. And watched in awe as William and his men broke into a heavy run and charged, heedless to all danger, across the open ground before the castle, sweeping Mercadier's men out of their path, bounding up the gore-greased stairway and into the steel fence of the breach.

William and his knights smashed into the line of defenders and I could hear the crunch of wood, the squeal of metal and clash of blades as the two lines collided. The enemy line sagged, pushed back by the force of fresh men pressing against it; and I saw Mercadier, limping a little, shouting at his men from below the walls, urging them to add their weight to this fresh attack. Sword drawn, he joined his raggedy warriors scrambling up behind the Marshal's fresh troops. I saw William himself, taller than other men, on the very lip of the breach, laying about him with a long sword, and dropping enemies with every stroke. And beside him his superbly trained household knights, their mail gleaming silver in the sunlight, hacked and carved their way forward, inch by bloody inch.

The resistance began to melt, the Marshal and his men were pushing forward, the defenders' line was buckling backward; there was a tremendous howl and a surge forward by Mercadier's men as they pitched in behind the Marshal's knights, adding their fury to the mêlée, and suddenly they were all through the breach, like a great dam bursting, our men flooding forward, washing the enemy from my sight.

The slaughter after the taking of Loches was appalling. William the Marshal's men and Mercadier's rogues—those who had survived the horror in the breach—killed every living soul they could find inside the castle. The castellan and his wife and baby daughter, and a pair of priests, managed to surrender to the Marshal himself when he and his closest knights had fought their bloody way to the top of the tower—and they were the lucky ones. Everyone else inside the walls of Loches perished. Mercadier's men, who had shown immense bravery in attacking that hellish gap, showed the other side of the *routiers'* reputation when they had broken through the outer wall, and overcome the slight resistance of a few young squires in the smashed northwestern corner of the keep. They sank to the level of beasts: a group of *routiers* discovered the cellars and they drank deeply of the rich yellow wine of the region, and this fueled their depravity in the captured stronghold. Men, whether armed for war or not, servants, priests, monks—were all put to the sword. Women, old and young, were raped by long queues of *routiers*, who shouted jests and drained tankards of wine while they waited their turn to defile some unfortunate belledame, whose only crime was to have been married to a French garrison knight.

Loches was ours by mid-afternoon—it had only taken King Richard a matter of hours to reduce this formidable stronghold—but the looting, raping and murders continued until long after midnight.

At dawn the next day, King Richard set about restoring order. He had a gibbet set up in the bailey of the castle and hanged three of Mercadier's men that his household knights caught in the act of raping an old woman. And the message to all the troops was clear: that devilish playtime was over; the King's army was being called to heel.

As ever, the sight of the hanged men put me in mind of my father's death. And I gave thanks to God that Robin's men had not been called upon to perform the executions. But an execution of a wholly different sort had taken place, which I only discovered when I returned to my tent later that evening accompanied by Thomas and Hanno.

Under a large blanket at the back of the tent, where he had been resting, and keeping the weight off his burned feet, I found the skinny, blood-sodden corpse of Dominic.

His throat had been cut from ear to ear.

8

WITH LOCHES SUBDUED, KING RICHARD LEFT a small garrison to repair the walls and drove south with the army into Aquitaine. After hearing of the bloody fate of Loches, castles now held by the foe in my lord's vast southern dukedom opened their gates to us and threw themselves on Richard's mercy; and, as ever, it delighted the King to be magnanimous in victory. The forces of Geoffrey of Rancon, Richard's enemy in the south, and Philip's ally, dissolved before us; some surrendered, were forgiven and renewed their allegiance to our King, others fled east into Burgundy. None could stand in the face of Richard's righteous wrath—and the might of his castle-breakers.

We had buried Dominic in the monastery churchyard inside the walls of Loches before we left that sad citadel, and the old man lay next to some hundred or so of the French garrison who had died so bravely in its defense. As Hanno shoveled the earth over his shrouded body, and one of Richard's priests mumbled prayers for his soul, I could feel a deep rage rising in my stomach. I felt almost certain that I knew who was responsible for the death of this good man—Mercadier. He could not have accomplished the deed himself, of course; we had all seen him heroically storming the breach with his men, and then less than heroically sacking and looting the castle. But

I was sure that one of his *routiers*, one of his cutthroats who had not taken part in the assault, had done the deed to strike back at me for killing his redheaded man-at-arms.

There was nothing I could do. Nobody could remember seeing one of Mercadier's men entering my tent while we were watching the battle. But then, encamped shoulder to shoulder with at least two thousand other souls in a vast township of woolen tents and roughly built shelters, and living on top of each other as we were, there was a constant stream of people—soldiers, squires, farriers, whores, peddlers—walking past my tent day and night, and nobody would notice one murderous *routier* among that throng.

I told Robin and he was characteristically uninterested.

"That will teach you to annoy Mercadier," he said, with a shrug. "You should count yourself lucky that he didn't decide to cut *your* throat at the same time."

But despite his apparent callousness, I heard later from Little John that the Earl of Locksley had been to see Mercadier privately, taking John with him, and had told the mercenary captain quite bluntly that if any harm at all were to come to his friend Sir Alan of Westbury, he, Robin, would take it as an act of provocation and there would be very serious, painful and fatal consequences for Mercadier.

"Give the black-souled bastard his due, he didn't turn a hair when Robin threatened him," Little John told me. "And Robin can be very unsettling when he chooses to be. The man just smiled, cool as a trout, and said: 'I hear you, my lord—young Westbury is your man, and is under your protection.' And he flatly denied having anything to do with the old priest's murder."

I was touched that Robin should take my side, but a little irritated too. Did he think I could not take care of myself? And, in our tent, I noticed that Hanno and Thomas also took turns to stay alert all through the next few nights—Robin was not the only one who seemed to believe that I needed protection.

Then word reached us that the King of France, Philip Augustus himself, was heading down toward us with an enormous army to confront Richard and to try and salvage something, after the fall of Loches, from the collapse of all his carefully wrought schemes in the south.

So we turned back north to meet him and, by the beginning of July, Richard and his entire force of knights, footmen, mercenaries and mighty castle-breakers were camped outside the gates of Vendôme—and I must confess that I was well pleased. I felt that finally I might have the chance to arrange an audience with His Grace Cardinal Heribert of the Holy Trinity Abbey to ask about my father, the theft and his fateful visit to Paris two decades ago.

The city of Vendôme was held against us by a small and presumably rather nervous French garrison—like Loches, it had been handed over to Philip by Prince John while Richard was imprisoned the year before—but the garrison was attempting to hunt with the hounds and run with the hart, and it was in almost constant communication with Richard's heralds, sending costly gifts to Richard, and dispatching embassies from the various city guilds and religious institutions. The feeling in our camp was that, if we were to beat the French in the coming battle, Vendôme would happily surrender to King Richard without a fight and accept his magnanimous forgiveness. If we were to be beaten by Philip—and I could not for a moment imagine that we would be—then Vendôme would remain in French hands, and would no doubt welcome Philip with flower-strewing maidens and sung hosannas. It was a truly practical, unsentimental arrangement—Richard did not have to waste lives and *matériel* capturing Vendôme, which would fall into his arms like a swooning virgin if he managed to see off the French King. This unspoken agreement also meant that there was a large amount of daily traffic between Richard's camp and the great men of Vendôme; negotiations of all kinds were taking place, knights inside the walls were looking for future favors from the King, merchants were making discreet deals with the army's quartermasters to supply them with food and equipment that was badly needed. And I had decided to take advantage of this unofficial accord to go myself into the city of Vendôme, and pay a visit to Cardinal Heribert.

I had been quite prepared to make a clandestine visit to the town, a knotted rope flung over the walls on a dark night, perhaps, or a quiet purse of silver passed to a venal sergeant manning a gate, but I was aided in the accomplishment of my desire by a most unexpected source. Robin mentioned that Sir Aymeric de St. Maur and his Templar entourage were making an official embassy to the knights and burgesses of Vendôme, on behalf of King Richard, a formal mission to prepare the ground for the submission of the town after the French defeat. On hearing this, I approached the Templar and asked his leave to accompany them into Vendôme. When he asked why, I stretched the truth and said that the Cardinal had been a friend of my father's when he lived in Paris, and I wished to pay my respects. To my surprise, the Templar readily agreed.

"Certainly, Sir Alan, if I can be of service, I should be happy to oblige you," said Sir Aymeric, smiling at me in a benevolent, avuncular fashion.

I was slightly unnerved by this—we had met on several occasions and he had never been this friendly. The last time I had been this close to him, he had threatened me with torture with red-hot irons to persuade me to reveal the whereabouts of the notorious outlaw Robin Hood.

"And how is the noble Earl of Locksley? In excellent health, I trust," Sir Aymeric said gravely as we parted, having agreed that I would join him and his embassy the next day before dawn and we would ride into Vendôme under the Templars' black-and-white banner together. I assured him with the utmost courtesy that his former mortal enemy, and the object of his almost diabolical fury one year earlier, was in the finest fettle.

The next dawn, Sir Aymeric was just as cordial. Hanno, Thomas and myself joined their party, which comprised his beaming lieutenant Sir Eustace de la Falaise, six sergeants, and several of King Richard's senior barons and clergymen. I nodded a stiff greeting at Sir Eustace, a good-looking young Norman knight whom I did not know well but who had a decent reputation as a fighting man if not as a deep thinker, and Sir Aymeric inquired with infinite concern whether I had broken my fast that day. When he discovered that I had not, he pressed a cup of wine on me and a perfectly delicious honey cake.

I had told Robin of Sir Aymeric's extraordinary affability the night before. "I don't think there is anything sinister about it," said my lord. "He merely wants to put the unpleasantness of the past behind him. We are reconciled, Alan, remember that. Whatever he has done, we are all supposed to be amicable now. I expect you to be on your very best behavior—"

"Yes, you play nicely with Sir Aymeric," interrupted Little John, chuckling heartily. The big man had been listening to our conversation from the corner of Robin's big tent. "Let him share your toys, but don't let him bully you."

I was irked by both Robin and John's attitude. Of course I would behave myself. Did they think I was going to brawl over some harsh words the previous year?

"So you have completely forgiven him, have you, Robin, for attempting to have you burned at the stake?" I said, a little truculently. Robin was not a man known for his abundance of Christian forgiveness.

"If ever I get the chance to do him some damage—or shove a blade into any of his sainted Order of bloodthirsty, God-struck maniacs—I will gladly do it; as long as it doesn't put my people at risk or harm my interests in any way. But, for the moment, it suits me to treat him as an ally. So behave yourself, Alan. As John says, play nicely with the Templars like a good boy—for now." And he grinned at me, his eyes twinkling with vicious amusement.

As Hanno, Thomas and I joined the column of mounted men that morning and began to ride out of the camp and toward the walls of Vendôme, less than half a mile to the south, I pondered Robin's description of these Templar knights as "bloodthirsty God-struck maniacs"—it seemed a bit too harsh to me. They were the vanguard of Christian knighthood: superbly trained in all forms of combat, deeply committed to the cause of Our Lord, and aloof from the petty squabbles of the princes of Europe. They served a higher cause: Christendom itself. Much feared by the Saracens, and merciless in battle against all infidels, they were men that I felt a good deal of admiration for: men I looked up to as an example of how to be. I would have no trouble "behaving myself" in their company.

Vendôme is built into the crook of a bend in the River Loir, where that great artery of trade divides into three streams. Vendôme itself seemed to be almost floating on water; and I imagined the inhabitants must have a good deal of trouble with flooding in wintertime. We approached on the main road from the north through brown-yellow fields of ripening barley and halted our horses outside the gates of the city, which lay on the far side of the first bridge across the Loir. One of the Templar sergeants walked his horse across the bridge and in a loud, officious voice announced who we were. As if pushed by an invisible giant's hand, the huge wooden gates of the citadel swung open to receive us.

Once through the portals, we entered the crowded, narrow streets of Vendôme, bustling with traders and ringing with the cries of its citizens. Apart from the occasional jovial curse as we forced our horses through the throng, we were almost ignored. The people seemed to have no fear of us, which I found rather odd, given that we came from a mighty and victorious army that was camped less than a mile away. Ahead of us, I could see the tall spire of the Abbey Church of the Holy Trinity—seat of Cardinal Heribert—and beyond, half a mile to the south of the abbey, the stone walls of the castle, glowering over the town from a prominence at its most southerly point. Shortly we clattered across a second wooden bridge and found ourselves riding beside the walls of the abbey itself.

I called, "God be with you, sir," to Aymeric de St. Maur, who was at the head of the column, and he turned in the saddle and raised a friendly hand in salute. I had told him that, rather than accompanying the embassy to the castle, where the negotiations were to take place with Lord Bouchard, Count of Vendôme, I would be heading straight for the abbey. And a few moments later, Hanno, Thomas and I were dismounted and pounding the big brass bell outside the porter's lodge of that venerable religious house.

I gave my name to the hosteler, whose duty it was to welcome guests to the abbey, mentioning briefly that I had been acquainted with Brother Dominic. He greeted me with joy, embracing me and thanking me for saving the old monk's life. Evidently the poor fellow had been in communication with the abbey while his feet had been healing. Then I had to deliver the sad news that Brother Dominic was dead—murdered by unknown hands—and I told the hosteler that I needed to speak to the Cardinal, hinting perhaps just a little dishonestly that it concerned Dominic's death. I felt guilty about that, but reasoned that if I told the Cardinal my true reason for wanting to speak to him, and he had something to hide, I might well find myself escorted out of the abbey, never to be admitted again. Needs must when the Devil drives.

The hosteler sent a novice scurrying away to relay my information to the Cardinal's secretary and to see if I might be granted an audience. In the meantime, our horses were taken away and stabled, and Hanno, Thomas and I were ushered into the refectory, offered cold spring water and rye bread with butter, and asked to wait.

After a while, the hosteler returned and told me that His Grace would see me, but only for a few moments as he had been summoned to the castle to take part in the negotiations for the surrender of Vendôme to King Richard. I nearly kicked myself—I had made a silly mistake. Of course the Cardinal would be required to receive the embassy! But I quickly stammered out my gratitude that I might be permitted a few moments of the prelate's time before he departed for the castle.

Leaving Hanno and Thomas in the refectory, I followed the hosteler across a large well-swept courtyard to the Cardinal's palace, a huge stone building on three stories that, after the abbey church, was the largest structure in the vicinity. Once inside, I was swiftly shown into the presence of the great man himself.

Cardinal Heribert was enormous—perhaps the fattest man I have ever seen, a mountain of flesh with a baby's head on top, dusted with light brown hair. I knew that he must be at least fifty, but he had the face of a man half that age. Had it not been for his huge, wobbling bulk, he could almost have been a young fellow of my own generation. When I was shown into his private chamber on the second floor, he was seated in a vast chair by a bay window, wrapped in a scarlet robe but bareheaded, clutching a big goblet of wine in one hand, while stroking a fluffy, white-haired lapdog with the other. I was announced, I bowed, and then went forward to kiss the hand, and the enormous jeweled golden ring squeezed onto his pudgy middle finger, that was extended toward me; it smelled of damp dog.

"God's peace be upon you, my son," said the Cardinal in a kindly tone. He had a surprisingly high voice for such a large man, and he wheezed slightly when he spoke—but his beady bright blue eyes, sunk deeply in the flesh of his face, glittered with a feverish, cruel intelligence.

"Thank you, Your Grace, for seeing me," I said, releasing his massive, doughy hand and standing straight and tall in front of him. I was wearing my finest clothes—a dark blue tunic, scarlet hose, and soft black kidskin slippers—my jaw-length blond hair had been washed the previous day, and well-combed before dawn, I had been shaved by Thomas and I carried no weapons save for a small eating knife in a sheath at my waist.

"I can only spare you a few minutes, my son, but I did wish to thank you personally for saving the life of our dear Brother Dominic—may he rest in Heaven. He was a good man called to God before his time. Do you have any knowledge of who it might have been who murdered him?"

"Your Grace, I must confess that I do not, although I have my suspicions . . . But I must admit that it is not truly the matter of Brother Dominic's death that brings me to you today. My name is—"

"I know who you are," the Cardinal interrupted me; his voice had lost its kindly tone and cracked like a rotten branch breaking under a weight of winter snow. "And I know what you want. You are Sir Alan

Dale—*trouvère,* former outlaw and liegeman of the Earl of Locksley. I know who your father was, too—that accursed thief Henri d'Alle—and I did not believe even for a moment that you came here to console me for the loss of one elderly monk."

He glared at me, wheezing slightly in his passion, his tiny blue eyes like chips of smashed glass.

"Let us speak plainly now, Sir Alan," he said, clearly trying to master himself. "I know the true reason why you are here today. You have it, do you not? You have that wondrous object that your father stole from me. You have it—and you wish to sell it back to me and make your fortune, that's your grubby little design, is it not, you thief-spawned wretch? Tell me now, do not waste any more of my time, what is your price?"

I was stunned by the Cardinal's words, and utterly bemused by his angry tone. I had to haul my jaw shut to stop myself looking like a straw-chewing yokel.

"No, Your Grace," I stammered. "I swear to you, you are quite wrong. I do not wish to sell you anything. I have nothing to sell—nothing; I come to you seeking only information about my father."

The Cardinal cocked his baby's head to one side and examined me. For a long moment he remained silent and then he said: "Nothing to sell? Nothing?" He peered at me for a while longer, his glass-chip eyes running up and down the length of my body. "Then you truly do not have it? You do not possess the . . . object?"

I shook my head.

"I believe you, by Christ's wounds, I honestly do—" The Cardinal sounded as if he had surprised himself. "You might be the greatest liar in Christendom, and I the greatest fool, but I believe you. You really do not have it, do you?"

"I do not know what this object is to which you refer." I was thinking: *another candlestick? Whoever described a candlestick, even a golden one, as wondrous?*

"It leaves a mark, a special mark on all those who possess it—and you have no sign of that, none at all. But tell me: why should I indulge you in this? Why should I help you? You—the son of a man who stole from me; the son of a God-damned thief? I should have you whipped and thrown out of here this instant!"

I straightened my shoulders and locked eyes with him; a rougher edge entered my voice. "I believe my father was falsely accused. He is dead now—murdered in England these ten years past—and I believe that he was killed on the orders of the real thief. He is a powerful man, this true thief—a 'man you cannot refuse.'

"You ask why you should help me: I will tell you. If I am able to discover the identity of the true thief—and I shall in time—then I may be able to return to you this 'wondrous' object of which you speak, whatever it is. Is that not a reason why you should aid me?"

The door of the chamber opened and a monk came into the room, a secretary of some kind. "Your Grace," he said, "Your Grace, it is time. We must be away."

The Cardinal ignored the interruption completely and continued to stare at me. "Yes, I see that," he said. "Yes, you have given me good reason. I cannot think what you might seek to gain by coming here, were you a liar. Very well, I will make you a bargain. I will tell you everything that I know about your father this evening after Vespers when I return from greeting the King's embassy at the castle—and for your part you will do a service for me in return. Are we agreed?"

"Your Grace," said the monk by the door, "we really must make haste . . ."

"What is it that you wish for me to do?" I said. I could not imagine what this fat, old, immensely wealthy and powerful prelate could possibly want from me.

"I want you to sing for me," he said, his tiny blue eyes in that oddly young face twinkling in the sunlight from the window—and suddenly I could imagine what he must have looked like as a boy, a naughty young boy. "Will you do that, Sir Alan? I have heard that you—like your father—have an exquisite voice. 'The finest *trouvère* at King Richard's court,' I heard you called the other day. Sing for me and I shall tell you all I know. Do we have a bargain?"

I smiled; it pleased me that my fame as a musician had traveled so far, and I bowed deeply in acceptance.

Heribert, the Cardinal of Vendôme, left for the castle in an enormous chair suspended from two stout poles and carried by four brawny porters. The chair was surrounded by a gaggle of brown-clad monks and guarded by four yawning men-at-arms in the Cardinal's livery. It was mid-morning when the procession bearing the great man left the abbey gates and began to make its way through the crowded streets of Vendôme, south to the castle. I returned to the big refectory to await the midday meal with Thomas and Hanno; I did not expect the Cardinal to return until after dark. After we had eaten, Hanno, Thomas and I changed into rough clothes and entertained the abbey folk with a demonstration of armed combat in the courtyard—a worthwhile practice for Hanno and myself, and a daily lesson for young Thomas. As the monks of Vendôme stood around in a circle and gawped at us delightedly, Hanno and I mock-fought with sword and dagger, mace and shield, until we dripped with sweat; and Thomas was made to perform a repetitive series of maneuvers with sword and shield to burn the basic patterns of attack and defense into his very muscles. I had learned this way myself, from an old Saxon warrior in Sherwood—and while I had hated it at the time, the old man had carved the lunges, blocks, strikes and parries of the swordsman into my soul. And when I am attacked with a blade, even to this day, even now that I am an old man myself, the block and counterblow comes to me as naturally as my next breath.

However, the learning did not all flow in one direction. Thomas, although he was still a lad, and not yet come into his full strength, had devised a method of wrestling entirely by himself that, he claimed, cunningly used a bigger man's strength against him. And so, in time, we put away the blades, bludgeons and shields, and Thomas instructed us in a few of his simpler moves: tripping an opponent over backward; grappling him and throwing him over your hip; and a move to combat a man who attacks you from behind by leaning forward, head down, and pulling him over your right shoulder, a move that much resembles a man-at-arms taking his hauberk off after a day's hard fighting.

We passed the afternoon in sport; then we washed in the abbey bathhouse. I had resumed my outer finery, and was just settling down in a quiet part of the cloister with my vielle, tuning the strings of the instrument and preparing a few of my favorite verses for my recital for the Cardinal, when a great hubbub erupted from the courtyard. The cries grew louder—a wailing and shouting that almost certainly indicated extreme grief—and so I replaced my vielle in its velvet bag, slung it on my back and went to investigate.

The abbey courtyard was in total uproar—monks were running here and there, shouting their sorrow to the skies. The bell of the abbey church was tolling a slow, dolorous beat; the senior monks had fallen to their knees on the beaten-earth floor of the courtyard and were praying aloud—and in the center of that space was the Cardinal's huge chair, with the Cardinal still enthroned upon it. His little eyes were half-open, his head cocked to one side and lolling backward, the front of his red robe was sheeted with wet blood and it was clear that the big man was dead. I walked toward the chair and its vast dead occupant, but when I got to within a yard or two, I felt a hand on my arm that stopped my progress and turned to see the anxious face of the hosteler at my shoulder.

"Sir Alan," he said, "it is not seemly that you disturb His Grace."

I looked at him, feeling as if I was in some kind of awful dream, and said: "I believe that he is well beyond disturbing now, Brother; I only wish to see how he died."

The monk frowned: "I think that in the pain of our loss, perhaps inquisitive strangers should not be among us," he said. "We must wash our Cardinal, and bind up his wounds, and prepare his body for burial. I beg you to allow us to be alone with our grief." It was polite, I must admit, but I was being firmly asked to leave the abbey forthwith.

"Before I go, can you tell me what happened to him?"

The monk seemed to hesitate for a moment, and then he said: "Cardinal Heribert was set upon by footpads in his own city. He was returning to the abbey from the castle after dinner and a gang of armed men, *routiers*, gutter scum, men of the lowest sort, attacked his procession. His men-at-arms were swiftly killed and the monks driven away by these vermin—may God strike them down!" The hosteler paused and gulped; there were tears in his eyes—and I had no doubt that his grief was genuine.

"They stole his ring," the hosteler blurted out, and I turned again to the gigantic corpse in the chair. I saw that the index finger, the damp, dog-smelling finger that had once borne a proud jeweled ring, had been roughly severed at the knuckle. I looked further up his body, and saw through the blood-crusted scarlet robe a dark hole, a stab wound a little to the left of his sternum, made by a dagger thrust directly into his heart.

Hanno was at my shoulder: he leaned forward to peer closely at the wound in the Cardinal's chest. "It is perfect," he said. "It is the perfect kill—a single blow, exactly on target, resulting in instant death. Perfect!"

I gathered up my men, our horses and possessions, and we made our way as quickly as we could out of the city of Vendôme. The sun was touching the western horizon and I knew the town gates would be closed at dusk; but I had worse concerns than being locked inside the city for the night. As the three of us cantered through the gates, across the wooden bridge and onto the road leading north toward King Richard's encampment, one thought was flapping around in my head like a panicked bird trapped in a bedchamber. Three clerics were dead; three innocent men of God had been murdered, and every time I tried to find out about my father, another man died. Somebody was trying to prevent me from learning any more about the life of Henri d'Alle—and that somebody was prepared to kill indiscriminately, even to kill those protected by Holy Mother Church, protected by God himself, to prevent me from finding out the truth.

9

THERE WAS NO SIGN OF ROBIN when I reached our camp. I found Little John with two of the Locksley farriers, helping the men to shoe a dozen of our company's horses. I only heard about half of that conversation with John, for it was punctuated by ringing blows of a hammer on an anvil as the head farrier struggled to get his task done as quickly as possible. We were expecting to fight the French in the morning and Robin wanted his cavalry all to be well-shod for the coming encounter. The Earl of Locksley himself, I gathered through the clanging of red-hot iron and the hiss of burning hoof, was out scouting the enemy positions and would not be back in camp anytime soon, and so I left Little John to his work and retired to my tent to think.

It seemed to me that Father Jean in Verneuil and Cardinal Heribert in Vendôme had both been killed by the same man, and in the same manner—a single dagger thrust to the heart. I was not sure about Brother Dominic—I still felt that it might be possible that he had been killed by Mercadier. And then it occurred to me that all three might have been Mercadier's victims. But why? I could understand—though not, of course, forgive—the murder of Brother Dominic. That was a strike at me to pay me back for spoiling his vicious fun when I rescued the old monk from his tormentors; I could see that I might have injured Mercadier's pride or his standing before his men by my actions and that he might wish to make a statement about his power. But why should he also want to kill a powerless small-town priest or a powerful cardinal? It made no sense.

As I lay on my pallet thinking hard, I found that there was something digging into my back. I fished around behind me in the blankets and pulled out a hunting horn. In the guttering light of a tallow candle, I examined its long, twisted shape, the sheen of the polished cow's horn, and the elegant silver mouthpiece—it was the horn that Robin had given me on the march through the Perche, telling me to sound it if I needed any help while I was flushing out phantom ambushers. In my contemplative mood, I turned this object over in my hands. In a way, I thought, it symbolized Robin himself: elegant, even beautiful, a noble shape yet twisted, and dependent on silver to make it work.

I chuckled to myself: these were not thoughts that I would have been happy to articulate aloud to my lord himself. I hung the horn by its leather strap on the pommel of my saddle, which was on its stand beside the bed, and wrenched my mind back to the subject at hand.

Someone—presumably the "man you cannot refuse" or one of his agents—had killed three men of God to prevent me from discovering any more about my father. And it had worked. I had found out little enough about his time in Notre-Dame and his expulsion from Paris. All that I had learned from Heribert was that whatever had been stolen had been "wondrous"—a relic of some sort, perhaps, a drop of milk from the breast of the Blessed Virgin Mary, a fragment of the True Cross, a hair from John the Baptist's beard or some such treasure; whatever it was, it was certainly something that the Cardinal was very keen to have returned to him. It seemed clear that the candlesticks, however valuable, were not the real objects of the theft after all. The relic was—but why should a relic be so important that someone was prepared to kill three men of God to keep me ignorant?

At that point I fell asleep.

The next morning the whole camp was alive with the news: the French King was withdrawing his forces. Philip was running away! I had barely had time to splash my face with water from a basin held by Thomas before Robin poked his handsome head through the flap in my tent and said: "Come on, slugabed, we are summoned to the King. Get moving!"

The King was in a fine mood that morning, full of bounce and energy, issuing orders in rapid succession to his clerks and to various knights and barons who appeared briefly in his grand pavilion and then hurried away to do his bidding. When Robin and I presented ourselves, the King wasted no time in pleasantries, and just said to Robin: "The Marshal met a strong force of Philip's best knights early this morning, and while he took a mauling, he broke them, and drove them off. They are all running now. Philip's entire army is on the run. Get after him, Locksley—your men are the vanguard. Harry him, chase him, and don't stop for anything. We've a chance to capture the King himself—and end his ambitions for good. But I need you to be quick. Go on, catch him for me. I'll be following you, hard on your heel with the rest of the army, but for the love of God, go now!"

It was not hard to follow the retreating French army; they withdrew up the main road toward Chateâudun, heading northeast and roughly parallel with the River Loir, leaving a broad trail of debris in their wake. Robin had left his bowmen in camp to pack up and follow us as best they could, and I had left Thomas there with similar duties; on this pursuit my lord took with him only his light cavalry—more than a hundred well-mounted lancers—and we moved fast. The road, a wide, gently meandering dusty track through thick woodland, with a broad swath on either side of it, had been much disturbed by the passage of thousands of feet and hooves—and it was littered with equipment and possessions abandoned by the French army in their haste to escape. As we galloped along, we even passed a few sick and wounded men and women lying by the side of the road, but we paid them no mind: we had our orders to harry the enemy, chase them hard, and not to stop for anything. We traveled as fast as we were able, in a great dusty, sweaty, jingling mass of men and horses, stopping once an hour to let the horses breathe and to snatch a mouthful of water to wash out our caked throats.

I was puzzled by King Philip's apparent cowardice. Why, I asked Robin—at one of these brief pauses, when we were about six or seven miles northeast of Vendôme near the hamlet of Fréteval—would Philip bring his army all this way south to confront Richard, then run away with his tail between his legs after only a brief skirmish with the Marshal?

"I believe he was trying to intimidate us," said Robin, wiping his sweating face with a linen cloth, and taking a swallow of water from a leather bag. We were all dismounted and gathered in a clearing in the forest at the side of the road, the empty thoroughfare winding on before and behind us. "A big battle is a very uncertain affair," my lord continued. "It should be the very last resort of any commander to commit his men to the hazards of a full-pitched conflict—it's like rolling the dice to determine whether you live or die, not something anyone who has any other option would choose to do. I know you would prefer to believe that warfare is all about glory, valor, great deeds and the thunder of charging horsemen, but, Alan, nobody wants to get killed or maimed, or captured and made a pauper with a crippling ransom. In war, you maneuver; look for advantage; try to find a situation in which you have the upper hand. And if you are wise, you avoid battle altogether, unless you are absolutely certain to win."

"I know all that," I said irritably, wiping Ghost's sides with a damp cloth to cool him. "But why did Philip come all the way down here with his army, seeming to seek battle with us, and then run like a craven after one skirmish?"

"Philip had to come down here. Richard has been winning too consistently in Maine, Touraine and Aquitaine for him to stay away. He has to keep the rebellion in the south alive—otherwise Richard will close down the southern front, having utterly destroyed the rebels, and then our victorious King would be free to turn all his forces loose on the north, on Normandy. Philip's army coming here was a threat—and it partially worked. Richard came north to face him, leaving several castles in Aquitaine still in rebel hands. I also believe Philip hoped to trap Richard between a rock and a hard place; between a strong Vendôme garrison loyal to Philip, and the French royal army itself. But the citizens of Vendôme believe Richard will win, ultimately; and Richard is not easily intimidated. So when Richard did not retreat south, as Philip expected him to do, but instead decided to confront the French head-on, Philip panicked and withdrew. It was the sensible move, I think. Richard would probably have beaten him here, and Philip can't afford a defeat. I suspect the French King will try to arrange a truce—and I think Richard may grant it him."

"Why would Richard agree to a truce, if we are winning?" I said.

"Oh, it would be in his interest, too. He needs to rebuild the castles he has captured; give his men time to rest and heal their wounds; perhaps recruit a few more knights to his side. This war will not be one giant pitched battle; it will stop and start, truce and war, a castle captured here, and lost there. We will win eventually, I believe; we will push the French back and reclaim Richard's lands, but it will not be swift."

I pondered Robin's words as we mounted up and set off again, thinking what I might attempt to do if a truce were declared. But I soon drowned my thoughts in the rhythm of the chase, pounding up the dusty road at a canter with thick forest forming a cool green curtain on either side. Then we rounded a bend, and at a hand-command from Robin we all drew rein and slid to an abrupt halt, with much snorting and cursing and one beast barging into another. Ahead of us, perhaps fifty paces away, was a thin line of mounted French knights, barely a score of them, drawn up knee to knee across the road as a fragile barrier.

Clearly they had heard us coming, and what they were attempting to protect was a massive train of wagons and carts, pulled by oxen and heavy horses and stretched out along the road for almost a quarter of a mile—gigantic, lumbering wagons piled high with goods, weapons, sacks of grain, barrels of wine. Round-topped carriages rumbled along carrying women—a knight's mistress and her maids, perhaps, or a traveling brothel, or a contingent of nuns; light donkey carts carried horse fodder, great mountains of hay packed tight under ropes but still towering ten feet in the air; strings of pack mules ambled along carrying chests of coin or bales of fine cloth; and every kind of transport imaginable filled the road ahead in a long river of beasts and men—and plunder. We had come up unexpectedly on what appeared to be the entire French royal baggage train—which was now defended by only a handful of knights.

"God in Heaven!" said Hanno from my right shoulder. To my left, Robin turned to me, a look of savage delight on his handsome face, like a starving peasant presented with a dripping roast on a silver platter. "Oh, Alan," he said, "your God—or whomever it is sitting on that cloud up there—he truly loves me! Be so good as to sound the charge!"

I was pleased to see Robin happy, though a little alarmed that he should choose this moment, just as we were to go into battle, to make a jest about Almighty God, the Lord of Hosts. Nevertheless, I unhooked the twisted horn from my pommel, put it to my lips, and gave two short blasts and then a long one; repeated twice. The signal to charge: ta-ta-taaaa, ta-ta-taaaa.

I lowered my lance, slammed my heels into Ghost's gray sides and surged forward—and Robin's entire force of more than five score loot-hungry outlaws-turned-lancers charged forward with me and poured down onto the thin line of enemy knights like an avalanche.

We swept them away in a matter of moments. I lunged at a knight directly to my front with my lance, aiming for the killing blow to his belly, but his warhorse took a sideways step at the last moment and I missed. My lance smacked into the high wooden cantle at the rear of his saddle and snapped in two. Suddenly he was on me with his sword swinging at my head. I blocked his first strike with my shield, simultaneously dropping my shattered lance and groping for Goody's mace, which was slung from the pommel of my saddle. He hacked at me again and I caught it again on my red shield, returning his blow with a hard overhand chop with the mace, which crunched sickeningly into his left shoulder joint. The knight dropped his shield—marked, I noticed, with a strange device: a light blue cross on a white background, with a black border around it—used his spurs and made off up the road, his left arm loose and useless, and I was content to let him live. The rest of the enemy knights had either been cut down or had run from the field, except for one Frenchman who had been knocked off his horse, half-stunned, and had managed to surrender himself to a delighted Little John. A few footmen, men-at-arms, crossbowmen and the drovers and carters were running from the wagon train in all directions, heading for the cover of the trees on either side of the road.

But Robin's troop were oblivious to their fleeing foes; they had already begun to loot the baggage train with a gleeful lack of restraint that reminded me of a pack of wild dogs on a fresh sheep carcass. That dusty stretch of forest-hemmed road rang with the joyful shouts of men-at-arms, the crunch of axes as they knocked the locks from money chests and opened wide holes in the heads of wine barrels. Handfuls of bright coins were thrown through the air—causing a scramble wherever they landed. Blood-red wine was guzzled like water. Precious silks and gold-embroidered cloths flapped in the light breeze, the men wrapping themselves in priceless materials and parading and prancing for the amusement of their friends. Gold and silver vessels were grabbed, examined, briefly admired and then used to scoop more dark wine from the opened barrels. There were snatches of singing and bawdy jests—some men had found stores of food and were cramming choice morsels, preserved fruits, fine cheeses and pickled vegetables into their mouths; some men already seemed to be drunk. From time to time I heard a woman's scream, and tried to close my ears. It reminded me of the last day of a raucous county fair at the end of summer, with food and wine abundant, the smell of sweat and animal dung and easy money in the air, and brightly colored, fabulous trade goods that tugged the eye wherever you looked. Every Locksley man seemed madly happy, seeing himself rich and carefree for the rest of his days.

And that included Robin himself.

"My lord," I said, "what about the French army?"

"Hmm? What about it?" My master was distracted. He suddenly bellowed: "I want piles here and here of all the gold and silver items, silks too—any item worth more than . . . oh, I don't know, one shilling, is to be collected over there; and any bastard who steals from it will be flayed alive; I swear it. John, get them organized, will you. The rest of the damned army will be here before long. We must hurry."

"My lord, the French."

"What about the damn French?" Robin rounded on me.

"We should be pursuing them, my lord. We have our orders: to harry them, to chase them and to stop for nothing. We must leave this wagon train until later, and keep on pressing the French."

"Are you mad?" Robin rarely raised his voice in anger but his bull-bellow at my quiet words nearly lifted me off my feet. "Leave all this? Abandon the spoils to Mercadier's scum? Have you taken leave of your senses?"

"My lord, we have our orders. It is our sacred duty to the King." I did not care to be shouted at, and my own tone to the Earl of Locksley had become cold and formal.

Robin controlled himself: his silver eyes glittered at me dangerously. "Do not seek to instruct me in my duty, Sir Alan. I command this battle of men. Not you. And you will remember that. If you wish to go chasing off across country after the fleeing French—I will wish you Godspeed, otherwise you will hold your tongue—and learn to obey *my* orders. Do you hear me? I have had quite enough of your schoolboy morality, your endless talk of right and wrong. Of my damned duty. From now on you will be silent."

The sensible thing to have done would have been to have held my tongue. But, of course, young and reckless as I was, I did not do that. My eyes clouded with rage, I said: "I, at least, am obedient to my King. I am his loyal man, even if you are not!" And with that I turned Ghost and began to walk him up the line of the wagons, past the drunken, joyful Locksley men who were happily wallowing in their extraordinary good fortune. I came across Hanno by a huge barrel of ale: he had smashed in the top with his fighting axe and was downing huge drafts of the brown liquid from a golden, jewel-encrusted chalice.

"Come, Hanno; we have our orders from the King," I said pompously. "We must pursue the French." Hanno stared at me with sheer disbelief. His stubbled jaw fell agape, exposing the yellow-gray wreckage of his teeth, the golden cup held loosely in his hand. Then he tilted his head to one side, and looked down at the ale barrel, and then at the magnificent jeweled vessel in his hand.

"Come, Hanno, we must be quick," I said. A large part of me recognized my unbelievable stupidity—there was a small fortune in silver coins alone scattered about Ghost's hooves—and yet I could not stop myself. It was utterly foolish for two men to chase after an entire army. What if we caught up with them? What then? But I was set on my course and my pride meant that I could not deviate from it.

I have never felt quite so much love for Hanno as I did in that next moment: he swilled down the last of the ale in the gorgeous cup, tossed it casually over his shoulder, as if it were no more than a gnawed old chicken bone, walked to his horse and mounted smoothly. And with that ugly old Bavarian murderer at my shoulder, I galloped up the line of the wagons and onto the empty road ahead.

After a mile or two, I began to calm down, and reflect soberly on my conversation with Robin. I had in truth behaved absurdly, like a spoiled little boy: it was a foolish burst of temper and I deeply regretted it. But there was something about the glee with which Robin and his men had ripped into that royal baggage train that set my teeth on edge. It was undoubtedly a rich prize—the personal possessions of the King of France; his treasury, all the silver he needed to fund his war against King Richard. It was a prize of staggering magnitude, and any sane man would want to partake of it. So why had I reacted the way I did? Sheer boneheaded stupidity; but it stemmed, I knew, from my relationship with Robin. I so badly wanted him to be the shining Christian knight, the *preux chevalier*—noble, honest, devout, courtly—and when he revealed to me the man he truly was, as tempted as any other man by the glittering lure of Mammon, I found myself reacting badly. What I needed to do, I told myself, was halt the horses, turn around and ride back to Robin and beg his pardon. And help myself to a share of the spoils. Another mile passed, and another, and I was just about to give the order to Hanno when my Bavarian friend put a hand on my arm, and we both reined in.

"Listen," said Hanno. And, over the jingling of our horses' accoutrements as we slowed to a walk, and our own heavy breathing, I heard what Hanno had made out: the pounding thuds of cantering horsemen on the road ahead. And they were coming closer.

Perhaps if we had immediately turned our horses' heads and galloped back down the road, we might have escaped; perhaps. But it is hard for a fighting man to run without even having glimpsed his enemy. So we stayed there in the center of the road for another twenty heartbeats—while I was rendered immobile with indecision. It was Hanno who broke the spell: "They are too many," he said. "We must go."

And, at that moment, a mass of enemy cavalry, a *conroi* of perhaps twenty riders, came into view around a shallow bend in the road.

"Come, Alan, we must go—now!" said Hanno again, more urgently. The enemy knights were less than fifty paces away. They saw us, and at a gleeful shout from their leader, they began their charge.

10

THEIR HORSES WERE FRESH, AND OURS were not. We were two men, they were a force of twenty. It was as simple as that. We ran. We put our heels into our horses' sides and ran for our lives. But after a bare quarter of a mile at a full gallop, I knew that Ghost was tiring, and glancing over my shoulder I could see the enemy knights closing on us fast. I noticed one other strange thing too; all of the knights bore the same device as the man I had fought at the baggage train—a blue cross on a white field with a black border.

It was not the blazon of a northern French noble, of that I was reasonably certain—I was as familiar as most knights were with the great barons on either side of this conflict, but this blue cross was new to me. And yet there seemed to be so many men bearing these arms that they had to belong to a powerful man, an earl or count or even duke.

As Hanno and I pounded along that dusty road, leaning over our horses' necks and trying to urge the maximum speed from our tired mounts, I could imagine the points of the knights' lances almost tickling my back. I snatched a quick glance over my shoulder, and saw that the leading knight was only a few yards behind. Hanno was slightly ahead of me, and I could sense Ghost beginning to founder, his smooth galloping gait suddenly changing, the horse stumbling with exhaustion for a pace or two, and then regaining its rhythm. He was a valiant beast, my Ghost, but I knew he was near the end of his strength. We were only a mile or two from the baggage train and I realized that I was leading this pack of galloping enemy knights straight to Robin's men. Unhorsed, scattered, every man probably as drunk as a bishop by now—our troops would be easy prey. These mail-clad killers on my tail could cut the Locksley men to shreds if they came on them unexpectedly. By leading the knights directly to Robin's force I would be responsible for the deaths of many of my friends.

That thought was unbearable; I had to warn them. I plucked the twisted horn from where it had been bouncing on the pommel of my saddle, managed to get it to my lips without slowing Ghost's thundering pace, and sounded it, once—twice—three times. The leading knight of the blue cross was right on top of us by now; from the corner of my eye I saw him draw his lance for a strike, and lunge forward, the needle-pointed blade licking out toward my lower back on the left-hand side. I saw the strike coming over my shoulder, and swung in the saddle and dropped my shield to take the blow. I felt a jarring smack, and looked down in horror to see that the lance had been deflected by my shield—and had plunged deep into Ghost's pale belly.

The knight had released the shaft of his spear, now wedged deep in my poor mount's entrails, the shaft drooping and tangling with Ghost's hind legs, and the next thing I knew I was sailing high in the air, over Ghost's neck and head, and landing with a crash on my back in the ashy dust of the road.

Stunned, winded but with, as far as I could tell, nothing broken, I lifted my head and saw that Hanno had halted his headlong flight and turned to protect me, God love him. He was engaging the leading blue cross knight with axe and sword. There was a flurry of blows, a hack, a crunch, and the knight slumped, boneless, lolling in his saddle. Hanno turned again and was shouting something at me, but in my fuddled state I could not comprehend him. He leaned down in the saddle and reached out a hand to me, urging me to rise and mount up behind him. His mouth was moving; I could see his awful teeth and the lips curling to form sounds, and yet I could make nothing of his speech. I got to my knees and reached out an arm toward him and suddenly his horse lurched a step forward, struck by a massive blow, and I saw Hanno look behind him. There were knights all around, tall shadows in the sunlight, and horses too; kicked dust swirled in the air and the shouts of angry men flew above me—and Hanno was slipping off his horse as it collapsed under him, lanced in the belly like my poor Ghost; then he was beside me, lifting me, helping me to my feet, his face concerned. A knight on horseback loomed over us, I saw the glitter of his sword raised to strike, and Hanno was pushing me on my stumbling feet under the horse's neck. The sword whistled down inches from my shoulder—and with a sudden rush my senses came back to me fully.

"Into the trees, into the trees," I found myself shouting. I had lost my shield, as had Hanno, and we sprinted unencumbered the few yards into the thick woodland on the eastern side of the road—closely followed by a dozen or so eager horsemen. By God's good grace, the woodland was ancient, thickly tangled with underbrush and low branches that much impeded the horsemen. We drew our swords and, by a combination of scurrying, ducking and slashing at the legs of the knights, Hanno and I somehow managed to dodge the questing lances of our enemies and squirm into the gloom of the forest. We survived to find ourselves fifty yards from the road, back to back, blades in our hands, panting and partially sheltered in a sort of dell made by two huge fallen oak trees that formed the sign of the cross on the forest floor. The fallen trees guarded our rear, but the horsemen surrounded us. They could not easily approach through the thick trees, scrubby thorns and bushes; but neither could we escape. There were perhaps a dozen of them by now on all sides around our pathetic wooden half-fortification, and they walked their horses closer all the time; and then things took a turn for the worse—they began to dismount. Hanno and I were dead men. On foot, these knights could close with us and then their numbers would tell and we would be finished in a few moments. The knights approached silently, their faces under their conical helmets grim and bearded—eyes showing no sign of mercy.

I stepped forward, away from the rudimentary cover of the oak-tree cross, and said in French in a loud carrying voice: "My name is Sir Alan Dale, a knight of Westbury in the English county of Nottinghamshire. You have killed our horses and we are at your mercy: under the laws of chivalry, I offer my surrender to you for ransom, on condition that you spare my life and also the life of my man-at-arms, here."

The leading knight, a handsome man with a bushy blond beard, who was by now no more than half a dozen paces from me, paused and looked directly at me. I saw a brief glimmer of compassion in his eyes. Then he spoke: "Alas, Sir Alan, there can be no surrender for you today."

I was puzzled: "Why not, sir?" I asked. "I have told you who I am and I have offered to yield to you—will you not accept my surrender?"

The knight merely shook his head and repeated a little sadly: "There can be no surrender for you." Then he rushed forward, in three long-legged strides, lifting his sword two-handed and swinging it in a great downward blow at my head. I swept my own sword up and around in a circle to the right, my blade deflecting his blow; at the same time I stepped in close and punched my misericorde hard into his side, through his white surcoat and mail, and deep into his liver. He fell at my feet, shocked, dying, white surcoat reddening quickly, bearded mouth working silently.

Then the remaining knights of the blue cross all charged forward together, and Hanno and I found ourselves battling half a dozen knights apiece in a murderous blizzard of blades and blows, shouts and curses. A sword hacked at my face and I ducked just in time. A lance speared at my chest and I somehow managed to deflect it with my misericorde. One of the knights clambered up onto the dead trunk of the oak tree behind my shoulder. We were dead men. And then I heard a sound that made my heart bound with joy.

A horn.

A hunting horn blown with two short notes and one long one, repeated twice: ta-ta-taaaa; ta-ta-taaaa. And in an instant Hanno and I were no longer fighting alone.

Robin's men came hurtling through the trees on foot—silent, deadly, their green cloaks merging into the forest and making them all but invisible. I saw Robin's lean face contorted in a snarl of rage as he sliced his sword into the back of a knight on the outskirts of the circle around Hanno and I. Much the miller's son, a pace or two behind Robin, let out a roar as he carved a knight from shoulder to opposite hip with one blow of his long sword. And the Locksley men were swarming everywhere, tackling the knights, two or three to each enemy, hacking with sword and knife, lunging with spears. The wise knights fled deeper into the woods—and some escaped, though many were pursued and savagely cut down—the unwise knights died where they stood.

Robin stopped before me, breathing great heaving lungfuls of air, but smiling at me, his merry gray eyes dancing. "You are a childish, stubborn, high-minded prig, Alan Dale," he said, when he had caught his breath. "But I would not care to be without you. I'm glad at least that you had enough wit in you to summon us with your horn."

The next day, shortly before noon, I poked my head inside Robin's tent, and my lord cheerfully invited me to enter. I wanted to thank him formally for saving my life. I had survived the encounter with the knights of the blue cross miraculously unscathed, except for a few bruises caused by falling from Ghost. I had recovered the body of my loyal animal friend and, although some of the Locksley men had sniggered at my sentimentality, Hanno, Thomas and I had dug a grave for Ghost and buried him at the side of the road, near the spot where he had died. I could not bear the thought of wild animals eating his carcass—or worse, hungry men of the lowest sort from King Richard's army cutting bloody chunks off his noble frame. So we buried him deep, and I wept over his grave.

Hanno had been lightly wounded in the knights' attack by the crossed oak trees, just before Robin's men had arrived—a bloody score up his left forearm. But Elise, the Locksley wise woman, had washed the cut, packed it with cobwebs, stitched it and bandaged it neatly.

Robin was in a cheerful mood when I entered the tent: although the sound of my horn had forced him and two score or so of the more sober men to abandon their looting of the royal baggage train and come to my rescue, and the rest of the army, including Mercadier's rapacious mercenaries, had come up while Robin was away, Little John had remained behind and had managed to secure a sizable amount of loot for our company. And Robin had been praised by King Richard for having captured such a great prize; so my lord was quite content with the day.

When I entered it that hot July morning, Robin's tent was taken up with a vast mound of scrolls, books and parchments, and half a dozen dusty clerks were on their knees by the pile, pulling out items, examining them and occasionally giving sharp little bird-cries of delight. One of the wagons of the baggage train had been found to contain the royal archives—letters and deeds, charters and correspondence, some of which stretched back to the beginning of King Philip's reign fourteen years ago. And Robin had been asked by Richard to go through the correspondence and discover which of the King's vassals had secretly been corresponding with the French. Robin was enjoying himself enormously, I could see, and I watched him as I awaited his attention, sipping a cup of light wine on a stool in the corner of the tent.

"Here's another one, Alan," my master called out, waving a piece of parchment that one of the King's clerks had handed him. "William de St. Hubert is offering to do homage to King Philip for all his lands in Normandy—the disloyal little weasel. He was having breakfast with our King this very morning, I believe. Lamb's kidneys and eggs. This letter will make him squirm when Richard reads it, that's for sure."

I was glad to see Robin so happy; our quarrel of the day before over the looting of the royal train seemed to have been completely forgotten.

"This one might be of interest to you," said Robin, and he lobbed a scroll overhand to me across the tent, narrowly missing the tonsured head of a clerk who was rummaging through the pile of parchments. I caught the scroll one-handed, and carefully untied the ribbon that secured it and unrolled the thick yellow cylinder. It contained a charter from His Royal Highness Philip Augustus, by the grace of God, King of France, and so on . . . to one Thibault, Seigneur d'Alle, granting him the right to build a hotel on the Rue St. Denis in the Ville de Paris. The charter was dated just over a year ago. It took me a few heartbeats to recognize what this meant: my uncle Thibault, the man who had refused to help my father in his hour of need, was now favored enough by the French King to be allowed to build a large town house in the center of the royal capital.

"I have to go to Paris," I said.

Robin frowned. "Why? Do you care so much for your French relative? You've never even met the man."

"Cardinal Heribert was murdered," I said, "and so was Jean the priest. The only two people that I know of who knew my father—and who are still alive—are in Paris: my uncle Thibault d'Alle and Bishop Maurice de Sully."

Robin was still frowning at me. "You are dimly aware, Alan, are you not, that we are in the middle of a war with the French?" he asked in a mocking tone. "And that Paris is the capital of the French King—our sworn enemy?"

I didn't deign to answer. So Robin continued: "This is madness, Alan. Your duty is to serve me and serve the King, and remain with the army. All this talk of exonerating your father is pure foolishness. He is dead, Alan, dead! He does not care whether you clear his name or blacken it. I urge you; I am in truth begging you—please stop this foolishness. No good can come of raking up the past like this. Leave it alone."

"I understand how you feel, Robin," I said, evenly. I was determined to be calm about this subject, even though I found Robin's opposition to my quest hurtful and more than a little baffling. "But I must resolve this mystery—or it will cost me my own life."

"We've found another one, sir," said one of the clerks, holding up a large sheet of parchment. "Robert de Dignac in correspondence with King Philip last year—"

"Not now," said Robin to the clerk, but he was staring at me. "What do you mean, cost you your life?"

"Those knights yesterday—the men with the blue crosses on their shields—they hunted us like wild animals. And when I offered my surrender, they would not accept it. They wanted me dead—and I would be, too, were it not for your intervention. Somebody, most probably this 'man you cannot refuse,' is trying to prevent me finding out about my father. Those knights of the blue cross serve this 'man you cannot refuse,' I am quite certain of it, and while initially he was content with silencing those who might tell me about my father, now, it seems, he has decided to have me killed too."

Robin put his head to one side, and half-smiled at me: "Mysterious knightly assassins hunting you down? A sinister, all-powerful 'man you cannot refuse'? Are you sure this is not some addlebrained fantasy?"

"Those knights of the blue cross wanted me dead—and not just because I was their foeman in a skirmish. They wanted me, Alan Dale, dead. Cardinal Heribert is dead; so is Father Jean—so too is poor Brother Dominic. I'm not inventing this; this is no addlebrained fantasy. I *must* go to Paris. If not, the knights may succeed at the next attempt."

Robin gave a long sigh and stared at the floor of the tent for a while. "Well," he said finally, "if you can persuade the King to release you, I won't stand in your way."

I found the King at the horse lines, inspecting a dozen fine new warhorses that had been sent to him as a gift from Count Geoffrey of the Perche. Clearly, that wily nobleman, currently sitting up the road behind the walls of Chateâudun, and shortly expecting to give shelter to Philip's retreating army, was sniffing the wind and attempting to assure himself of a welcome should he decide to change sides and renew his allegiance to our King.

Richard was gracious enough to receive me and listen once again to my petition to take my leave of the army. I told him that it was urgent that I speak with Bishop Maurice de Sully, who must now be an aged man, before he died. But I did not mention my uncle Thibault—having a close relative, and a rich one too, on the side of the French King might, I felt, cast some doubt on my devotion to Richard. As the Lionheart seemed in a jocular mood that morning—I even essayed a jest to sweeten my request.

"If I may make so bold, Sire, it is entirely your fault that I need to embark upon this journey. Were it not for your hasty actions in Nottingham, I would already know the name of the man who ordered my father's death."

The King looked at me quizzically. "So it is all *my* fault, is it, Blondel? How so?"

"Well, Sire, had you not ordered Sir Ralph Murdac to be hanged as a lesson to the other traitors in the castle, he would have been able to tell me the man's name!"

The King chuckled. "You cannot blame me fully for that," he said. "It was at your master Robert of Locksley's suggestion that I had the man hanged. If Robin had not bent my ear, that rascal Murdac might even be alive today. I might well have pardoned him." And the King laughed.

I tried to match his merriment, but I felt as if a dark storm cloud had crept over the sun. The King carried on speaking, oblivious to my sudden discomfort. "Well, Sir Alan, because I am an exceedingly kind and generous lord—and because I have this very morning heard that the French are seeking to negotiate a truce with us—I shall grant your request to depart, and I will go so far as to wish you luck in your quest. May you return soon to my side, wiser and more content with your place among my best men."

I managed to make my bow, and leave the royal presence with some dignity. But my head was reeling like a drunkard's after downing a barrel of wine.

Robin had urged the King to summarily hang Murdac! Robin had silenced Murdac and prevented him from speaking to me about the orders to kill my father. A monstrous, unthinkable idea was growing in my mind. Robin himself was the "man you cannot refuse." Robert Odo, Earl of Locksley, my liege lord and master, my dear friend and mentor—Robin Hood was the man who had ordered my father's death.

Part Two

11

I have shown these pages to my grandson Alan and, while he read them without pausing and with seeming enjoyment, he is a little bemused by them, I think. He has difficulty in seeing the young warrior that I once was, valiantly defending castles for kings and skirmishing with bands of murderous knights, in the white-capped, dry stick of a man I am now. I believe that he feels I must be playing some sort of trick on him, perhaps weaving too much romance in with the truth. But he tells me that he likes the tale, so far.

"I am glad that you went to seek vengeance for your father," he told me gravely. "That is what I would have done—it is a knight's bounden duty to protect his honor."

Why is vengeance so appealing, particularly to the young? There is no material reward that springs from it; a man is not richer, or healthier, or even happier as a result of it—quite often the reverse. Why does a young man's heart beat faster at the thought of bloody vengeance taken for a hurt received? Why do we thrill at a tale of revenge? I know that we do, or at least that most men do; so many of the great lays and stories of knights and warriors are built around this idea. Is it because all men have been wronged at some point in their lives but few have ever received just recompense for their hurts? Is that why the male heart eternally thirsts for vengeance? Perhaps.

I remember on one occasion, when I was newly come to Robin's band of outlaws and about the same age as my grandson, my lord spoke to me of the virtue of vengeance. I had been weeping over my father's death and Robin had spoken to me quite brutally: "A man does not snivel when a member of his family has been murdered," he said. "A man does not cry like a babe, seeking pity from those around him for a wrong he has suffered. He takes his revenge. He makes the guilty men, the men who took that kinsman's life, weep in pain; he makes their widows sob themselves to sleep at night. Else he is no man."

As a youngster, I had absorbed Robin's simple but savage message, I had thought on it often in my private moments, and it had become part of my warrior's creed.

"And was the Earl of Locksley really the 'man you cannot refuse,' Grandpa?" young Alan asked, when he had finished reading the parchments. "And did you ever have your vengeance on him?"

"You will have to wait until I have written my whole story down to find out," I told him.

"But I must return to my duties at Kirkton tomorrow," said young Alan, quite cast down. I confess I was slightly pleased by his sorrowful tone; but then, what storyteller does not delight in delaying the pleasure of his audience?

"You shall read the whole tale on your next visit to your mother—perhaps at Christmastide," I said.

"That is six months or more away," protested the boy.

"As a knight, you must learn to bear a vast degree of suffering without complaint," I said, smiling fondly at him. And young Alan, to his credit, tried very hard not to sulk.

Within an hour of receiving permission from the King, I was on the road. I was heading for Rouen, Richard's Norman capital, and mounted on Shaitan, with Thomas on his brown rouncey and Hanno reduced to riding a packhorse and leading a mule that bore my possessions, kit and weapons. One should not really ride a costly destrier when merely traveling, but I possessed no other horse, and I would not even contemplate taking one from Robin's string: I felt the absence of Ghost as an ache in my heart.

I had left the army without speaking to Robin, or any of his men. I could not face him; I was almost certain that he was the "man you cannot refuse" and I knew there would have been bloodshed if I had set eyes on him. My gut roiling with rage and confusion, we took the road west toward Le Mans and I ran over in my mind the workings that had made me believe that my lord, my hero, the man I looked upon as a respected older brother, had, in effect, killed my father.

King Richard's words rang like a church bell in my head: *It was at your master Robert of Locksley's suggestion that I had the man hanged. If Robin had not bent my ear, that rascal Murdac might even be alive today. I might well have pardoned him.*

Robin was well aware of our sovereign's vast appetite for forgiveness—he had been pardoned himself by the King when he had had the sentence of outlawry lifted five years earlier. Did Robin fear that if Sir Ralph Murdac was not hanged he would ultimately go free? Was that why Robin urged the King to execute his enemy Ralph Murdac? Or was there some deeper reason? Did Robin secretly wish to prevent Murdac from revealing any more information to me about this "man you cannot refuse"—because he himself was that very man?

I pondered what I knew about Robin's history. Ten years ago, when my father had been ripped from this world, Robin had already been a powerful man; living outside the law, to be sure, but a much-feared warrior with a ruthless reputation for killing and mutilating anyone who stood in his way. He was then known as the Lord of Sherwood, and he held absolute if unofficial sway over a hundred thousand acres of England, from Nottingham to South Yorkshire. But

Murdac had been his hated foe. Or had he? I remembered Robin telling me a few years previously that he had once had the Sheriff of Nottinghamshire in his grasp in those days and had demanded a ransom for his life—one that Murdac had subsequently failed to pay. However, Robin had said that for a year or more after that incident, Murdac had acknowledged Robin's authority over Sherwood, despite his outlaw condition, and had left him and his men in peace to run their larcenous affairs as they saw fit. During this unspoken truce between the two most powerful men in central England, could Robin have asked Murdac for a favor or a boon? Could the outlaw have asked the sheriff to have one insignificant peasant summarily hanged? It was possible—Robin would not shy away from ordering a man's death, if it served his purposes. And Murdac had been the sort of creature who would have a man hanged in an eye-blink purely for his own vicious amusement. I cringed in the saddle: I knew that it was entirely possible that Robin was thc "man you cannot refuse." There was nothing in my master's character—and I knew him well—that would disavow this supposition. But was it probable?

Why? I asked myself. Why would Robin seek my father's death? They had known each other, Robin had admitted that when he and I had first met, and they had liked each other, or so he said. What could have happened between them to cause Robin to resort to making a deadly agreement with his enemy Murdac? I had no answers for that—or for the many other questions tumbling around in my head.

There was, indeed, something to my mind that seemed to strongly indicate Robin's guilt: ever since I had told my lord that I wanted to track down my father's killer, he had tried to discourage me from the task. He had told me on at least three occasions to let the matter lie, insisting that no good would come of my investigations. Was he protecting himself? Was he trying to prevent me from discovering that it was his secret hand that had caused my father's death? And there was one more thing: Robin had been present in the castle when Father Jean had been murdered at Verneuil; he was at Loches when Brother Dominic was killed; and he had been missing from the army on a private "scouting mission" when Cardinal Heribert had been stabbed in his chair. Could my lord have accomplished these murders? Certainly, he was capable of them. Had he committed them? Was he even now trying to accomplish my death?

These questions chased themselves in weary circles for the next seven days, as Hanno, Thomas and myself made our way in easy stages, careful to spare Shaitan's costly legs, on the main roads west to Le Mans and then north, through Alençon and Bernay, to Rouen. The weather was mild and cloudy but with only one rain shower during the entire journey, and we slept rough in hayricks, woods and remote barns, eschewing the company of other travelers. I was very aware that I had the best part of five pounds in silver in a broad leather money belt around my waist, the proceeds of Robin's milking of the Tourangeaux, and now that we were away from the army, I had no small fear of meeting a well-armed gang of footpads. Large organized gangs of such lawless men infested many of the wilder regions of France, robbing and murdering unwary travelers, just as they did in parts of England. Some of these bandits were *routiers* who had grown bored with army life; others were peasants forced into outlawry by bad harvests, the ravages of war or by their own cruel lords. Some were simply evil men.

I did not want to meet any of them.

On the outskirts of Rouen, we stayed for one night in a monastery, and I discovered from one of the monks that what Richard had told me was indeed true: the French King was holding talks with King Richard's Chancellor, William Longchamp, and a truce between the two sides now seemed to be imminent. The agreement was likely to allow each side to retain what territory it had. Both sides, the monk said, were exhausted by months of warfare; there would be a cessation of hostilities for a long while, God be praised.

I was weighed down with fatigue myself; Richard's hard campaigning in the south had worn me thin, and my suspicions of Robin dragged at my spirits. I could not decide what to do about them: I knew that I must avenge my father, but challenging Robin was an unthinkable prospect. I needed to know more about the events around my father's expulsion from Paris; and that knowledge could only be obtained by traveling to that great foreign city and demanding answers from Bishop Maurice de Sully and my uncle Thibault, the Seigneur d'Alle. I vowed that I would not leave that place until I had fathomed this mystery; and, furthermore, if it proved that Robin was responsible for my father's death—despite my long friendship with him, and all that I owed him—I would seek a fitting revenge.

While the truce talks between Chancellor Longchamp and the French were taking place at the castle of Tillières, ten miles east of Verneuil—and King Richard, we heard, was continuing to win a series of minor but brilliant victories against the rebels in the south—Hanno, Thomas and I found ourselves accommodation in the stone castle of Rouen. Things were not at all well in the Norman capital: Prince John had been holding the city for Richard for the past two months, but while Richard had been covering himself in glory in the south, Prince John had been struggling to hold his own in the duchy against King Philip's marauding men. A few weeks before our arrival, the French had captured the small stronghold of Fontaines, a bare five miles north of the walls of Rouen. Worse, Robert, Earl of Leicester, a renowned and reliable warrior—who had been charged with the defense of Normandy along with Richard's brother—had been captured by the French while raiding the lands of Hugh de Gournay and was now being held for ransom. There was an air of defeatism in the castle, servants tiptoed, knights wore long faces and talked among themselves almost in whispers. Prince John, on the other hand, complained long and loud to anyone who would listen that Richard had not given him sufficient men-at-arms to hold the duchy, and was to be heard suggesting that the string of reverses that his men had suffered were, in fact, no fault of his but a result of Richard's meanness with his available troops.

I had determined to stay out of Prince John's presence, and I came to his attention, I believe, only once during the ten dull days I spent there. At dinner one day—a surprisingly lavish feast, given our circumstances, of swan baked in its feathers, stuffed crane, roast boar's head and stewed lampreys—I found myself staring with deep contempt at John while he talked loudly in his harsh croaking voice about secret traitors within the walls of Rouen who were undermining his heroic defense. The look I gave him was unguarded, betraying all the derision that I held in my heart for the man, and he caught my eye while he was in mid-flow about the suspected perfidy of the Jews of the town. Our eyes locked for an instant, then I quickly glanced away—it does not pay to confront royalty, it can be as dangerous as teasing a wild bear—and I saw a glow of dark anger in his eyes. Clearly he had not forgotten me, and my "betrayal" of his cause a year earlier. But he said nothing, and neither did I, and the talk between him and his cronies passed to other matters, chiefly, the hunt—for John, if he was a poor warrior, was extravagantly fond of sport, war's tamer shadow.

I took care to stay away from Prince John for the remainder of my stay in the castle, and filled the hours with battle practice with Hanno, and in the training of Thomas, who was becoming at least half-decent with a sword and shield, for all his tender years. I also took the opportunity to re-equip myself and my men, spending some of the Tourangeaux silver on new shields painted with my boar device and bundles of lances, fresh provisions and other necessities, and buying a spirited palfrey for Hanno to ride and a swift, well-mannered, three-year-old courser for myself.

When the news arrived in late July that Chancellor Longchamp had indeed secured a truce with the French at Tillières, which was agreed by both sides to last until November the following year, Hanno, Thomas and I were rested, ready and equipped to take advantage of the cessation of hostilities and make our way onward to Paris.

We rode out of the walls of Rouen on a blustery summer morning heading for the manor of Clermont-sur-Andelle, which stood about fifteen or so miles to the east of Rouen. This was the manor that Richard had endowed me with after the siege of Nottingham earlier that year, and as Robin had rightly pointed out, it was largesse with very large strings attached. The manor stood at the eastern edge of Normandy and it had been one of the first to be gobbled up by the French during their initial advance. It was a royal gift that I could not enjoy until King Philip and his barons had been pushed out of Richard's domains; certainly I was not receiving its rents and the fruits of the worked land—and after the truce of Tillières, which stipulated that each of the two warring sides should keep the territories that they had captured, it looked as if I might never receive them. But I was curious, and although it was out of our direct path to Paris, I wanted to see Clermont-sur-Andelle to know the lands that one day, with God's help, I might possess.

By late afternoon, Hanno, Thomas and I were sitting astride our mounts at the edge of a patch of thick woodland, almost completely hidden from human sight, and gazing down at a broad water meadow beside the reedy banks of the River Andelle. In the distance, on the far side of the slow river, on a low hillock, I could see the manor that was rightfully mine: a spacious compound, well fortified with a stout wooden palisade, a large L-shaped, thatched, timber hall inside it, and a scatter of other buildings. By the river, a mill wheel turned in the race and half a dozen figures could be made out moving around the mill itself, some burdened by large sacks of grain or flour. On this side of the river, across a narrow wooden bridge, was a fenced orchard of pears and apples—it was too far for me to see, but, at that time of year, I could imagine that the first tiny fruits must be beginning to show. Standing in my stirrups, I could also make out a high cross atop a small wooden church beyond the fortified compound of the manor and a score or so of villeins' hovels scattered between the two. Beyond the village, as far as the horizon, were broad fields, some greeny-yellow with standing wheat and barley, others fallow and thick with weeds. But it seemed an orderly place, did Clermont-sur-Andelle; not perhaps as prosperous as Westbury under the care of my efficient steward Baldwin but remarkably untouched by the ravages of war.

In the foreground, perhaps three hundred yards from our position in the trees, were four well-mounted horsemen; by their trappings and clothes, at least two of them were knights, the other two grooms or servants. The knights were bareheaded and they appeared to be related by blood—a father and son, perhaps. I could not see their faces clearly at that distance, but both men had a similar posture in the saddle and shared the same shade of pitch-black hair. As we looked on, the younger of the knights launched a large blue-gray peregrine falcon from his wrist, and we joined in watching that majestic bird soar up into the air and circle almost beyond the range of human sight.

My hands on the reins of the courser tightened into fists, and the big horse moved under me, feeling the stirrings of my outrage, but unsure of my intentions. Who were these men, and by what right did they hunt my lands? It crossed my mind, only for a brief moment, I swear, that I should ride down to them and take my sword to them for their impertinence. Hanno and I could handle the knight and his son, I was sure of it: we were armed for war, and clad in mail, our weapons keen. We could very soon have overcome these men who were accoutred only for a day's pleasant sport. I would teach them to appropriate my fief!

The moment passed. We were here on enemy territory. Even if I were to kill these men, take the village and occupy the fortified compound, I did not have enough men to hold it against the vengeance of the French King. And my own King Richard would not be best pleased if, after agreeing a sacred truce with the enemy, one of his unruly knights were to break it in a rage. No, I said to myself, I will keep the truce, as a true vassal should. I loosened my grip on the courser's harness and felt the beast relax.

Dusk was not far away. One of the servants released a liver-and-white water dog and it galloped eagerly into the forest of reeds beside the slow-moving river, barking with joy and sending up ribbons of brown water with every hectic stride. It quested round for a moment or two, taking the scent, and then charged forward and launched its body into the deeper water. A pair of mallards burst out of the reeds, their wings slapping the air as they hurried to escape the splashing canine. The pair of birds beat strongly away from the Andelle, making for the wood in which we were hidden. But one duck at least was not fated to escape. A long blur of blue-gray, like a javelin flung down from the heavens, and the peregrine struck, hurtling into the right-hand mallard and striking with an explosive puff of bright green feathers, killing the bird instantly. The falcon bore the duck to the ground, no more than fifty paces from us and, spreading its dark wings over the limp water bird like a cloak, as if from some avian shame it wished to hide its actions from the world, it began to feed. The hunting party spurred their horses toward the peregrine, now mantled over its prey, pecking and tearing at the mallard's flesh. Eager to confiscate the falcon's plump victim for their larder before that noble bird had eaten its fill, the horsemen were heading toward us at a gallop. I nodded at Hanno and Thomas and the three of us turned our mounts back into the wood and slipped quietly away into the gathering gloom.

The next morning, after a cold night under the stars, we found ourselves on the arrow-straight Roman road that led through the border county known as the Vexin and into Paris. We were not the only travelers on the road, and we soon fell in with a gang of rowdy, joyful English students, a little younger than me, who were heading for the great University of Paris to study under a renowned teacher: Master Fulk du Petit-Pont. The students' leader, Matthew of Oxford, was slightly older than the others; he was a dark-haired fellow, too mocking and worldly wise for my tastes, but a clever man, and he had been to Paris before; indeed, it seemed that he had studied at several places in Europe: Modena, Montpellier and even in Rome. I never warmed to Matthew—there was something about him, a kind of shiftiness, that made me distrust him instinctively—but he was a fund of information about our destination, and he was certainly a diverting companion. He and his four fellow students were much given to pranks and japes, to jesting with each other in Latin, and to drinking. I liked them, and their sober clerical robes and high spirits put me in mind of my father's youth in Paris. Had he been anything like one of these carefree tonsured youths? I imagined so.

As the bells were ringing out for Vespers, we drew rein, my party of three and the five young students, at the gates of the enormous Priory of St. Martin-des-Champs. To the south, less than a quarter of a mile away, I could see the tops of the larger churches and houses of Paris under a smear of smoke from the cooking fires of a multitude.

The hosteler of the priory was summoned and he showed us where we could stable our animals, and the location of the dormitory. After a very fast wash in the horse trough in the yard in front of the church, we joined the monks of St. Martin's, who were streaming out of church after the evening service, for supper in the refectory. It was simple fare but in generous portions—a rich bean stew, loaves of barley bread and a hard yellow cheese. The monks also supplied several earthenware jugs of wine to wash the meal down. I was tired and a little out of sorts—the riddle of the "man you cannot refuse" was preying on my mind—and I wanted to be away from other folk, no matter how congenial. And so, after supper, I left Hanno and Thomas with the students—passing around a big glass wine cup called a *henap* and calling "Wassail! Drink hail!" before every draft in the old English manner—and went to scale the bell tower of the priory church.

It was very nearly full dark on that warm summer night by the time I reached the top of the tower and found a little shelf that served as a seat for the lookout. I could see for miles in each direction. To the south was Paris and, while I knew that it held as many as sixty thousand souls, I was still surprised by its size and its strange beauty when I saw it first that night—the watch fires in the streets, and as-yet-uncovered family hearths, and candlelight leaking from a thousand windows, where earnest young clerics were hard at their books after supper. It looked like a carpet of stars, spread out before me, or a vast field of burning embers.

Somewhere in that sprawling mass of humanity was the answer to the mystery that tormented me. Half of my heart told me that Robin could not truly be the "man you cannot refuse," and the other half told me I was fooling myself because I cared for him. I knew that Robin had some feeling for me, too: he had saved my life on several occasions, at very great risk of his own—and therefore he could not be the man who had sent those knights of the blue cross to kill me. Yet the evidence against Robin was there; and had been there all along. Had I been so blinded by my affection for my lord that I had failed to see it?

I fell to my knees in that high bell tower, bowed my head and prayed to St. Michael, that Robin might not prove to be the man responsible for my father's death, and that my old friend would not be revealed to me as my secret enemy. I would find the truth in Paris, I vowed, and I swore a holy oath to St. Michael, alone, in the darkness above the edge of Paris, that I would not leave that city until I had found out the truth. I am certain the saint heard me, for having so sworn, I felt eased in mind and spirit and descended the tower with a much lightened heart to seek out my bed. And for the first time in weeks, I slept like a newborn.

For me, Paris shall always be associated with the acrid smell of masonry dust and the shrill ringing of metal chisels on hard stone, for the city that we rode into early the next morning seemed to be one huge builder's compound. The chink-chink-chink of tools cutting into limestone blocks began shortly after dawn, drifting on the cool air from the new headquarters of the Knights Templar that the Order was building a quarter of a mile to the east of the Priory of St. Martin, in the broad fields there outside the city.

As we approached the half-built wall of the city of Paris, the metal-stone chinking sound intensified and mingled with the cries of workmen, the sharp crack of axe on wood, and the rumble and crash of falling rubble. At the Porte St. Martin, I announced myself as a pilgrim wishing to pray at the cathedral of Notre-Dame before a most sacred relic, a lock of the Virgin's hair. I paid the toll to the Provost's men-at-arms and entered the city itself. As we emerged from the gatehouse, I looked to my right and beheld a huge finished wall, four times as high as a tall man and dotted with strong round towers every sixty yards, which curved around and down to the right toward the River Seine. It was a fortification to daunt even King Richard's mighty castle-breakers. To my left, however, there was a stretch of half-built wall, thirty yards long and teeming with workmen even at that early hour, and then, almost shockingly—nothing; only the wide vegetable gardens of the householders of this suburb of Paris, open to the world, with no obstacle to an invader more impressive than an occasional sheep hurdle, low garden wall and rickety wooden hut.

We rode almost due south down the Rue St. Martin into the city of Paris, our horses making easy progress on the broad stone-paved road, which Matthew told us had been laid down hundreds of years ago by the Romans, although the stones were now covered with a thick layer of dried black mud. This part of the French capital, to the north of the River Seine, sometimes called the Right Bank, or the Ville de Paris, was its mercantile heart—and evidence of the city's trading wealth was everywhere. The houses that lined the street on either side were mostly tall, well-built structures of wood, wattle and lime-plaster, two and sometimes three stories high, the wooden beams and corner posts carved and decorated in neat geometrical patterns. There were numerous churches too, the wealthier ones, and the grander houses, being built of pale local stone. Sudden wafts of incense made the horses snort, and the singing of monks could be plainly heard as we passed these houses of God and clopped along down the Rue St. Martin.

The ground floors of many of the larger dwellings we passed served as shops, with a counter opening onto the street displaying the wares of the owner: wrought gold and silver trinkets, bright orange Scandinavian amber, fine Spanish swords and costly armor, exquisite Italian glassware for the table, fat beeswax candles and pungent spices from the Orient, beautifully worked leather goods—all were on offer, should we have a mind to buy. Pastry sellers, with huge square trays hung around their necks, strutted through the crowds, offering delicious-smelling savories of chopped ham with pepper or soft cheese and egg in fragrant flaky casings. The shouts of a dozen wine-criers from the taverns filled the air, promising the delights of such-and-such a wine available at such-and-such a price at such-and-such a tavern. One of these men, beating loudly on an earthenware jug of wine with a stick to bring attention to his wares, lifted the jug toward Thomas for a sniff of the deep red liquid, and I saw my squire blanch and gag—almost to the point of vomiting up his breakfast. He was suffering this morning after a night of revelry with the students—although the young clerks themselves seemed to be unaffected by their drinking bout, which had kept them up long past midnight.

We were within a bow-shot of the Seine by now, and we turned sharply right onto Ruga Sancti Germani, the long road that ran almost parallel with the river. After two hundred yards, riding past the bloody reek of the shambles, a wide open space where the city's meat was slaughtered, its stalls bedecked with swinging carcasses and red-raw joints encased in creamy fat, we stopped at a crossroads where the other great north–south road of Paris, the Rue St. Denis, crossed the Sancti Germani. To my left, a short way down the Rue St. Denis, was the mighty Seine and ahead of it rose the strong tower of the Grand Chastelet—the fortification that guarded the northern part of the Grand-Pont, the gateway to the water-lapped, beating heart of Paris, the Île de la Cité.

The Grand-Pont was where Father Jean had last set eyes on my father Henry, before he had set out for England. But it was no lonely spot for a tearful leave-taking between friends who would never meet again, as I had imagined it in Normandy. As we rode through the portcullis under the imposing bulk of the Chastelet tower and onto the bridge itself, I saw that the Grand-Pont was a hive of activity, even busier than the merchant-teeming Ville de Paris that we had just ridden through. About eighteen feet wide and a hundred yards long, the bridge was lined with narrow, shallow houses on each side. A few, a very few, had the look of dwelling places; most were given over to the *changeurs*, the men who made their living by exchanging foreign coins into Parisian silver pennies. I stopped my horse and, digging a handful of the Tourangeaux silver out of my money belt, perhaps half a mark, I changed it into *deniers parisis*—frowning at the fee that the Frenchman demanded for this slight but essential service.

There was a constant stream of traffic crossing the bridge; a few men like us on horseback, but many others afoot—traders leading pack animals, one fellow herding a flock of unruly sheep northward toward the slaughter yards we had recently passed, dozens of clerics in their black robes, students or young priests, it was hard to tell. Packs of filthy street urchins dodged between our horses' legs offering more services than the ear could comprehend—and some involving their sisters that it is better not to contemplate, if you wish one day for a reward in Heaven. Even with Thomas and Hanno between me and the crowds, and our student friends waiting patiently a few yards ahead, I was jostled by the throng of passersby, buffeted and bustled; the noise of a hundred throats dinning in my ears. I had a strong sensation of being in a strange, disorientating world—an unreal place, almost like a dream battlefield. It was not a pleasant feeling. Not for the first time I longed for the broad open dales of Yorkshire or the clean woodland of Westbury. Then my eye alighted on a knight, or rather on the departing back of a knight. He was at the north end of the bridge, about fifty yards away, pushing his horse through the throng, preparing to ride under the arch below the Grand Chastelet and out of sight. He was in full mail covered by a white surcoat, and he had his shield strapped to his back, a normal way to carry it when the prospect of battle was remote. But it was a shield I knew: a blue cross on a white field with a black border.

It was the device of the knights who had tried to kill me at Fréteval. And the sight of an enemy brought me back into the real world like a dash of icy water in the face.

12

I SHOUTED "HOY!" AND POINTED AT THE back of the knight, just as he was passing under the Chastelet portcullis and away north into the Ville de Paris. Hanno followed the direction of my arm and nodded to himself.

"Shall I follow him?" he asked me, pulling his palfrey with difficulty around to face the direction we had come from.

The press of the populace around us was too thick and the knight of the blue cross had already disappeared from sight into the maze of streets in the Right Bank; knowing it was useless, I shook my head.

"It is well that we know that these fellows are in Paris, too," I said to my Bavarian friend. "We are forewarned. And one day, Hanno, we'll have a reckoning with them."

Matthew the student called over to ask what we were so excited about, but I had not yet told them of my quest in Paris, and for some reason I did not wish to speak of it then. So I merely said that I had admired the knight's helmet and wished to possess one similar myself. Then we all moved off the bridge and entered the Île de la Cité—the pulsing heart, the very core of Paris.

Paris had two masters in those days, each almost the other's equal in pomp and power: the temporal lord, Philip Augustus, the King, and his spiritual counterpart, Bishop Maurice de Sully. And just as the city of Paris was shared between these two puissant lords, so too was the Île de la Cité. The western part of the island was the preserve of the King and his court: a vast palace for Philip himself, apartments, private chapels and grand halls for his family and servants; the eastern half of the island belonged to Bishop de Sully, and was dominated by the cathedral of Notre-Dame—only as yet half completed—but it also contained the episcopal palace, where Bishop de Sully and his people lived and worked, and a hospital, or Hôtel-Dieu as it was called, as well as innumerable smaller churches, and a never-ending complex of cloisters that housed the throngs of clergy belonging to the cathedral. It was Notre-Dame, of course, that I was most eager to see: this great godly edifice was the Bishop's life's work. It was also the place where my father had made his music, and perhaps been briefly happy before his descent into peasanthood, poverty and ignominious death.

As we came off the Grand-Pont and onto the island, the royal palace, with its high tower and fortified walls, was directly to my right, but we turned almost immediately left into the Rue de la Draperie—a bustling street filled with sellers of all kinds of cloth, from shining samite in peacock colors to drab fustian, from soft oriental silks to rough workman's canvas. The mason's-yard chinking once again echoed through the streets, above the animal hum of thronging humanity conversing, disputing, buying and selling. The drapers cried: "What do you lack; what do you lack, mistress?" to every goodwife who hurried past their shopfront. Porters, struggling under the weight of vast bundles of colored cloth tied to their backs, forced their way through the press, shouting for passage, their language sharp when their way was blocked, their elbows even sharper.

Up ahead, I could already catch brief glimpses of the high slanting roof of the choir of Notre-Dame above even the tallest houses. We turned right and rode on for a hundred yards through a slightly less populated street that had once been the Jewish quarter, Matthew told us, until Philip had expelled the Jews fourteen years previously and confiscated their wealth. The street was now the preserve of the furriers, and rich pelts of sable, mink and fox—and skins of cat and squirrel, too—hung from the stalls we passed. Then we turned right again and came into a broad space, entirely cleared of shops and houses, and I checked my courser and stared, agog at what lay before me.

There were huge piles of creamy limestone blocks, both dressed and roughhewn; groups of men clustered around the great stones, sometimes drawing on them with lead, carefully, precisely, sometimes a lone man chinking away delicately with his chisel or a muscular pair laboriously sawing the larger blocks into smaller ones. Dust puffed and plumed in the air, occupying it in dense clouds along with workmen's cries, the shouts of the overseers and the harsh creak of a giant windlass as a finished block was winched ponderously via a network of pulleys and ropes toward the sky. Rough, very dirty workmen bustled hither and yon, some burdened with heavy bags of sand and rare earths on their shoulders, bundles of wood, or long, well-cared-for cutting tools. A scaffolding of logs and tree branches, lashed together with rawhide, crawled up the half-finished north wall of the nave like a sprawl of brown ivy or the veins on an old man's hand.

It was noisy, filthy, chaotic and yet breath-stealing—the exquisite beauty of the finished part of the cathedral, the choir at the eastern end with its huge columns, standing like stone trees, their branches curving out impossibly high to meet and support the vaulting roof; the round apse, dim and cool beyond the choir, lit only by the slim candles of pilgrims; the transepts, which gave the building the holy shape of the cross, had their spreading masonry worked and carved in wonderful designs; the vast windows along each side of the church, filled with colored glass and glowing like jewels in the shafts of summer sunlight; even the half-built nave before me so majestic and elegant, gigantic and yet delicate—its buttresses outside the walls sprawling like massive spiders' legs supporting the tall thin body of the cathedral itself . . . The sight of it all, the bustle and the ethereal beauty, the squalor of the building yard and the soaring wonder of Notre-Dame, made my head spin. I felt tiny in comparison to that wondrous, enormous, heavenly building—as if I were an ant in the presence of a mighty bull; and humble, just as one should feel in the presence of God. And I felt His presence then; as surely as I now feel this smooth parchment under my calloused fingertips.

I was gawping, transfixed, as I gazed upon a grand project that had already been in the building for more than thirty years. The men I saw, those grubby workmen, the shouting overseers, the burly middle-aged masons, those folk would never see their cathedral completed, not if they lived to be three score and ten. It was a staggering, awesome monument to man's skill and sweat, his perseverance and ingenuity—a most fitting offering to the divine creator of the Universe himself.

"Big, isn't it?" said a voice at my elbow; it was Matthew. "And it must cost a king's ransom to keep all these workmen on, year after year—but I am afraid, Sir Alan, that we may not tarry. We need to be at the widow's house before the dinner hour. You can come back and gawp at this dusty madhouse anytime you care to. But for now, sir, we need to keep moving along, if you please."

I suppressed my irritation at Matthew's interruption: he was right, I would be in Paris for some time, and I would come here again, at my leisure, to gaze at this miraculous House of God. Right now it was more important to secure suitable lodgings for myself and my men.

The Widow Barbette's house stood at the beginning of the Rue Garlande on the Left Bank of the Seine, a hundred yards from the Petit-Pont that connected the Île de la Cité with the southern portion of Paris. The house was close to the church of St. Julien-le-Pauvre, where I went to hear Mass as often as I could over the next few weeks. Matthew had a connection of some kind with the widow; I believe his family in England were involved in some sort of commerce with hers, and while he and two of his fellow students took one large room on the second floor of her big timber-framed house, Hanno, Thomas and I took another and we all shared a common *salle*, where we took our meals, and which had a big fireplace and a single scribe's chair and desk for the students. Two of the students, Luke and Henry, would also sleep in the *salle* at night on light, low beds that they dismantled each morning.

Our room was spacious and comfortable, with a cool black-and-white tiled floor, a set of green velvet curtains, finely embroidered with red and gold silk, drawn around the walls of the room to keep out the drafts, and a large bed of intricately carved wood in the center of the room with a huge wool-stuffed mattress, which seemed to me luxurious after months of hard campaigning. A shuttered window opened out onto the street below, and as I poked my head out, I could see a groom leading our horses away to the stables at the rear of the building. Hanno and Thomas had simple straw pallets made up for them on the floor of the chamber, which could be stored under the big bed in the daytime. The room contained a strong carved oak chest with an iron lock, a chair, a table, two stools and a long pole suspended from the ceiling from which we could hang our clothing; the ceiling itself was painted with weird and delicate depictions of the signs of the Zodiac. I must admit it was one of the most elegant chambers I have ever occupied: I felt more like a visiting prince than a man seeking vengeance on a murderer.

Although I never got to know her well, the Widow Barbette seemed a respectable woman, round, neat and always busy, and she was certainly an accomplished cook. She occupied the kitchen and storerooms on the ground floor, and for a modest payment provided a meal for all of us twice a day: dinner shortly before noon, and supper in the early evening. On that first day, once we had settled the rent, she served a fine meal of roast saddle of mutton with a garlic sauce, fresh bread and a large dish of boiled peas. Her manservant Léon, a near idiot, was induced to go out and buy wine for us and we made a convivial meal with the five students in the *salle*—before taking a short nap, as Matthew assured me was the custom in Paris, and then rising again and setting out to see some of the city in the late afternoon.

We accompanied the students to the Petit-Pont, where they were planning to meet up with their new teacher, Master Fulk. I did not like the look of him, at first. He was a big, hulking man, hairy as a wolfhound on his body, with a head that was nearly bald as an egg, with only a few gray wisps to indicate his tonsure. He was not at all how I had imagined one of Christendom's great minds, a celebrated teacher at the University of Paris, to look. He wore a dirty black robe, his nose had clearly been broken in a long-ago brawl, and when I came close to him I found that he had a rancid odor of old sweat about his person that almost made me gag.

The Petit-Pont itself had been a surprise, too, when we crossed it that morning. It was nothing like the crowded, endlessly moving thoroughfare of the Grand-Pont to the north of the Île de la Cité. It was quiet, for a start, with only a few houses belonging to the members of the university set upon it, and large open spaces between these lodgings where one could sit on stone benches and look out over the slow-rolling Seine. It was in these spaces that Master Fulk conducted his lessons. I whispered to Hanno that I could well understand why Fulk's students preferred to meet him outside: how could anyone stand to be in an enclosed space with that stench? But Hanno did not find my jest in the least amusing, and frowned at me, clicking his tongue at my disrespect of a man of learning.

We bade farewell to the students on the Petit-Pont, leaving Matthew and his friends clustering around the brawny form of Fulk the Scholar, and already beginning to argue in Latin. Hanno, Thomas and I made our way north over the bridge on foot back onto the Île de la Cité and headed toward the great cathedral of Notre-Dame.

I was allowed, this time, to indulge my eyes on that wondrous sight to my heart's content. I spent more than an hour just gazing at its exterior before entering that vast and holy space and lighting a candle for St. Michael at a little shrine in the apse. I prayed once again that the archangel would help me find out the answers to the mystery surrounding my father, and sat for a while looking upward at the majestic, soaring ceiling, and thinking of the happy times I had spent in the rude cottage in Nottinghamshire that my family had called home. Thus comforted by my communion with the saint and with the spirit of my father, I led my two men to the episcopal palace, the residence of the venerable Bishop of Paris, Maurice de Sully, a mere stone's throw to the south of the cathedral.

The sky was darkening as we entered the palace by a door opposite the south transept of Notre-Dame; it was perhaps a mere hour before Vespers and I had spent far longer in the cathedral than I had realized. We were greeted at the door of the palace by a young monk, who asked our business and then conducted us into a chamber off the main hall. While we waited, a servant brought us cups of green wine and delicate sweet pastries, a Parisian speciality, and I ran over in my mind what I would ask the prelate, if he should be good enough to grant me an audience that very day.

After a wait of perhaps a quarter of an hour, a tall thin man came into the room. His hands were folded across his slim waist and tucked into the sleeves of his long brown monk's robe and his dark hair was neatly cut in the tonsure.

"I am Brother Michel," he said, smiling. "I have the honor of serving the Bishop by helping to make his appointments, among other matters. I understand that you seek an audience with His Grace, is that right?" He had a kind face with intelligent bright blue eyes and a frail, youthful air—in truth, when he first came into the room I had thought that he was a young man, but as he drew near to us, I saw that he was a man in his late thirties, with a scattering of pockmarks and the first lines of care only now beginning to appear on his lean, handsome face.

"I need to speak to His Grace the Bishop on a private matter, a family matter," I said. "It is also a matter of some urgency."

"I see," said the monk. "Is there perhaps some way in which I could help you? If it is a question of alms, or perhaps a small advance . . ."

I flushed, embarrassed that this man of God should think that I had come to the Bishop seeking money. He pulled out his right hand from its sleeve and indicated a long table at the side of the chamber.

"Why don't we sit, make ourselves comfortable, and you can tell me what the problem is," he said. I trusted him instinctively—he radiated a kind of inner strength and goodness that was truly comforting to a troubled man—and before I knew it, I was seated on a stool across from him and telling him the tale of my father's time at Notre-Dame twenty years ago, and of the visit by Bishop Heribert, and of the theft of the candlesticks, and my father's expulsion from the cathedral, his exile in England and his mean death at the hands of Sir Ralph Murdac. The tale came pouring out of me like a torrent, and I realized how much I had wanted to confide in someone sympathetic and helpful. Of course, I had told Hanno and Thomas the nature of our business in Paris, but they were in no position to help me solve the mystery. This kindly man of God, I believed, might hold the key.

Brother Michel nodded and frowned and looked at me, his clear blue eyes now filled with compassion. When I had finished my tale, he sighed deeply. "So much suffering," he said. "So much pain." And I swear I saw a gleam of a tear in his eye.

"Well, Sir Alan," he continued, "I have no doubt that His Grace will wish to hear about this matter in full from you personally. And I am sure that he will do his utmost to help you in your quest to find the real thief. I will speak to the Bishop this very evening and I will urge him to find the time to see you; but he is an extremely busy man, as I'm sure you must know, with a great many calls on his good nature. So I think the best thing might be for you to tell me where you are lodging and I will have a servant bring you a message when His Grace is at liberty to attend to this. Would that be acceptable to you?"

I nodded, and he smiled, and I felt a wave of relief flow through me, now that this godly man had shouldered my burdens.

"It may take a few days, I'm afraid," said Brother Michel, as he ushered us out of the chamber, "but I pray it will be no more than a week or so. Be patient, be strong, and trust in God that we may bring this matter to a happy conclusion." And he gave me another smile before he left us in the care of the hall servants.

As I walked back over to the cathedral, flanked by Thomas and

Hanno, to say an extra prayer for the soul of my father, I was satisfied that Brother Michel would champion my cause to the Bishop. Between us, through reasonable discussion, and with God's help, we would unravel the mystery of the Heribert theft and exonerate the memory of Henry d'Alle, once and for all.

The call that I paid on my uncle Thibault, Seigneur d'Alle, was far less satisfactory than the encounter with Brother Michel. His house on the Rue St. Denis, next to the church of St. Opportune, was a very grand edifice of timber and brick, three stories high and set back a little from the road. It reeked of money. Thomas and I banged on the big front door in the middle of a violent rainstorm the afternoon of the day after my meeting with Brother Michel. We were admitted, well soaked by the downpour, by a richly dressed servant and shown upstairs to a solar on the second floor.

The Lord of Alle, my uncle Thibault, was playing chess with a much younger and very handsome fair-haired man when I was ushered, dripping, into the opulent room. A pair of long hounds snoozed by the fire at the end of the room. The men were seated at a table in the center, hunched over the board. I saw that the board was inlaid with squares of ivory and ebony, and that the pieces were decorated with tiny jewels. As I came in, the younger man moved a piece and said: "There, I have you, Father; your king is dead!"

The Seigneur d'Alle's face mottled with anger: "Again? God damn this cold-blooded, womanish game!" And with a blow of his arm, he swept the board off the table, sending it crashing to the floor, the pieces skittering away across the wooden surface. One of the hounds lifted its refined, pointed head, gazed at me for a minute out of deeply stupid eyes, then went back to sleep.

"Father," said the handsome young man, in a warning tone, "we have company!"

The Seigneur swung his large head round toward me: under a mop of brown hair, his face was ruddy, pouched and touched here and there by whitish, faded scars. He glared at me angrily, then rose from his chair, turned and stood facing me, his hands resting easily on his hips. He was a big man, taller than me, with broad shoulders and long legs, and while he was dressed in costly finery, a gold-embroidered tunic and a black sable-lined mantle, and not equipped as if for the battlefield, I could tell from a glance that he was a fighter. This was no city-dwelling lordling with soft hands and mild manners—this was a seasoned French knight, a man of blood and iron. He seemed familiar, the resemblance with my father being apparent—but he also reminded me just a little of my beloved sovereign, King Richard. Not in looks, but in his belligerent masterfulness and total confidence.

"My lord," I began, after making my bow, "I am Sir Alan Dale, the son of Henri d'Alle—I am your nephew."

"Are you now?" said the Seigneur. "Are you indeed?" There was a slight, uncomfortable pause while he stared at me. "And what is it that you want with me—nephew?"

I was taken aback; I had assumed that my ties of kinship, the fact that we shared the same blood, would be enough to guarantee some civility. Evidently, I was wrong.

"What he wants," said the younger man, getting up from his seat and coming around the table to approach me, "is a dry towel." The young man, who was clearly the Seigneur's son, looked beyond me to the servant hovering by the door of the solar. "Gaston, be so good as to fetch this gentleman a clean, dry towel. Immediately!"

Turning his gaze back to me, the fair-haired young man said: "I am Roland d'Alle. Perhaps you and your man would care for a glass of wine to warm your hearts on this miserable day?" He smiled, but only with half of his face, and I saw then that the left-hand side of his head, which had previously been turned away from me, was disfigured by a large red mark, raw and ugly, a recent burn for sure, only partially healed—what had once been a remarkably good-looking face was now quite disfigured by that wound.

"I asked you—Sir Alan, is it?—what you wanted here," said the

Seigneur, his voice brusque, like a man accustomed to giving orders and having them instantly obeyed. "So—what do you want? You pop up out of nowhere and claim to be a long-lost relative; what could you possibly want, I wonder? Could it be that you are hoping for a little advance to tide you over in a difficult time?" His tone was very close to a sneer; and I bristled. This was the second occasion in my two days in Paris that strangers I had met had assumed that I had come to beg money. I peered down at my shabby, damp and travel-worn clothes. And then looked back up into my uncle's brick-red face. I could feel the stirrings of a raw anger that I'd hoped so much to keep suppressed.

"I do not come seeking anything from you, my lord, least of all money," I said coldly. "All I require is some information. I wish to know about my late father, your brother Henri d'Alle. Who was wrongly accused of theft, and hounded from Paris, abandoned by his *family*"—I gave that word its due weight—"and, once outcast by the Church, lived in poverty in England until his death at the hands of an unknown enemy."

"You seem to think you possess all the facts," growled the Seigneur. "What more do you wish to know?"

"I wish to know why you did not help him."

"That is no God-damned business of yours."

"My father, my family, my business," I said, struggling to keep my temper; fighting the growing urge to step over to my uncle and knock him to the floor.

"And I have no more information about your father and his relations with *my family* that I care to give you," the Seigneur said. "Now, I will ask you—"

"He was a fool," said a new voice, a woman's voice, and I turned toward the door to see a servant carrying a tray of wine cups and a slim, elegant shape in a long green fur-trimmed silk robe offering me a large white linen towel. Thomas was already scrubbing at his damp head with a similar item.

This was the Lady of Alle, I assumed, and the first thing I absorbed about her was that she was truly, incandescently beautiful; even approaching her forties, as she must have been, she stole the living breath from my lungs: raven hair peeking from under a neat white coif, deep green eyes, pale, almost translucent skin, a swelling bosom above the waist of a sixteen-year-old. From half a dozen yards away I caught a waft of her perfume: something floral yet creamy—she even smelled utterly delicious. I found my anger at her boorish husband washing away as I drank her in, like a thirsty man downing a full jug drawn from an icy well. She kissed me on the cheek, a cool, brief touch of her lips that made the hair on my arms stand up, and said: "Good day, nephew, I am Adèle—what a pleasure it is to finally meet you."

And I found myself seated at the table, with the Seigneur and Roland and this heavenly creature in human form, while the servant poured wine for us all.

The rain rattled against the closed shutters of the solar, and brought me back into the world. When I had taken a sip of the wine, I turned to Adèle and, trying to control my fluttering belly, I said: "Why did you call my father a fool?"

"I'm afraid he *was* a fool. He could have come to us at Alle, and lived with us, after the . . . the incident. We could have found a way," she said. "I'm sure we could have found a way for all of us to live together. There was no need for him to run off to England like that—"

"*You* are the fool," the Seigneur d'Alle interrupted his wife brutally—and I glared at my host, hating him for his rudeness to the lady. The Seigneur completely ignored my look and continued: "After what had passed, there was no earthly way that I would have allowed Henri within a mile of the castle. And you know why!"

What sort of brother *was* he, this Thibault, this Seigneur d'Alle, to condemn a member of his own family for a trifling misdemeanor—without even ascertaining whether the accusation were true or not?

I got to my feet, and put my hand on my hilt. "I do not believe my father was a thief," I said. "By my sword, I say that he was innocent and wrongly blamed for this crime. And I have vowed that I will find the real culprit, and I will fight any man who says that Henri d'Alle was a thief—any man!" And I looked at Roland for a moment, and then locked my gaze with the Seigneur. He stared back at me, his blue eyes unwavering—but I saw a mocking smile on his mouth. He said: "You would fight for his honor, would you?" Then he said: "Hmm-mm . . . ," a two-toned nasal grunt through closed lips, but no more.

"Come, Thomas, I can see that we are wasting our time here. These . . . people . . . do not wish to help us clear my father's name and we cannot force them to. Let us go."

We were halfway to the door when Adèle caught up with us. "Do not leave in anger," she said. "The Seigneur is always out of sorts on days like this."

"Days when his relatives come to call?"

"No, only when it rains. He cannot go out; his old wounds plague him so in this weather, and he says he feels like a caged bear. He certainly has the temper of one. Please, I beg you, call again some other day. I would like . . . I would very much like to know Henri's son." And her smile was so beautiful that I felt my heart melt. "Promise me that you will visit us soon," she repeated.

I nodded and mumbled something, and she warmed me again with her look. "Roland here will show you out." I saw that her son was standing, unnoticed, at her shoulder. "And you must not forget your promise to come again."

Roland escorted us to the front door, opened it and stared doubtfully out at the rain, which was sheeting down. The Rue St. Denis was flowing with water, a raging black torrent in the center of the broad road washing the filth of the city down toward the Seine.

"Are you sure that you would not prefer to wait a little while before departing?" he said.

For a moment I hesitated, imagining how pleasant it would be to rest in a cozy parlor by a glowing brazier with a cup of warmed wine, but then I thought of having to endure the company of the Seigneur, and I steeled myself and bid my host goodbye. Just as Thomas and I were about to step out into the downpour, I turned to Roland and said: "Forgive me for asking, sir, but how did you get that mark?"

"This?" he said, pointing to the raw oozing patch that covered half of the left-hand side of his face and a portion of his neck. "I got this in battle; I got this at the Castle of Verneuil in Normandy. It was made by the touch of burning oil dropped from above—this, Sir Alan, was your work, I believe." And he smiled at me, crookedly, painfully, with the unwounded half of his handsome face. I saw young Thomas's cheeks go pale, and his eyes widen. But I could find nothing to say to an enemy in peacetime, a man who three months ago had been trying to kill me; so I merely shrugged and stepped out of the door.

"I fear we must postpone a discussion of the fortunes of war until another occasion," Roland said. "God be with you, sir!" And he firmly shut the door.

13

THE RAIN FELL LIKE THE BIBLICAL deluge—on a day such as this, even Noah, snug in his ark, would have looked at the sky and been convinced that God's wrath would never end. Thomas had had the foresight to bring thick oiled-wool cloaks for us, but they were sopping wet and heavy as lead copes before we had gone fifty yards. It was like walking under a waterfall. We stepped gingerly down the very edges of the Rue St. Denis toward the Grand-Pont, marveling at the black river of refuse that poured down the center of the street—muck, leaves, rags, old shoes and bones; I even saw a dead dog tumbling past me in the thick, dark porridge-like flow. The shops of the city had closed their counters when it became clear that the rain had set in for the day, and all honest householders were indoors warming themselves by their hearths. The streets were almost entirely deserted. It was hard to believe that it was August—high summer; it felt more like January—and though it was only mid-afternoon the dark clouds overhead made it feel as if dusk had fallen. We walked slowly down the Rue St. Denis, watching our footing on the rain-greased paving slabs, and saw hardly a soul . . .

Thunder cracked, and a bright stab of lightning illuminated the rain-battered road with an eerie blue glow. Fifty yards ahead, on the far side of the road, I saw four figures lurch out from the shelter of the porch of the church of St. Leufroy and into the fury of the storm; they began to forge up the sloping street toward us. They were dressed in beggarly rags, hooded and very wet—and yet they seemed to be remarkably well-fed and able-bodied beggars, and the way they walked, with a springy purposeful stride, suggested men at the peak of fitness. I grabbed Thomas's shoulder and pushed him behind me, between my body and the stone wall of a large house, then I drew Fidelity. I blessed God that I had chosen to wear my sword that day, reasoning that, as I was visiting my noble relatives, I should make the point that I, too, was a knight.

The beggar-men spread out and crossed the street, coming directly toward me: I could see weapons in their hands now: cudgels, knives, and one man had a short mace—all weapons that could be easily concealed beneath their rags, for who has ever seen a mendicant beg for alms with a long sword or a spear at his side?

Four soldiers—for they were very clearly soldiers—against one man and a boy whose voice had yet to break. They were not good odds, but I had faced worse and survived. The anger that I felt at the house of the Seigneur d'Alle was still lapping in my belly. The four men, their young, bearded faces peering at me intently from beneath their dripping hoods, paused for a moment, at a distance of five paces or so, spread out in a line in front of me, hemming me in against the wall behind. I did not wait for their attack but shouted: "Come on then!" in English and leaped into battle.

I blocked a cudgel blow from the man on the extreme left with Fidelity, whirled and hacked the sharp blade into the calf muscle of the man next to him—and he was down, his right foot all but severed. I ducked a mace blow, bobbed up again and killed the man wielding that iron bludgeon with a lunge to the throat. Two down. Out of the side of my rain-blurred eye, I saw that a knifeman had lunged past me, grabbed Thomas, wrapped a brawny arm around him and was holding the blade to his throat. I jumped toward Thomas, slipped on the wet stone paving slabs, skidded, and had barely managed to regain my balance, my arms waving wildly out on either side, when a cudgel slammed into my lower back, at the level of my kidneys. If it had been a sword, it would have cut me in half—instead, the explosion of pain drove me to my knees. My long wet hair was in my eyes, and I sensed rather than saw the next blow from that great oaken club, and swayed my head just enough to avoid it. The cudgel crashed down onto my shoulder with numbing force, though I believe the thick sodden wool of my cloak saved me from a shattered joint. I tried to rise, slipped on the wet road again, and found myself on my back; my left arm was useless, the man with the cudgel was standing over me, his knotted club raised to strike again. Still down, breathless with pain, I jerked my torso off the wet ground, and lunged up with my sword, spearing Fidelity's sharp point hard into his groin and beyond, deep into his lower bowels. The cudgel-man fell to his knees, mouth wide, blood draining from his face; he dropped the club, hands cupping his privates, and blood pissing through his fingers, instantly washed away by the driving rain.

Beyond him I could see Thomas in the arms of the fourth man, who was looking about madly, unable to believe that none of his three comrades still stood. Regardless of the sharp blade at his collarbone, Thomas reached up and behind him with both hands, and took a bunch of the man's wet rags in his fists. My squire twisted his shoulders, bent forward suddenly and pulled hard, and the knifeman—to his considerable surprise—was thrown over the boy's shoulder and crashed onto the slick paving slabs, flat on his back. Thomas leaped on his fallen foe, his own small eating knife in his fist, and the boy began to savage the prone man with a speed and ferocity that more than made up for his lack of skill. Within a few moments Thomas had plunged the knife a dozen times into the man's face and neck, the blade sinking deep, the gore jetting upward, and as the man lifted his hands to his face to protect himself, Thomas's dagger punched and sliced into fingers and palms, too, in his fear-spurred killing-rage.

By the time I had regained my feet, my squire was weeping and panting, spent and still kneeling over the body of a man whose upper regions had been transformed into a mash of chopped meat. Thomas's hands were red to the wrists, as if dipped in paint; but the blood was not his, God be praised.

All four men were down. The fight from first to last had taken only a couple of dozen heartbeats. The first man I had struck down had tried to crawl away from the fight and now sat half a dozen paces away, facing away from me, howling in agony, clutching his half-severed foot as it pumped blood to join the black flow in the center of the street. I shambled across to him, growling, my left arm completely numb, and took his head off with one low hard sweep of Fidelity. As I stepped back from his squirting neck stump, and watched his head roll bumpily into the torrent of filth in the center of the road, I realized that my anger had led me into making a mistake: I needed information. Turning, I saw that the second man, whose throat I had skewered, lay sprawled on the paving slabs, the rain falling relentlessly into his still open eyes. The deluge was beginning to wash the blood from Thomas's victim, but the knife-mangled neck that was revealed made it clear he would never speak again. The cudgel-man whose bowel I had pierced was still alive, but only just. His face was a waxy yellow, knotted with pain, and he was breathing in short, hard gasps. I knew he too had only a few moments left in this world—and I badly needed him to talk to me.

I knelt beside him and gently smoothed the wet hair from his forehead, out of his eyes. The rain fell like spears. I put my mouth to his ear. "What is your name, sir?" I said quietly in French. "And why did you seek to attack me?"

He seemed not to notice my questions, although his breathing slowed a little—the end was very near. I repeated my questions, slightly louder this time, giving his shoulder a gentle shake. And this time, he managed to turn his head and look at me. "Forgive me," he panted.

"Tell me your name and whom you serve, and I will forgive you," I said. "Tell me now."

"For . . . forgive me," he forced out again. "We had our orders from the Master. You had . . . to die. But I ask your forgiveness, Sir

Alan . . . for the sake of Our Lady, Our Mother, the ever merciful Queen of Heaven, forgive me."

For all that he had been trying to kill me a few moments before, I did feel pity for him. I was moved by his unusual way of begging for forgiveness. He slumped against my body, his breathing ragged, pumping, the pain riding him. I said: "I forgive you; but tell me whom you serve. Who is this Master you speak of—and why does he wish me dead?"

The man gave no reply but let out one long shuddering breath. He twitched once, his head fell forward, chin on breast, and his immortal soul left the cage of his body.

I laid him down as gently as possible in the street, made the sign of the Cross above him, and looked over at Thomas. He was still kneeling beside the corpse he had made, the rain splashing in the gore puddles around him. I levered myself to my feet, my back and shoulder shrieking with pain.

"Come, Thomas, we must go. Before long the Provost's men will come and we are strangers here, and foreigners to boot—we will be seen as enemies. I do not want to answer questions in the King's dungeon about these men's deaths; questions that I cannot answer. Let us leave their souls to Almighty God, and their bodies to the Provost's men."

Extremely bad weather, my bruised body and a stinking cold—brought on no doubt by our violent exertions in the rain that day—kept me housebound for the next week. But I did not grudge the inactivity; it gave me time to think.

I was no longer convinced that Robin was the "man you cannot refuse." Twice now I had been attacked by men who sought my death; on each occasion the men involved in the attack were of the same quality: trained soldiers, most probably knights. I had been close to Robin for six years, and even assuming that he sought my death—which I did not really believe—if he had a company of murderous

French knights at his beck and call I was certain that I would have had some inkling of them. So these were not Robin's men, they belonged to somebody else: somebody they referred to as "the Master." Presumably the Master and the "man you cannot refuse" were the same man, and he was not Robin.

On the other hand, Robin had silenced Murdac, and had tried to prevent me from pursuing the man who ordered my father's death. So Robin might well have some connection with this murderous Master—but what?

My reasoning could go no further.

There had been no word from Brother Michel—but I was not overly concerned. From Maurice de Sully's point of view, I was a man inquiring into a twenty-year-old crime—it would not be high on the list of duties that needed attending to. And I had confidence that Brother Michel was a man of his word and that he would find an opportunity for us to meet with the Bishop. As he had said, I must be patient.

The students too were housebound during these unseasonably wet days. As their lessons were usually held on the Petit-Pont in the open air, they had been canceled while this stormy weather continued. Matthew and a few of the others spent their free time in a local tavern, the sign of the Cock, and came back to the room after nightfall, rosy-faced and cheery with wine. But one of the students, Luke, a slight chap, who cared less than the others for wine and games of dice, preferred to stay in the Widow Barbette's *salle* and improve his skills as a copyist. He sat for long hours at the scribe's desk, copying out a text in Latin called the *Institutiones Grammaticae* by a long-dead Roman pedant called Priscian.

I was fascinated by Luke's work—not the book he was copying, which was a turgid exposition on Latin grammar, full of advice on inflexion, word-formation and syntax, but by the process of writing. Luke bought the parchment from a dealer on the Left Bank and he would cut it to the right shape and scrape it smooth with a knife, polish it with a boar's tooth, and then when it was ready to receive the ink, he would rule neat lines across the parchment, and down the margins, with a lead point. He bought goose quills by the sheaf from another shop nearby, and he would cut the quills with a sharp knife to make a nib, dip it in a cow's horn of black ink and begin, in tiny precise strokes of the quill, to copy out Priscian's dull text.

I knew my letters, of course—I had been taught by Robin's own brother, years ago in Sherwood, and I had a decent command of Latin, too, but there had been little time for writing in the past few years of war—and I had spilled far more blood than ink since I was a boy. All the same, I loved the idea of transmitting my thoughts and feelings, and of recording deeds, and some of my better songs and poetry for future generations to read. Luke occasionally and rather reluctantly allowed me to practice my writing on the offcuts of his pages, and I believe it was then that I conceived the idea of writing this memoir that now strains your tired eyes. You have young Luke to thank for this tale, for his work in Paris gave me the idea to make a book all of my own, and fill it with my own adventures; although he was horrified by my eccentric plan to compose the story in English, my own mother language, rather than in French or good, honest Latin.

"But, Sir Alan, Latin is the language of proper literature," he protested. "All educated people read Latin."

"And what of those who are not so well educated?" I said. "Should I not share my songs and stories with them?"

"If they are not educated they will not be able to read, whether it is written in Latin or English or Ethiopian," shot back Luke. I could see his point. They were sharp boys, my young student friends, and ruthless wielders of the formal logic they were taught; I could never manage to best them in any argument. But he did not dissuade me from setting down this tale in English—and if none can read my story in the years to come, so be it. It is all in God's hands.

After a week of almost constant thunderstorms, the August sun returned and Hanno, Thomas and I set off for the Ville de Paris once again, this time through clean, gently steaming streets, on horseback and fully armed. My bruised back and shoulder were still stiff, marked yellow and brown and purple, and remained very painful—but I was able to move. As Hanno had pointed out, I should be grateful that I was not in my grave. My Bavarian had reproached himself severely for not being with me on the day that I had visited the Seigneur d'Alle, although I had not asked him to accompany me, and the attack had come with no warning at all. Nevertheless, Hanno felt that he should have been there to protect me. He did have a thoroughly good reason to be absent from my side, though—he had discovered a Flemish alewife living in Paris, and although she was fat, middle-aged and married, he had fallen in love.

"Oh God, Alan," Hanno had told me in mock despair, "she is so wonderful; sweet and plump as fresh butter, and her heavenly brew, her ale—strong, brown, bitter and clean—and tasting a little of hazelnuts. It is perfect! I love her! I think I should kill her man, that good-for-nothing Provost's lackey; I should cut his throat and take her for myself."

I knew that Hanno was not serious—at least, I hoped he was not. However I made him promise not to molest that unfortunate ale-husband—I did not wish to bring the wrath of the Provost upon us. This powerful royal official, who resided in the Petit Chastelet, a small fortress on the south side of the Petit-Pont, was famously corrupt and lazy. But he was responsible to the King for the maintenance of law and order in Paris and he had over a hundred men-at-arms at his command. We had heard nothing more of the men Thomas and I had killed on the Rue St. Denis—Matthew had passed by the spot shortly after dawn the day after the fight and he had reported that the bodies had been removed by someone, but what became of them I never discovered. May their souls rest in peace.

So, on a gleaming day in late August, Hanno, Thomas and I crossed the Seine at the Grand-Pont, turned right on the Ruga Sancti Germani, and left again to head north on the Rue St. Martin. We were retracing the steps we had taken almost two weeks earlier when we entered Paris—but I was not reneging on my vow to St. Michael to remain in the city until I had discovered the identity of the "man you cannot refuse." We were heading to the Paris Temple, the huge new compound of the Order that was being constructed just outside the northern boundary of the city, next to the Priory of St. Martin, where we had spent the night on our arrival. I had a broad and bulging money belt around my waist, which held nearly four pounds in silver, and I wished to make a deposit at the Temple, so that the money would be secure from thieves—footpads like the men who had so recently attacked me. At least, that was what I would be telling the Knights of the Order when we presented ourselves at the gates and demanded entry.

In truth, we were on a scouting mission: while I had been idle during the past few thundery days thinking about the mystery, a single word kept popping into my head. The word was "Templar." The one thing that all the knights who had attacked me had in common, both in Paris and at Fréteval, was that they were bearded. Now, of course, the Templars were not the only hirsute knights in Christendom, but most of the members of the Order of the Poor Fellow-Soldiers of Christ and the Temple of Solomon favor beards. I believe it may even be one of the many vows they take when joining the Order.

And there were other signs, too. The cross was a well-known Templar symbol, although theirs was red not blue, and the black border on a white field echoed the famous black-and-white flag under which the Templars fought. The knights of the blue cross, I reasoned, might well be Templars of some kind, or have some link with them—and by going to the Paris Temple and making a deposit of money into their safekeeping, I would have a perfect excuse to inspect the inside of their stronghold and perhaps learn something about my enemies.

As we rode up the crowded Rue St. Martin, I saw that Hanno kept glancing behind us. After a while, he put out a hand and the three of us reined in and stopped, allowing the heavy traffic to push past us on both sides.

"What is it?" I asked my Bavarian friend, who was twisted in his saddle and scanning the street behind with narrowed eyes.

"I do not know," he said. "Perhaps it is nothing, but I have a feeling in my backbone that someone is following us, watching us."

I looked behind me and saw shopkeepers, tradesmen and workers striding up and down the street, going about their lawful business, a monk or two, a knot of black-robed students, laughing together and drinking wine from a large earthenware jug, a pair of glum men-at-arms standing outside a church. A very dirty man was tending a herd of pigs, who were foraging in the remaining muck in the center of the thoroughfare that had not been swept away by the storms. A lone mounted man, evidently a rich townsman by the quality of his clothes and horse, was coming closer; but he showed no interest in us and when I looked into his face I realized I had never seen him before. I had never seen any of them before, as far as I could recall.

"There is nobody following us," I said to Hanno, releasing the hilt of Fidelity.

"I cannot see him," my friend replied, scowling, "but I feel him in my marrow."

Jumpy, I thought, *he's jumpy, that's all—and perhaps he feels a little guilty because he was with his butter-sweet alewife when I was attacked last week. Nothing to worry about, Alan, just fix your mind on the task at hand.*

We were admitted to the enormous Templar compound, and once again my ears were assaulted by the ringing of chisels on stone and my nostrils clogged with fine white dust. The knights had recently completed a very strong, three-story stone tower as the core of their defenses, and a big round church, which reminded me painfully of the Temple Church in London, where Robin had been tried for heresy by this same Order the year before. And they had also recently finished building the encircling walls of their stronghold, but the huge compound, perhaps six acres in size, still resembled a mason's yard. The knights were constructing a grand palace for the Master of France in the south of the compound, next to the great tower, and a hospital further to the north, and a dozen buildings of wood and stone—conventual houses, cloisters, farm buildings, stables, chapels—were slowly rising into the sky. But while the Paris Temple might have been unfinished, it still represented a formidable fortification; perhaps as strong as any castle in France. And the Brother Sergeant who manned the powerful gatehouse admitted me through a portal guarded by two round towers, a portcullis and an iron-studded oak gate.

After hearing my story, the gatehouse guard indicated that we should take our business to the largest stone building to the front of the Temple Church, the Counting House, where all the Order's money matters with outsiders were transacted.

I had the utmost respect for the fighting abilities of the Templar knights, and I had never met one who was not an extraordinary man, in one way or another—but the Order was cunning, too, and full of guile. And they were wealthy. Despite the vow of poverty that each knight took upon entering, the Order itself had amassed an abundance of treasure in the seventy years of its existence, and wide lands and estates, too, across the breadth of Europe. It was said that many a king or duke envied the coffers of the black-and-white knights—and part of the reason for their wealth lay in the nature of the exchange that I was about to make with them.

The Templars had preceptories all over Christendom and each was staffed by the Order's knights and their sergeants, clerks, chaplains and servants. For decades, the Templars had been conveying goods—food, wine, clothing, building materials, weapons and so on—to their bases in remote parts of the world, from Syria to Scotland, from Denmark to the Douro, and in doing so they had also, naturally, begun to take part in commerce. Moving goods over the face of the earth, and selling them here and there, had meant that sometimes the members of the Order needed to carry large sums of silver coin; and they thus laid themselves open to attack by bandits and thieves in the wilder regions. So the knights had devised a simple method of money exchange: a traveler would not carry money in the form of specie or coin, he would carry a letter, written in code, which commanded a Templar clerk when he arrived at his destination to hand over a particular sum of money on receipt of the parchment. This proved to be a great success—as a piece of parchment could have no value for a back-country thief—and soon the idea spread to other knights, who were not members of the Order, and then to townsfolk and traders who were traveling to far-flung markets and wished to safeguard their own silver.

On that fine morning in August, when Hanno, Thomas and I rode into the Paris Temple, there was nothing at all unusual in a knight with a large sum of money in heavy silver coin wishing it to be converted into a simple letter, to be redeemed in another preceptory, in another town, in another land, or indeed, almost anywhere in Christendom.

The scouting plan, as such, was that while I conducted my business with the Templar treasurers, and perhaps reassured anyone who cared to listen that I believed that I had recently been attacked by mere footpads, Hanno would reconnoiter the interior of the fortress, wandering off in a casual manner like a bored man-at-arms stretching his legs, while Thomas looked to the horses. Hanno was my eyes and ears; he would explore the compound on foot, perhaps chatting to some of the Templar sergeants or some of the lay brothers and servants, and seeing if he could discover any evidence of the knights of the blue cross.

When I had explained the plan to Thomas and Hanno, my squire had voiced the sensible worry that, if the knights of the blue cross were indeed Templars, and we were within their precincts, they might decide simply to kill us, and I had to agree that there was a risk attached to our stratagem. But not, I judged, a large one. At Fréteval, in a dense patch of wild woodland, secluded, miles from the main armies, the knights of the blue cross had felt confident enough to show their identity and display their animosity toward me. But when they had attacked me in the streets of Paris—in public—they had made an attempt to hide their status as knights and had pretended to be beggars. It had not been a very impressive masquerade—I have found that soldiers often stand out from the common run of men—but it demonstrated that they did not wish us to know, or anyone who saw us fighting to know, that they were knights. We would be safe in the Paris Temple, I argued, because they wanted to hide their identities. The knights of the blue cross could not openly attack us in this big, open semi-public place without being observed by many eyes, and this was something they were most unwilling to allow. We were as safe here, I told my friends, as we would be anywhere in Paris. This was my logic, anyway, and I prayed that it might be true.

I left Hanno and Thomas with the horses outside the Counting House and walked inside. It was cool and airy—I came through a great wooden double door into a tall stone hall with a double row of columns supporting the huge roof, and a series of doors at the back leading, I assumed, to private chambers, perhaps treasure vaults or rooms where parchment rolls and accounts might be stored. Two Templar sergeants wearing black surcoats over mail and with long swords belted at their waists stood guard on either side of the main door. In the center of the room were four long tables covered in green cloth, and at each table sat a pair of clerks. At two of these tables, the clerks were in the process of transacting business with clients: at one, a French knight was passing over two small linen sacks of coins to the clerks; at the other a wealthy merchant was carefully reading a parchment document, holding it close to his face and frowning at the words written upon it.

I marched up to one of the vacant tables and by way of greeting wished the two clerks there the peace of God. The clerk on the left replied with a similar blessing and then asked who I was and what was the nature of my business that day. I told them that I was Sir Alan Dale, an English knight of Westbury in Nottinghamshire who had recently been attacked by thieves in the streets of Paris, and that I wished to lodge some monies with the Templars that could be redeemed at the London Temple at some future time.

The clerk on the left nodded and asked if I had any money already lodged here in the Paris Temple, or at any other Templar preceptory, and when I admitted that I did not, he said that it was no matter and then explained the procedure to me and told me that a small charge would be levied for the service. The clerk on the right said nothing but scratched away on a scroll of parchment, presumably recording the size of the deposit and my personal details. I duly handed over three pounds of Tourangeaux silver from my money belt and the clerk weighed the entire silver horde on a set of scales in front of him, bit into several of the coins gently with his incisor teeth and noted the depth of the indentations, and muttered something to his fellow clerk that I did not catch. Finally, he counted the money out into stacks of twenty coins—each stack with the value of one shilling. The clerk then arranged the shilling stacks into three rows, with twelve stacks in each row—which made up a pound. And when he had finished this ordering, he again murmured to his colleague, then looked up at me.

"These coins were minted by Count Bouchard of Vendôme and I'm sorry to say they are a little debased."

I looked at him, mystified.

"They have been debased with lead," said the clerk. I was still none the wiser. "Some lead has been added to the silver in the smelting so that more coins may be minted from a certain weight of silver bullion."

"Are they no good?" I said, suddenly alarmed.

"They are not the worst I have seen, nor yet the purest coinage either—do not be perturbed, sir, they still have a certain value, but if you took them to London you would not be able to exchange them for the equivalent weight in sterling silver English coins."

"So how much will I get in London if I hand them over to you here and now?"

The clerk conferred with his colleague; again, irritatingly, I could not hear what was said between them.

"We will give you four sterling silver pennies for every five of your Tourangeaux coins; and there will be our fee of three shillings in addition to that. Do you accept our offer?"

"So what will I receive in London?"

The clerk did not hesitate this time—he had made the calculation entirely in his head: "In London you will receive two pounds, one shilling and sixteen pence."

I was taken aback; this business was going to cost me nearly a pound. I could well understand how the Templars had amassed such riches. If I accepted their offer, I would have walked into this hall with three pounds and be walking out with a piece of parchment worth only a little over two. But I nodded my head and through gritted teeth agreed to the deal. I was worried that if I refused I would look foolish, unworldly. The Templars had a reputation for scrupulous honesty and I reminded myself that I would be exchanging my lead-tainted Tourangeaux coins for sterling silver, and that the risk of my being robbed on the way home had been eliminated. The risk that I was being robbed right here and now in this airy hall, however, I did not like to think about.

I waited no more than half an hour, pacing the long hall and staring up at the high arched beams that held up the roof, and then the clerk summoned me back to his table and showed me a parchment letter, some of which was written in fine, clear Latin, including my name and the manors I held, and some in a gibberish of Latin letters and numbers all jumbled up so that it made no sense to me at all, but which the clerk assured me would be the key to releasing my silver when I presented the letter to the Templar knights in England. Then he folded the letter, placed it in a waterproof pigskin pouch that he sealed with wax and presented it to me with another blessing for a safe journey.

The first person I saw when I walked out of the Counting House, feeling somewhat dazed after what had just transpired and a good deal lighter around the waist, was Sir Aymeric de St. Maur, the Templar knight who had threatened me with fiery torture the year before, and the man who tried to have Robin burned at the stake for heresy.

"Sir Alan," he said, "I had heard that you were headed for Paris, but what great joy indeed to run into you here."

And his mouth smiled.

14

I AM NEVER AT MY BEST WHEN I run into people unexpectedly and refined conversation is required in an instant and, I confess, I gawped a little at Sir Aymeric before I managed to clasp his outstretched hand and summon enough wit to pretend that I too was delighted to have encountered him. At the back of my mind, a fierce debate was raging: was his presence here outside the Counting House, on the day that I had chosen to visit the Paris Temple, a coincidence? Or did he have some sinister design in mind? He had every right to be here—more than I did: he was a Templar, he had only been following Richard's army as an observer, and now that a truce had been declared, it was only natural that he should take the opportunity to visit his brethren in Paris. But I was not convinced. At Sir Aymeric's shoulder stood Sir Eustace de la Falaise, his dull-witted lieutenant, who beamed at me as genially as ever. I dipped my head in salute.

"Are you in Paris for long?" Sir Aymeric was asking. "If you are staying for a while, then I would take it as a great boon if you would dine with me. I should very much enjoy your company over a good meal—with some decent wine. And I have something I wish to discuss with you."

I found Sir Aymeric's affability disconcerting. We were not friends, in any sense of the word; nor yet jolly dining companions. I had attached myself to his diplomatic mission into Vendôme out of necessity—not because I sought his company. What was wrong with the man? One day he was threatening to have me writhing under red-hot irons, and the next asking me to dine and drink heartily. Was he touched in the head?

"I shall be in Paris for a few weeks," I said, smiling stiffly at him, "but I am not sure of my plans exactly."

"We must make it soon, then," said Sir Aymeric. "Let us say a week from today, at noon. If you come to the main gate and ask for my apartments, the Brother Sergeant will show the way. Excellent! It's settled. Till we meet again."

I said, "Ah, well, you see . . . ," but Sir Aymeric was already striding away. Sir Eustace smiled cheerily at me: "God be with you, sir," he said, and went after his master.

You may ask why I did not protest further, or call out after them that I would not be available—but the simple truth is that I did not think of it at the time. My wits were scattered by his suggestion that we should break bread and drink wine together, and I was quite disarmed by his friendliness. Besides, why not dine with him? I wished to know more about the Templars, and here was a potential ally who might enlighten me about the knights of the blue cross.

Or have me murdered.

In the event, when I walked over to join Thomas and Hanno by the horses, the first thing I did was to tell them that I would be returning at the same time the following week: for a feast with a Templar. The first thing that Hanno said to me was: "They are here—these knights of the blue cross have a place here in this very stronghold. Our enemies are Templars, Sir Alan, I swear it."

We waited until we were well clear of the Paris Temple before I allowed Hanno to speak. "They have many chapels in that place, many, and I go in one, a small one to the north of the hospital, and say a prayer. It is an old chapel, made before all this new building is happening, I think; very dusty, not so well cared for now, but dedicated to the Blessed Virgin Mary. And when I go inside I see their shields, two of them hanging on the walls, old ones, the faces very faded. But I saw the blue cross in a black border, for sure. And so I begin to look around the chapel, I search it, and I find a little stone, set in the wall by the chancel for the remembrance of a dead knight: Rodrigo of León. The stone was carved and painted, and bore the knight's arms and the blue cross and black border. This dead Spanish knight is a member of an order: the Poor Fellow-Soldiers of Our Lady and the Temple of Solomon—it says so on the memorial stone. And I think this is the order that the knights of the blue cross also belong to. And I think they must be Templars, or an order similar to the Templars, for sure."

Hanno was rightly proud of the information that he had gathered. We had ascertained a Templar connection, and knew that these killers were dedicated to Mary, the Mother of Jesus—which tallied with the dying beggar-knight I spoke to asking me to forgive him in the name of the Queen of Heaven. We were beginning to know our foe.

On the way home, I stopped by the palace of the Bishop of Paris to see Brother Michel and ask if the Bishop had set a date for our meeting. After only a short wait, Brother Michel appeared looking flustered. He apologized handsomely for the delay and said that the Bishop had been especially busy during the past week but that his duties were lighter in the next few days and he was sure that there would be an opportunity for a meeting then. As I was leaving, I told the monk, as a form of security, that I would be dining with Sir Aymeric de St. Maur the following week. I'd be less likely to be murdered, I reasoned, if a senior member of the Bishop's personal staff knew my whereabouts. And if I was murdered, the monk's knowledge of my engagement might allow my friends in Robin's ranks to take a suitable revenge on Sir Aymeric.

Brother Michel seemed stunned when I explained this to him: "You suspect that Templars—our own warriors of Christ—are responsible for your father's murder?"

I outlined to him my two encounters with the knights of the blue cross—or the Poor Fellow-Soldiers of Our Lady and the Temple of Solomon, as we now knew they were called—and how on two occasions they had tried to kill me. Brother Michel was deeply angered: "This is quite insufferable, Sir Alan. Have you informed the Provost of this crime? I thought we were dealing with a tale from twenty years ago, but now this! We must bring these men to justice immediately. The Bishop is a close friend of Sir Gilbert Horal, the Grand Master of the Order—I will have him arrest these blue knights and drag them before the Provost in chains. We shall demand answers from them."

Brother Michel had become quite incensed by my words; two twin pink spots adorned his pale cheeks. I thought to myself: *I have been in war and around warriors for so long now that violence has become commonplace, but this man of God has reminded me that not all of us live with a gore-slicked blade permanently in our fists.*

"Calm yourself, Brother," I said to the rage-trembling monk before me. "We must not seek to involve the Provost nor call hysterically for the Paris Temple to be ransacked—we have no proof. And they may not truly be Templars after all—merely affiliated to them, or a group that seeks to ape them. I have been thinking a little on what I have seen of their fighting prowess, and I must conclude that it is not up to the very high standard of true Templars. Besides, it would be viewed as a preposterous accusation from one English knight, a foreigner and enemy, unsupported by any other evidence. I'm afraid I must continue to seek the proof myself—but if you could hasten the time when I might have an audience with the Bishop, I would be grateful."

"Well, if you think that is the best course, Sir Alan," said Brother Michel doubtfully. He seemed to have swiftly regained mastery of himself. "I will support you, of course, and keep my counsel. I will certainly speak to the Bishop about your case this very day. And I shall pray for your soul—and your father's too."

"Thank you, Brother," I said, and left him.

We spent that evening in a tavern with our student friends. The sign of the Cock was a bright, cheerful place much frequented by the young scholars from all over Europe who had come to hear the masters of Paris dispute. Matthew had invited us, saying that since I had been paying for the wine we consumed in the Widow Barbette's house, it was right that he and his friends should stand me a cup of wine at the Cock to show their gratitude. The students had barely any money between them, and I knew that by the end of the evening I would be settling a sizable account with the tavern keeper, but I did not mind. I enjoyed the company of these young, clever people and, even after depositing such a sum with the Templars, I could afford to be generous.

Matthew told me that their teacher, the famous Master Fulk, would be dropping in to join them later in the evening and urged me to stay and hear him speak. "He is a very brilliant man, Sir Alan, perhaps the best mind in Paris," said Matthew earnestly. "We are lucky to be his students."

As I have mentioned, I had little proper education, save in the arts of war, and despite my unenthusiastic first impressions I was curious to see more of this thinker that my young friends seemed to prize so highly.

We were drinking merrily and swapping stories about our adventures—I had told the boys the full story of my father and the theft of the candlesticks—when the air in the tavern seemed to chill slightly, and the lively chatter of the young men ran suddenly dry. A group of students, perhaps half a dozen big, boisterous lads, had come into the tavern and were seating themselves noisily at a table on the far side of the room, shoving each other and shouting jests. My friends were whispering to each other, and seemed nervous. "What is the matter?" I asked Luke, who was seated beside me.

"It is those German fellows—we had some trouble with them a few nights ago. Just a bit of shoving and shouting, but they told us that they would beat us black and blue if they ever saw us again."

I studied the German students: a big one, presumably their leader, was shouting jovially to his fellows and shooting his index finger over at our table.

"What are they saying?" I asked Hanno.

"They want to fight with these little English boys," my Bavarian friend replied coolly. "They are making insults and calling them weaklings and women, the usual things."

"Let's go and talk to them," I said, and stood up.

Since the attack by the Knights of Our Lady, I had worn my sword wherever I went in Paris; I also had my misericorde at my waist, but wore no mail. Hanno was armed to the teeth, as usual, with a sword, a dagger and a small axe shoved in his belt at the back. With his strong squat body, shaven head and scarred face, he looked the picture of the formidable warrior that he truly was.

We walked toward the Germans, and they fell silent at our approach. "I want you to translate everything I say into German, Hanno. I don't want them to misunderstand me."

Hanno grunted something, and I said to the table: "God be with you on this fine evening," and Hanno translated it into German for their benefit.

I continued: "These English boys here are friends of mine"—I waved a hand toward the table of students behind me—"and I understand that there has been some unpleasantness between you. And so I would like to buy you all a drink to make amends for any insult that you believe has been offered to you."

While Hanno translated my words, I pulled out an old scuffed leather purse from my belt and dropped it on the table. The purse was dark brown, worn smooth with the touch of my hands; it was very nearly worthless and contained only a few Parisian pennies, just enough for them to buy a *henap* or two of wine, perhaps something to eat.

"I hope that you will accept this gesture of amity, and that this will be the end of any trouble between you and my friends." I casually put my hand on my sword hilt, to indicate that if they did not wish to be friends then there were other options. But I also grinned at them in what I hoped was a kindly, avuncular fashion and made sure that I looked every man there squarely in the eye.

Hanno's translation seemed to be taking rather a long time; he picked up the flaccid leather purse and shook it at the German students—and I saw every one of their faces suddenly blanch. Then he dropped it on the table, uttered another phrase or two, and we both turned our backs on them and returned to the table of our friends.

The German students did not touch the purse of money. They all got up, as one man, and filed out of the tavern without a single word; though a few did give our table oddly fearful glances on their way out of the door.

"What did you say to them, Hanno?" I asked.

"I only say what you told me."

"Hanno, what did you really say to them? Come, my friend, please tell me."

Hanno sighed: "I say what you say and I add a bit. Just to make sure they pay attention to you. I tell them that you are an English knight known all across Christendom for his bloodlust and ferocity in battle. I say that it is your custom always to cut off the testicles from your enemies, and to cure the ball bag, the scrotum, in salt and use it as a money purse. Then I told them that *this* purse, taken from a Saracen in the Holy Land some years ago, is now nearly worn out and you are very much hoping to cut yourself a new one."

Our laughter was interrupted by the arrival of Master Fulk. With tears in my eyes, I stood to greet the students' teacher, and it was only when we had found him a place, and settled again and ordered more wine, and sent a boy out to fetch some beef-filled pastries from a nearby cookhouse, that I was able to take proper notice of him.

He was a big man in his forties, with battered features and sharp brown eyes below his bald head. His robe was even dirtier than the last time I had met him, and the stench of it as he sat beside me made my eyes water. But, though he may not have been fond of changing his clothing or washing his body, as Matthew had said, there was nothing wrong with his mind.

He engaged the boys almost immediately in a conversation about the true nature of the Bible that dazzled me with its wit and elegance. Master Fulk maintained that the Bible was only part of the scriptures, the most important part for sure, and the part that contained the keys to Salvation, but merely a part of the teachings of God and His only son Jesus Christ. He cited the Gospel of Nicodemus, a book that I had never heard of, though the students all seemed to be conversant with it, and suggested that it should be included in the Bible as it offered an alternative version of the Crucifixion story that was a valuable addition to the lore of the Church. Matthew, typically, took up the opposite position, and claimed that if the Bible already contained the true and full instructions on how to attain Heaven, there was no need for any Gospels other than the four already contained within it. I lost track of the argument on several occasions—and found it again, and lost it once more, and as a result I said nothing, listening quietly in awe as Fulk demonstrated the depth of his learning, and the keenness of his mind. Matthew was drinking too heavily to be a true match in argument for Master Fulk—and after a while the student conceded his position with a laugh, and much jeering from his fellows.

It was at Luke's suggestion that I put the mystery of the "man you cannot refuse" before Master Fulk, and, with only a little reluctance, I was persuaded to do so—for the wine had warmed me, too, and made me loquacious.

When I had finished my tale, to which Master Fulk had attended with complete concentration and in silence, the teacher gave me a strange, almost shamefaced look: "I thought that you seemed familiar," he said. "I must tell you now that I knew your father twenty years ago, and I remember well his expulsion from Notre-Dame. Have people told you that you resemble him?"

I nodded and I remembered where I had heard his name before: at Verneuil, Father Jean had told me that Fulk was the name of the bully whom my father had thrashed.

"I was not a very good student in my youth," said Master Fulk. "I drank too much, I was loud and loutish—you should all learn a lesson from my youthful sins." The teacher pointed a powerful finger at the flushed, unlined faces gathered around the table. "Your father taught me a lesson, Sir Alan. We fought with our fists and he bested me; but more importantly he taught me to mend my ways. I was headed down the path of sin to certain destruction, and your father showed me the error of my ways." The teacher smiled at me a little shyly and I saw the honest truth of his statement in his eyes. "I honor your father's memory," said Master Fulk, his voice gruff with deep feeling, and he lifted the *henap*, the big wine cup we were all sharing. "To Henri d'Alle!" he said, and drank. I felt the choke of emotion in my own throat as he passed the cup to me and I took a long swallow from the vessel.

"Perhaps you should give these sinful rascals a good beating one day," Master Fulk said, waving a hairy paw at the students gathered round the table. "It might teach them to mend their contumelious, dissolute ways!"

"Well," I said, "I do have need of a new purse!"

The table erupted in laughter, and once the joke had been explained to the teacher, he laughed the loudest of all.

Toward the end of the evening, when one or two of the students had slipped away to bed, Fulk leaned in toward me and said: "I do remember something concerning Bishop Heribert's visit that may be of interest to you. It was mere rumor, of course, but we young monks whispered about it a good deal at the time. Heribert was supposed to possess a great and holy relic, a magical device that could defeat death itself. It was supposed to have the power to cure any hurt or illness and grant youth and everlasting life to the man who possessed it. I think the Bishop may have been heard boasting about his fantastical possession to de Sully by one of the novices who served at their table. Heribert may even have shown it to his host."

I was intrigued—it put me in mind of the "wondrous" object that Heribert had mentioned to me before his death. Surely this was the relic that my father had been blamed for stealing.

"Do you know anything else about it?" I asked him.

"No, and it was merely a rumor; perhaps completely unfounded. None of my friends had ever laid eyes on this relic. It may not even have existed outside of Heribert's mind, for he was not always entirely *compos mentis.* But if it did exist, it would have been fairly small; there was some talk of it being contained in a box about so big." Fulk made a gesture with his hands, holding them a foot apart. "But, as I say, it may have been pure invention—a fantasy concocted by a half-mad old man."

I was less than completely sober when I stumbled the short distance to the Widow Barbette's house from the sign of the Cock; and it may have been the wine or the darkness—or just my own fevered imagination, but when Hanno stopped to urinate in an alleyway, and I idly gazed around the neighborhood, I thought I saw a hooded figure, no more than a tall, man-shaped shadow, a hundred yards further up the street leaning casually against the side of a house. I rubbed my eyes, looked again, but it was gone.

15

EARLY ON THE MORNING BEFORE I was due to dine with Sir Aymeric de St. Maur at the Paris Temple, a maidservant called at Widow Barbette's house. She was a very pretty, delicate girl with incongruously large breasts for her slight frame, which she evidently found most embarrassing. And while the students, who were helping Luke and Henry to pack up their beds in the *salle*, eyed her without attempting to hide their lust, she conveyed her message to me with a very becoming blush mantling her cheeks.

"Sir Alan," she began, "I come directly from my mistress the Lady d'Alle, who beseeches you to meet her this morning after Prime in the choir of the great cathedral of Our Lady, on the northern side. She wishes to speak to you urgently about a family matter and hopes that you will agree to the rendezvous and tell no one of this affair."

She glanced around at the staring students. "I hope these young gentlemen can be trusted to be discreet?"

I said that they could, but in truth I had my doubts: they would probably be gloating to their friends about the visit of this petite angel before noon. But it could not be helped. I dispatched Luke, the least lascivious of the students, to escort the maid back home to the Rue St. Denis, and prepared myself to meet the lovely Lady of Alle.

It might seem from my descriptions of her that I had fallen in love with Adèle—and, if I had not sworn to tell the truth in all matters in these pages, I might have made a pretty romance of the "affair" as the maid described it—a young lusty knight who was not yet twenty and the beautiful wife of an older lord. I have written many a *canso* on this popular theme myself. But I swore to tell the truth, and the truth is that my heart belonged to Goody, my betrothed, as it always has—and always will do. My own lovely girl might have been far away in England, and we might have done no more than kiss each other, but I loved her. And as soon as I had solved this mystery concerning my father, my heart's desire was to be wed to her and to hold her in my arms forever. To be sure, I was almost as prone to bouts of lustful thoughts as my student friends, but I swear, as Almighty God is my witness, I did not lie with any other women during my long absence from Goody.

Having said that, Adèle's beauty squeezed my chest when I saw her in the cathedral of Notre-Dame two hours later, sitting on a corner of one of the square pediments that support the mighty pillars. She wore a silk gown the color of young leaves, and even through her white mesh veil I could see it perfectly matched her eyes.

"Oh, Sir Alan, do not stare at me so," she said when I stood before her seat under the pillar on the north side of the choir. "Sit here, quickly now and do not look at me, we must pretend that we are strangers. I do not want to heap yet more humiliation on my husband with vile rumors."

I perched on the adjacent corner of the pediment, the carved stone already worn smooth by countless pairs of weary buttocks before mine. Adèle's slight maid—she of the bountiful breasts—waited just out of earshot and spent the time with her back to us, praying at a small shrine to St. Botolph. The arrangement of the seating on the pediment meant that I was facing northwest, and Adèle was facing southwest; we were not in each other's line of sight, so it would appear as if we were not known to each other and had no connection either—and yet a quiet word spoken by one could easily be heard by the other.

"I thank you for coming, Alan," said Adèle. "And I'm sorry that we should have to meet this way—but you did promise to come and visit me again, and I waited and waited, and you did not send word. So I had no choice but to summon you here. Do not speak, now, but only listen, for I must tell you a tale so that you may understand something about your father—and your uncle, too."

Out of the corner of my left eye I could see that beneath her veil her lips were hardly moving as she spoke. Directly in front of my eyes, along the side aisle of the cathedral, passed a constant stream of humanity: pilgrims, priests, men-at-arms, mendicants—men, women and children of all ranks and conditions and from all over Christendom. All were coming to marvel at the splendor of the rising cathedral and to say a prayer or light a candle or purchase a saint's medal at one of the little alcoves that lined the northern wall of the choir. As the lady spoke, and I listened, I watched this stream of souls all seeking something, and many finding it, in God's holy house.

"I first set eyes on my husband Thibault on the day that we were betrothed—twenty, oh twenty-five years ago. I was very young and the match was arranged by my father, and by Thibault's father, who was then the Seigneur d'Alle. I liked Thibault well enough, and I wanted to please my father, and so I consented to the match. A month later, we were wed.

"I first set eyes on Henri, your father, on the day of my wedding, and from that moment onward I knew what true love was. I was very fond of Thibault—he was a fine man, a strapping fellow, lusty and well made—but your father I loved with a mindless yearning passion. It was a soul-hunger; I wanted him so much it was an ache in my chest: when I heard him sing, I nearly swooned from the sheer beauty of his voice. And I knew that I must have him or I would surely die.

"At this time, both Thibault and Henri were in training to be knights. Your father was about your age, and a truly beautiful man, but I persuaded Thibault that he must be allowed to teach me music, which was always his first love. And so for an hour a day after the noon meal, I would be with Henri in a small chamber on the third floor of the castle, while he tried to teach me music. I lived for that hour; it was the center of my life; for me that was the only hour in the whole day in which I felt alive. All morning long, I trembled as I waited for the music hour to come; and when it was finished I longed for the afternoon, evening and night to pass so that I might be with Henri again for that fleeting, thrilling, wonderful patch of time.

"Though I tried to hide my feelings, your father must have realized that something was amiss. He was fond of me, he liked me, I am sure, but he did not feel the same passion in his heart that I did. And I had no ear for music—none at all. Henri realized soon enough that trying to teach me was an impossibility—and so he went to Thibault. I heard them laughing and joking about my lack of ability, and so inevitably the lessons came to an end.

"I was at my wits' " end: I loved Henri with my very soul but I knew that he did not love me, although I sometimes saw him looking at other women—my God how that cut into my soul—and I knew that he had carnal desires like any young man. I was in black despair, and in that melancholy state the Devil entered my mind, and inside it he deposited a cloud of dark spawn that hatched into a plan that nearly destroyed us all. Perhaps it did destroy your father."

I stirred uneasily on my stone seat. I have to admit that I was shocked by Adèle's words. I did not care to think of my father being pursued by another man's wife; I did not care to think of him in sexual terms with anyone but my mother, if the truth be told. But I held my tongue and Adèle carried on with her sad tale.

"One night, after Thibault and Henri had been drinking late together following a long day of hunting, I went to your father's chamber while he slept and—oh, I was shameless—I crept into his bed. I am not sure Henri could tell whether he was awake or dreaming, but he was naked and that night I took him hungrily in my arms and we made love. For one stolen night he was mine . . . And then the foundations of my world came crashing around me.

"In the chill light of dawn, Henri saw that I was beside him naked in his bed, and he knew that what he had done had been no drunken dream. He cursed me and threw me out of his chamber, shouting that

I was the Devil's whore, and then he went straight to Thibault that very morning and confessed to his crime.

"I thought Thibault would kill him—and I think he would have liked to have done so, but his roaring at Henri and the blows that he struck roused the whole castle. The Seigneur, torn from his bed in the great chamber, only just managed to separate his two sons and prevent a murder. Henri was banished, packed off to Paris and a life in the Church that same day—and I never set eyes on him again."

I heard a sob, and despite the lady's instructions, I turned my head toward her and saw that she was weeping. I had the strongest urge to enfold her in my arms, but I knew that to be seen in public in the arms of another man would not be helpful to her already much besmirched honor. Then, shockingly, across on the other side of the cathedral, I caught sight of a tall, familiar shape, the face partially hidden by a deep hood, but, I could tell, a face dark as a Moor's: it was the watcher I had seen from the night at the Cock. For a moment, I thought that I recognized him from somewhere, but my mind, awhirl after Adèle's lustful revelations, could not grasp that eel-slippery memory. The crowds of pilgrims grew thick on that side of the cathedral and when they cleared the figure was no longer visible. Was I imagining this fellow; was my fear giving me visions? Or was he another assassin awaiting his chance? Either way, as I scanned the faces of the passing pilgrims, I could see his dark face no more.

I had to wrench my attention back to Adèle: she had composed herself and was continuing with her tragic story.

"And so, you see, Alan, when you came to us and told us that you believed that we had abandoned Henri because of some silly accusation of pilfering, I had to tell you that you were wrong. After he was expelled from the Church, Thibault would not have Henri in the castle—because of me, because of my passion for him. He did not trust me with your father. It has nothing to do with some petty crime. I wanted you to understand this, so that in understanding, you might forgive us."

I was moved by her story, but it was clear to me that, while I had been blaming the rough-tongued Seigneur for my father's exile, the true blame lay with this woman, or rather with her passionate younger self. It was she who had ruined my father—she was as much to blame as anybody for his sad life and miserable end. Yet I could not hate her. The Church teaches us that women are weak and lustful; they are the daughters of Eve and it is in their nature to seduce men from the path of righteousness.

"I must think on this matter," I said, rising to my feet.

"Please, Sir Alan, I beg you to forgive me. It was not easy for me to tell you this. And I know that I have done you and your father a terrible wrong. But I was young and foolish and in love—have you never made a mistake in these circumstances? Many people have. I would like us to be reunited as a family again; d'Alle and Dale, English and French together. Please, look deep into your heart, seek and find the compassion to forgive us!"

Her words struck a chord: *I was young and foolish and in love—have you never made a mistake in these circumstances?* Yes, I thought. I have made mistakes in love: poor mutilated Nur sprang into my mind; and a lovely Jewish girl who was killed in York a few years ago. Yes, I had made mistakes in love. Who has not?

Adèle's exquisite tear-stained face and beguiling bright green eyes were beseeching me—and I knew that I would not be able to refuse her request of forgiveness if I stayed under such a powerful enchantment for long. But she had destroyed my father—her shameless lust, her selfish urges, her wanton actions had spurred him toward his untimely death. And so I merely muttered, "I must go, my lady; I have an appointment to dine with a Templar. I will think long and hard on what you have told me. God be with you."

And I turned my back and hurried away before her green eyes and bewitching beauty could break my resolve.

The dinner with Sir Aymeric de St. Maur was a private affair: just we two knights at the board, and served by half a dozen silent servants—

but, as the Templar had promised, the food was lavish and the wine excellent. I had been shown to his guest hall in the north of the Paris Temple compound shortly before noon, and Hanno and Thomas had been led away to the servants' quarters to be fed separately—which gave me a moment's pause—but Sir Aymeric's affability reassured me, and there were several trustworthy people in Paris who knew that I was being entertained by this Poor Fellow-Soldier, and so I felt reasonably secure. I gave my sword to Thomas for safekeeping—but I kept my misericorde at my waist, and I had a stout eating knife at my belt, too. But, in truth, I did not seriously fear that I would be murdered over the many different, and quite astoundingly delicious, dishes that the English Templar had ordered to be served.

Sir Aymeric and I sat close together and, after an interminably long prayer of thanksgiving, we ate from the same bowls, my host serving me with the choicer cuts of venison and beef, and urging me to try the sauces that his cooks had prepared to accompany the roasted meats. If the food was good, and I could not deny that it was, the wine was truly exceptional, pale yellow, tart and refreshing, coming, Sir Aymeric told me, from vineyards that the Order cultivated in the region of Champagne. Once again I was impressed with the reach and power of this organization, and reminded of its wealth. We spoke of inconsequential things, platitudes and gossip, for the first part of the meal. I praised the food and the wine, and my host told me how impressed he was with my growing reputation as a knight. Harmless stuff. I mentioned how thunderstruck I had been by the cathedral of Notre-Dame, its beauty, the majestic scale of the project, and my host concurred. But then he said: "Do you think, Sir Alan, that God wants us to expend so much treasure and time on these great edifices? Surely they serve to aggrandize Man and not Our Lord—surely the whole world is God's masterpiece and anything Man builds can only be a pale, imperfect imitation of the wonders of Nature that Almighty God has already made."

I choked on a large piece of peppery roast beef. I had never thought of it that way before. But how could building churches be wrong? And this was coming from a Templar, a warrior dedicated to the service of Christ.

Sir Aymeric took a frugal sip of wine and continued: "Consider a tall tree in a wood; see how glorious it is, soaring, magnificent and yet alive, providing shade for mankind and a place of shelter for all God's creatures—birds, squirrels, spiders and tiny insects. Can one of de Sully's big stone columns, most cleverly carved in the image of a tree, whose purpose is merely to prevent an absurdly high roof from falling on our heads, ever truly compete with a mighty hundred-year-old oak? And de Sully is, in fact, felling trees by the thousand on his lands to use in building his cathedral. Is de Sully not destroying something truly beautiful, which reminds us of the perfection of God, to create something artificial that is but a monument to Mankind's ambition—and a rich source of revenue for the Church from the swarms of pilgrims who come to gawp at it?"

For an instant, Robin leaped into my mind: he too preferred trees to churches, the clean wildwood to the venal priest-ridden city. And then I remembered the Templar clerks exchanging my three pounds in hard silver for a piece of parchment worth only two, and I said: "And does Notre-Dame truly bring in rich revenues for the Church?"

"Ah, you have me there," said Sir Aymeric, chuckling. "I see some of the disputative air of the University of Paris has sharpened your wits. I must confess that no, it does not: Notre-Dame's pilgrims bring in a small amount, and in future years they will undoubtedly bring in more, but the costs of building the cathedral must be almost beyond reckoning. Indeed, many people wonder how Bishop de Sully can afford such a vast expenditure of treasure. No one knows how he manages it—except the good Bishop himself! And God, of course." The Templar laughed to show that he did not mean his words to be taken seriously.

A suckling pig was brought into the room, carried high by two servants, with a baked apple stuffed under its crisp snout. The Templar carved into it with his own knife and helped me to a portion of its unctuous melting flesh and a piece of the glossy brown skin. It was astonishingly good. Then Sir Aymeric said, in an altogether more serious tone: "Sir Alan, I imagine you are wondering why I have invited you to dine with me—particularly after the unpleasantness last year with"—he paused, swallowed with some difficulty as if the words were choking him—"the inquisition of my lord the Earl of Locksley."

"I did ponder it a little," I said dryly.

"Well, I must confess I have an ulterior motive for seeking your company. I meant what I said earlier about your prowess as a knight; it has been noticed in the highest circles that you are a warrior of unusual skill and courage. Did not King Richard himself dub you? And so I have asked you here to plant the seed of an idea in your head—but first I must ask you an important, nay, a vital question; a somewhat intrusive question, which springs partly from our unfortunate encounters last year. May I ask it?"

I nodded warily, saying nothing.

"Are you truly a devout and humble Christian?" said Sir Aymeric. "Do you reject the Devil and all his demons and love the Lord Our God and His only son Jesus Christ with all your heart and soul?"

He looked at me intently, his brown eyes burning with the passion of his faith. I answered him with full honesty.

"I do believe with all my heart that Jesus Christ is my Savior and the Savior of all Mankind. I cannot answer for my lord of Locksley, except to say to you again that he is no demon-worshiper, but *I* try to be as good a Christian as I may—though I am of course a sinner like any other man, and I pray that God will have mercy on my soul."

Sir Aymeric was smiling broadly at me: "That is a good answer, Sir Alan. Then I will plant my idea, if I may. Have you ever considered joining the ranks of the Poor Fellow-Soldiers of Christ and the Temple of Solomon? A man of your talents on the battlefield, if he wished to take our oath and accept the discipline of the Order, would receive a warm welcome among the Brethren."

I was stunned. Me, a Templar? I was flattered and outraged all at once: this brotherhood was made up of the best fighting men in the world, the very best, and to be asked if I would join them was an almost unbelievable honor, a compliment of the first rank; and I must confess that, in that moment, the idea of a life serving God with a humble heart, with a guarantee of a Heavenly reward, was most appealing, too. But the Order had clashed several times with my liege lord, and while they had made peace earlier in the spring and were now officially reconciled, less than a year ago they were seeking to have him burned alive for what they described as his heretical beliefs. Did they really expect that I would abandon my master and go over to his enemies? Did they think I would join up with an Order that Robin described as "bloodthirsty, God-struck maniacs?" It was almost beyond belief . . .

Another thought crawled out from the back of my mind: could this be some sort of ruse to trap me, or a stratagem to ensnare Robin? Either way, I could not accept the offer. I was betrothed to Goody, for one thing; and Templars were celibate—which seemed to me then, as a lusty young man, a very high price to pay for a place in Heaven. But a part of me was flattered, and it occurred to me that it might be wise not to turn them down with a curt refusal.

I said: "I am sensible of the great honor that you do me by making this proposal—and I believe that I could be a contented man as a member of the Order, but I must think about it deeply, and pray, of course. I am certain that God will show me the true path."

"Of course, of course, it is not a thing that a man can decide lightly over dinner. But may I tell you something that may influence your decision. I know that you fought, and fought with courage, against the Saracens in Outremer during the Great Pilgrimage—but I suspect that you, like many of the men who survived it, feel that it was not a well-managed expedition, that too many Christian lives were sacrificed for naught."

He had struck the target full on: I felt that the Great Pilgrimage, for all its good intentions and for all the valor of the men who took part, had achieved nothing but an ocean of spilled blood—Christian and heathen alike—but I did not generally trouble to express this unpopular opinion to my fellow men, unless they too had experienced the mindless carnage of that ill-fated campaign.

Sir Aymeric continued: "It is not generally known, but our new Grand Master, Sir Gilbert Horal, has set his heart on finding an acceptable permanent peace with the Saracens in the Holy Land. He is one of a new breed of Templars, which I must say includes myself, who feel that the years of useless slaughter in Outremer must come to an end, and if it is humanly possible we must learn to live with Saracens as our neighbors, and undertake to share the blessed land where our Lord Jesus Christ lived and died."

I was moved by his speech: Robin was wrong—these men were not "bloodthirsty, God-struck maniacs" but good men trying to serve Christ and find a reasonable solution.

"It would make my heart glad to become a Brother of the Order," I said quite truthfully. "I am deeply touched by your offer, and I thank you for it. But I must contemplate quietly on it and pray for guidance first."

And there we left it.

The servants brought more wine, rich puddings and tarts, and fruit—golden oranges from the southern lands, sweet as nectar. And I asked Sir Aymeric the question that had been in the back of my mind for most of that fine meal.

"Sir Aymeric, what do you know of the Poor Fellow-Soldiers of Our Lady and the Temple of Solomon? Their badge is a blue cross on a white field with a black border."

"The Knights of Our Lady? Ah, Sir Alan, now you are taking me back to my days as a novice. I have not seen that badge or heard that name for many, many years."

"But you do know of them?" I persisted.

"Oh yes, they were part of the Order once—and famous, too, for their deep faith and prowess in battle. It was our new Grand Master himself who formed the Knights of Our Lady, oh, a good thirty years ago in Spain. Sir Gilbert was a fiery young man back then, and very devoted to Mary, the Mother of God. He formed a company of knights—a hundred or so young, devout Templars, men of exceptional skill and dedication—who vowed that they would fight in the name of the Queen of Heaven to the last drop of their blood to clear the Moors from Spain. They compared themselves to the fabled knights of King Arthur—fearless warriors for Jesus Christ and his Blessed Mother Mary. Sir Gilbert was their first Master, of course, and he designed their badge, using his own family emblem, the blue cross on white—argent, a cross azure, as the heralds would have it. For ten years or so they had a powerful influence on the war against the Moors, pushing them back in several notably bloody engagements, if I recall rightly, and doing great deeds of valor. Sir Gilbert was a very different man then—full of passion and rage, with a burning desire to rid the world of all nonbelievers. He's quite different now, of course, older and wiser—but I shall remind him of those days when I see him next. It will make him smile."

"Where are these knights now?" I asked. "Who commands them today? Who is their present Master?" I found I was holding my breath as I awaited the answer.

"Oh, the Knights of Our Lady are no more. They were disbanded long ago—perhaps fifteen years ago, I think. The Grand Master of the time—Odo de St. Amand—completely suppressed them; he felt, I believe, that there should only be one Order of Templars, that these chapters within the Brotherhood, dedicated to this saint or that, were bad for morale, caused unnecessary rivalry and diluted our sense of purpose—and he was quite right, of course. By the time they were suppressed, many of the Knights of Our Lady had perished in the Spanish wars, some were then absorbed back into the ordinary ranks of the Brotherhood, others left to join other Orders—the Hospitallers, mainly. Some retired to the cloister and became monks. It happens to all men; we lose the zeal that we had as youngsters, and become shamefully fat and lazy." Sir Aymeric smiled and slapped at his belly, which had only the tiniest suggestion of a paunch; hardly shameful for a man in his late thirties.

"So if I were to tell you that I saw a *conroi* of these knights outside Vendôme two months ago, and another knight bearing a shield with a blue cross two weeks ago in Paris, that would surprise you?"

"I would be astonished!"

I stared hard at him. He did not look as if he were lying.

"You do not believe me? I will swear it for you, by my faith, if you wish me to," said Sir Aymeric. He seemed hurt that I should doubt his word.

I waved away the suggestion: as far as I could tell, Sir Aymeric de St. Maur was telling me the truth. The Knights of Our Lady, as this open-faced Templar had known them, were in their graves, or scattered to the winds; it would appear that the original fellowship that had fought the Moor so bravely in Spain had been dissolved fifteen years ago.

16

THREE DAYS AFTER MY DINNER WITH Sir Aymeric, in the late afternoon, I was invited to Master Fulk's home on the Petit-Pont. It was Luke who brought the invitation after his lessons had ended, and who offered to act as my guide to the narrow house on the bridge, where I was greeted with great affection by his huge, hairy and malodorous teacher. When Luke had departed, Fulk offered wine and sweet cakes and we sat in his cramped downstairs room, with the shutters flung wide on that warm September afternoon—for which I was grateful, given that it appeared that he had neither bathed nor changed his robe in the weeks since I first met him—and we watched the boat traffic gliding down the brown Seine, our conversation occasionally interrupted by the coarse oaths of the boatmen passing through the arches of the bridge beneath us.

"After I left you the other week, Sir Alan," Master Fulk began, "I started to think hard about your father's story and the goods that were stolen from Bishop Heribert all those years ago. And I remembered something, which I think may be significant. You recall the magical object—the wondrous relic that defeats disease and holds back death—that Heribert was rumored to possess?"

I said that I did.

"Now, let me ask you another question: have you heard of a *trouvère* known as Christian of Troyes, who used to serve Philip, Count of Flanders? He died a few years ago."

I nodded. "I read one of his poems called 'Erec and Enide' and I was impressed. He was good, very good, some of his poetry was truly lovely."

"And have you read *Le Conte du Graal*?"

I sat up straighter on my stool. "No," I said, "but I have heard other *trouvères* speak of this bizarre story. Indeed, they speak of it with something approaching awe."

"It is the tale of a young knight called Perceval and his adventures. I have a copy here: will you allow me to read you a little from it?" Master Fulk pulled a small, fat book bound in brown leather from the sleeve of his robe. He muttered to himself as he leafed through the vellum pages until he found the passage he wanted.

"Perceval has been invited to dine in the castle of a mysterious fisherman king," Fulk said, "they are sitting together on a great bed in the hall. Listen to this!" And he began to read:

"*While they talked of this and that, a young attendant entered the room, holding a shining lance by the middle of the shaft. He passed between the fire and those seated on the bed, and all present saw the shining lance with its shining head. A drop of blood fell from the tip of the lance, and that crimson drop ran all the way down to the attendant's hand. The youth who had come there that night beheld this marvel*—he means Perceval," Fulk said, interrupting himself before continuing—"*and refrained from asking how this could be. He remembered the warning of the man who had made him a knight, he who had instructed and taught him to guard against speaking too much. The youth feared that if he asked a question, he would be taken for a peasant. He therefore said nothing.*

"*Two more attendants then entered, bearing in their hands candelabra of fine gold inlaid with niello. Handsome indeed were the attendants carrying the candelabra. On each candelabrum ten candles, at the very least, were burning. Accompanying the attendants was a beautiful, gracious, and elegantly attired young lady holding between her hands a* graal. *When she entered holding this* graal, *such brilliant illumination appeared that the candles lost their brightness just as the stars and the moon do with the appearance of the sun. Following her was another young lady holding a silver carving platter. The* graal, *which came first, was of fine pure gold, adorned with many kinds of precious jewels, the richest and most costly found on sea or land—those on the* graal *undoubtedly more valuable than any others. Exactly as the lance had done, the* graal *and the platter passed in front of the bed and went from one room into another."*

Fulk paused and looked at me meaningfully. I looked back at him, not entirely sure how I was supposed to react.

"What exactly is a *graal*?" I asked. Like the knight in the story, I was concerned that in my ignorance I would be taken for a peasant.

"Normally, it's a serving dish, about so big," Fulk replied, holding his hands a foot apart. "It is the kind of serving dish that you might use to bring a large cooked fish to the table. The word is a southern one, an Occitan word—we would call it a 'grail' in French."

He was beginning to exhibit a little excitement: "But that is not important: in this story the *graal*, or grail, is a wondrous object that can bestow eternal youth, defeat disease and grant immortality. Does this not strike you as significant, in the light of what you know about the theft of the goods from Bishop Heribert?"

"Well, it is a rather odd story . . . ," I began.

But Master Fulk had become fully animated, his eyes were shining with excitement and he brusquely interrupted me, speaking to me as if I were one of his slower pupils: "The candlesticks, the silver carving platter . . . come on, Sir Alan, come on . . ."

"You think that Bishop Heribert had somehow gained possession of these marvelous objects from a poet's fairy story—you believe that they actually exist?—and that they were subsequently stolen from him in Paris?"

"Exactly so, and only the candlesticks and the carving platter were recovered—the least valuable, the least miraculous items were planted in Henri d'Alle's cell to throw the blame on him. They were sacrificed so that the Grail—the most holy and wondrous of all of these objects—and perhaps the lance, too, might be retained by the thief."

"But surely Christian's poem is just a story, an allegory, a fantasy—I have composed a few fantastical tales myself and I'd not expect any man to take them as Gospel truth."

"Quite so," said Master Fulk. "Quite so." He seemed suddenly deflated. "You may very well be right, Sir Alan. But I thought that you might be interested in hearing the tale." The light seemed to be dying in his eyes, and he was once again his solid, pungent, rational self. "I am in the process of making further inquiries into this Grail; I have heard tell of a young man in Burgundy called Robert de Boron who is said to be investigating these matters. And I've written to him to seek his advice. We may learn more."

Master Fulk's theory seemed preposterous at first hearing. But as I sat there and thought about it, it occurred to me that maybe, just maybe, there might be something in this tale. Many a man has invented a fantastical tale to amuse a rich patron, but, equally, many a man has taken an old tale and used it as the basis of his own story. Perhaps there was some grain of truth behind this *Conte du Graal*.

The sun was sinking in the west, behind the towers of the palace of the King, which cast long shadows over the river, and I soon took my leave of the big man, after thanking him warmly for taking such an interest in my own quest—and for a very interesting and informative afternoon. Before I left, I asked him a final question: "Tell me, Master Fulk, how did Christian, this excellent and inventive poet from Troyes, come to die? Was it peacefully in his bed in quiet old age?"

"I had a student from Champagne who came to me last year and he told me a curious story about Christian the *trouvère*," said Fulk. "Apparently, the man was working quietly in his house one evening, alone—working on the *Graal* story, in fact—when thieves broke in and killed him for his purse. But they were most singular thieves: they did not bother to take all his valuables—leaving his deep money coffer untouched and only taking the few objects of value that were close to hand—and the manner of his death, my student told me, was also highly unusual. Christian of Troyes was stabbed, only once, and killed instantly by a dagger-blow directly to the heart."

I needed time to think and so I went to the church of St. Julien-le-Pauvre, which was on the corner of the Rue Garlande. The priest was beginning to say Vespers as I slipped through the door, and I joined the meager congregation and stood at the back of the church, half-listening to the comfortingly familiar Latin words and half-filling my mind with dark thoughts of magical fish dishes and murdered poets. Although Master Fulk's theory—that this Grail had been the real object of the theft that my father had been blamed for—still seemed to be far-fetched, it did at least fit all the facts. Somebody was going about merrily murdering people in an attempt to preserve this secret, and therefore it had to be a secret of great magnitude to be worth killing so many for. Could this wondrous serving dish, this Grail, really hold back death? If it were true that the Grail could bestow eternal youth, defeat disease and grant immortality, then it clearly would be the most miraculous object in the world. And I could easily imagine the "man you cannot refuse" and his cohorts—the apparently disbanded but still very real Knights of Our Lady—killing to keep it in their possession; and killing again to prevent anyone from discovering their secret.

It occurred to me that there was one man in Paris who might be able to enlighten me about whether Bishop Heribert had claimed to possess the Grail or not. It was the man I had been waiting to see since I had arrived in Paris all those weeks ago, but who seemed to be reluctant to talk to me about the matter: Bishop Maurice de Sully.

As the priest concluded the service of Vespers, and all were joined in the final prayer, I resolved that I would seek out Bishop de Sully the very next day; I would go to his palace and demand to see him—I had waited long enough. I would go there and refuse to leave the hall until I had been granted a few moments of his time.

"Sir Alan, I am so sorry, please forgive me, as God surely knows, you have been more than patient—but the Bishop cannot see you today, and he may not be able to see you for some time." Brother Michel's kindly face was a picture of misery; he seemed to be taking this news harder than me.

I had consumed a light and hurried breakfast at the Widow Barbette's and had then marched over the Petit-Pont, turned right past the Hôtel-Dieu and, without even taking a minute to gaze in awe at the cathedral, which had been my unfailing habit these past weeks, I strode up to the wide doors of the episcopal palace, knocked loudly and demanded to see Brother Michel.

"He is avoiding me," I said to the harassed-looking monk, determined that I would not leave until I had been granted a personal audience with the Bishop himself.

"He is not, I swear it—I swear it by Almighty God and the Blessed Virgin. May I be struck dead if I lie. His Grace the Bishop of Paris is not trying to avoid you."

I looked at Brother Michel's face and, in spite of myself, I believed him. He seemed worn out, the lines of age cutting deep furrows in his still handsome face.

"The Bishop is not avoiding you," he said, after a long pause, and with a resigned sigh. "The truth is that he is not well. He has been ill for some weeks now, but I was commanded to keep this a secret from the world. I had hoped that he would recover in due course and then might have time for an audience with you. But I am afraid that he has taken a turn for the worse."

"Perhaps I might be allowed to visit him, very briefly, at his sickbed," I said, though without much hope. "Just a few moments; I swear I will not badger him."

"His Grace is not here—he has retired to the Abbey of St. Victor, beyond the city boundaries, where he keeps a house. He has long been a benefactor of St. Victor's, and he plans to live out his remaining days there in prayer and contemplation. I am sorry, Sir Alan, but I am afraid it is impossible for you to see him. His doctors have insisted on complete rest, no excitement or upsets. We will pray for him, of course, night and day, but I fear that His Grace, that good and holy man, will soon be gathered to God's side."

It did not occur to me to argue any further; something about the honest way that Brother Michel had opened his heart to me stilled my tongue. As I walked back to the widow's house, my head hanging low, I felt a great weight of despair settle around my shoulders. I felt that I should never manage to unravel the mystery surrounding my father's expulsion: the little I had discovered seemed to have taken me no further toward revealing the identity of the "man you cannot refuse." And wild tales of magic serving bowls and secret knightly orders only seemed to confuse the matter. I felt as if I were being mocked by Paris itself for my fumbling attempts to find the truth about my father. It was as if the very stones, the bricks and beams of the city were laughing at me.

As I trudged over the Petit-Pont, approaching Master Fulk's house, I heard a shout that jerked me out of my doleful reverie. "There! There he is! Catch him—he's the murderer. Catch him!"

There was a knot of people, I saw, gathered outside Master Fulk's house, including half a dozen men-at-arms. A student in a dirty black robe, a fellow called Benoît whom I knew only by sight, was pointing at me and shouting: "He's the murderer! He is! I saw him leaving Master Fulk's house yesterday evening. It must have been him." Then the men-at-arms were running toward me. I felt a passerby grab my arm. Someone shouted: "He's a murderer; don't let him get away! Catch him, you fellows!"

Murderer? My stomach grew icy. For an instant I thought of drawing Fidelity and cutting my way clear—but there were too many people in the press around me, and I would have had to kill or maim dozens of unarmed folk to make my escape. And so I stayed still as a rock and when the youngest and fleetest man-at-arms came running up to me, I asked, as coolly and calmly as I could: "Tell me, sir, is Master Fulk dead?"

"That he is," panted the man-at-arms, grabbing my shoulder with his sweaty hand.

"Was it a stab wound to the chest—here?" I asked, pointing to my own breast, about an inch or two to the left of my sternum.

"You should know," said the man, taking a firm grip on my arm. "Folk on the bridge are saying that you're the one who did this foul deed."

I have been unfortunate enough to spend time in more than a few jails—the damp, rat-infested dungeon below Winchester Castle, a pitch-dark storeroom in the fortress of Nottingham, and several others besides—but the crowded stone cell at the foot of the Grand Chastelet on the north side of the Grand-Pont was easily the worst of them all.

I had been stripped of my arms and fine outer clothing, bound and led ignominiously north through the streets of the Île de la Cité to the Grand-Pont by the men-at-arms. I caught a glimpse of Hanno and Thomas in the crowds that followed me, and that gave me some heart, but the black feeling of despair continued to dog me. At the Grand Chastelet, the men-at-arms presented me to the provost-sergeant on duty, and I was informed that I would be held until the grave charge of murder had been thoroughly investigated. I had been the last person seen to leave Master Fulk's house the evening before, and he had been killed—as I had rightly feared—by a single dagger thrust to the heart at about that time. It occurred to me that the real killer must have watched me leave, and entered Master Fulk's house shortly afterward.

The provost-sergeant ignored my protests of innocence, and when it was revealed that I was an English knight taking advantage of the truce to visit Paris, that knowledge seemed to blacken my name even further. Despite the fact that I had never tried to hide my identity, I heard the word "spy" whispered more than once by the men-at-arms. Somebody, it seemed, had informed on me to the Provost's office, and suggested that I was not only a murderer, who had quarreled with Master Fulk and then killed him in rage, but that I was also an agent of King Richard's, bent on causing any amount of murder, mischief and mayhem in Paris.

The charges were clearly absurd, and would have been laughable, save for the fact that I was now being bundled through an iron-bound door into a small chamber packed almost to its dripping ceiling with the human scum of Paris.

Mercifully, my hands had been freed, and I sprawled on the floor of that tiny cell onto a carpet of legs. I was immediately kicked and stamped on by dozens of feet, shod and bare, for the jail, which was no more than six feet wide by eight feet long, contained eighteen men in various stages of degradation. They were seated on the stone floor hip-high in noisome ooze with their backs against the slime-covered walls while their outstretched legs filled the entire space in the middle. The stench was indescribable. There was no place for me to sit and, after having been kicked and pummeled to my knees, then to my feet, I found myself crouching in the middle of that tiny box, unable to stand fully upright as the ceiling was a mere five feet from the floor. I have been in beds that were bigger than that prison and the reek and squalor of the place would have made an ordure-eating scavenger-pig swoon.

Within an hour or two my back was aching from standing in such a stooped position. By the time that the light from a tiny barred window high on the wall was fading—and I calculated that I had been there for six or seven hours—I was in agony, the muscles of my legs and back burning. And I knew that if I was going to survive my incarceration in that stinking hell, I'd have to find a space to sit, and to do so in that rock coffin, I was going to have to behave like a beast—a ferocious creature of the wild.

I am not proud of what I did next—and although I have killed many men in my long life, the man who lost his life that evening in that cramped and stinking pit is one of the souls that haunt my conscience most regularly. I picked a small man, for the ease of it, a thin and sickly one—may God have mercy on me—and hauled him bodily out of his place by the wall and clubbed him down with my fists. He saw me coming for him and, knowing the likely outcome, he fought like a madman, scratching and trying to bite me, kicking wildly with his feet. I steeled my mind and battered him unmercifully, punching at his head and body, cracking his ribs and breaking his nose and jaw, until he was down and, as he lay moaning, bleeding in the six inches of slurry on the floor, the other men in the cell finished the job and kicked and stamped him until he lay silent and still in the muck. The other prisoners did not say a word to me about the fight; a few eyed me indifferently, but each was sunk too deep in his own personal Hell for fellow human feeling. A few had pulled their legs in to give us room during my fight, or to avoid being stamped upon, but no one suggested that I was not within my rights to tear that little man apart and take his place, most gratefully, God forgive me, against the slime-streaked wall.

The battered corpse lay in the center of the floor, with other men casually resting their legs upon it, all through that long and terrible night. During the last few minutes of daylight, while I could still see their gaunt, bearded faces, I tried to make some conversation with the men whose shoulders were squeezed next to mine, but one of them, the man to my left, was seriously ill, coughing violently from time to time and expelling a wad of bloody mucus with each hacking retch. I knew he was not long for this world. The man on my right, a big-boned man, now as thin as a broomstick, seemed to be more than a little crazed. I asked him how long he had been in that cell and he asked me in return what month it was: when I told him it was September, he laughed wildly and shockingly loudly, then said: "March, I came here in March. In spring when all the world was fresh and new! Ha-ha!"

He was a thief, the big crazy man, a house-breaker called Michael, and I told him that I too had followed the path of a cutpurse in my youth. We talked a while during that long, long night, though my throat was badly parched, and for most of the time he made some sense. He told me of the laws and customs of that God-forgotten cell, such as they were, and my soul was chilled by their simple brutality. Every man was for himself, the strong would live and the weak would die—Devil take the hindmost. Every few days the guards would come and call out a name, and that man would be taken out, briefly tried by a judge and then hanged. Nobody ever returned after their name had been called, nor were they ever heard from again. At dawn, it seemed, we could expect the guards to bring sustenance. "There is not much of it, and you must fight for every drop and morsel, as there will be no more until the same time next day," Michael warned me.

There was yet another unpleasantness in store for me—there was no provision for our waste. The prisoners, I learned, merely voided themselves where they sat, and after holding my bladder for most of the night, shamefully but with a sense of guilty relief, I followed their example and released my water to join the slurry that washed around my legs.

In the dirty gray light of dawn, I saw that the man to my left—the cougher—had died in the night. I bundled his corpse into the center of the cell without even thinking, and shifted my body to take advantage of the increase in space. I extended my long legs, and found them resting on the dead man's head. They were comfortable, and half out of the lake of filth, and I left them there, propped up on the cadaver. It had taken me less than a day, I thought ruefully, to discover the true savagery of my soul, a pitiful few hours to sink lower than a wild animal.

Soon after dawn, the guards entered the cell—two of them, crouching under the low ceiling with drawn swords, kicking the men's legs out of their path. One of them shouted behind him, through the opened door: "Two more for the river today," and a pair of ancient wretches in leather coifs and aprons came shambling into the cell to take the corpses away. Once the dead men had been cleared, and presumably dumped in the Seine, the two old men returned with big, rough wooden buckets slung over their shoulders on yokes—each bucket filled with a sloppy mixture of stale bread, watery soup and a little vinegary wine. As the guards retreated, we fell upon these four buckets like wolves upon newborn lambs; I got an elbow in the cheekbone, and returned it with a punch, but I got my head over a bucket and managed to scoop a handful of watery bread sops into my mouth, and a second and third one, too, before somebody hauled me by the shoulder away from the bucket and forced his head into the space that mine had so briefly occupied. I saw that it was the thief Michael, and allowed him to claim his share, as payment for taking the trouble to speak with me through the long night.

My thirst had only partially been assuaged by the time the buckets had been scraped clean. I retook my place against the wall, reflecting gloomily that if I did not get out of here soon I would not last long. On only a couple of mouthfuls of soggy bread a day, I would lose my strength in a few weeks. Then I would be the one to be plucked from the wall and beaten and kicked to death by a still-powerful newcomer.

The ancient yoke-men retrieved their empty wooden buckets an hour later, and all the prisoners settled down for the day. I dozed a little that morning myself, leaning against the wall, my buttocks and legs submerged in filth, and wondered what my friends were doing. Hanno and Thomas knew that I was in that stinking midden of death and I was certain that they would be striving to secure my release. There was still plenty of money at the Widow Barbette's house, if some sort of surety was needed, and surely if approached by Brother Michel or Sir Aymeric de St. Maur, or even by my squire Thomas, the Provost could be persuaded to set me free in exchange for a generous contribution to his private coffers.

At about noon, the door of the cell opened, and in the bright sunlight that flooded the dim cell, I could see the hulking shape of a man. He was tall and well-made with broad shoulders and a mane of dark hair, and he was not, as I had been, hurled down the steps by the jailers to sprawl onto the floor of the cell; he descended slowly, cautiously, on short, muscular legs. The door slammed behind him, but in the light from the barred window I could see his face clearly for the first time: unshaven with brutish features, cunning eyes, and several whitish scars around the jaw.

"That is Guillaume du Bois," Michael whispered in my ear. "I never thought they would take him alive: he is a bandit from the wild woods south of Paris, a killer, and the leader of a gang of cutthroats. He is a man to be feared."

This Guillaume stood, so far as he was able, in the center of the cell, his big head sunk on his shoulders and thrust forward, turning this way and that. He was scanning the faces in that dim place intently—he seemed to be looking for someone. His flat glaze slid over my face and moved on to Michael's beside me—and I heard my comrade draw in a quick frightened breath—but the big man's head carried on turning, as his questing continued. Then it stopped and his gaze returned along the line of faces against the wall—to me. He fixed his eyes on me and I stared straight back at him. I knew full well what was going to happen next.

"You," said Guillaume, in a rough, guttural accent that was barely French at all. "You are in my place."

And the big man reached down to his boot and pulled out a broad knife.

I had my legs underneath me by that point but I stopped myself from diving at him—he would have gutted me like a fish. Instead, I half-stood and took a step toward him—and swayed to the right just in time as his blade plunged toward my belly. His right arm passed through the space between my ribs and my left arm, and I clamped his forearm with my elbow against my waist, and curled my left hand around to grasp his upper arm—so trapping his right arm and knife immobile against my body. My right hand had been moving at the same time, and I plunged a hard index finger into his left eye, and felt a popping squelch that caused him to scream with rage and pain. He wrestled his knife arm free, and roaring, his left hand cupping his damaged eye, he slashed at me again with the blade, and I pulled back to avoid its slice. Then he stabbed again, lunging forward with his right leg, like a swordsman, and I moved with him, forward and left, dodging the strike, my weight on my right leg. I lifted my left leg chest high and stamped down as hard as I could on the inside of his forward right knee, pushing the joint outward, dislocating it with a brisk pop, and causing him to splash screaming to the cell floor, half-turned away from me. I punched down hard, using all the weight of my shoulders, and smashed my fist into the back of his neck. There was a muted crack and a bolt of agony shot up my wrist—but he flopped down face-first into the filth, and I was on him as fast as a hunting weasel. Both my knees crashed into his back, with my full weight behind them, pinning him to the cell floor. I punched him again, hard in the back of the neck—and then leaned my left forearm on the base of his skull, grabbed a handful of greasy hair with my right hand, and kept his face firmly pressed into the slurry on the floor. His knife was lost, but his arms flailed wildly about him as I bore down with my full strength, mashing his head into the six inches of liquid sewage that covered the stone floor. He wriggled and kicked, but I held him there. He gave one last desperate heave that nearly unseated me, but I kept my place, my fifteen stones of weight between his shoulder blades—and his mouth and nose below the stinking surface.

Finally, he moved no more.

When I was certain he was dead, I scrabbled around in the slurry and found the knife. Tucking it in belt, my chest still heaving, my right hand a blur of agony, I retook my place against the wall and offered up a long-overdue prayer to Almighty God, St. Michael and all the other saints who, between them, once again had preserved me from the wrath of my enemies.

The door crashed open; again light flooded the cell and two of the Provost's men-at-arms stood in the doorway.

"Which of you is Sir Alan Dale?" said one of the guards.

I lifted my aching right hand.

"You have been called," he said, looking at me doubtfully. "Will you come with us peacefully, or must we come down there and bind you?"

17

WHEN I STUMBLED OUT OF THAT cell, dripping, stinking, half-blinded by the daylight, I was astonished to find that the first person I saw was Roland d'Alle.

"Good day to you, cousin," he said.

I squinted at him, and then I saw that beyond this knight, who had just publicly acknowledged our kinship, were the familiar figures of Thomas and Hanno. The Bavarian was grinning like a gargoyle, and Thomas was frowning and holding out a large blue cloak for me to wear. I waved my young squire and his voluminous cloak away. And ignoring the insincere offer of a supporting arm from Roland, I walked, head high, out of the arched gates of the Grand Chastelet and a dozen yards to the right by the riverbank.

"Wait here," I said, and fumbling at the linen belt that secured my braies, and the ties that kept up my hose, I walked down the earthen bank and plunged into the river.

If I had spent a week in the Seine, scrubbing my body raw with soap and a stiff brush, I don't think I would have felt truly clean, but after I had removed shoes, hose, braies and chemise—and let them float away downstream, and splashed and washed as best I could in the cold, brownish water, I did feel a little better. And, wrapped in

Thomas's large cloak and naked as a baby underneath, I walked barefoot up the Rue St. Denis, and explained to Roland and my men what I thought had happened in the jail.

It all came out in a gabbling, barely intelligible rush, for I was feeling the mind-spinning effects now of my dance with Death. "It was another attempt to murder me—obviously. The 'man you cannot refuse,' the Master, or whatever you want to call him—my enemy—that bastard—he sent a bandit called Guillaume in there with orders to kill me. That fucking bastard. He had Fulk murdered to stop him helping me, then had me arrested, and while I was in that hellish hole, he sent in a man to kill me, with a fucking knife. Of course he did. The cunning bastard. And if he killed Fulk, it means that Fulk's theory about the Grail is correct. It must be right. Don't you see, it must be!"

"The what?" said Roland. Thomas and Hanno were looking puzzled, too. And I realized that I had not yet had the chance to explain poor Master Fulk's idea to them.

I took a deep breath. "Never mind about that for the moment," I said. "How did you get me out of there?"

"When we saw where they had taken you, we went first of all to the episcopal palace to enlist Brother Michel's help," said Thomas. "But he was not there—the servants said that he had been suddenly called away that morning to the Abbey of St. Victor to attend Bishop de Sully."

"So then they came to see me," said Roland cheerfully. "The Seigneur called on the Provost of Paris—they are old friends, of course—they had a quiet chat, a little silver changed hands, and the Provost dispatched me with a docket for your release. Quite simple really."

"I am most grateful to you . . . cousin," I said.

And I was. Roland and his father had pulled me out of that stinking hell of a jail; they had undoubtedly saved my life—and for that I would be forever in their debt.

We arrived soon enough at the Seigneur's big house, and I had no sooner washed myself thoroughly again, and finished dressing in Roland's spare clothes, when the Lady d'Alle came in. We were in

Roland's small chamber at the top of the building, and I had been telling an admiring audience of Hanno, Thomas and Roland how I had defeated Guillaume with my bare fists, when the lady of the house entered. "Are you well, Alan?" she said, full of concern. She was even lovelier than I had remembered.

I told her I was unharmed—and did not bother to mention that I feared I had broken the third finger on my right hand, which Hanno had strapped tightly to the little one beside it.

"Such an awful place; such awful people—it is a miracle that you survived it."

"It might appear so, my lady," I said. "But it was in truth a miracle wrought by your family."

There was a slight pause, and the lady said: "The Seigneur has asked me to tell you that he would very much like to speak with you downstairs when you are fully restored to your comforts."

"I will be down directly," I said. "But first I would like to have a word with you in private, if I may be so bold."

When Hanno, Thomas and Roland had left the room, I said: "My lady, I owe you an apology. When you told me about your, um, friendship with my father, I confess I was angry with you. But I now see that I was wrong: love is a strange madness, sometimes a curse, sometimes a blessing, but it is not ours to command. I also believe that it is an affliction that comes from God and His son Jesus Christ, and so must be honored even when it seems destructive."

"Do you forgive me, then?"

"With all my heart," I said, and she stepped forward and took my hands in hers.

I could see that her eyes were wet, but she smiled at me and said: "Then all is well."

The Seigneur greeted me gruffly, self-consciously in the downstairs chamber and gave me a cup of wine and began reciting a little speech that he had obviously spent some time preparing.

"I think you are an honorable man, Sir Alan," he began, staring hard at the floor between us. "And doubtless a brave and puissant knight. And I do not believe that you seek anything from my family except that which you demanded at our last meeting. I apologize for my rudeness—I was . . . in a bad humor, and suspicious of your intentions, but by your conduct then and since, I am satisfied that you mean me and the members of my family no harm. Therefore I must say this . . ." He cleared his throat, and lifted his gaze to my face.

"I formally acknowledge you as my nephew, the son of my brother Henri, whom I once loved. And while you are in Paris under a flag of truce you are also under my personal protection." He gave me a small, chilly smile before continuing: "But, as God is my witness, you are also an enemy, a knight who is bound to King Richard, the mortal foe of my King, and if there comes a day when this truce is over and we must face each other on the battlefield, on that day I shall treat you as I would any other enemy knight. Is that understood?"

"I understand, sir," I said.

"But until that sad day arrives, nephew, you are a welcome guest in my house." And the old warrior almost crushed my chest as he embraced me in his powerful arms.

We dined together then, the Seigneur, Roland, Adèle and myself—and I told them a little of my father's life in England, and of his death, and I recounted my quest so far to find the "man you cannot refuse." The Seigneur became grave when I mentioned the name of my enemy. "I have heard of this man," my uncle said. "I have heard the Provost speak of someone who goes by that ugly title. He is said to have the wealth of Crassus and to command the loyalty of a number of gangs of bandits and thieves in the wild lands in the south of the Île de France."

"The man I killed in the Grand Chastelet—Guillaume du Bois—he was one such bandit," I said. Uncle Thibault's information seemed to confirm what I had suspected: that the "man you cannot refuse" had sent Guillaume into that stinking cell with specific orders to kill me.

"There are other stories about this 'man you cannot refuse'—strange tales that tell of his possession of a magical relic that makes him all-powerful, impervious to death, impossible to kill," said the Seigneur, "although I doubt there is any truth in them."

"I am not so sure," I said. "A friend of mine, now with God and the angels, suggested something similar recently."

"I can easily see why he has claimed that title: the 'man you cannot refuse,'" said Roland. "It is rather dashing—mysterious, commanding, awe-inspiring . . . And with the degree of wealth that he is rumored to have, he could buy whatever he wishes, or if his demands were ignored, enforce his will with his bandit-rascals or these knightly assassins that you spoke of before. Truly he is a 'man you cannot refuse.' And having a supernatural gewgaw only adds to the impression of awe he is trying to create, I suppose."

"So what will you do next?" asked Adèle, fixing me with her lovely green eyes. As she spoke to me, I could see the Seigneur gazing at her with quiet, complete adoration.

"Well, I must speak with Bishop de Sully—no matter how enfeebled he is. And so I will be visiting the Abbey of St. Victor as soon as I can arrange it."

"If there is any way in which I can be of assistance—I have a handful of loyal men-at-arms, a little money, some useful connections . . . ," said the Seigneur.

I smiled at my uncle. "That is most kind, sir," I said. "And I thank you for your offer from the bottom of my heart. But I am merely planning to pay a brief visit to a sick old man."

There are some decisions that a man makes which he must live with, for good or ill, for the rest of his life. One such was my decision to take Hanno with me when we set off two days later, for the Abbey of St. Victor. It was early morning when we left, and Hanno had come home late the night before after visiting his alewife, and he was sleepy and more than a little hungover on that fateful morn. For a few moments, I considered leaving him behind with Thomas at the Widow Barbette's house, and going alone to St. Victor's. A part of me said that I was merely going to see an invalid—and what need could I possibly have of a bodyguard in a House of God? Another part of me whispered that there had been three attempts on my life in the past three months, and the "man you cannot refuse," if he discovered my plans, might well try to prevent me meeting the venerable Bishop. In the end, I waited while he had splashed his face, drunk a pint of watered ale and collected his weapons, and we rode off together. It was a decision I have weighed many times since then.

We headed southeast, just Hanno and myself, he on his palfrey, I on my courser, making our way along the southern bank of the River Bièvre beyond the boundaries of Paris for less than a mile until we came to the high walls and stout gates of the abbey. It was quiet and deeply peaceful out there, away from the bustle of the city streets and, as the fields outside the abbey walls had been carefully cultivated by the canons over many years and sown with homely cabbages and leeks and onions, the whole area had a sleepy, village-like feel.

We told the porter at the gate, a half-deaf canon who must have been eighty or even older, that we had come from the cathedral of Notre-Dame with an urgent message from the Dean for Bishop de Sully. As I had hoped, it was enough to get us inside the gates and the old man pointed out a path to follow that would lead us to the south of the abbey, where the Bishop had his apartments.

The abbey sprawled over a very large area; it had almost as wide a precinct as the Paris Temple, though of course it was much older, and had filled the space within its walls with dozens of stone buildings, including a huge abbey church in the center, as well as scores of humbler wooden constructions. And inside the high walls, it was as busy as a small market town, and nearly as populous. Wide roads drove through the abbey in a cross-shaped formation, meeting at the center, and were trod by canons, scholars, merchants, workmen and men-at-arms; several well-laden carts clopped along these thoroughfares too and a haze of dust hovered above them in shifting brown clouds.

To the north of the abbey, where the River Bièvre flowed toward the Seine, there was a broad wooden dock and two large ships were moored there unloading and loading goods. Clearly the abbey was rich—and I could assume that old Bishop de Sully would not lack for material comforts in his final days.

The Bishop's lavish apartments, we were told by a passing canon, were tucked away in a secluded corner behind the abbey church: they comprised a large stone house on two stories, with outbuildings, a kitchen, a bakery, a private chapel for the Bishop's use, and a big, square walled herb garden where food and medicines might be grown, which was surrounded by a well-swept path paved with flat yellow stones.

At the simple wooden gate of the garden, we were stopped by a servant, an old man, who demanded to know our business with the Bishop. Once again I lied and said that I came from the Dean of Notre-Dame with a message, and we were admitted, without further questioning. I was dressed in my finest clothes, a new silk tunic with a velvet-trimmed mantel, mounted on a fine horse and accompanied by an armed attendant—so I was clearly a knight and a man of consequence—but it was nonetheless surprisingly easy to obtain access to the most powerful man in Paris after the King.

We left the horses tied to a stunted apple tree outside the garden, and Hanno and I pushed through the simple wicket gate. Bishop Maurice de Sully was sitting on a low stone bench in a patch of September sun with a bowl of cut thyme in his lap and he was carefully separating the tiny green leaves from the spindly stalks. He looked truly ill, thin and worn; his gray hair sparse, his face deeply cut with the marks of long years and hard struggles. He was perhaps seventy, I guessed, and in no little amount of pain. The heavenly smell of crushed thyme—fresh, woody and sweet—filled the air of the herb garden.

As we made our way over to the Bishop, I glanced around that square open space, admiring the blocks of plants arranged in the center in neat geometrical patterns, and I noticed a figure in a dark robe on the far side, just leaving the garden and entering an outbuilding.

He was a tall man and although he was turned away from me, and I glimpsed him for only a moment, there was something about the way he moved that stirred my memory.

"Your Grace," said the servant, and Bishop de Sully glanced up from the thyme bowl. "I humbly beg your pardon for disturbing you, but this gentleman says he has a message from the Dean; he says—"

"Your Grace, I must speak to you about a very urgent and private matter," I interrupted, and Maurice de Sully looked directly at me for the first time. He had pale, almost colorless eyes and seemed wary, even rather alarmed at my words.

I hastened to reassure him: "I mean you no harm, Your Grace," I said, "and I admit I lied to your servant about a message from the Dean. But I have a great need to speak with you about my father, Henri d'Alle, who was once a monk here in Paris. I only wish to trouble you for a few moments and then I will gladly leave you in peace."

That was true: I had told the Seigneur that I would dine with him and his family that day, and had sworn to be at the Rue St. Denis by noon for the feast. The servant, a slight, elderly man, was now looking between Hanno and myself, his mouth working soundlessly, his arms waggling jerkily from the shoulders: he seemed not to know whether he should make an attempt to lay hands on us and forcibly eject us from the Bishop's presence. He hesitated, flapping like a bird, torn between fear and his duty to his master.

"It is quite all right, Alban," said the Bishop to his man. "Calm yourself. Please be so good as to go and fetch us some wine, and perhaps a little bread and cheese." Then to me: "Be seated, young man, here, sit beside me, and tell me how I might be of service to you."

The Bishop put the bowl of thyme down on the warm yellow slabs at his feet, and I took a seat beside him on the stone bench. Hanno stood behind me, his back leaning comfortably against the sun-warmed bricks of the garden wall, alert and yet relaxed at the same time.

"I have an ailment of the stomach," the Bishop said. "It discomforts me a good deal and my new doctor—a Jewish fellow, but very well regarded among the brotherhood of physicians—advises that I drink an infusion of honey and thyme every night. I pick the herb myself each morning, and tell my servants that it is part of the cure but, in truth, I come here mostly so that I may be alone with my thoughts for a while. So you have chosen a good time to speak to me, my son—we will not be disturbed. You said that this matter concerned your father, yes?"

"Do you remember him, Your Grace? Henri d'Alle; a singer in the cathedral twenty years ago, a tall, blond man who I'm told has a good deal of resemblance to me?"

De Sully looked closely at me, his pale eyes crawling over my face, and then let out a long heavy breath. "Yes," he said, "oh yes, I remember Henri d'Alle. And I see him in you. I remember well the manner of his leaving us, too—I may be old and not in the best of health, but my recall is still reliable."

"Would you be so kind as to tell me the circumstances leading up to his departure from the cathedral . . ."

The Bishop picked up his bowl of thyme and began plucking the leaves from the stalks again as he spoke, his white fingers and thumbs moving with speed and delicacy to strip off the tiny green rounds from the woody stalks.

"Henri was not comfortable being a monk," he began. "I don't think it was his true calling; I think God did not mean him for that, although He had endowed him with an exceptionally fine voice. Your father was, I recall, unruly and disobedient—and I think lecherous, too. I know that the Dean was forced to discipline him on a number of occasions for minor transgressions. Having said that, I believe he was a good man and a true Christian."

The Bishop paused for a moment, and put down the bowl of thyme again. He laid an almost translucent, blue-veined hand, blotched here and there with the brown spots of old age, along his cheek, remembering. "The visit of Bishop Heribert, God rest his soul, was a grand affair—it must have been in the thirty-sixth year of the reign of King Louis, oh, twenty-one years ago—it smacked of rather too much pomp and ceremony for my liking, but Heribert came from a powerful family in the south, and his wealth allowed him to make an occasion of his visit—and he was an important man, after all, a bishop, one mustn't forget that. His money also allowed him to indulge his two great passions in life: Heavenly music and holy relics.

"He came to Paris to hear the monks of Notre-Dame sing—your father being one of the leading choristers at the time—and I believe he found the experience rewarding. He spent many hours in the old cathedral listening to the holy offices being sung—and in my grand new cathedral, too, though in those days only the choir had been built and it was hellishly cold in wintertime. But while he was in Paris he also purchased a sacred relic—I think it was supposed to be a toe bone of John the Baptist—from a trader in such items and he had it mounted in a beautiful golden reliquary with a crystal top and sides, so that the bone could be viewed—and venerated. He had a collection of such pieces—a hair from Christ's beard, the dried arm of St. Gregory of Tours, and as many as four fragments of the True Cross—and he took them with him wherever he traveled, which I thought foolish. Indeed, so it proved to be.

"I am afraid that I am somewhat wary of relics—perhaps it is a foible of my upbringing, or perhaps I merely lack the proper amount of faith—you young people all seem to be very keen on them and rush to pray before them whenever they are revealed, but I have always felt that, while there are undoubtedly some genuine relics, which do indeed have tremendous spiritual power, there are also a goodly number of charlatans offering items for sale that are no more than midden-fodder in a golden box. I have twice personally been shown a scrap of dried leather that was claimed—each time in earnest by a most pious and respected high churchman—to be the foreskin of Christ. And yet there is nothing in the Holy scriptures about Our Lord being so unusually endowed as to require two circumcisions!" The Bishop gave a dry chuckle—but Hanno shifted uneasily behind me and when I turned to glance at him I swear that tough old Bavarian warrior looked deeply shocked by the Bishop's crude words.

"And so, when Heribert showed me his newly acquired holy toe at dinner one day, I was not as awestruck as perhaps I might have been. The good Bishop sensed this and my indifference to it seemed to make him desperate to impress me with the sacred grandeur of his collection. He mentioned this item and that, and extolled the special powers of this object and the rarity of another—I am afraid he did not command my full attention. And while, God knows, I tried to show the proper enthusiasm for his collection of old rags and bones, I was not successful. And eventually Heribert became quiet and sulky, and spent the rest of the meal indulging his prodigious appetite.

"I regretted it the next day, of course, for that same night someone broke into the storeroom where the Bishop's possessions were kept, and the thief made away with several of his much-vaunted relics—and it was the ones that were closest to his heart that were taken."

"Do you remember which particular relics were stolen?" I asked, interrupting the old man for the first time.

"Yes I do," he said, looking at me with his colorless eyes. "He was reluctant to tell me at first, but I pressed him and it all came flooding out eventually."

"And what were they?" I asked. I could feel my pulse beating faster; a bead of sweat ran down my spine.

"They were the most preposterous cluster of costly rubbish imaginable: a silver carving plate, a pair of golden candlesticks, an old lance head, and something he called a '*graal*,' a sort of serving bowl. I never fathomed the significance of the carving plate and the candlesticks, though Heribert claimed they had vague miraculous qualities—but the lance head, he told me, came from the weapon that a Roman soldier used to pierce the side of Our Lord Jesus Christ while he suffered on the Cross—and this *graal*, well, that was the vessel that Christ used at the Last Supper and also, rather conveniently, I must say, it was the vessel used by Joseph of Arimathea to collect the blood of Christ after he had been cut down from the tree at Calvary."

Despite the Bishop's dismissive, almost blasphemous tone, I felt a jolt of lightning run down my spine at his words. This *graal*, this

Grail—if it were indeed the true artifact—was claimed to be the very bowl that Christ had used and drunk from and blessed with the touch of his hands; and as if that weren't enough, it had held his sacred blood! If it were real, I could scarcely imagine an object more worthy of deep veneration. This Grail had held the sacred blood of Our Lord, it had cradled the life fluid of God himself! To those who believed, it was indeed a wondrous object—that would be well worth killing for. Indeed, for some, it would be worth dying for. It was without a doubt the holiest thing that I had ever heard of.

I pulled myself together and dampened my excitement—though I noticed that Hanno had stepped a little closer, to listen, and that his face seemed to be all eyes. Then I asked the question that had been nagging at the back of my mind. "Who else was at this dinner when Bishop Heribert spoke so eloquently of his collection of holy relics?"

"No one—it was just Heribert and me. And the duty monks who served the meal, of course."

"And my father, Henri d'Alle, was he one of the monks who served at the dinner table that day?"

"He was—him and some of his young friends had been chosen to serve. I don't recall exactly. It was one dull meal, with a dull, greedy, credulous fool, twenty-one years ago."

"Do you believe that my father was the man who stole this *graal*?" My question came out flat and heavy, like a sheet of lead being dropped on wet turf. At first I thought that Bishop de Sully would not answer me, so lengthy was the pause between my question and his response.

"A bishop must be a man of God, a devout follower of Christ's teachings," said de Sully, "and as such, I shall answer you truthfully: no, I do not now believe that Henri d'Alle stole any of Heribert's ludicrous collection of relics. But a bishop is also a lord of men, and a power in the land, and sometimes it is necessary to do things that a good Christian would not normally countenance. I shall answer to God for my actions, of course, but at that time I deemed that it was necessary for your father to shoulder the blame for that crime. I was not certain of his innocence, I may even have convinced myself of his guilt at the time; but I knew that I needed Heribert's goodwill. And Heribert demanded a scapegoat for his loss. You must understand that the Bishop of Roda was a very wealthy man, absurdly wealthy, and he had agreed to make a vast contribution to the building of the cathedral, to Notre-Dame, to my life's work. I decided that the building of a sacred monument to God's greatness, a sublime edifice that would proclaim the glory of Our Lord, which would stand as a testament to the Christian faith for a thousand years—I decided that this work was more important than the continued employment of a young monk who did not have a true vocation for a life in the Church. Would you have made a different decision? I think not. So I sent Henri d'Alle away—he was not punished for the crime; he was asked to leave Notre-Dame and make his way elsewhere in the world. And, as I say, God will judge me for this, but I think not harshly."

"You are mistaken," I said, rising to my feet. "Henri d'Alle was punished—he paid for that crime, a crime he did not commit, with his life. He was put to death by someone who calls himself the 'man you cannot refuse' because he was innocent. He was innocent and this 'man you cannot refuse' was guilty, and was attempting to keep his guilt a secret. Your negligence in seeking out the true perpetrator of the crime led indirectly to my father's death!"

I found I was jabbing my index finger at Bishop de Sully, my voice rough and barely quieter than a shout. De Sully looked up at me as I ranted at him, his mouth open in surprise and showing his few remaining teeth. All the authority seemed to have gone from him and I recognized, quite suddenly, how old and tired and sick he was, and dropped my arm, feeling ashamed.

"Peace, my friend, peace," said a familiar voice behind me, "this garden is meant as a haven of tranquility." And I turned to see Brother Michel standing behind me, smiling serenely, his arms folded across his belly, his hands tucked into the opposite sleeves of his simple habit. Beside him stood the servant Alban, astonished at my rudeness, but bearing a tray of wine and cheese. "It is time, Your Grace, for your nap," said Brother Michel in a soothing voice. The sun was approaching the meridian.

"But I must explain to this boy, I must tell him . . . ," quavered the Bishop.

Brother Michel smoothly interrupted him: "You know what the new doctor has said about complete rest, Your Grace—and you may talk again with Sir Alan later. Perhaps this evening. Perhaps we can even persuade him to stay with us for a while."

The Bishop nodded, and got obediently to his feet and began meekly to walk toward the corner of the garden and the house, shepherded by Brother Michel with his right arm around his shoulders.

I said: "Your Grace, I cannot stay, I am afraid—but I would ask one more question, if I may: do you have any idea of the identity—"

But the monk turned his head back to me: "Be patient, Sir Alan, I beg you—refresh yourself: eat, drink, and I shall be with you very shortly. Then we can discuss the right time to arrange another interview with His Grace." And then he caught sight of the bowl of thyme that the Bishop had left on the stone pathway. "We mustn't forget your medicine," said Brother Michel, and he took two steps back toward us and reached down with his left hand to pick up the fragrant clay bowl.

I looked at his hand as it descended, grasped the bowl and picked it up, and it was all I could do to prevent myself from crying aloud in surprise. In a blinding flash, I knew the identity of the "man you cannot refuse"—for I saw with a sense of chill horror that the left hand, which Brother Michel had used to collect the bowl of thyme, had two tiny thumbs, each perfectly formed and sprouting from a single thick root.

18

AS BROTHER MICHEL AND THE BISHOP walked away toward the big stone house, it took all my self-discipline to turn to the servant and say: "Just set the tray there, please, and leave us in peace for a few moments." And while Alban, the serving man, slowly walked away, shaking his head at the foolishness of his betters, I whispered to Hanno: "We must go, now; we must leave immediately." So many pieces of the puzzle had suddenly fallen into place that my head was reeling. I had to find somewhere safe and quiet to think. "We must get out of here, right now!"

Hanno did not argue. As soon as the servant had disappeared into one of the outbuildings, we began to saunter casually toward the gate in the garden wall, and the waiting horses, not hurrying, certainly not running.

"Why do we go?" said Hanno quietly.

"Brother Michel is the 'man you cannot refuse,'" I said. "I am certain of it. He was a friend of my father's when they were at Notre-Dame together, and he is the one who stole the relics from Bishop Heribert. He is the one who has been killing clerics, or rather ordering their deaths, and he is the one who's been trying to kill me these past months."

Hanno stopped. "Maybe I just go and kill him now." We were a dozen paces from the garden gate, and before I could answer, it swung open and a tall knight strode into the walled garden: it was Sir Eustace de la Falaise, the dull, cheery Templar I had last seen with Sir Aymeric de St. Maur in the Order's compound north of the city.

He was not alone.

Behind Sir Eustace came a file of men-at-arms; half a dozen men each carrying a loaded crossbow—and pointing it at Hanno and myself. But it was not the sight of so many men aiming their weapons at my unarmored body that gave me pause—it was the clothing that they wore. Each man, including Sir Eustace, wore a white linen surcoat with a shield depicted on the chest: a blue cross on a white field with a black border.

They led us out of the garden, in silence, through the house and out the other side—the crossbowmen keeping their weapons trained on us at all times. I knew that it was useless to protest, and the slightest wrong move would leave us lying pierced and bleeding on the ground. We were ushered by Sir Eustace into a private chapel beyond the Bishop's palace, near the abbey wall, and made to stand with our hands in the air while the men-at-arms appropriated all our weapons, even the dagger Hanno hid in his boot-top. The men-at-arms stripped us down to our under-chemise and braies and tied us tightly to two heavy, high-backed oak chairs by the wrists, waist and ankles. Sir Eustace checked the ropes, then without a word they all filed out of the chapel, leaving us bound and helpless, in that House of God. Alone in the chapel, both Hanno and myself spent a futile few moments struggling against our bonds, and both discovered that we were well secured. I raised my eyebrows at him, and he gave me a half-shrug—there was nothing to say—and so we waited in silence, contemplating our surroundings and our likely fate.

The chapel was small but stone-built, with the main door set in an arch at the western end, a font in the center of the space and a large altar at the eastern end. On the altar was a huge golden cross, and set before that was a wooden box, slightly larger than a foot square, nestled on a vast purple velvet cushion. The box was of dark brown wood, polished with beeswax, and seemed to be the center of veneration on the altar. Beyond the altar, in the northeastern corner of the chapel, I saw a wooden door, perhaps a discreet entrance for the priest, perhaps leading to a vestry or storeroom of some kind.

The rest of the chapel was sparsely furnished, a couple of benches pushed up against the far wall and the two impressive chairs that held Hanno and I captive—but it was filled with the most marvelous light, shafts of red, brown, blue and green, which streamed through a large stained-glass window directly opposite our chairs, in the southern wall of the chapel. The window occupied almost all the wall before our eyes, beginning perhaps four feet from the ground and soaring up to the high domed roof of the chapel sixteen feet above. It was about four feet wide and constructed of small colored panes of glass held in place between delicate strips of lead. Perhaps inevitably, it depicted an image of Our Lady, cradling the infant Jesus and looking with deep compassion at the miserable mortal sinners huddled at her feet. It was breathtakingly beautiful, a masterpiece of light and colors; a true visual treasure. And I found that I could not look away. As the hours passed and the sunlight shifted, I grew mesmerized by that exquisite colored image of Our Lady; I prayed to her, asking for her to intercede with Almighty God for my sins—for I felt certain that I would soon be meeting the Lord—and I vowed that I would be a better man if I managed to survive this encounter with the three-thumbed "man you cannot refuse." I do not know if I slept or dreamed, but as time passed the face of Our Lady seemed to change—and began to resemble Goody, my beloved. I realized that I had not seen her in so many months, and I felt the absence like a void in my soul. A part of me wished that, instead of coming to Paris to track down this evil man who had ordered my father's death, I had instead forsworn vengeance and gone home to Goody. Perhaps Robin had been right: if I had been content to let the matter lie, I might now be in Goody's arms instead of anticipating my death like a bound pig awaiting the November slaughter, in a foreign land far from all those whom I loved.

After three or perhaps four hours, Sir Eustace entered the chapel by the big door to my right. He stood in front of us, still wearing his amiable idiot's grin, but his eyes, I noted, were cold black shards in his handsome face. His hand toyed with something that hung from the right-hand side of his belt.

"You are a persistent fellow, Alan Dale," he said. These were the first words that he had uttered since capturing us in the garden. "Persistent even for a gutter-born busybody who can't keep his nose out of better men's affairs."

I said nothing but looked down at the object he was toying with at his belt. It was a weapon of some kind, unlike any I'd ever come across. A wooden handle in the shape of the capital letter T protruded from a broad leather scabbard about eight inches long. His blunt fingers stroked the horizontal crosspiece of the handle as he spoke.

"You were warned to leave well alone, and by your liege lord, no less, your superior before God, but you refused to listen to him," he said, his words humming with anger. And I thought: *Robin—he knows that Robin told me to drop my inquiries. This angry moron and the three-thumbed freak, and the rest of the murderous Knights of Our Lady, are all acquainted with Robin, and their relationship is such that they can ask Robin to tell me not to investigate my father's death.* A cold, black pit opened up in my stomach. But Sir Eustace was still speaking.

"You were thoroughly warned, but you would not let it pass; and now we have all had enough of your meddling. You are a hard man to kill, I give you that, Dale, and you have the luck of the Devil in battle; but today your luck has run out. Today is the day that you will die. Today you will see the face of God."

Sir Eustace paused, and took a gulp of air; he had worked himself up into some sort of state, and was trying unsuccessfully to control himself. When he spoke again it was in short panting breaths. "But you are blessed, too; more blessed than you deserve or than you can imagine. Your death will be swift and painless; and your Salvation will be assured."

He stopped. I said nothing, but Hanno then spoke.

"You talk too much," said my bold Bavarian. "When you have some killing to do, you don't talk—you kill. Only a fool talks before he strikes. But you, you are a talking fool. Talk, talk, talk. I will tell you this for nothing, talky fool: you threaten us, you'd better kill us good while you have the chance, because when I get out of this God-damned chair, I am going to rip out your cowardly liver and choke you with it. That will stop your talky mouth!"

The fury on Sir Eustace's face was now obvious: he pulled out the strange weapon from its sheath and brandished it in front of our faces. "You see this, you sacrilegious scum! You see this"—he was shouting, and I felt a speck of his hot spittle graze my cheek. I stared at his weapon; truly I had never seen its like before. It was the head of a broad-headed lance, an elongated diamond shape about two inches across at its widest point and tapering to a wicked needle tip. The iron of the lance head looked ancient, pitted here and there, but had clearly been well cared for and burnished brightly. In the socket where the long shaft would once have been fitted was a stubby wooden T-shaped handle, approximately four inches long, fitting snugly. Sir Eustace gripped the wooden crossbar in his palm, and made a fist, so that the lance head protruded from between his second and third fingers.

"You see this!" Sir Eustace bellowed, his words again accompanied by a storm of spittle. "This is the instrument of your deaths. And while you are not worthy to even look at it, by the mercy of the Blessed Virgin, and her son Our Lord, you shall receive death from it; and solely because of its sacred power, you shall be received into Heaven. This is the Holy Lance that pierced Our Savior's body on the Cross; this blade has been anointed with the blood of Our Lord Jesus Christ! Christ's holy blood . . ."

Eustace had a light froth around his mouth now; his black eyes gleamed with madness. And while I stared mutely in hopeless fascination at the extraordinary object in my enemy's hand, Hanno spoke.

"Talk, talk, talk . . . ," he said. "That is all you can do, you talky fool . . ."

Sir Eustace took two steps toward Hanno, his right fist lashed out like a bolt of lightning, and he punched the lance-dagger deep into Hanno's chest. It was a single thrust, snake-fast and perfectly accurate, an inch to the left of the sternum, directly into my friend's living heart.

I heard the door opening to my left, and a voice from the east end of the chapel shouting: "Eustace, no! I told you to leave them be!"

Sir Eustace stepped back, ripping the bloody lance-dagger free of Hanno's punctured chest. Thick dark blood was bubbling from the wound. And I twisted my head to stare into my old friend's eyes as he died. There was a slight smile on his lips, and he managed to utter one word, just a whisper, before his eyes rolled and he slumped unstrung against his bonds.

The word was: "Perfect!"

Something of myself died with Hanno that day. And the memory of his ugly, battered face and his proud final word still makes my eyes prick and burn four decades later. But I console myself by thinking that Hanno died happy: no sane man wishes to die, but many a warrior I have known has spoken to me of the manner in which he would prefer to depart this earth. Usually, these men say "in battle, with a ring of enemy slain around me, like the heroes of old" or something similar; but I think Hanno—who always strived for perfection in everything, and especially in the arts of war—would not have been dissatisfied by the manner of his passing. He was killed by a skilled enemy; by a man who must have made a considerable study of the perfect way to kill. I think that perhaps Hanno was content to die at his hand, and may even have provoked him for that very purpose. But I pray that Sir Eustace was right, and that the Holy Lance did indeed have the power to confer entry into Heaven with its lethal punch. I also silently vowed that I would split Eustace's cowardly heart one day, if God gave me the opportunity, and look in his eye while he died.

Those were not my uppermost thoughts at the time, however. I was more concerned with my own demise. Sir Eustace stood before me as I sat there bound and helpless, the dripping lance-dagger in his hand and a killing gleam in his mad black eyes. He was breathing heavily, like a man who had just run a race. And I was certain that nothing would restrain him from plunging that blade into my breast.

The voice spoke again, nearer this time. "Eustace, command yourself! You will step away from Sir Alan."

I wrenched my gaze away from the madman in front of me and glanced left toward the chapel door. Brother Michel was approaching fast, his sandals slapping the stone floor of the chapel like brisk applause. But it was the man walking beside him, a tall dark man in a long black robe, who made me gape in surprise. It was the man whom I had glimpsed in the garden, and the same man I had seen lurking round and about me in the streets of Paris.

It was my old friend and comrade Reuben of York.

I was dimly aware that a dozen men wearing the white linen surcoat of the Knights of Our Lady had filed into the chapel behind these two men, but my eyes were locked on Reuben's dark face. Was he friend or foe? What was he—a Jew—doing in this Christian abbey? And why had he been following me so relentlessly through the Paris streets?

Brother Michel stepped forward and placed his hands on the shoulders of Sir Eustace—and I could not help but stare in horrified fascination at the twin thumbs on his left hand. Brother Michel was oblivious to me; he was murmuring quietly to Eustace and eventually he turned him and led him away from my chair to a dim corner of the chapel, where he began speaking to him urgently and yet rhythmically, the half-heard drone of his voice oddly soothing. I pulled my attention back to Reuben, standing before me, smiling sadly—his kindly brown face a little more worn, his dark hair now streaked with threads of gray—he looked far older than the last time I had seen him in the Holy Land. But I took comfort from his presence and from his first words:

"I imagine that you must have many questions, Alan, my friend, but for the moment, keep your silence, I beg you, and know that I am here as Robin's representative, and that I speak for him. I am so very sorry that I could not save Hanno—but I swear that, if it is in my power, I will not allow any harm to come to you. Hold your tongue and husband your courage, and we will see what can be salvaged from this situation."

"Cut me free, Reuben, and give me a weapon," I said, glancing at Hanno's corpse, still slumped gorily against the restraining ropes, and my own voice sounded thick and clogged. I had it in my mind that I would kill Sir Eustace without delay—and Brother Michel too, if I could manage it—before the assembled Knights of Our Lady, now standing quietly and watching us from the shadows of the chapel, cut me down.

"Alas, Alan, I cannot do that yet," said Reuben. "I have told Brother Michel, in the most forceful terms, that killing you would certainly bring the wrath of the Earl of Locksley, and all his considerable might, down on his Order, ensuring its destruction, and possibly Robin's too—and he has agreed to discuss the matter with me. But I cannot cut you free, not yet. Be patient."

"What are you doing here?" I was still quite astonished to see him in front of me.

"I am Bishop de Sully's esteemed new doctor—I have been for three days now. But I fear that the poor man is slowly dying. The Crab is in his stomach, and he may last another year, maybe two at best. There is nothing I can do but make him as comfortable as I can."

"I don't care about de Sully. I mean, what are you doing here in Paris?"

"Robin summoned me from Montpellier and sent me here to watch over you—but no more questions now, Alan. Stay silent and allow me to see whether I can extricate us from this predicament."

Over his shoulder I could see Brother Michel striding toward us, his handsome face serene. I was suddenly struck by something that had been in the back of my mind since I had first met him: he resembled Robin. But the resemblance was not one of flesh and bones, or in the angle of eye or mouth, but rather he had that air about him of invisible power and utter, iron-cast confidence, the conviction that whatever task he was about, however wrong it might appear to lesser men, it was the right thing to do because he was doing it. I had the bizarre sensation that if he ordered something, anything, I would obey him.

"I fear you have upset poor Sir Eustace," he said.

I opened my mouth to reply, but caught Reuben's eye and shut it with a snap.

"I think perhaps it would be best," said Reuben, "if we all considered our positions in a calm and reasonable manner. First of all, let us have poor Hanno taken away for burial, and let us release Alan from his bonds, and then perhaps we could discuss this over a glass of wine."

"He stays there," Brother Michel said quietly. "Sir Alan is a formidable man, even unarmed—I am told he dispatched my Guillaume, an iron-hard fellow and skilled with a knife, in a matter of moments. Sir Alan, I'm afraid, must remain bound till we have determined his fate."

"But my dear Brother Michel . . . ," Reuben began in a soothing tone.

"You may call me Master—Jew. I am the Master of the Order of the Poor Fellow-Soldiers of Our Lady and the Temple of Solomon." The monk's voice was icy, and he drew himself up to his full height and made a bold gesture with his right hand behind him to the exquisite stained-glass window. "I serve the Queen of Heaven, the Blessed Virgin Mary, Mother of Our Lord Jesus Christ. And, knowing this, Jew, you will accord me the appropriate honor to my station and address me as Master!"

"Very well, 'Master' it shall be," said Reuben, with a wide agreeable smile. "Now, Master, could we perhaps—"

"You fought in Spain," I said, looking directly at Brother Michel. It was somehow hard to look at him, as if he were a bright and shining light that burned my eyes. Of course, it came from the low sun shining through the magnificent window behind him, but still its glare was painful and I closed my eyes and continued: "And you scrambled to the top of the dung pile, to the title of Master, over the bodies of your comrades. Even when they disbanded the Order, you kept it alive, in secret; a handful of knights at first, and then more, younger ones, men who wished to serve God with their swords but would never have been accepted as true Templars."

"You are insolent, my friend, but not inaccurate—do you think knowledge will help to save your life? Keep talking and we shall see. What else do you know?"

I opened my eyes and squinted at him through the harsh light. "I know that my father protected you from bullies at Notre-Dame and that you repaid his kindness by blackening his name and allowing him to take the blame for your crime against Bishop Heribert. I know that you are Trois Pouces!"

The superior smile on the Master's face was wiped away by my words. He tucked his hands across his chest, back into their habitual position in the sleeves of his robe, and stared at me stone-faced.

"I have not been called that for a long, long time," he said slowly. "And were it not for the dire threats that this Jew has made to me on behalf of the Earl of Locksley, I would kill you now, this very instant, for those words."

He paused for a few moments, and I caught Reuben's eye. He was frowning at me, glaring and shaking his head—it was almost comical. Then Brother Michel said: "But God has taught us that to lie is a sin, any lie, and indeed I must own my actions. Yes, I did steal from Bishop Heribert, and yes, I did allow your father to take the blame for my crime, and yes, I did order his death at the hands of Sir Ralph Murdac because I feared that he would expose me. I admit all of that, freely. And I will answer to God for it on Judgment Day—but, I tell you, Sir Alan, I would do it all over again, a hundred times, if I had to. For I serve a higher purpose, one that soars above the concerns of petty morality, above the life or death of one man, even a dozen men, a hundred; I serve the highest purpose of all. I serve the Queen of Heaven! I serve Our Lady! All that I do, everything, from the moment I wake to the time I fall exhausted into my miserable cot, is directed toward that one aim. And every day, when I contemplate my sins, I can look out of my window and see that monument to her greatness, the superb embodiment of her majesty, that goal that I strive for, rising, slowly, inexorably, week after week, month after month—"

"The cathedral of Notre-Dame," I said.

"Yes, Sir Alan, yes. The cathedral! It will be the most magnificent church in Christendom and a fitting tribute to the Mother of God. When I returned to Paris from Spain, my Order disbanded, destroyed by those blind fools of the Temple, I found that the work had almost ceased on the cathedral for lack of funds to pay the workmen. It was almost too much to bear: the Order gone, the grand church of Our Lady half-built, abandoned and silent. It was I who found the necessary silver for de Sully to continue the work; and it was I who breathed new life into the Knights of Our Lady. I saved them both—all for her glory!"

"And does the venerable Bishop de Sully know that the money for the cathedral comes from banditry? That it comes to him stained by the blood of the travelers robbed and murdered by the likes of Guillaume du Bois?"

Brother Michel remained silent.

"Does he?"

"The cathedral is everything, nothing else matters. That impious old fool closes his eyes. I tell him the money comes from the donations of pilgrims, from the thousands of faithful who come to see Notre-Dame and pray before its holy relics, and he chooses to believe it. It is not important. Only the work of building for her glory is important."

"Your cathedral is built on the bones and bodies of murdered men and women; its stones are cemented with their blood—it is an abomination—" I said, my anger rising like a red tide.

But the Master cut me off, saying too loudly: "You could not possibly understand the wonder of Our Lady and the gift of love she brings to the world . . ."

I stole a glance at Hanno's body. "I understand that you are a gore-glutted monster, a ghoul whose soul is crimson with the blood of innocent men—" I was almost shouting.

The Master goggled at me: "You do not speak to me in that manner."

I kept my eyes on my dead friend. "I understand that you are a weakling and a coward, who caused the deaths of men whose boots you are not fit to lick," I said very loudly, my anger making me insanely reckless.

"Be silent or I will have you gagged!" The Master was shouting now, too.

"Alan, please, we must be reasonable about this," said Reuben.

"You caused the deaths of my father, and the priest Jean of Verneuil, and Cardinal Heribert, and Master Fulk, and my loyal friend—" my voice was harsh, crackling with rage.

"Sergeant! I want him gagged, now." The Master was beckoning to one of the white-surcoated men-at-arms.

"Alan, please moderate your language; it cannot do us any good to abuse the Master in his own chapel." I noticed that as Reuben spoke he was jiggling a small round clay pot in his hands, the kind of common vessel in which doctors store rare ointments. But I was beyond moderation by then: "You are a filthy worm, a soft, gelatinous, gently steaming turd! A man you cannot refuse? I refuse you. I refuse to give you the slightest shred of respect; the would-be killer who cowers in the shadows and orders other men to do his bloody work, urging them on to their slaughter in the name of the Mother of God. You are a God-damned, cowardly, three-thumbed, child-fucking pimp—"

The sergeant had managed to wrestle the gag around my mouth by then, a thick, musty-smelling woolen cloth that made it very hard to breathe, let alone rant and rave.

And I was finally silenced.

The Master was glaring at me: "You call me a coward? Do you

think I am afraid of your master's wrath? Do you think that I do not dare to kill you for fear that the Earl of Locksley will fall on me with all his power and might? You are quite wrong!"

He turned to the sergeant standing behind me, and said: "Cut his lying throat, this instant!"

And Reuben moved. His arm went back and he threw the small round ointment pot, hard and fast, and directly at the gorgeous, stained-glass window that I had been staring at for the past few hours. The missile smashed straight through the glassy face of the Mother of God, destroying it and leaving a jagged yellow hole of streaming sunlight, an empty space in the spot from which Our Lady had once gazed down so compassionately.

Everything happened very fast.

The Master gave a huge shout of horror at Reuben's throw. I felt a hard hand on my shoulder as the sergeant behind my chair readied himself to cut my throat. And Reuben was moving again. His brown hand dipped into his robe and emerged bearing a slim black-handled knife. In one smooth flowing movement, Reuben's hand went back and flicked forward, and for a moment I thought the knife was coming for my face. It whirred past my cheek and I heard a thunk, and a wet, gurgling cry and the rough hand clamped on my shoulder slipped away.

The knights and men-at-arms of the Order had all begun to move toward us the moment the Master had screamed at the desecration of the lovely stained-glass image. They were pulling swords from their scabbards. Reuben had pulled another knife from somewhere. I tugged at my bonds once again but still could not move them.

The huge window exploded into a thousand pieces as a giant black-clad form smashed through it, scattering shards of jewel-like glass in all directions.

Everybody in the chapel froze as the giant figure rose from the wreckage of the window, shrugged off the thick black woolen canon's robe that had protected him from the broken glass and revealed itself to be a huge man with an ugly, red, battered face framed by two blond plaits. In his hands he carried an enormous double-headed war axe, and a round iron-bossed shield.

Little John threw back his head and bellowed a war cry that seemed to shake the stone foundations of the chapel, then turned and, almost gracefully, sunk his mighty axe into the head of the nearest Knight of Our Lady, splitting the helmeted poll in two. He wrenched the blade free and, almost as a continuation of the same stroke, sliced into the waist of another unfortunate soldier. Now more dark figures were leaping through the smashed window—and there was Roland of Alle, and his father the Seigneur, swords in hand—and last of all a smaller figure that revealed itself to be Thomas, my brave squire.

My heart banged at the sight of so many friends; and their battle skill was a joy to watch. Roland ran a man-at-arms through the belly, pulled his sword clear, whirled and blocked a scything blow from a yelling Knight of Our Lady. The Seigneur, though past his prime, was clearly still a fine warrior: he engaged a pair of knights simultaneously, swiftly dropped one with a slash to the ankles and stunned the other with a smashing pommel blow to the head. Little John killed another knight, and another, and within a couple of heartbeats a full-pitched battle was in progress. Reuben hurled a knife that smacked into the chest of a crossbowman who was aiming his weapon at Little John's back—and by now there were half a dozen dead and dying soldiers of Our Lady sprawled across the floor.

The Master shouted: "Eustace! Eustace!" and the black-eyed fiend burst through the main door at the western end of the chapel, leading a crowd of men-at-arms. The soldiers rushed at my friends, engaging them in a mad, hacking mêlée—a whirl of sharp cries, clashing metal, glittering sword sweeps, and bright sprays of blood. My friends advanced in a line, Little John in the center, his great axe swinging with a terrible rhythm; Roland on his left moved with a sinuous grace, his sword flickering out like a reptile's tongue to steal men's lives. The Seigneur d'Alle's style was old-fashioned, but he killed with a relentless ferocity and surprising energy. And all about the enemy knights were staggering, falling, bleeding, dying. I remember thinking: *These men, these Knights of Our Lady, could never have been true Templars, never.*

The Master shouted once more: "Eustace, the Grail!" and rushed toward the altar at the east, shoving the slight form of Thomas out of his path. And without a moment's hesitation, Sir Eustace left his men to their fate, coming fast on the Master's heels. He gave my reeling squire a kick in the belly as he came level with my chair; Thomas, winded, sat down abruptly on the stone floor and dropped his knife, his plan to cut me free thwarted. I saw the Master reach the altar, grasp the square wooden box on its purple cushion and without the merest backward glance to see his men dying under the swords of their enemies, he headed toward the door in the northeastern corner of the chapel and disappeared through it.

Sir Eustace took three paces after him, then stopped. He turned toward me—bound, gagged and helpless in my chair—and swiftly pulled the lance-dagger from its broad leather sheath at his right side. He advanced on dancer's feet and the killing blow, when it came, hurt no more than a heavy punch to the breast, a feeling of hard pressure rather than pain. I looked down in surprise to see Sir Eustace's mailed sleeve, and his fist on the wooden handle, and the Holy Lance embedded deep in my chest, perhaps an inch or two to the left of my sternum.

He pulled it out with a wet tearing noise, a gust of stale lung air, and a gush of bright blood. And with the blood, the pain came roaring through me.

I looked up at his face, and he smiled at me, his amiable idiot's grin. He saluted me by lifting the blood-smeared lance-dagger to his brow, and then he ran to the northeastern corner of the chapel, and disappeared through the same door that had swallowed his Master.

Part Three

19

Young Alan is back with us again at Westbury a mere month after his last visit. He has been sent home in disgrace after savagely beating a fellow squire with his fists during some petty boys' disagreement in Kirkton. The other lad's father, Lord Stafford, is said to be extremely angry. And Marie, Alan's mother, blames me.

"It is your silly stories that have made him behave in this barbaric way, you old fool! You should know better at your age. I told you that you shouldn't be wallowing in your violent past again, dredging up your blood-hungry tales; I told you that no good would come of it. And wasn't I proved right?"

Although I dearly love her, she can be something of a shrew, my daughter-in-law.

"Boys fight," I told her. "It is quite natural, but, if you wish, I will speak to young Alan about the matter."

My grandson was unrepentant about his victory over the other boy: "He insulted the honor of our family, and so I was obliged to punish him," he said, and when I inquired further, he told me that the boy had been spreading the word among the other noblemen's sons at Kirkton that Alan's great-grandfather, my own father Henry, had been a villein who had been hanged as a thief by the Sheriff.

"I told him all about the tale you are setting down, Grandpa, and the search for the 'man you cannot refuse' who ordered your father's death, and he went off and told everyone else. They all started to call me 'plow boy' and 'dirty serf.' And so I took my vengeance on him. I paid him back for his insolence. Tell me honestly, Grandpa, would you not have done the same thing yourself?"

I found it difficult to answer him: I might very well have done exactly the same in those circumstances; I well remembered a bully who called himself Guy who had tormented me when I was Alan's age, and how I had been revenged upon him, but I knew that Marie would make my life a living hell if I did not try to teach the boy to behave himself in a civilized manner among his peers.

I scowled at him: "You are supposed to be learning how to be a knight, up there in Kirkton," I said sternly. "And a knight is a gentleman; he does not brawl like a tavern drunk with his fellows. Furthermore, Our Lord Jesus Christ has taught us that it is better to turn the other cheek when we are wronged. A true Christian knight would have forgiven his enemy for the wrong that had been done to him—he would have meekly turned away and given up his wrath for the sake of peace."

At my age, after all that I have been through in this long life, I had thought myself beyond shame. But I felt the burn of shame then—it seemed as if my prating hypocrisy to my grandson were choking me—and young Alan could sense my falseness as keenly as a pig smells buried acorns.

"Would you truly have forgiven a man who blackened your name like that; who insulted you and mocked you behind your back?" asked Alan, his face blazing with innocence. He was honestly seeking the truth, desperately wanting to know how to be. I couldn't look him in the eye:

"The fruits of vengeance are almost always death and sorrow—for all concerned," I said, and I picked up a bundle of parchments. "Read this and you will see what happened to my good friend Hanno, and to me, as a direct result of my seeking vengeance on the 'man you cannot refuse.' And perhaps this will persuade you that revenge is a futile path, and that there is a greater wisdom for Mankind in Christ's teachings." And I shoved the second part of this tale at him; partly for his education, partly to get him to stop looking at me that way.

I did not pass out, at least, not then. I watched, gagged, bound and bleeding, as the Master and Sir Eustace de la Falaise made their escape from the side door in the Bishop's chapel in the Abbey of St. Victor. The skirmish was over; the surviving Knights of Our Lady, only three or four of them, seeing their Master flee, made a fighting retreat to the main door and ran for it themselves, and Little John let them go. Presumably they went to summon reinforcements or raise the hue and cry within the abbey—we did not tarry long enough to find out.

My bruised and weeping squire Thomas cut my bonds and, under Reuben's direction, he made a rough pad from the altar cloth and strapped it tightly over the wound in my chest. The gag had been removed and I was free to speak, but, convinced that I had only moments left to live, I kept repeating to Reuben the same phrase over and over: "You must get word to Goody—you must tell her how I love her. Tell her I am sorry . . ." But my breath was short and I could feel puffs of wet air seeping through the bloody bandage on my chest every time I tried to utter a word.

"Shush, shush, now, Alan! Be quiet and save your strength," Reuben said to me, as he felt for the pulse in my neck. I could feel his cool hand on my skin, and the throbbing of my vein under his fingers. Reuben was frowning, looking at me oddly, almost with a kind of awe.

When the last wounded Knight of Our Lady had been dispatched, Little John came across to me. His blue eyes in that ruddy face stared into mine, and for once he didn't make a crude jest. "We must go now, Alan," he said. "You grip on tight to my neck. I shall carry you."

"What about Hanno?" My breath hissed in my throat. Little John looked at my friend, sprawled in the chair next to mine, and he said: "The canons will give him a decent burial." And then he leaned forward and scooped me up in his arms, as if I was no heavier than a child's doll.

We left the same way that Little John, Thomas and the d'Alles had entered: through the ruin of the window, the glittering shards crunching under their boots.

I was laid in the bed of a straw-filled wagon, and I saw Little John and my friends donning the robes of monks once more, five anonymous clerics and their wagon among the hundreds that streamed about the abbey in the last few hours before Vespers and the closing of the gates.

And *then* I passed into oblivion.

I awoke to Robin's long, handsome face, and a look of infinite concern in his gray eyes. I was in a narrow bed, in a small whitewashed room, a cell of some kind. It was nighttime and cold, and the room was lit by a single candle. But I knew somehow that it was not the same night as the fight in the chapel; I knew that I had been there for many days. I had a raging thirst, and a crushing ache along the whole of the left-hand side of my chest; a full bladder too.

"I'm not dead," I said wonderingly. And then I said it again. "I'm not dead—am I?"

"No," said Robin with a half-laugh. "You are not dead; and I sometimes think that you must be indestructible."

"Why am I not dead?"

"Somebody stands a very good guard over you: God, the Devil, one of your myriad saints, the Blessed Virgin Mary . . ."

"Not her."

"No, not her," Robin agreed.

"You do. You stand guard over me."

"Well, I try to," he said, the candlelight turning his eyes to silver.

"I cannot for the life of me say why: you are seldom grateful, you are far too willful; you will not obey even the simplest of orders from your lord—I told you to leave these people alone, but would you ever listen—"

"They told you to tell me to leave them alone."

He said nothing.

"How long have you known that it was Brother Michel who ordered my father's death?" I asked. "How long have you known that he was the Master, the 'man you cannot refuse?' "

Silence.

"And why did you never tell me?"

Another pause.

"We will talk about it in the morning," said Robin finally. "You are not going anywhere for a while; and neither am I. Here"—he lifted a clay cup from the table beside the bed—"Reuben says I am to make sure that you drink all of this."

And he cupped my neck and helped me to drink. Then he gave me water and, without a shred of embarrassment, he helped me to relieve myself into a chamber pot below the bed. These simple actions exhausted me, and I fell back into the cot, barely able to keep my eyes open. My chest was a jagged cage of fire, but I could feel whatever it was that Reuben had prepared for me to drink beginning to soothe and ease my pains, spreading its soft, supple fingers, kneading the pain away around my whole body.

"Where am I?" I asked Robin as he picked up the candle and prepared to leave.

"In the Hôtel-Dieu, on the Île de la Cité," Robin replied with more than a suggestion of a twinkle in his eye. "We are guests of the venerable Bishop Maurice de Sully."

"Situs inversus viscerum," said Reuben, relishing the three Latin words. "Your insides are the wrong way around, Alan. And for that reason you are breathing today, and no other. You have a perfectly normal

heart, lungs, liver and lights, they are just on the opposite side of the body from most other people. Your heart is on the right-hand side of the body, not the left as usual. I should have known in Cyprus three years ago when I removed that crossbow bolt from your right side, and couldn't find your liver. This is the second time your life has been saved by your condition."

"That's it? He stabbed me in the heart but my heart wasn't where it was supposed to be—so he missed?" I said. It sounded wonderfully absurd.

"Well, he also missed the major veins and arteries, but yes, that's it. It's not even all that uncommon—I remember reading a treatise in Montpellier recently by a much-fêted Arab physician who claimed that one person in ten thousand had been made by God this way. Think of it as being left-handed, but inside your body. No more sinister than that. Ha-ha!"

I acknowledged his feeble joke with a smile. But then Reuben's face turned grave: "I'm not saying it was easy for me: your left lung collapsed and filled with fluid, and I had to drain it with a hollow reed, through a water valve—you will have noticed that beautifully stitched cut under your left armpit—but I won't confuse your simple brain with the details of my extraordinary skill as a surgeon, nor of my miraculous healing powers as a physician . . ."

"Or your world-renowned modesty . . . ," I murmured.

". . . but in short, you are alive because of the way your organs are arranged—that is it!" Reuben's dark face was lit by a grin. And I could not but be warmed by his smile and comforted by his presence at my bedside.

"I thank you," I said, smiling wanly back at him, "and I give thanks to God for your miraculous healing powers."

And I meant it, but while I was grateful to Reuben and his skill, I knew in my heart that I had been saved by God, and that St. Michael, the warrior archangel to whom I often prayed, must also have had a hand in my deliverance.

It was then three weeks since the fight in the chapel, and I had spent all that time recovering from my wound in the small cell in the Hôtel-Dieu. A rib had been smashed by Eustace's strike, my lung had been punctured, and I had lost a lot of blood—but, by the grace of God, the assistance of St. Michael and, of course, my undeniably skilled physician friend, I was still alive.

I was not, however, in very good shape. I was as weak as a crippled baby mouse, and it still hurt very much even to breathe—but worst of all was the soul-crushing guilt.

I recalled the moment when Hanno was killed over and over again in my head. It was entirely my fault that he was dead: I had foolishly led him into extreme danger and he had not survived it. And, only a little less troubling than the passing of my friend, when Reuben's drugs allowed me some shallow sleep, I saw the faces of all the men who had died as a result of my quest to clear my father's name: Owain the Bowman, Father Jean of Verneuil and those other scores of Locksley men who died on that castle's walls and in that gore-steeped stable; Brother Dominic, Cardinal Heribert, Master Fulk; the nameless man in the Grand Chastelet jail, whom I killed with my empty hands just so as to have somewhere to sit—even the Knights of Our Lady that I cut down in the rainstorm, who for all their violence believed they were serving the Mother of God.

These shades crowded around my sickbed in the small hours of the night, and silently scolded me for my pride. Sometimes Sir Eustace de la Falaise appeared too, with his lance-dagger projecting from his fist, and he would plunge it into Hanno's ghostly chest again and again. And I would awake, covered in sweat, my pounding heart threatening to tear my chest apart. These dead men would be alive today had I not been so determined to seek revenge.

The Master—or Brother Michel or the "man you cannot refuse" or Trois Pouces or whatever name he was now traveling under—had fled Paris with Sir Eustace and a handful of the Knights of Our Lady. No one knew where he had gone to, but a safe wager was that he had found refuge with his gangs of bandits in the lawless woods south of Paris. The Master, once the strong right hand of the second most powerful man in Paris, had become a *hors-la-loi*, an outlaw. But I felt no satisfaction; indeed, I felt like a hapless hunter who had been thrashing blindly in the undergrowth seeking a hare, and who had stumbled upon an angry wild boar, been brutally savaged for his temerity, and then had allowed the beast to escape unharmed.

Robin had visited me daily with news and tidbits of Parisian food that he felt sure would restore my strength: delicate pastries, sticky sweetmeats and expensive wines. Many of them I could not eat, for Reuben's drugs killed my appetite along with my pain, and so I passed them on to the elderly monk who brought me gruel and water and washed my body and changed the bedding. Robin was staying as a guest of Bishop de Sully in the episcopal palace—while the old man himself preferred to remain in the Abbey of St. Victor and nurse his ailing health. I gathered that Robin had pressured the Bishop into caring for me, and into providing him with accommodation. I would receive the finest care in the Hôtel-Dieu, while I recovered from my wound, I was made to understand, and Robin would remain silent about the fact that de Sully's trusted amanuensis had been a murderous gang-master, and that the building of the cathedral of Notre-Dame had been funded by blood money stolen from innocent travelers.

Reluctantly, and only after a certain amount of undignified pleading for the truth on my part, Robin confessed that he had known about the activities of the Master, and the identity of Brother Michel, for more than a decade. Indeed, while Robin had been an outlaw in Sherwood, robbing churchmen and thumbing his nose at the law, the Master had been, to a certain extent, his counterpart in France. They had met face-to-face three times, twice in Paris and once in London, and had agreed a pact of sorts that included the stipulation that neither would attack or harm the other—or any of the other's lieutenants.

Robin had been aware that the Master had ordered my father's death—although he insisted that he did not know why. In fact, part of the reason why he had taken me into his care when I was a penniless thief on the run from the Sheriff, was because he had known and liked my father and felt pity for his orphaned son. But when I had discovered that Sir Ralph Murdac had merely been following the instructions of the "man you cannot refuse," Robin had become concerned. He realized that I would not rest until I had discovered the identity of the Master and attempted my revenge.

Robin's fear was that the Master would snuff me out as easily as a man extinguishes a bedside candle, if he suspected that I was even the smallest threat to him. And so Robin had tried to shield me, and had sent a message to Paris that I was not to be touched, and he had at the same time tried to dissuade me from pursuing my inquiries. When it was clear, after the attack by the Knights of Our Lady at Fréteval, that the Master planned to ignore their long-standing pact and eliminate me anyway, and when I deserted Robin's men and the relative safety of the army and began to make my way to Paris, Robin summoned Reuben from Montpellier and dispatched him to follow me and to act as my protective shadow. When Robin heard from Reuben, who knew Paris well, that I had been slung in the notorious Grand Chastelet jail, there to rot for the rest of my life, my lord had sent Little John to Paris with orders, if necessary, to recruit men and break me out of the jail as soon as possible: Robin knew that the longer a man remained inside the Grand Chastelet—and it would have been a matter of days rather than weeks—the less chance he had of ever emerging from that filth lapped stone coffin.

Robin had indeed watched over me like a mother hen.

On the morning of his arrival in Paris, Little John had gone directly to the Rue St. Denis and discovered from the d'Alles that I had set off for the Abbey of St. Victor that morning but had not returned, as promised, for dinner at noon. Knowing of the Master's connection with Bishop de Sully, and suspecting that he too might be at St. Victor's, Little John had ridden as swiftly as possible to the abbey with the Seigneur, Roland and Thomas. Once there, he had hurriedly colluded with Reuben, who was inside the Bishop's quarters, and they had effected my rescue in that dramatic, if destructive, manner.

"Tell me, Alan," said Robin, munching idly on a fig that he had brought for my delectation that day. "If I had told you from the beginning that the Master had ordered your father's death, would you have left him alone?"

"If I knew then what the cost in lives would be, I think so . . . I hope so," I said.

"Truly?" my master asked, swallowing his fig.

"Truly?" I thought for a moment, then sighed. "No. In truth, at some point, I would have come here and tried to bring him to justice in any way that I could."

"So I was right to keep this knowledge from you," said Robin.

"You used to extol vengeance as a virtue, as a man's duty," I said, thinking of one of my first encounters with Robin, a musical evening with Marie-Anne.

"Only when it is public."

"What?"

"Vengeance only has meaning if it is a public act. If someone wrongs you, and everyone knows that they have wronged you, you must take revenge or people will think the less of you. You will lose your honor in their eyes and will soon come to be thought of as a weakling, a man of no account. Then you are finished. But if somebody wrongs you in private, secretly, away from other men's eyes—revenge is pointless. You may take vengeance in an attempt to make yourself feel better, although that is not much of a balm, in my experience, but in truth revenge serves no real purpose unless everybody around you understands the circumstances under which it is taken. What I'm saying is that vengeance taken in private is an indulgence. In fact, seeking revenge on a man like Brother Michel for something he did in the greatest secrecy ten years ago, and in the knowledge that he has no plans to do you any further harm, is plain idiocy. Actually, it is closer to suicide. Look at you, lying there with a hole in your chest, and poor, faithful Hanno cold in his grave. What have you achieved by pursuing your manly revenge on him?"

I said nothing. My chest throbbed. He was right. And perhaps oddly, I no longer felt the burning urge for vengeance against the Master. Hanno was dead, I was alive, barely, and the Master was gone. I had not the strength for revenge: this time I would let it lie.

After a while Robin stole another fig from the bowl and said: "Did you ever lay eyes on this wondrous object that was the cause of all this trouble, the relic that the Master stole from Heribert as a young man—this Grail thing?"

"No, but I believe it was in the box on the altar in the chapel. And the Master took it with him when he fled."

"And do you think it is real?" Robin said, cocking his head to one side, eyes bright and looking more than a little like his avian namesake.

"I think the Master believes it to be real, and Sir Eustace and the Knights of Our Lady—it is real to them."

"What would a holy relic like that be worth, I wonder?" Robin mused. Then he added: "I've read Christian of Troyes's poem; he describes it as being made of pure fine gold and being adorned with many kinds of precious jewels. It should fetch a pretty decent amount at market, I would have thought."

I looked at him; he had on his acquisitive expression, a glimmering flame of larceny behind his silver-bright eyes. And, for one reason or another, I badly wanted to dowse it.

"If it is real, it is beyond price," I said. "A vessel that was used at the Last Supper and that also once held the blood of Our Lord Jesus Christ? Men would die for it, kill others for it—it would be the most wondrous, valuable and powerful object in the world, but not something that could be bought or sold with mere money. On the other hand, if it isn't real, it is no more than a golden bowl worth a few pounds—after looting the French King's wagon train at Fréteval, I'm sure you already have several better pieces."

Robin caught my eye and, sensing my impatience with him, he dropped the subject. Instead, he pulled out a blood-spotted parchment letter, and waved it under my nose. "When Reuben was cutting you about, we found a money belt around your middle and a sealed pigskin pouch, and this letter inside. It is none of my business, I know—but I'm rather curious. Can you tell me what it is?"

I noted that Robin had been rummaging through my most personal possessions while I was unconscious. But the man had saved my life, and so I suppressed my irritation. In fact, I was happy to talk about a subject other than the Grail or the Master, so I explained to Robin how the Templars took a traveler's money at one preceptory, and returned it at another, in another country, perhaps years later. Robin listened intently; he seemed fascinated by the process, and asked innumerable questions. I answered him as best I could, and when I had finished, Robin said: "And they charged you three shillings for this service? No wonder those God-struck bastards are so damned rich."

Then he made a strange request: "Alan," he said, "might I ask a favor from you? Could I borrow this letter for a week or so? You will not be needing it until you return to England, and I would like to show it to a friend of mine. I swear I will not lose it."

The days passed, the weather grew colder and before long it was November, and although the flesh of my chest was healing, I caught a dangerous chill that went straight into my lungs. Thomas and Reuben rarely left my bedside in those fever-racked weeks and Reuben admitted afterward that I came closer to death in that sweat-drenched whirling nightmare of oozing bloody phlegm and racking coughs than I had done in the immediate aftermath of the stabbing. My dead visited me night and day, clustering around the bed but rarely speaking: merely looking at me imploringly. Men I had killed in battle years before and very nearly forgotten came to me then; they sat at the foot of my bed, their wounds fresh and bleeding: their quietness chided me. I screamed for their forgiveness; I begged them to leave me be; but they returned my fevered shouts with a vast, aching silence.

November became December and the Feast of Our Lord's Nativity came and went without my being conscious of that holy celebration: Robin and Little John had been called away to attend King Richard, who was keeping Christmas at Rouen, but Reuben and Thomas remained with me, and I realized that I was receiving the attention that a prince of the Church would receive from the monks of the Hôtel-Dieu; whatever Robin had said to Bishop de Sully had had a profound effect. I was all but pampered like a lapdog, brought fine foods and wrapped in costly furs, read to by the monks each day—mostly dull homilies and sermons, but I knew that they meant well—and with a brazier almost constantly burning in the small cell to keep the winter chill at bay.

The great man came to see me himself, one gray afternoon in January. I was standing beside my bed—the fevers had left me pathetically weak, but I forced myself to get out of the warm, comfortable cot each morning and stand by the window for as long as I could, staring out over the vast building yard of the cathedral of Notre-Dame. It was abandoned by the gangs of workmen in the very coldest season; the mortar could not be mixed and set properly when frost and ice ruled the night. That morning, it had snowed and the high roof, the buttresses and the canvas-covered sections of the scaffolding of the cathedral bore a crust of white that resembled a giant nun's wimple.

"It is even more beautiful in the winter," said a voice behind me. And I turned slowly to see the Bishop, very gaunt but smiling, standing in the doorway of the cell. He was alone, but holding a large earthenware pot in his hands. I could see a ladle poking from the open top, and tendrils of steam, but it was the hot, fruity, spicy smell filling the room that allowed me to recognize the Bishop's burden.

"I have brought you some warmed wine—Doctor Reuben has recommended it; he says it will do you good, and it may quite possibly help me, as well. May I enter?"

It was a curiously humble speech from this most powerful churchman who was the master in this Hôtel-Dieu, and therefore my host.

"Please come in, Your Grace," I said. "Be welcome!"

With a good deal of effort, the Bishop put the pot on the table by the bed and fumbled two clay cups from a pouch at his waist. He served us both a steaming portion of the rich red liquid, clumsily, spilling some of the liquor and splashing his long white fingers. We both sat on the bed, and after a mumbled benediction from the Bishop, we drank to each other's health. He was nervous, I saw, which surprised me, and very thin. He looked even more ill than the last time I had seen him. And he did not know how to speak to me. So I tried to make it easier on a sick old man.

"Your Grace, I must thank you for your hospitality, and for the kindness your servants have shown me here in the Hôtel-Dieu. I believe they have saved my life and I am most grateful to them—and to you."

He regarded me with his pale, empty eyes over the rim of his steaming cup.

"You are a good man, Alan Dale—I can tell that. As was your father, I recall. You may not think me such a good judge of character after, after . . ." He tailed off; then rallied. "But I never wished any harm to come to you, or to your friend—Johannes. We buried him with dignity in the graveyard at St. Victor's, you know. The monks sang a Requiem Mass for him, and I pray that Almighty God has taken him to his bosom."

I felt a jab of raw grief at his words. "We called him Hanno," I said, fighting back the burn of unmanly tears.

He nodded and we fell silent for a moment or two.

"How much did you know," I finally asked, "about Brother Michel's activities? Did you know he possessed the Grail? Did you know about the gangs of cutthroats?"

"Those bandits? No, never in my wildest dreams," he said, sounding shocked that I should suggest it.

"And the Grail?" I persisted. "Did you know that Brother Michel possessed the Grail?"

He gave a long deep sigh. "The Grail, that God-damned, devilish Grail . . . yes, I knew he had something that he believed was the bowl that had once contained Christ's blood. But that was later: your father was long gone by then. And when Michel came to me after his service in Spain—it must be fifteen years ago, now—he was the finest, the most hardworking and intelligent assistant that I have ever had. He was pious too, and humble. I found out much later that he thought he possessed the true Grail, but I was wholly convinced that it was a silly, harmless fancy."

The Bishop rose and began to pace the small cell. "I think I must have known in my heart that he had stolen it from Heribert, and that your father was innocent; but I suppressed that thought. He had such youthful energy and enthusiasm and faith in my cathedral as a grand ideal. And then, later, when he began to find the resources, the money to continue the building work, when mine had run quite dry—well, I did not ask too many questions, I was aware that he was using the Grail in some way as a method of raising revenue. But for such a good cause, I did not want to discourage him. I thought he was displaying it to pilgrims, allowing rich, pious knights to drink from it for a fee, that sort of thing. I had no idea that he had constructed an entire secret order of killers and thieves, upon one old dish. I turned a blind eye, I admit it; I believed, as I still do, that the cathedral is a worthy cause and I confess I was prepared to condone a little relic-mongering to achieve that aim."

The Bishop was standing now by the window, staring out at the snow-covered cathedral: "Look at it, Sir Alan—just imagine its splendor when completed! It is my life's work; it is the fruit of a life dedicated to Almighty God. Is that magnificent monument to the Mother of Christ not worth a little mummery with an old bowl?"

I stood and looked past the Bishop's shoulder and saw . . . a building—an enormous, very grand, beautifully constructed, three-parts-built, snow-covered building. But just a building nonetheless—and one that had indirectly caused the death of my father and my friend. I made no reply to the Bishop but sat down on the bed again, suddenly overwhelmed with a great weariness.

The Bishop turned and regarded me for a while: "I came," he said, "to make an apology to you. And perhaps to try to explain myself, and seek your forgiveness for what has passed between us. But I can see that you would not welcome that little speech. And so I will leave you with a gift of information. It is this: if you seek Brother Michel—and I suspect that even if you do not wish to encounter him again now, you or your hard-faced master will decide to seek him out one day—you will find him in the south, in Aquitaine. Viscount Aimar of Limoges is his cousin; they were boyhood friends—and he told me once, after he had taken too much wine, that it was in those lands, and those lands only, that he felt truly happy and at peace. When he has no other place to run to, Michel will go south, and you will find him under his cousin's protection. And, if you do meet him again, you may give him my curse."

I thanked the Bishop for his counsel, and once again for his hospitality, although I could not find it in my heart to utter words of forgiveness, and he blessed me and took his leave. And then I thought about the information that he had given me, and felt a heavy weight on my heart. I could not even contemplate a journey so far to the south on a mission of vengeance. Robin was right: revenge was an idiotic indulgence. Besides, the thought of another encounter with the Master chilled my stomach. I finished the wine, crawled into my blankets and, although it was not yet noon, I was asleep in an instant.

I left Paris in the spring, still weak and low in spirits, but at least able to ride the ambling horse that I had purchased for the journey—Robin had sold the courser and had arranged for Shaitan under the care of two grooms to be sent back to Westbury months ago. Before I left, I bade farewell to the noble French family in the big house on the Rue St. Denis—my family. Adèle had visited me often in my cot at the Hôtel-Dieu, bringing me hot soup and egg possets and fresh fruit, and fussing over me in an irritating but also deeply comforting way. Reuben had departed in February, with my heartfelt gratitude, saying that he could do no more than that which the monks at the Hôtel-Dieu and my own constitution might achieve. And he had business matters to attend to in Montpellier, anyway; he could not spend the rest of his life fussing over me like a mother. Roland and the Seigneur had visited me twice at the Hôtel, but they were both uncomfortable in a sick-room, as I have found many fit and active men to be, as if my wound could somehow weaken their own robust bodies. But they made an attempt at joviality, and shrugged off my thanks for saving my life as if breaking into an abbey and battling deluded would-be Templar knights was nothing out of the ordinary.

When I called on them before my departure from Paris, the Seigneur greeted me in the big dining chamber on the ground floor with a bear hug, Roland clasped my arm warmly and beautiful Adèle kissed me on both cheeks. I was pleased to see that Roland's face had healed and the scar—a large pink shiny patch on his left cheek—was not as disfiguring as it might have been.

My cousin seemed to hold no grudge against me for marking him in such a cruel way: "In battle a man will do what he must to defeat an opponent," he told me. "I might have done the same to you, had our positions been reversed. But God forbid that it should ever come to that again." I felt a rush of affection for my newly discovered cousin and his chivalrous attitudes. He would never stoop to petty revenge, and I was certain that he would be a very good man to have beside you in the battle line.

We dined simply, as Thomas and I were to leave Paris the next morning and we had much to do before our departure, taking only a little wine and cold meat and cheese at the Seigneur's board.

The talk turned, inevitably, to the war. While the truce between Richard and Philip had been largely observed—apart from some discreet castle-rebuilding on both sides and a few reckless raiding forays by the wilder knights in both armies—we all knew that it could not last forever. It was March by now, a month rightly named for the Roman God of War, and the beginning of the campaigning season. The warmer spring weather would bring the bellicose spirits on both sides bubbling up to the surface. A raid would lead to a skirmish, and that might end in a battle or a siege. A truce was not a peace, after all—and as long as King Philip's men occupied large parts of Normandy, Richard was bound by his sense of honor to fight him. It was his patrimony, after all, granted him by God and his father, Henry—it was his duty to recover the territories for himself and for his as yet unborn descendants.

"I am pleased that you will not be arrayed among the English knights who will oppose us when war does come, Sir Alan," said the Seigneur, with a wry grin. And I was glad too. Reuben had told me that I must rest for a good long time, to allow my body, and particularly my lungs, to fully recover. My wind was bad, and I knew that I would not be fit for campaigning this season, and for the first time in my life I felt a strange reluctance to don mail and ride into battle ever again. I was going home to England and to Goody. And that pleased me a very great deal.

It took us two weeks, Thomas and I, to ride to Calais, for we traveled slowly, making sure that we stayed somewhere warm every night for the sake of my lungs—a safe conduct from Bishop de Sully easing our path and commanding the finest hospitality at any religious house we visited. Matthew the student accompanied us on this journey. Since the death of Master Fulk, he and his friends had found other teachers, and we had enjoyed one more evening at the sign of the Cock before my departure, a brief affair, it must be said, for I was soon exhausted by the young men's high spirits and begged off early to go to bed. Matthew had told me he had tired of Paris and wished to travel back to England, to Oxford, where he had heard there was a renowned new teacher of Philosophy that he wanted to study under. I believe, in truth, that he owed a good deal of money to some very unpleasant people in Paris, but I was content for Matthew to come with us on our journey north. He provided some youthful company for Thomas, for I was a morose and irritable companion. Even a few hours in the saddle wearied me, and though we three rode out each morning at dawn, by noon, as often as not, I had traveled as far as I wished to for one day. We lingered at Beauvais, Amiens and St. Pol-sur-Ternoise, for a full day's rest. At Calais, it took another three days to find a ship that would take us to Dover. But, at the beginning of April, the year of Our Lord eleven hundred and ninety-five, I was once again on English soil. We traveled up to London, and I paid a visit to the Temple on the western outskirts of the city, and redeemed my silver from the knights there when I presented the letter from the Paris Temple. My silver was delivered to me in small white linen sacks no bigger than my fist but each marked with a neat red cross on the side. The clerks at the Temple seemed to take it as a matter of course that I should walk into their precincts with a piece of parchment, and walk out with more than two pounds of bright metal. It was a marvelous system, to be sure, but I was glad once again to have specie about my person and—once I had unpacked it from the linen sacks, counted it and packed it into my broad leather money belt—to feel its comforting weight on my hips.

We bade farewell to Matthew at St. Albans, and while he took the road west to Aylesbury and on to Oxford, Thomas and I headed north. A week after that and Thomas and I rode through the open wooden gates of Westbury, in the County of Nottinghamshire, and I slipped out of the saddle and into the arms of my beloved.

20

I HAD NOT SEEN GODIFA, MY BETROTHED, my fiery blonde darling, for almost a full year. And I found that she had changed a good deal in that time: I had left her a coltish girl, and returned to find her a beautiful full-grown woman. While I could still span her waist with my big hands, her hips and breasts had blossomed into soft curves. I took her into my arms and we kissed for a long, long while, our tongues intertwining like mating snakes, with a passion that made my head whirl and nearly cost me my self-control—I had it in my mind to drag her into her chamber and allow my lust free rein. But I did not: Goody was yet a maiden, and I'd sworn that she would be one until our wedding night.

I broke our honey-sweet embrace, held her in my arms, gazed into her lovely violet eyes. "Welcome home, my sweet love," she said, and I kissed her once more, briefly, on her soft lips before releasing her.

"The weary warrior is home from the battlefield," said a warm voice with just a hint of Wales in its tones. It was my old friend Father Tuck, beaming at me from a round red-weathered face beneath the iron-gray smear of his tonsure.

I embraced him too, and then the tall, chestnut-haired woman standing beside him. Marie-Anne, Countess of Locksley, had put on a little weight, though she was still a lovely woman, and the reason for that slight increase in girth lay sleeping in her arms. "This is Miles," she said, filled with pride, and I peered at the bundle at her breast and saw a pair of unmistakable silver-gray eyes staring out at me with ferocious interest from a chubby pink face.

Beyond Marie-Anne and her baby, I saw the tall figure of Baldwin, my steward, standing by the door of the hall. He nodded a respectful greeting at me, but did not move; he was resting his hands on the shoulders of a dark-haired boy, who stood immediately in front of him: it was Hugh, Robin's eldest son. And he stared at me without recognition, but with the curious gaze of any five-year-old.

It was wonderful to be back at Westbury, and for a few days the joy at homecoming managed to lift the black gloom that had enveloped me since my encounter with the Master six months ago. I had so much to tell Goody and Tuck and Marie-Anne, that although we sat down to eat dinner at noon, we did not rise from the table till full dark.

The next day, after a sleepless night, I found myself inexplicably restless, prowling around the manor on foot and a-horse, like a dog sniffing the air, seeing what had changed and what had not. Since I had taken my wound, I had been beset with a strange malaise of the soul: I was constantly in a state of wariness, as if danger were just around the corner. It meant that I could not sleep, or if I did manage to drift off momentarily, I awoke with my heart pounding and drenched with sweat. Images of Sir Eustace striking me with his lance-dagger often flashed into my mind; and of the Master's lean, pockmarked face, his commanding blue eyes. On waking, I was nervous, irritable, jumpy—but at the same time detached from my feelings. I had expected, now that I was back at Westbury, to be able to rest easily for a few months. But, to my deep frustration, I found I could not.

I have noticed that after battle or combat I have often felt a similar sensation—the sleeplessness, in particular, and the awful, blood-tinged dreams—but previously these feelings had gradually faded over several weeks, and I had regained my normal buoyant mood. Not this time. I was haunted by my experiences in France, by the deaths of Hanno and Owain, and by my own near escape from the yawning grave. Back at Westbury, I began to drink a little more each night, in an attempt to help me sleep, just another cup or two to begin with, and then whole flagons of good red wine—and another full one set by my bed, too.

It was to no avail.

It is true that after drinking deeply of the good wine that Baldwin purchased from the Aquitanian merchants, I would sometimes fall into a short sleep, but I would almost always awake past midnight, mouth dry as old leather, head beating and with a sour belly—unable to sleep again until dawn found me exhausted, sweaty and irritable.

I behaved badly in those months at Westbury, often snapping angrily at Tuck, Marie-Anne, Thomas or even at my beloved Goody. I found myself bristling with rage and snarling at the slightest thing: a dropped cup or a door left open, a dog barking in the night. And I drank more and more wine to try to calm my nerves. Looking back on that time it is a wonder that my friends bore my company at all: I would not have been surprised if they had all decamped for Robin's castle of Kirkton in Yorkshire and closed the gates in my face. When we all meet again in Heaven, as I am sure we will, I shall apologize to them and try to make amends. I could not explain it then: I did not understand it myself. I had faced danger and death many times before that episode in Paris. I was young, just turned twenty years, and my chest had healed to a thick pink scar—my wind was not good but it was slowly improving. But I could not shake the demons of memory that haunted my days and particularly my nights. And, although I knew I was playing the boor, I could not fathom why. I still do not fully understand it.

But if my rude and angry behavior were not enough, there were other dark forces at work to sour the air at Westbury that spring and summer. On the third or fourth day after my arrival, Tuck took me aside and explained why he and Marie-Anne had decided to move in with Goody and abandon Kirkton to Robin's army of servants.

"It is Nur, I am afraid," Tuck told me as we strolled through the long apple orchard, admiring the delicate blossoms that adorned the trees. "She has taken up residence in the old, deep woods over toward Alfreton, and she appears to be gathering followers to her; a sad crew made up of the mad and infirm, the dispossessed and rejected—all women, young and old."

"Has she bothered Goody in any way?" I asked.

"I'm afraid Nur has been making something of a nuisance of herself in these parts recently. She sometimes visits Westbury by night, usually at full moon, and leaves dead, mutilated animals in strange contorted attitudes—baby shrews, rats, foxes, even cats, hanged or crucified—and blood-daubed messages outside the walls. The villagers are all terrified of her and whisper that she is a witch and servant of Satan—and I am certain that, while she is surely mortal, it truly is the Devil who drives her wicked actions!"

"Has she hurt Goody?" I repeated, a little shortly.

"No-ooo, she has not," said Tuck slowly, his red face wrinkling with thought. "Goody says she is not frightened by that sort of nonsense—and has threatened to give Nur another thrashing if she ever encounters her again. But it must be wearing on her soul—having an enemy so close, and someone so filled with malice. Goody would not be human if she did not find that unsettling."

I felt a pang of guilt then. For Nur was a monster of my own making; it was my failure, my inability to love her after she had been mutilated, that had turned her toward evil. And I was certain that she meant to do Goody harm, if ever she could.

"Do not fret, Alan," said Tuck. "We have a dozen good men-at-arms at Westbury, and I have cleansed the hall and the courtyard buildings with holy water; we are safe from Nur's evil—I only tell you so you will understand if Goody seems rather tense."

I spoke to Goody about the threat from Nur, and she seemed to me to be quite calm: "I feel a kind of pity for Nur, rather than anything stronger," she said. "You loved her once but no longer, and she cannot let that go. I can understand that. It must be eating her up inside to know that, only a few miles away, I have you all to myself!" She gave me her lovely smile, and brushed my cheek with her lips.

"If you wish, I could raise a troop of men and we could scour those Alfreton woods, flush her out and drive her away," I said. "It would not be such a difficult task and perhaps we would be doing a kindness in expelling her from the area. If she were not close by, perhaps she would forget all about us and move ahead with her own life."

"No," said Goody, "let the poor woman be. She has already been exiled from her home once—in Outremer. We can survive a few dead rats every full moon—perhaps she will grow bored with this dark game and find some other way to fill the emptiness of her life."

And so I did nothing. And, in fact, at the next full moon there were no executed animal corpses strewn around Westbury, no foul messages scrawled in blood for all to see. And the next moon after that, too. I began to think that Nur had given up her attempt to scare us, and that she had perhaps gone away, or died of some fever, or just expired of plain starvation. I allowed myself to feel a little easier.

The months passed at Westbury, and the harvest was gathered in by the villeins and franklins of the village, under the efficient rule of Baldwin, my steward: it was a bountiful year, with soft rain to make the crops grow in April and May and then strong sunshine to ripen the ears all through June and July. On the first day of August, at the feast of Lammas, when the tenants were duty bound to pay their rents, I took some pale satisfaction at seeing the grain barns being filled to the rafters with the produce of Westbury, and after Mass in the village church, in which a loaf made from that year's harvest was consecrated by the priest, an owlish little man called Arnold, and given out with the wine at the Blessed Sacrament, I feasted my tenants with a roasted pig, two ewes, six dozen capons, innumerable puddings, and many barrels of fresh ale.

My squire Thomas spent hours by the ale barrels with the dozen or so Westbury men-at-arms, and became quite drunk, and not long after dusk, when a great bonfire was being lit, and the dancing was about to begin, Goody had to help him off to bed. The boy, I noticed, had changed in recent months: his voice had changed from the shrill treble of the year before and become deeper, though it still cracked and jumped from a high to a low register when he was excited. And he had grown too. He would never be a tall man, but he had added six inches to his stature since our time in Paris, and he undoubtedly would be a man before long.

A drum began to throb, and the wailing of a pipe pierced the twilight. When my tipsy squire had been put to bed—even in drink he was a grave and sensible youth, not given to giggling, singing, loud extravagant words or violence—Goody came and sat beside me. We shared a plate of roast pork with fresh wheat bread, and a large flagon of wine, and watched the villagers join hands in a circle and begin the intricate steps of the traditional Lammas dances. The night was warm and well lit by the bonfire that cast flickering light and shadow upon the circling dancers. It was a homely, peaceful scene, the red firelight, the wheeling dancers, a broad table, laden with good food—and yet there was something troubling my beloved, and I knew what it was. It had been a year and four months since we had become betrothed, and the celebration of our bountiful harvest had bent her thoughts toward her own fecundity.

"Hal's daughter Sally is with child, or so they tell me," my lovely girl said, as if she were merely making idle conversation. But even then I knew her better than that. I merely grunted through a mouthful of half-chewed pork and waited for her next sortie.

Sparks crackled and leaped from the bonfire, the music skirled through the darkness and the drums thumped on. We watched the ring of dancers break apart and reform as the spokes of a wheel, their left hands joined in the center, their faces flushed and smiling.

"And Aggie the Miller's wife has just had twins—two beautiful boys."

"What happy news," I said, in a carefully neutral tone.

The circle had formed again, but now a young man and a girl were dancing together, nimbly, in the center of the ring. The love between the young couple was almost visible, and they moved like one creature, arms linked, toes pointed in perfect symmetry, eyes fixed on the other's face.

"And little Daisy Johnson is to be married next week," she said. "To William the Thatcher, of all people—he must be thirty years old if he's a day! Twice her age!"

"He's a good man, a skilled craftsman, and a kind one. She will be well provided for in William's house—"

Goody snapped: "The Devil take you, Alan Dale—why are you being so difficult about all this?"

"You know why, my darling," I said calmly.

"One mad, unhappy woman utters a stream of pure moon-addled gibberish, nothing but hateful, hurtful ranting, and you take that as a reason not to fulfill your lawful promise to marry me and give me babies! You are scared of her, Alan, aren't you? You're frightened. Admit it. You—the big, tough, fighting man—are scared of her silly threats."

I was stung, and an angry retort sprang to my lips. But I managed to swallow it, something that I had failed to do on several occasions in the past few months. Besides, Goody was right: when I looked into my heart, I realized that a part of me *was* frightened of Nur's curse. When she had burst into our betrothal feast the year before, she had uttered these words: *"I curse you, Alan Dale, I curse you and your milky whore! Your sour-cream bride will die a year and a day after you take her to your marriage bed—and her firstborn child shall die, too, in screaming agony."*

The words had burned themselves into my brain, and if Goody did not fear the curse, I knew, deep in my unreasoning heart, that I did.

"We have not heard from that poor crazed woman for months now: there has been no sign of her at all since you returned," Goody continued. "She has likely gone away or curled up in a hole and died—she cannot hurt us, my love. Her words of hate have no power over us. Let us be married, and soon. And then in a while Miles shall have a playmate! And you will have an heir, a little Alan. Would that not please you, my love?"

Goody spent most of her days at Westbury with Marie-Anne, and while a wet nurse, a plump, plain village girl called Ada, tended to Miles's basic needs, feeding him and changing his soiled napkins, the two gentlewomen, my betrothed and Robin's wife, seemed to spend an inordinate amount of time clucking and fussing over the baby, playing with him, cuddling him. I could not understand it—he was a fairly pleasant infant, to be sure, with the correct number of fingers, toes and the like. But he did not seem to do anything except feed or cry or sleep. I was bewildered by Miles's ability to enthral the household females. Occasionally I would lean over his basket and examine him, to see if I could discover the source of his fascination, always without the slightest success.

Goody was staring at me expectantly, and I realized that I would have to come to some decision on this matter.

I cleared my throat to give me time to think.

While the threat of Goody's death a year after the day of our marriage alarmed me, I realized that my girl might have a good point. We had neither seen nor heard anything from Nur in the three months that I had been at Westbury. As Goody said, it was entirely possible that the Hag of Hallamshire, as she was sometimes known in these parts, might well have abandoned her feud with us and gone away. I looked into Goody's lovely pink-and-white face, and made my choice.

"My love," I said, "you know that it is my deepest desire to wed you, to take you into my bed and to fill your belly with a child. God knows, it is not a lack of regard for you that has restrained me thus far. You are entirely right, my angel, until now I have gone in fear of the curse—but no longer. I will make this pact with you: if we have heard nothing from Nur by Christmas Day, if she is truly gone from our lives, we shall make our plans to marry next Easter, with all the pomp we can muster: a lavish event, attended by every great person of our acquaintance, that will set the whole county a-twitter. I will take you as my bride the first Sunday after Easter, and to my bed that night. Would that please you, my darling?"

Goody made no verbal reply, but she gave a secret smile, leaned into me, and kissed me deeply on the lips, her hot little pink tongue flickering into my mouth. Suddenly, it seemed to me that Easter was a lifetime away.

Robin came to stay with us at Westbury late that summer, a week or so after Lammas. He arrived with his dunderheaded squire Gilbert and a hundred men—many of whom were old comrades of mine—in a cloud of dust and shouts and laughter. My lord was in high spirits, bronzed by the French sun, and very happy to be able to spend a day or so with his wife and children before resuming the fight. I had given orders to Baldwin to set up the guest hall the moment the message arrived about his visit, with a private solar at the eastern end that was to be entirely at their disposal for the length of his stay. And Robin's men were housed in a scatter of huts and stables around the courtyard.

My lord had been raising troops in Yorkshire and Wales following the resumption of hostilities in Normandy between King Richard and King Philip, and he came bearing an invitation to me to rejoin the struggle at his side.

"You're getting fat, Alan," was Robin's impolite and quite inaccurate observation. "You'd better get back into the saddle and bring your soft, bloated body south with me. A sharp bit of action would do you the world of good!"

It was then almost a year since I had been pierced by the lance-dagger, a year of very little activity on my part, and yet, perhaps strangely, I felt not the slightest urge to leave Westbury and take up arms again. In fact, I was still struggling unsuccessfully with my queer malaise at that time—I found it difficult to get out of bed in the morning and had to be chivvied into the daylight long after dawn by Goody or Marie-Anne. It was not helped by the fact that I was still unable to sleep well and, when I did, my dreams were filled with horror.

Robin had a rendezvous in Portsmouth in a few days' time with Little John, a company of his Sherwood archers, and the rest of King Richard's newly raised troops, and this fresh contingent was planning to take ship and assemble in Barfleur by the end of August. "You really should come with me, Alan," Robin said in a more affectionate tone, as we sat over our wine in the main hall long after the rest of the household had gone to bed. "The King has been asking for you: he misses your music, apparently. And you can't just mope here for the rest of your life. I take it that you are now fit enough for a campaign?"

I nodded miserably, and it was true: my chest had completely healed, and on the rare occasions that I did my duty by Thomas and engaged him in a lesson in swordcraft or on horseback with the lance, I found that my old skills, so hard won, had not deserted me. It was not my body that was ailing, but my soul. I struggled to explain to Robin the terrors that my nighttime mind threw up, the deep currents of rage and fear that washed through me every day; with the only respite an ever-increasing tide of wine in the evening and a few hours of drowned oblivion. It was hard to tell my friend and master of these things: we were men, and warriors, and I hated to admit my weakness to anyone and particularly to someone whom I admired so much. And when I had finally revealed my sorry state to him, I thought I saw pity in his eyes, and that made me feel even worse. I felt a flare of red rage, and it was only with difficulty that I managed to keep a spew of angry insults behind my teeth.

"I have known several brave men who have been plagued with this condition," said Robin softly, perhaps sensing my rage. "It is a soul-sickness of a kind that falls on a warrior who has seen too much of the raw face of battle. In each man, the illness and its cure is different. But you are not alone in this suffering, my friend, although I'm sure you must feel that you are. What does Tuck have to say about this matter?"

I saw then that Robin's pity was, in truth, compassion.

"Tuck says that I must have sinned greatly, and that God is punishing me—and perhaps he is right, there is much blood on my conscience. The Lord knows I have harvested many souls and not all of them deserved death at my hands. But I have done penance, as Tuck suggested, and prayed until my knees were numb, yet still I cannot find peace."

"Well, give it time," Robin said. "And rest here until you feel strong enough to take up arms again. I will say to King Richard that your wounds are not completely healed, which is true, in a way, and while he will miss you—as will I—he will not wish to embarrass us by inquiring further."

And then he changed the subject and told me of the doings of our King in France since my return to England. "He's a restless soul, is Richard," said Robin. "He cannot bear to be in one place for long: we've held court at Alençon, Tours, Poitiers, Chinon and Le Mans all in the past six months. Oh, and he has found time to buy a very pretty country estate for himself and his wife Berengaria at Sarthe, near Le Mans—though God knows when he will have the leisure to enjoy it. There is no end in sight for this war, as far as I can tell. The sides are equally matched and neither King will yield territory willingly. Still, it keeps our beloved sovereign happy—and out of mischief!" Robin grinned wickedly at me, a sliver of silver in his eyes, and I made an effort to smile back.

"Is there any news of Brother Michel?" I asked. I seldom thought of the Master in the daytime, but he was a regular attendant to my half-dreams in the long hours of night, standing over my bound body and shouting curses.

"None," said Robin, with a grimace. "I make inquiries, occasionally, but he seems to have completely disappeared. No one has seen hide nor hair of him, anywhere. Even in the far south, apparently."

He took a frugal sip of his wine, and looked at me out of the side of his eyes. "Your old friend Mercadier is in high royal favor, though." An image of that scarred and brutal figure flashed into my mind; the phantom mercenary seemed to be sneering at my weakness. "He's flourishing, in fact, quite the hero of the moment. He and his men have just taken the castle of Issoudun in Berry for the King—and by the way Richard talks about him, you'd think that scar-faced brute was the risen Christ."

I shrugged. I did not care for Mercadier, but while I was fairly certain that he had killed Brother Dominic, I could not raise the proper amount of outrage in my heart that this crime warranted. I shrugged again.

"And Prince John is back in favor, too," Robin continued. "Richard has restored to him the counties of Mortain and Gloucester, and there is talk of making him Richard's heir. So far, he seems to be behaving himself. But then, after last time, Richard was not so foolish as to grant him possession of any actual castles." Robin chuckled. "But he can now strut about calling himself the Count of Mortain and the Earl of Gloucester. To be fair, he does seem to have learned his lesson, and there has been no hint yet of disloyalty. But my point is, Alan, we need you in France—our enemies are prospering and growing more powerful. So as soon as you feel able, come south and join us, I beg you."

And with that he went to bed. I did not. I sat up late, burning a precious candle and drinking the rest of the wine.

21

ROBIN LEFT THE NEXT DAY, AND with him went his men-at-arms, Marie-Anne, the two children and Father Tuck, her personal chaplain. I found myself feeling strangely resentful at their departure, and barely managed a civil farewell at the gate. Westbury seemed deserted without them, the courtyard quiet, the hall echoing and empty. Goody wept when her friends left and for some unfathomable reason I felt slightly awkward to be alone with my betrothed.

After Robin's departure, I descended into a great, dark melancholy, which did not recede for many long months. My spirits had been temporarily lifted by the presence of hard fighting men and true friends, but when they had gone, I felt their absence like a hole in my soul. I also felt the shame of a coward, a warrior who has heard the trumpet call and refuses it, a man who has, in effect, deserted his comrades in the hour of battle.

Autumn came, and the ripe apples and pears from the orchard were gathered in, the hedgerows delivered up their purple bounty, and Goody made fools and puddings and crocks of preserves; and in November we slaughtered the pigs and salted the meat for the winter and made long loops of sausages and huge earthenware pots filled with brawn. But none of these normally joyous occasions could bring my soul back from the depths of despair. How Goody put up with me, I do not know; but she did—for a while.

She and Thomas and Baldwin worked ceaselessly to keep Westbury running smoothly, and myself diverted from my black moods. But sometimes I had had enough of their healthy company and their cheerfulness, even that of my lovely Goody—and I would retire into my chamber with my vielle and bar the door, saying that I wished to compose something special, only emerging after several days, unshaven, hungover, having come up with barely a line or so of bad poetry, to empty my piss-pot and seek more wine. In those dark months, I occasionally even wished that Sir Eustace had ended my life when he stabbed me with the lance-dagger; and one night in December I found myself sitting naked on the end of my bed, shivering with cold and holding my misericorde in both hands, the sharp point resting on the right-hand side, the heart side of my chest, opposite and level with the pink ridge of scar tissue on the left, summoning the courage for one hard final thrust. In the end, I was just too damned cold to kill myself, and merely buried myself under furs and blankets, weeping and swearing that I would do the fatal deed in the morning.

At dawn, after another sleepless night, I knew that I could not end myself. I was not yet twenty-one years old, and I told myself that I had to hold on, I had to hope that this Devil-sent soul-sickness would lift. I prayed to God, on my knees in that cold, fetid bedchamber, stinking of old wine, ancient sweat and farts, that one day I would regain my joy, and afterward, after beseeching God to save me from my own despair, I did feel a little better.

Christmastide came and went; I drank my way through the entire season, sitting for hours alone by the fire in the center of the hall, and sipping at mug after mug of warmed wine. In truth, I remember little of that time, although I do recall that, even fogged by wine, those short gray days and long tortured nights of late winter seemed to last an eternity. I was dimly aware of the other members of the household continuing with their daily tasks: Baldwin overseeing the demesne as if I were not there, which was true, in one sense, and Thomas exercising

Shaitan and taking command of the dozen men-at-arms who now lived with us—once Robin's men, but now, I dimly assumed, mine. I fed them, anyway, and housed them, and stabled their horses; and Thomas exercised with them and took them hunting on my lands to keep them fit for battle.

One washed-out morning in March, Goody came to me. I was sitting in my favorite X-shaped chair outside the entrance to the hall, watching the chickens scratch about in the dirt of the courtyard and thinking about a young English servant boy I had murdered in the Holy Land—God forgive me, I had cut his soft, white throat while he was tied and helpless. And, although it was long past dawn, I was still dressed in an old sweat-stained chemise, one that I had been wearing for many days and nights, and I was wrapped in a tattered blanket against the chill and sipping my customary morning mug of wine.

"I've had enough," Goody said, without preamble, and I blinked up at her like a newly awakened owl. "I have been waiting for you to say something about the matter since before Christmas, and now I've had quite enough. I've had enough of your moping, your silences, your drunkenness and your bottomless self-pity. And whether you like it or not we are going to end all that right now. I am holding you to your word: we shall be married at Eastertide. There has been no sign of Nur for nearly a year now, and I will not stand for any further delays. Baldwin and I will make all the arrangements: your job is to pull yourself together and turn up, clean, sober and cheerful, at the church. Do you think you can do that, my darling husband-to-be?"

I was astounded by the change in my betrothed: her normally loving violet eyes were sparkling like cold blue gemstones, her mouth was a grim line. I knew that she had a fearsome temper, but she had never directed it at me before then. I merely gawped up at her, and then recovered myself enough to dumbly nod.

Goody reached out and pulled the mug of wine from my unresisting grip. "For a start," she said, "no wine in the mornings. You may have a drop with dinner, if you must, but otherwise you will drink ale, well-watered, like the rest of us before noon. And get yourself to the bathhouse, you smell like a month-dead polecat. You are embarrassing yourself, and me, in front of the servants, not to mention your tenants in the village. Go on now, and if you can't cheer up, at least wash up."

"How dare you—" I began.

Goody brought her head closer to mine; her brilliant eyes bored into mine, and she said quietly but in a voice trembling with passion: "Alan, my dear, I do love you, but you *will* do as you are told—do you hear me? I want a real man as a husband, not a sweat-stinking sot and, so help me, I will have one, even if I have to fetch Baldwin and Thomas and some of the men to hold you down while I scrub you sober myself."

I was so surprised by her new demeanor toward me that I was rendered speechless. Which, I believe, was a very fortunate thing. I do not like to think what would have happened if I had defied her. And so I ordered the servants to prepare a piping-hot wooden tub in the wash house, soaped and scrubbed myself thoroughly, dressed in suitable clean clothes, and made an effort to wear the mask of a happy, carefree fellow.

I should like to tell you that Goody's irresistible words cleansed my soul of its malaise, and that after that I was a different man: cheerful, sober and filled with purpose. I should dearly like to tell you that. But the world does not turn in that way, at least not for me, and I have vowed to tell the truth on these pages.

I did make much more of an effort, though, to appear happy and normal; I rose early each day, whether I had slept or not, and I realized that my fondness for wine had passed an acceptable point, and banished the fruit of the vine from our table except at great feasts. But I was not cured; the soul-sickness lingered, filling my bones with lead, my stomach with vinegar and my head with bloody horrors. At the end of each long, dreary day, sober, sad and exhausted, I would retire to my chamber and huddle beneath my blankets, staring at the white plastered wall by the feeble light of a wax-dipped rush, both dreading and yearning for sleep.

Baldwin and Goody made all the arrangements for the wedding.

Easter was late that year and we were to be married the week after it on the last day of April. But two arrivals to the neighborhood in that crisp spring month blew all our plans apart like cobwebs in a gale.

In the first week of April, a dusty messenger arrived from Hubert Walter, Archbishop of Canterbury, Papal Legate and the Chief Justiciar of England. Walter was the man who held the country for Richard while the King did battle against Philip's forces in Normandy. I knew him by sight as a short, wide, muscular bishop, the kind of man who was equally at home slaughtering his foes from the back of a horse or delivering a solemn address in an incense-wreathed cathedral. He had a reputation across Europe as an able administrator, a ruthless ruler and a man utterly loyal to King Richard.

His messenger was a tired knight I had never met before, and whose name, I am ashamed to say, now escapes me. His message was simple: Richard needed more knights for the war in France, and all those landed men in England who owed him service were being summoned by Hubert Walter to a muster at London in May. The new force was expected in Normandy at the beginning of June. I held three English manors of the King's in the West Country, the manors of Burford, Stroud and Edington—I held Westbury, of course, from the Earl of Locksley—and also in theory the manor in France now occupied by the black-headed French knight and his son: I had little choice. Like it or not, I was going back to war.

The second arrival was even less welcome. On the day the messenger had left, to carry his news to other idle knights scattered about the north, Goody had bid me goodnight at dusk and had left me, with a cup of watered ale beside the banked hall fire, cleaning Fidelity with an old cloth, a smooth stone and a pot of goose fat, and made her way to her own apartments in the southern part of the courtyard. A few moments later, I heard her screams: three long, high shrieks of soul-shriveling fear.

I burst out of the hall with my sword in my hand and sprinted toward the two-room guesthouse that Goody had made her home. The outer door opened at one blow from my boot, and I found myself in a small, dark hall. To my left I could see seams of light coming from the other room, a bedchamber, and in a trice I had smashed that door from its hinges with a brisk shoulder charge. As I stood in the wreckage of the doorway, I saw Goody standing, apparently unharmed, in the center of the room, clutching a candle to her chest, her underlit face frozen in a rictus of fear. On the far wall, on the white limewash, some shaky hand had written in blood:

One year, one day
after you wed, you pay.

But that was not the horror of the room. On the bed, propped up on the pillow, wrapped in the swaddling clothes of a newborn child, was a day-old lamb, with a little white baby's linen cap tied to its head. The animal had been crudely skinned before being dressed in linen bands, and its pink, glistening flesh, pointed jaw, and bulging blue-gray eyeballs gave it the resemblance of a freakishly deformed human infant. Nur, it seemed, was back in our midst, her malice toward us undimmed.

The room smelled of blood and excrement and burned hair. There were people crowding into the chamber behind us, peering through the smashed doorway, muttering and crossing themselves, and the light of half a dozen candles made the crude lamb-baby look even more terrible. I strode across to the bed and swept the awful dead thing off the blankets with one sweep of my hand, and then I went and took Goody in my arms, pressing her wet face gently into the crook of my neck and shoulder.

She was no longer screaming, but her whole body was shuddering with the shock of the encounter. I held her tightly. We did not speak. Then I steered her, on unresisting feet, out of the guesthouse and back into the hall, and from there through into my bedchamber. And, holding her chastely in my arms, we both lay down on the bed and I gently rocked her until, some hours later, she found sleep.

I could not sleep myself: the words written on the wall in Goody's chamber marched through my head in a simple, endless drumbeat: *One year, one day, after you wed, you pay. One year, one day, after you wed, you pay . . .*

The next morning, at dawn, I rose, summoned a sleepy-eyed Thomas from his pallet, washed, dressed, armed myself with sword, mace and misericorde, saddled Shaitan, who was badly in need of some exercise, and took the road toward Alfreton. I was determined to speak with Nur and put a stop to this nonsense once and for all. I ordered three green-cloaked men-at-arms to accompany Thomas and myself on that mission, reckoning that five mounted warriors would easily be a match for one mutilated girl and whatever poor bedraggled followers she might have gathered around her in the deep woods. And, to be honest, it felt good, a warm satisfying feeling, to be well-armed and mounted on a mettlesome destrier, and surrounded by my loyal armed men, riding to war in defense of my woman.

We approached the lair of the witch Nur from the east, coming up the Great North Road from Westbury and turning left on a narrow path toward Alfreton into dense woodland two or three miles from that small settlement. It was an ill place, even on a bright April morning, and the trees, venerable oaks, tall alders and exuberant ash, grew close together, their trunks covered in the snake lines of vines. The trunks seemed almost to be huddled together in fear, or from cold. We were no more than five miles from my lands and yet I felt as if I were entering strange and hostile country. As we plunged into the trees, a raven cawed above our heads and flapped away on black, tattered wings, and from then on the wood seemed softly quiet, almost expectant in its thick silence. The path grew even narrower, thin questing shoots, spreading branches and catching brambles barring our path, and plucking at our horses' coats and our loose clothing; the ground underfoot was a deep mulch of dead leaves and boggy mud, our mounts' hoofbeats no more than dull thuds. Even in full daylight, only a little sunshine pierced the high canopy of leaves, and we moved through a green-tinged world, silent and close. Evil seemed to hum in the air with the midges and dragonflies. The men-at-arms pulled their cloaks close around their shoulders, though the day was warm. Even sturdy Thomas wore an uneasy frown on his young face.

We forged onward slowly, walking the horses, looking for some sign of Nur and her camp. But we found no trace of her, just a surrounding army of thick gray trunks and shifting walls of green dappled foliage. I knew that this patch of Sherwood Forest, an island of trees surrounded by farmland, was only twenty or thirty acres in size and yet we seemed to have been traveling for an age with no sign of leaving the woodlands—by now we should have ridden clear through these woods and be entering the broad open wheat fields around Alfreton. I began to regret my haste in sallying out after the witch without a guide: if I had paused and found a countryman, a good local man who knew this place like his own hearth, to lead us through this dank wood, we would not now be—I had to admit it—lost.

I looked down at Shaitan's feet and saw that the path had disappeared completely; we were merely threading our way through uncharted woodland, passing where we might between the trees. I could not see the sun, not even its vague direction; this opaque green world had swallowed it whole. We seemed to be within an enchanted fairy realm, a place of magic and evil. I had a brief moment of panic, a sudden breathlessness, and thumping heart, which I believe I managed to conceal from the men: I knew not where we were, or how we might escape with our lives, indeed with our souls, from that fell place. Eventually, I called a halt.

"I believe we must have scared her away," I said, attempting a brisk, confident tone but producing one that came out dull and eerily muffled by the closeness of the trees. "We will not see her this morning, I fear. And perhaps we may never see her again. But the day is drawing on, and I should like to eat my dinner back at Westbury. So we will now return the way we came and rejoin the Great North Road without delay. This way, men, and look lively for I am hungry for my own hearth!"

I turned Shaitan and urged him in the direction from which we had just come; but something was wrong with my senses, for after only a few moments I found myself facing a wall of dense greenery with no clear passage through it. Oddly, we seemed to be surrounded by the wood, as if the trees themselves had moved in around us, hemming us in. I dismounted and ordered my men to do likewise and, drawing Fidelity, I began to hack at the brambles and fronds, and the low swooping branches that blocked our path forward. It was slow going, and sweaty, aching work, and my sword arm was weakened by many months of inactivity, but we did make some progress. I slashed and swiped at the swaying woodland, moving forward only a yard at a time, the thick sap running down the fuller of my blade like the blood of wounded trees. At last, the boughs began to thin, and when I had hacked through a thick patch of head-high green ferns, I found myself—to my surprise—leading Shaitan into bright sunlight and a clearing no more than thirty paces across. My eyes were dazzled at first after so long in the gloom of the forest, and I found that I was standing at the edge of what could only be described as a small village. I was astounded: all around the edge of the clearing a ring of mean hovels had been constructed. There were huts, even tiny cottages of timber and turf, with trickling smoke coming from holes in the bracken-thatched roofs—and people, scores of people, mature women sitting by their doorways cradling babies, young girls tending pots by a fire-pit in the center of the space, skinny children in tattered clothes running hither and yon, squealing and laughing, playing catch-me-if-you-can in the warm sunlight.

I heard my men and their big horses crashing through the greenery behind me, then Thomas was at my shoulder, his own sword drawn, staring agog at the scene before our eyes. *These are the outcasts,* I thought, *these are the runaways, rejects and outlaws of the kind who had once flocked to Robin for protection. And they are all women.*

Apart from their sex, there were other characteristics that united these people: they were all ugly, some spectacularly hideous; deformed, crippled, lacking limbs or digits or ears; leprous, blind or ancient or just drooling mad. Only the babies, wrapped in filthy rags, appeared to be whole. I absorbed all of this in a few heartbeats, and while I was staring in amazement at the hidden village, the women in turn noticed me. A crone at the far side of the clearing, seated by the entrance to a sagging turf hut, gave a gibbering screech, pointed a bony finger at me, and fled into her hovel. The whole village immediately erupted in a chittering, babbling roar, and the placid, happy scene disintegrated into movement. Old women with flapping empty dugs scrambled to scoop up suddenly screaming babies and darted away into the forest; emaciated girls with filth-matted hair wailed and cowered behind the nearest trees. One lumpen woman, broad-shouldered but with an enormous purple goitre swelling from her neck, grasped a thick branch from the wood pile and, growling, took a pace toward us and shook it in our direction in a distinctly threatening manner. Everywhere were women scurrying and rushing; calling out in alarm and anger. The occupants of the sturdier hovels bustled inside and slammed their doors, throwing wooden locking bolts across with a thump.

But one door opened.

The door of the largest hut, almost a house in fact, burst open and a figure strode into the center of the clearing. She threw back her head and howled like a vixen in mortal agony, a long, booming shriek of limitless rage and pain. It was Nur, witch-chieftain of this women's village, the queen of the damned, in all her ragged majesty.

Her hair, long since turned ash-gray, had been shorn and spiked with dried mud so that it stood proud of her head and resembled the spines of a hedgepig; her skeletal body was draped in a filthy, ripped gray chemise that fell only to her thighs and exposed round swollen knee joints above spindly shanks; the nails on the ends of her long, knuckly fingers were overgrown and twisted into yellow curls; she held a tall polished staff in her right hand, its head a knot of roots encasing a rounded piece of granite in which thin seams of sparkling quartz glinted and shone; a necklace of tiny animal skulls bounced on her bony chest—weasel, shrew and mouse heads, painted a rusty brown and strangely marked in black and white with chalk and charcoal;

around her waist was a belt of half-cured snakeskin supporting a big furry pouch, the papery heads of two serpents dangling from the knot in the front where it was secured; her mottled yellowing skin, wherever it showed, was criss-crossed with fresh tiny red scratches and older healed and half-healed scars as if she rolled in a bed of thorns each night . . . But it was her face, her poor mutilated face, that drew the eye. When I had first known and loved Nur, she had been a shining beauty to shame the sun and the moon—but my enemies had taken her and had cut that transcendent loveliness from her, slicing off her nose, her lips and her ears. Her once wondrous face now resembled a living skull, the dark-burning eyes the only hint of humanity above the gaping red holes of her nose and the eternally grinning teeth. A smear of charcoal beneath each eye socket and along the cheekbone gave her an unearthly look, while the chalk paste that covered her lower jaw enhanced the skull-like illusion. In truth, she was terrifying to behold, and I heard the men-at-arms behind me curse and gasp, and begin to make the sign of the cross and mumble desperate prayers for their Salvation.

Nur advanced across the clearing toward me, leaning on her staff, one clawed hand held up in front of her, a hailing gesture, or a benediction, or a curse. I could hear that she was muttering words under her breath in a chanting rhythm, in a language that I recognized as Arabic; but my slight knowledge of that tongue had faded with time. I knew, though, that it was not a blessing. She stopped less than two paces from me, and said, in English: "Alan, my love, the light of my life, my darling man; welcome to Al Mara Madina. You have come at last to fulfill your promise, that can be the only reason for this intrusion."

I stared at her, speechless with mingled apprehension and disgust; her lipless mouth opened and I realized that she was trying to smile coquettishly at me. I finally managed to stammer: "Wh-what promise?" But I knew how she would reply.

"You have doubtless abandoned your milky whore and come to me to beg my forgiveness—and to make good your promise to love me forever and never leave me. The spirits of the wildwood have at last granted my request."

The poor, deformed, broken women of the camp were creeping out of their hovels by now, curiosity overcoming their fear, and groups of them were hovering, half-visible, at the tree line, reassured by Nur's calm conversation with me and my men. I was unmanned by the mutilated witch's words, and for a brief moment I remembered the beauty she had once been and the passion of our lovemaking, the wonder and the joy that we had made between ourselves; I had indeed promised many things in the first flush of young love that Mediterranean summer, foolish things, the poured-out promises of a pleasure-drunk boy, and I had indeed broken my word. Looking at her now, I understood the pity that Goody said she felt for her; this monstrous creature before me, daubed with chalk and coal-black, gathering her half-baked, childish pretense of magic around her like an invisible cloak: substanceless and pathetic, with only the power to cause a little nervousness in the feeble-minded; this was a poor woman made miserable by a cruel fate and unlucky circumstances, she was no enchantress, she was no true witch. She had no power beyond that of any ordinary human soul to hurt with words or deeds.

Staring at her in bright daylight, examining her tawdry rags and emaciated, crudely painted face, I found my courage returning like a river in spate, a rushing of hot blood through my arms and legs.

"Come now, Nur," I said briskly, "you know very well that I have not come here for that. Let us put aside these foolish games. I came here because you have trespassed into my home and hearth, and have frightened the good woman that I love with your silly tricks and ugly threats. And I tell you now that you must stop this attempt at intimidation. I will not allow you to continue to harass my wife-to-be. Do you understand? This foolishness must stop. Now. Else I shall be very angry."

For a moment Nur looked at me in stony silence. Then she said quietly: "You have become cruel, Alan. You were never like that before.

A demon is gnawing on your soul. I can see it. Your heart is now a shard of ice. And you are forsworn; a liar like all your sex; a wretched, lying, worthless man." And she turned her back on me and walked to the center of the clearing, by the pit-fire. She turned again to face me, thrust a hand into the hairy pouch at her waist, and pulled out a handful of dried herbs. Sprinkling them on the fire with her left hand, and holding up the staff in her right, she said: "One year, one day, after you wed, you pay." The herbs had caught fire and a thick, pungent, blue-greenish smoke was rising from the pit and enveloping her frail, raggedy body. The smoke seemed to cling to her skeletal frame as she repeated: "One year, one day, after you wed, you pay." But this time I could hear the murmurs of the other women repeating the refrain. It began low, but with each repetition the chant became louder. "One year, one day, after you wed, you pay." The women were swaying slightly with the rhythm of the chant, and I noticed that they seemed to be, almost imperceptibly, coming closer to the center of the clearing, moving toward me and my men with shuffling steps, quiet but purposeful.

I took a pace forward, Fidelity, still sticky with tree sap, naked in my hand, and I said loudly, clearly above the lapping waves of the baleful rhythmical chorus: "Nur, stop this now, I will not stand for this—"

Nur gave a high, clear scream, and pointed the heavy granite end of the staff directly at me. Her body was by now entirely wreathed in smoke. "He threatens me; he threatens a woman of the sanctuary! A man, a lying man, a forsworn man—he threatens me, he threatens all women!"

I glanced down at the bright blade of Fidelity in my fist. "No, Nur, I do not mean—"

A stone sailed out of the crowd of advancing women and smashed into my chest, cutting off my words abruptly.

I looked beyond the smoke-wrapped form of Nur, pointing her staff, like a lance at my head. A wall of raggedy women, scores of them—old, young, maidens, matrons, crones, goodwives, whores; all hideous in one way or another, all broken or deformed, and all chanting those hateful words: "One year, one day, after you wed, you pay"—was now moving across the clearing toward me. Another stone flew past my head, and another cracked painfully into my shin. Nur gave a long yelping cry, and gestured at me again with her staff. Then Thomas was at my side: "We cannot fight them all, Sir Alan, we must retreat," he said, his voice steady and calm.

And we ran.

I scrambled up onto Shaitan just as the first woman reached me. She was elderly, one-eyed, toothless and mangy and armed with no more than a rusty eating knife, but I had no time for mercy. She ran at me, ahead of the pack of her sisters, and I killed her, God forgive me, turning Shaitan in a tight circle and decapitating her with one sweeping blow of Fidelity. The women were screaming now in rage and fear, and they were nearly all upon us. And I put back my spurs and we five big brave men charged away into the safety of the forest.

Safety—that is an odd word to have chosen. True, we were away from the clearing and the terrifying advancing wall of chanting, stone-throwing women, but we were very far from safe. Our horses could not move swiftly in the thick undergrowth, and while one of the men-at-arms and I dispatched two more crazed women, a burly matron waving a carving knife and a slight pretty girl with one arm, who chased us into the trees, after that there appeared to be no one immediately behind us as we forced our horses through the gaps in the thick green wilderness. I could hear scurrying, however, and the cracking of sticks on either side of our path, and sometimes the gray blur of a figure slipping from tree to tree in the gloom of the forest; half-glimpsed and wraith-like. This was their territory, and we were the interlopers. Worse, I did not know which way to go to find the Great North Road and safety. My heart was beating like a tambour; my skin clammy with fear and the cloying warmth of the forest. The going was as hard as before, and we all took turns to hack a slender path through the undergrowth and create a road between the silent trees with our swords. I cursed myself again and again for my foolish haste in seeking to confront Nur. Rage filled me: I would return, I vowed, with a *conroi* of hard men, thirty mailed lancers, and scour this village of madwomen from the face of the earth with fire and sword—if God allowed us to escape with our lives today.

The attack came without warning: two dozen women, running in screaming from our left flank, two of them leaping onto the back of one of our hapless men-at-arms and dragging him from the saddle. They had no proper weapons to speak of—only sticks, stones and clumsy clubs, and one young girl wielding a heavy iron skillet. But they killed our comrade with their numbers. They used their teeth, when they were in range, and battered him bloody with rocks and broken tree branches, anything that came to hand. I killed another woman with a slash that opened her belly, and Thomas fought like a hero, slaying our enemies with short controlled strokes of his sword, but I had no time to admire his growing skills. A young girl of barely fifteen summers leaped down on me from the branch of a tree overhead. For an instant, her glaring, snarling face was inches from my own, her teeth snapping wildly at my nose like a mad dog's, and then I managed to shrug her off, hurling her down to the leafy ground to my left. Shaitan, who was usually a model of composure in any mêlée, lost himself so far as to buck dangerously, whinnying with terror, and almost causing me to lose my seat. As I tried to calm him, the young madwoman came at me again, and I crushed her skull with one overhand blow of my mace. The women were all around us now, screaming curses, clawing at our legs and battering at our backs with homemade clubs; we killed them as fast as we could—easily spitting skin-and-bone bodies on our swords, hacking clean through scrawny limbs—but still more of these demented creatures came bounding out of the trees, and those we killed too. We feared them and their reckless ferocity, but in truth they were no match for us and, in our fear, we killed without mercy. And we lost another good man in that frenzied, unequal battle, pulled from his horse by the howling pack, and Thomas took a flung stone hard to the face that rattled his teeth, but by the time we had cut ourselves free of them, a dozen of those poor demented women would never breathe again.

I saw Nur only once more that day, through a narrow passage amid the trees, both scratched, emaciated arms raised and the staff twitching as if urging on an invisible army of fiends. She caught my eye and gave a great bubbling cry and pointed the staff at me, but no crazed women came hurtling out of the greenwood to attack us, and I think she believed she was assailing us with magic, summoning evil spirits to accomplish her revenge.

By God's good grace, we found a path of sorts at our horses' hooves and we urged our mounts into a canter, and then a gallop. And we were free and clear. A quarter of a mile later, I reined in, my heart still pounding, and looked over what remained of my little patrol; Thomas was there, his cheek red, shiny and already starting to swell, and Alfred, the senior man-at-arms, but beyond that, two riderless horses, their empty saddles mutely accusing me. I'd lost two good men in that pointless woodland skirmish, and had been routed by a gaggle of unarmed women.

22

THERE WAS NO MORE TALK OF our wedding at Westbury. A few days later Baldwin discreetly told me that the mistress had asked him to unmake the arrangements; Goody and I never mentioned the subject at all. My beloved was a much-subdued woman for many days after the affair with the lamb-baby, and she listened to my tale of the disastrous foray in the Alfreton woods in silence. When I had finished my story, Goody asked one or two questions, and then she said: "You must kill her, Alan. I underestimated her—we both did; but she clearly has a terrible hold over the poor women in that place, and she will surely send them against us again. She will not stop until you and I are dead. You must take enough men this time—end this once and for all."

"I thought that you felt sorry for her," I said.

"I pity her, I really do, Alan—and I do not believe that she has any true magical power. But those outcast women in her encampment, they believe she does. And they are the real threat to our happiness. You do not know very much about women, Alan, but they are keenly aware of each other in a different way to men. When women come together in a group they can change and become quite unlike any gathering of single individuals. Something happens—perhaps it *is* just a little magical—and powerful bonds are formed; as strong, I believe, as any bond that a company of men can form in the face of battle. In a group of close, loving women, the power and support that each member feels can be almost visible—a great force for good. But it can also be directed toward evil. These woodland women, reviled, rejected by their villages, by their men, have formed such a group. Inside that tattered gathering, these poor women have found love and acceptance; and having tasted that happiness they will not allow an outsider, a man, to take it away. I am not surprised at their ferocity: they will willingly die for their sisters, just as men, I'm told, will give their lives for each other in battle. They will gladly die for their kind, and for Nur, who gave them a home. So you must kill Nur. You must kill her before she truly harms us. Go, Alan, gather the men, and destroy her."

But gathering enough fighting men was to prove difficult for me. I had only eleven surviving men-at-arms at Westbury, including Thomas, and that number was about to be greatly reduced. I had agreed with the messenger from Archbishop Hubert Walter that I would present myself, armed, mounted and equipped for war, at London in three days' time when the moon was full. And if I were to fulfill my obligation, I would have to set off the next day. But I did not wish to leave Goody alone at Westbury under the menace of Nur and her coven of demented harridans.

It was Goody who came up with the solution to my problem.

"Send Thomas instead," she said, when I was discussing it with her, on a sunny morning in late April. Goody and Ada, a servant girl from the village who had wet-nursed Marie-Anne's baby Miles, were churning butter in the dairy. It was a physically demanding job, requiring stamina and strong muscles, but Goody seemed to relish it, as she did so many humble tasks that another woman might have felt beneath her dignity as the lady of the manor. "Send Thomas and three men-at-arms," she said. "That way Archbishop Walter is getting four men for the price of one—he cannot complain too much, even though I am sure that he and the King would rather have the renowned and most puissant knight, Sir Alan Dale." She poked her little pink tongue out and I smiled back at her gentle teasing. "What other choice do you have?" she continued. "Either you go and leave me here to face Nur and her women alone, or you refuse the summons and incur the wrath of the King. It is simple. Send Thomas."

I looked out of the dairy window and saw my squire in the courtyard. He was training with sword and shield against Alfred, a veteran man-at-arms in his early thirties, and I realized, as I watched the strokes, counterstrokes, parries and blocks, that Thomas was not half bad. He rode well, I mused, and God knew he was a reliable, brave and resourceful fellow. He had not mastered the lance yet, which was my fault, for I had been neglectful of his training in recent months, but as a swordsman he was competent, even skillful. I struggled to remember how old he was at that time: he must be nearly fifteen, I thought, and I'd been of a similar age when I fought my first battle.

"I shall send Thomas in my stead, and two good men-at-arms under Alfred," I announced. "Thomas can report to Robin when he gets to France and my lord of Locksley will doubtless take him under his wing."

"What a very wise decision, my lord," said Goody, a suspicion of a smile twitching her lips as she pounded the pole of the butter churn up and down, up and down.

Although he did his best to hide it, Thomas was utterly delighted by the prospect of going off to France in my stead. When I gave him his instructions, and told him to report to Robin when he got to the army, he said: "As you wish, Sir Alan," and bowed formally. But he could not help a sparkle of joy lighting his eye and a grin stretching his mouth. I tried to dig up some special words of wisdom for him to take with him and, as usual, came up woefully short.

"Keep Alfred close during the journey to France, and obey Lord Locksley in all things when you get there. Do not try to be a hero on the battlefield—nobody expects that of you; obey orders, and keep your head down and your shield up. And, uh, stay away from the local women, they may harbor, uh, diseases. If you must indulge yourself, ask Little John's advice on which are the cleanest whores."

After that last gem, we both stood looking at each other in embarrassed silence. Until Thomas said, quietly and sincerely: "Thank you, sir, for this opportunity. I will try to be a credit to the proud name of Westbury."

And I suddenly felt a great lump in my throat.

We spent the afternoon outfitting Thomas and his men with hauberks, aketons, helmets, new swords and shields—and I gave them the pick of the best equipment in the armory; also warm cloaks and cooking kit, horse gear, spare clothing and bedding. The next morning Goody provided each man with a cheese, a bag of onions, and several loaves of twice-baked bread that would keep for weeks. I gave Thomas a small purse of silver and a few final words: "Tell Robin that I shall come as soon as I have dealt with Nur and her women and made Westbury safe; and, Thomas . . ."

I paused and put a hand on his shoulder. "Be careful, Thomas, and for God's sake don't get yourself killed!"

My squire saluted, smiled, climbed onto his horse and, followed closely by his three men-at-arms, he clattered out of the big gate and embarked on the long road to war.

I was sad to see him go, but at the same time I could not deny a surge of pride. He was not my son, it was true, but Goody and I were both very fond of him; he was a fine young man—a man, I realized, no longer a boy.

I had cause to regret the loss of four of my fighting men not two days later.

It was the night of the full moon, and our rest was interrupted by the sound of drums. I had been sleeping, unusually for me at that time, and awoke with a sense of irritation and grievance rather than fear. I knew that it was Nur before I stepped out of the hall with Fidelity in my hand and crossed the courtyard to climb up to the walkway that ran around the inside of the palisade. I saw Goody emerging from her guesthouse, tousled, rubbing her eyes and wrapped in a woolen shawl, as I hurried up the steps to the cloaked figure of the man-at-arms, a young fellow called Kit, waiting at the top.

Kit pointed, wordlessly and unnecessarily, at a pinprick of light about three hundred yards away to the west, a fire. It burned in front of a copse that stood beside the stream that ran through my lands. At that very stream, a mere quarter of a mile from the hall, Goody and the village women did their weekly washing, beating the cloth against the rocks and spreading it to dry on the sheep-cropped grass. In choosing that place for their midnight gathering, I felt that Nur was deliberately desecrating my lands, befouling them with her presence. I felt as insulted and perturbed as I might if she had emptied her bowels in the well in my courtyard. The drums beat a simple rhythm—and I realized that it was the rhythm of the curse: one-two, one-two, one-two-three, one-two—or one year, one day, after you wed, you pay.

I called loudly for Thomas, then realized stupidly that he was no longer with me, and sent Kit down the steps to rouse the manor; I wanted all the men arrayed for battle, armed and mounted as soon as possible. This was a gross provocation, an insult—one I could not ignore.

The courtyard, below and behind me, flared to light as torches were lit and soon began to echo with the shouts of men and the protesting whinnies of tired horses woken from sleep and hastily saddled. As I looked out over the palisade, I saw the distant fire leap higher and I could make out what appeared to be two posts planted on either side of the blaze, and slim figures dancing wildly through the firelight. The drumming continued and I heard snatches of song and shrieks and cries either of pain or ecstasy. Then a number of the figures lifted a pole, with a large lumpen shape in the center of it, and set it horizontally across the two vertical poles above the fire. Something was tied to the pole, a sheep, perhaps, or a pig for roasting—*These God-damned witches are having a full-moon feast from one of my slaughtered beasts*, I thought with a spurt of savage anger. I would not stand still and let it pass.

In the darkness, with sleep-dogged men and horses, it took an age to get ready to ride out and challenge the reveling madwomen. But finally we were prepared and, wrapped in righteous fury, I trotted out of the gates of Westbury at the head of six mounted men. Two of them bore burning torches, but the other four, and myself, carried twelve-foot man-killing lances. We had been openly challenged by Nur, and our response would be swift and deadly. I anticipated punching the steel point of my lance into Nur's belly, and imagined her expression of shock and surprise as the spearhead went home, and she writhed around the shaft in her final agony.

But the women did not wait to receive our charge; they fled the very moment they saw our cantering horses approach. And I did not catch even the merest glimpse of my former lover. The women melted silently into the copse at our advance and, when we arrived at the fire, there was not a living thing to be seen.

There was however a sight that chilled our very souls. The lumpen shape that had been roasting over the fire, while these women cavorted about it, was no pig, nor sheep: it was the naked body of one of the men-at-arms who had ridden with me in the disastrous foray against the women's woodland village the previous week. I could see by his tortured frozen expression that he had been alive when he was lowered over the flames and that he had subsequently died, slowly, in screaming, unquenchable agony.

And there was worse: some parts of his half-cooked body had been cut away by sharp knives, several strips from the brown, crisped buttocks, arms and thighs. Until we interrupted them, the witches had been gorging on his poor roasted flesh.

My head reeled, and I had difficulty keeping my supper where it belonged. This was a monstrous, demonic, almost unbelievable act. I ordered two men to cut down the body and wrap it in cloaks, so that we could bear it back to Westbury for a decent Christian burial. One of the men I detailed to cut our comrade free suddenly bent double and vomited copiously beside the dying fire, and I had to fight the urge to do the same myself. I was helped in my task by a distraction.

"Sir Alan, sir," cried Kit, perhaps the sharpest-witted of my men. "The manor, the manor—it's burning," he said, pointing away behind us toward Westbury, where the first yellow flames were licking the black night sky.

Three days later I went to Nottingham Castle, a notional begging bowl in my hands, and a very real and heavy purse of silver in my saddlebag.

We had vanquished the fire after a long, long night of brutal hard work by every living soul in Westbury who could hold a water bucket. The guesthouse was utterly destroyed, as was a storeroom next to it, and the stables were also badly burned, but by dawn it had been completely quenched and one quarter of the Westbury compound was a charred mess of burnt beams and soggy cinders. Goody was not harmed, thank God. Rather than going back to bed, when we rode out for the courtyard so boldly, Goody had decided to go into the hall and find something to eat from the sideboard there. She was eating by the light of a single candle at the long table when the fire broke out in her guesthouse. Nobody had seen any strange folk around, but we all assumed that one of Nur's madwomen had crept into Westbury and set the fire in Goody's apartments while all the fighting men were busy charging out to challenge the witches at their awful feast.

I had not credited Nur with such cunning, and I had made a bad mistake. Now it was time to end this deadly game before my beloved was seriously hurt.

I presented myself to the Sheriff of Nottinghamshire, Sir William Brewer, in his private chambers in the Great Tower of Nottingham Castle. I did not know the man, except by reputation: he came from a family of hereditary foresters in Devon, and was said to be vigorous, ambitious—and utterly venal. He greeted me graciously, insisted on feasting me in the big hall in the Middle Bailey—which I knew of old—and for a consideration of five pounds in silver, he lent me a *conroi* of twenty of his best cavalry for a month.

For two weeks, aided by a man from Alfreton, who knew the land well, we scoured the woods in search of Nur and her gaggle of God-cursed wretches. In vain. We swiftly found the clearing and its circle of mean huts and hovels, and burned everything in it to the ground—but the only soul we found there was an aged woman, blind, and unable to walk, who revealed nothing under questioning except that Nur and her coven, some forty females of varying ages, from barely ambulant children to toothless hags, had left some days ago and headed north. The old crone seemed almost to welcome the knife, wielded efficiently by a Nottingham sergeant, that slit her throat and ended her miserable existence on this Earth.

It was a frustrating time. I had been out-fought by a woman with no deep knowledge of war nor the stratagems of battle, and made to look an utter fool. She eluded me, and left no trace. I sent messages north to Kirkton and Robin's garrison there, but nothing had been seen or heard of the Hag of Hallamshire or her coven. We scoured the wilder parts of Nottinghamshire and South Yorkshire by night and day, and found nothing. I was at a loss. After four fruitless weeks, I dismissed the *conroi* men back to Nottingham, and returned, shamefaced, to Westbury and Goody. Perhaps Nur had worked some kind of charm of concealment. Or maybe, more simply, after years of living wild without the comforts of civilized life, she was adept at moving through the countryside without disturbing a soul.

There was one great boon that my otherwise fruitless struggle with Nur had bestowed on me. That embarrassing contest with the witch had cured me of my malaise. I worked hard in that time; I slept little, but deeply, and drank hardly at all. Without knowing it or wishing it, the mutilated Saracen bitch had cured me of my melancholy, when no other remedy could.

Nevertheless, that summer saw the beginning of a long period in which I never truly managed to find ease. A time of nervous uncertainty, of general but constant fearfulness, a time that frayed the nerves and made everyone short-tempered and quick to anger: it was the season of the witch.

Country folk are superstitious. They always have been and always will be. So in Westbury, from the summer of the Year of Our Lord eleven hundred and ninety-six until the early spring of the next year, every minor disaster was an attack of witchcraft, every accident must be black magic: if a cow gave birth to a stillborn calf, it was Nur's malice; if a bucket of milk, left out too long in the warm sun, went sour, it was her sorcery; a frail grandfather of four score years died suddenly in the village—Nur must have stolen his soul. Every misfortune, every setback—even those with patently obvious causes—was laid at her door; and folk whispered that it was in truth my fault for angering her. People spoke openly—though wisely not in my presence—of the curse that lay over Westbury, and wondered how it might be lifted. To make matters worse, the harvest was bad that year—Nur had clearly brought the rain clouds in August and a succession of heavy, pounding storms to crush the standing wheat.

I asked Arnold, the local priest, to exorcize any evil spirits that inhabited the village and the manor, and the little man made a great show of bumbling about the place in his best robes with his servant holding a huge leather-bound copy of the Holy Bible, mumbling prayers in bad Latin and splashing holy water about with enthusiasm. But the villagers refused to believe it had worked, and when a nervous girl claimed she had seen Nur and her witches riding broomsticks across the face of the full moon, nobody was inclined to disbelieve her.

We saw no sign of Nur at all in that period, but there was evidence from time to time that she had not forgotten us and that she had agents of her evil in the area. Not long after the meager harvest, in late August, Goody found a figure made from plaited wheat straw in her bed in the newly rebuilt guesthouse; long black thorns had been stuck in the belly of the doll, and through its eyes. Goody was shaken and brought the horrible object to me, and I burned it—and from then on Goody abandoned the guesthouse and slept in my chamber. Chastely, I hasten to add, with a long round pillow separating us in the big bed. Though I did on more than one occasion feel the stirrings of an almost overwhelming lust, watching her lovely sleeping face, or catching a glimpse of her white body as she dressed in the morning, I restrained myself. It was a small price to pay for the reassurance of having her under my watchful eye.

In October, we received a letter from Robin telling us that Thomas was impressing all in the army with his courage and prowess, that Little John had been ill with an ague but had now recovered, and that the Bishop of Paris, Maurice de Sully, had finally succumbed to the Crab that had been slowly eating his belly, and all Paris, all France, was in mourning for him.

Robin's letter brought the events of my time in Paris back into my mind; it felt long ago and far away—as if those terrible occurrences had happened to another man, a stranger. I wondered idly where the Master was hiding, and whether he would surface now that his old spiritual lord was dead. But I could not bring myself to care overmuch; my time in Paris seemed like a bad dream, and one that I had no urge to recall. Hanno's death was still a deep and painful wound, only lightly scabbed by time.

The months passed with a surprising swiftness. The Feast of the Nativity came and went, and in January I was forced to dole out grain from my storehouses and open several casks of salted pork to distribute to the poorer villagers of Westbury in the harsh winter months, else they would have starved to death. But I received scant credit for my largesse. Even that cruel winter, with drifts of snow covering the iron-hard fields, was said by some to be the work of the black witch. And, of course, it was I who had rashly brought her wrath down upon our community.

Our spirits began to lift with the coming of spring, as they always did. And I began to feel restless. I thought of my friends in Normandy and began, for the first time in many, many months, to feel the pull of war.

I broached the subject with Goody after dinner one blustery March day while she was spinning wool sheared from our sheep into fine thread—a seemingly endless task—by the hearth in the center of the hall.

"Yes, we are rather stuck," she said. "We fear the curse too much to be married, and yet we cannot find that wretched woman either to make her lift it or, indeed, to kill her. And while she is out there somewhere, you fear that by going off to war, to do your duty as a knight to the King, you will leave me in danger. We are trapped by our fears."

I looked at Goody with no little surprise. It was an intelligent, candid, merciless expression of our situation. And one that was absolutely true, of course.

"So what should we do?" I asked.

"We must do what good men and women have always done when beset by fear. We face it, we walk up to it, nose to nose, and spit in its eye—and we do what must be done regardless of our fears. You must go to Normandy; I will pack up Westbury and go back to living with Marie-Anne in Kirkton until you return. And when you return victorious from the war, my dearest love, we shall be wed here, in our home, and to Hell with that foul bitch and all her works."

I took Goody into my arms, and at that moment I loved her as much as I had ever done. It was a deep love, a love of the soul, not inspired merely by her beauty, although she was truly as lovely as the dawn, but by her courage and strength, her clear-eyed intelligence and certainty.

I departed from Westbury a month later, having spent the intervening weeks training half a dozen or so of the more adventurous local lads as men-at-arms. We had not the leisure for sophisticated teaching but by the time we left they could all wield a sword and shield with moderate competence, and hit a man-sized straw dummy with a lance in two out of three passes from the back of a galloping horse. In fact, I was pleased with my little troop. I left three of the older men-at-arms with Baldwin to help him in his duties about the manor, and the Countess of Locksley had agreed that she would send a strong party of bowmen to escort Goody to Yorkshire, when she was ready to move in with her friend at Robin's castle. And so it was that I led ten fully equipped men-at-arms south with me that April—although the majority of the men had been farm boys the month before—and I must confess, for the first time in many, many months, my heart was light.

We took one of the ships that now regularly plied between Portsmouth and Barfleur supplying Richard's army, and after a rough day's passage, which was the first sea journey for most of my men, and an occasion for much gray-faced groaning and vomiting, we arrived on Norman soil. Almost the first person I saw on the quay at Barfleur was my lord of Locksley. He had been waiting for me.

23

ROBIN SEEMED TIRED AND THIN, THE skin stretched tightly over his cheekbones, but his gray eyes sparkled with pleasure as we clasped hands in greeting. He put his hands on his hips, looked me up and down and said: "Well met, Alan—you look like your old cheerful self again. I'm glad to have you back among us where you belong." And I felt the familiar glow of affection at seeing my lord.

Beyond Robin stood Little John, a blood-and-muck-stained bandage wrapped around half his face covering some cruel injury. "About bloody time, too," growled the big man. And then he spoiled the effect by grinning at me. "God's rotting toe-rags, lad, it's good to see you! I was worried that you had given up the noble profession of arms and decided to spend your days as a stay-at-home, wimple-wearing milksop."

He laughed and hugged me, and I broke away and tried to lift up a corner of the bandage that covered the right-hand side of his face. "What's this, John? Did one of your catamites get jealous and try to scratch your eyes out?"

Little John actually blushed. "It's just a scrape; a French knight got lucky with his lance at a tiny dustup we had near Vernon. It will heal in a day or two."

"You're getting old and fat and slow, John," I said, grinning cheekily at him, and poking a finger into his big, steel-hard belly. He nodded in agreement and then, noticing my disappointment—I had been hoping for our usual friendly exchange of insults—he added quickly: "Not too ancient to put you across my knee, you, you, you . . . battle-dodging brat!"

I could tell by this lackluster response that even Little John was weary to the bone; and I felt a sense of shock and sadness. I had never seen the big man flag before, either physically, mentally or verbally. He had always been a pillar of strength and I was oddly embarrassed, even a touch shamed, by his weakness.

Then I was engulfed by a crowd of familiar smiling faces, my back slapped, my shoulder pounded and my hand shaken vigorously by calloused archers' paws. Robin's warriors were making me welcome. Lastly I spotted a mounted figure in red at the back of the sea of green-clad men-at-arms, a tough, lean-faced fighter armed with lance and sword, and bearing a red shield marked with a fierce wild boar device; I almost didn't recognize my squire Thomas.

He dismounted and greeted me shyly and I saw that he had grown taller in the year since I had seen him. He would never be as tall as me, but I was standing in front of a man—and a formidable one at that.

Robin took me aside: "We have work to do, Alan, I'm afraid," he said. "Nothing too onerous, but we're to escort a pack of chattering English masons and a train of building supplies to Château-Gaillard, and we must make haste, the King insists that we make haste."

Château-Gaillard—the "saucy" castle. Even far away in northern England there had been much talk of the cunningly fashioned, gigantic, apparently impregnable stronghold that Richard was constructing on the very edge of his territory, right on the threshold of the French King's possessions. Rumors of the vast expenditure in silver that the King had poured into this undertaking had reached my ears, even in such a backwater as Westbury, as had stories about his feud with Walter de Coutances, Archbishop of Rouen, who had once been his staunchest supporter. The rift had come about because Richard had insisted on building his huge new "saucy" castle on the Archbishop's land—at a crook on the River Seine in the manor of Andeli—without that venerable prelate's consent. In protest, the Archbishop had gone so far as to place an interdict on the whole of Normandy, which in effect caused all offices of the Church to cease. But Richard had taken the case to the Pope in Rome and, there, old Celestine had sided with the Lionheart. It had been smoothed over now, and King and Archbishop were reconciled: probably because Richard had promised Walter two other rich manors and the port of Dieppe as a *douceur.*

"How go things with the King?" I asked Robin, as we walked our horses along on the road south from Barfleur at the head of a lumbering train of supplies and a marching double column of burly masons in square white aprons, their precious tools slung in sacks on their broad backs. At first Robin did not answer: he merely frowned down at his hands holding the reins. "Between you and me, Alan, last summer was disastrous for Richard," said my lord finally, in a low voice. "Philip got his tail up, and snatched the advantage in the field several times; and now the French have made alliances with the counts of Boulogne and Flanders . . ." These were two very powerful princes, I mused, lords of the rich lands to the north of the French King's domains, and with very strong trading connections to England, in wool and cloth and wine, mainly. This was bad news indeed.

Robin was still quietly speaking: ". . . and no doubt emboldened by this diplomatic coup, Philip sallied out last July and besieged Aumale. He's learned a lot from Richard since the early days of the war—he's still cautious, but when he moves, he moves very fast. And now his siege train is even bigger than ours—with at least two dozen 'castle-breakers,' I'm told. It was certainly powerful enough to knock the mortar out of the walls of Aumale. When he heard the news of the attack, Richard rushed up there with too few men, in his usual gallant, reckless fashion; he took Nonancourt, and ravaged Philip's territories, but when the French King declined to come away from Aumale and fight him like a man in open battle, Richard charged in and attacked him before its walls and got himself very badly mauled. The French were prepared for him, well dug in behind ditches seeded with wooden spikes, and our knights got handed a bloody whipping—our Locksley boys weren't with Richard that time, mercifully, but the Marshal's men were badly cut up. Richard had to withdraw and shortly afterward the Aumale garrison was forced to surrender to Philip. To make matters worse, Richard got himself wounded a few weeks later—shot in the knee outside Gaillon by a crossbowman—and that put him out of action for the rest of the summer."

"Is he recovered?" I asked anxiously. A wound, even a small one, could easily become infected and gangrenous on campaign. I had seen several good men die from mere scratches in the Holy Land, and quickly too, sometimes only in a matter of days.

"Oh, you can't keep Richard down for long," Robin laughed. "He's back on his feet now and still taking big risks as if he were some brash young knight trying to make a name for himself. Come to think of it, he reminds me of you! But he has changed his strategy of late. The few weeks he was incapacitated gave him time to think: since then it's been more about diplomacy than mad dashing about." Robin glanced about him quickly to check that we were not overheard. "Richard's planning to suborn Philip's new northern allies. If we can get the counts of Boulogne and Flanders away from the French and onto our side, Richard believes that we can outflank the French King and attack him from the north and the west simultaneously."

We had left the coast behind us and were entering an area of scrubby woodland. Robin halted his horse and summoned his fatheaded squire Gilbert from the column of a hundred or so men behind him. He issued a rapid series of orders; Gilbert seemed not to understand them, but after several repetitions the oafish lad finally managed to grasp what was required and galloped off to the rear of the column.

Robin looked at me and grimaced: "He's very nearly an idiot; but I can't get rid of him. His father is an old friend. Where were we? Oh yes, the King. The other thing that is greatly occupying our sovereign's mind at the moment is his damned 'saucy' castle."

"What's wrong with it?"

"Nothing. Brilliant idea—a large forward base, packed with well-armed knights and powerful enough to resist a siege for months, if not years. A big, looming threat right on the edge of the French lands. It's an inspired strategy. But the King seems to want to have it constructed in a matter of months. A castle that size, with its many layers of defenses, might ordinarily take ten years to construct; Richard wants it done by tomorrow morning—before breakfast. He is stripping materials and men from across Normandy and sending them to Andeli, and now bringing in craftsmen from England too"—Robin jerked a thumb over his shoulder at the marching masons behind us, who were singing a jaunty song in time to their steps.

"He is spending everything he has on Château-Gaillard, and more—he seems to have no money left for anything else. No money for bribing Boulogne and Flanders to come over to our side; no money to feed the troops; no money to spend on new siege engines or weapons or replacement horses. Mercadier's ruffians haven't been paid for months. They take their living by force from the French lands—or from our own Norman peasants, when they can get away with it. And the other paid men are drifting away from the army day by day. Meanwhile, the rest of us are being worked to the bone to keep Philip's men at bay. On top of that, he asked me to make him a large loan."

I gave an involuntary snort of laughter, and regretted it immediately. "It's not funny," Robin said crossly. "All the barons were asked to make a contribution to the building of his precious Château-Gaillard and I had to hand over five hundred marks. No way of getting it back either. Richard hinted that he knew about the Tourangeaux arrangement—you remember that?—and also suggested that I had hogged more than my fair share of the booty from the royal wagon train we took at Fréteval—and when I countered that the manors he had 'given' me were deep in French territory, and that I had many hungry mouths to feed, he merely replied that that should inspire me to strive harder to drive back the French and claim what is rightfully mine."

I stifled a grin, and said: "But surely, Robin, as the Earl of Locksley, you can easily spare the money . . ."

"Is that what you think?" Robin glared at me. "When you grow up a little, Sir Alan of Westbury, you will realize just how fragile the dignity of a title really is. What counts is land and revenues and cold, hard silver in your coffers. Thanks to Richard, I have given up the golden frankincense trade, and have not been recompensed for it, and Locksley is a minor honor, compared with some English earldoms, and the income it provides is relatively meager. And it could be taken away from me like that"—he snapped his fingers under my nose—"at the whim of the King. I cannot spare the money for Richard's grand designs. For the security of my family, for my sons, I need to keep every penny. But I cannot afford to refuse him either."

We walked our horses on for a while in silence. I had never really concerned myself with money—having been truly penniless as a young boy, my small fiefs seemed to me to generate an abundance of wealth. But then I was not an earl with a certain style to be kept up at the royal court, and the lord of several hundred men who needed to be fed and clothed, armed and encouraged, housed and horsed.

"I am sorry for my shortness with you, Alan, and for my ill humor," said Robin unexpectedly. "I am bone weary—we all are—and this campaign against Philip seems as if it will never be decided."

I looked at him in surprise: it was very unlike him to apologize to me, or to admit any weakness.

"It is I who must beg your pardon, my lord," I said. "I have been absent from the fight for too long, but I shall try from here on to take up my share of your burdens."

"You are welcome to them, my friend," said Robin. He gave me a brilliant smile that almost belied his exhaustion.

We approached Château-Gaillard from the southwest, with the River Seine rolling slowly along on our left flank. After five days of talk with Robin's troops about Richard's extraordinary building endeavor as we trundled uneventfully across Normandy, I was eager as a schoolboy to see this "saucy" castle. In truth, I was not disappointed.

The castle rose before us on the far side of a bend in the river with all the *gravitas* of a mountain—gray, massive and brooding over the landscape. Even unfinished it was a formidable presence, and as we drew nearer I could see hundreds, in fact thousands, of men swarming around the castle's roots and scaling the half-built walls. An army of workmen, summoned from the four corners of Richard's empire to unite with one purpose: to build this mighty fortress in the shortest possible time. We stopped at the far side of the bridge across the Seine that led to the castle, and gazed up in wonder at our King's pride and joy. I heard the muttering and gasps of the workmen behind me, and unbidden, an image of the cathedral of Notre-Dame in Paris flashed into my head: both that great church and this monumental stronghold were extraordinary structures, awe-inspiring, colossal and conjured up by the will of one man.

We crossed the bridge, our necks cricked back as we gazed upward at the castle, and passing through a gatehouse on the other side of the Seine, where we were briefly challenged and then allowed to pass, we rode past a village for the workmen and their families that cowered under the huge bulk of stone above it, and took the narrow road in front of Château-Gaillard, between the castle and the Seine, that wound up to the main entrance.

Above us, atop sheer limestone cliffs, the inner bailey at the north end of the castle with its gigantic towering keep was already constructed and I could see bright banners flying from the battlements and the stick-like figures of men-at-arms standing guard a hundred yards above my head. The walls of the middle bailey were almost complete, but hundreds of men still labored to construct the circular towers that punctuated its stout fortifications. As we rode up a steep track toward the main gate I saw that an extra layer of defense, an outer bailey, roughly triangular in shape with the beginnings of massive towers at each corner, was in the early stages of construction at the south end of the castle, joined by an arched passage above our heads but separate from the middle bailey. We rode through the narrow road between the middle and outer baileys and turned left to enter the castle through the main gate. The noise in that enclosed passageway was deafening, the shrill ringing of steel chisel on masonry, the shouts of overseers, the crack of raw stone splitting, and the dry stench of dust filling my nostrils—memories of Paris flooded my mind and I felt once again the ache of Hanno's loss.

King Richard greeted us in his big, round audience room on the first floor of the mighty keep. He was in very high spirits, as usual, but I could see too that while he was animated, he was tired, and more than a few silver flecks were now plainly visible in his red-gold hair. He greeted Robin jovially, slapping him hard on the arm, and laughing hilariously, almost maniacally, at some comment from my lord of Locksley, and then turned his feverish brightness on me and said: "Well, my good Blondel, you are here at long last—and what do you think of my one-year-old daughter?"

The world shimmied and seemed to rock beneath my feet. Had the King run mad? Surely he had no children. We would have heard about a royal daughter, for certain, long before she had survived a twelvemonth.

A quiet voice murmured at my shoulder. "I believe His Royal Highness is referring to this castle, sir," said Thomas. "He only began its construction last summer—and so it is very nearly one year old."

The world righted itself. I stammered out something along the lines that it looked to be in a good strategic position, easy to defend . . .

"Easy to defend?" roared the King, half-laughing, half-shouting. He seemed rather put out by my tepid answer. "Is that all you can say, Blondel? When this place is finished, I could defend it with one old man on a lame donkey. Why, I could defend this place if these walls were made of butter!"

Robin stepped in smoothly: "People speak of the Château-Gaillard as the greatest fortress in Christendom, Sir Alan," he said. And the King beamed at him, and slapped him hard on the back again. "And so it will be, Locksley, so it will be, if I'm only allowed to finish it."

"It is most impressive, Sire," I said, the courtier in me finally coming awake. "A noble achievement."

The King was mollified. "I am glad that you approve of it, Blondel," he said. "It is the key to our fortunes in Normandy, I believe. From here we can sally out and attack Philip's castles with impunity. And if those French rogues challenge us in vast numbers, we can withdraw here, and defy them for months. It is from here, from this fair rock, that I shall retake Gisors! And when I have Gisors again, I shall have the whole of Normandy and the French Vexin in the palm of my hand. Do not get too comfortable here, Sir Alan. Tomorrow we shall leave for Gournay to show the enemy a thing or two about warfare, and I want you beside me. Reminds me, Locksley, I need to ask something . . ."

The King gave me a curt nod, and I was dismissed. I bowed, and withdrew a few paces. But as I was turning to go, the King spoke again, in a softer, less abrasive tone: "My good Blondel, did you remember to bring your vielle with you from England?"

"I did, Sire."

"Will you give us some music after supper tonight?"

"Gladly, Sire."

The King nodded, and I bowed again and walked out of the keep into the weak May sunshine of the inner bailey.

In a castle bustling with hundreds of knights, squires and men-at-arms—not to mention the innumerable swarms of low-born workmen: carpenters, quarrymen, masons, smiths, diggers and carters, who were hurrying to complete the fortifications—I was very glad to run into an old friend. While Thomas was organizing accommodation for me and my men, and stabling for Shaitan and the other horses—I had brought a palfrey and a pack animal with me from England—I wandered into the courtyard of the middle bailey and watched a knight in a dark-blue surcoat with three golden scallop shells and a dolphin on the chest putting two dozen men-at-arms through their maneuvers with sword and shield. The knight—my old friend Sir Nicholas de Scras—was demonstrating various cuts to the men-at-arms on a paling, a stout pillar of wood set into the ground in the center of the middle bailey. I was struck, once again, by Sir Nicholas's mastery of the art of the blade; his flowing cuts and parries, as he demonstrated a variety of blows on the paling, and the dancer's grace of his footwork.

As I paused in the shadow of a wine-seller's awning to admire Sir Nicholas's skill, I sensed a presence beside me. Turning my head, I saw a tall man with mop of jet black hair atop a lean dark face bisected with a long white scar: Mercadier was watching with me.

For a few moments neither of us spoke, as the line of men-at-arms advanced, slashing the air with their swords, killing an army of invisible Frenchmen. Then the mercenary leader looked directly at me with his blank brown eyes and said: "Hoping to pick up a few new tricks, Sir Knight?"

His tone, with its slight Gascon twang, was just on the polite side of sneering, and though it irked me a good deal, I was determined not to allow him to provoke me into a fight. "A gentleman can never learn too much about the skill of arms, I believe. One never knows what scrap of knowledge may one day save one's life in battle."

"A gentleman," said Mercadier. "Is that what you call yourself now?" He stared at me, and despite myself I could feel the first spikes of rage blooming behind my brow.

"I am Sir Alan Dale of Westbury, a knight of Nottinghamshire . . . ," I began, hating my own foolish pomposity even as the words tumbled from my mouth.

"I know *what* you are and *where* you come from," said Mercadier. He paused, and then drawled: "Sir . . . Knight." There was almost no emotion in his voice: he might have been remarking on the price of the wine in the vats behind us. But I could sense a deep, deep fury inside him; a volcanic anger that he kept from erupting only with some difficulty, only by exerting a vast icy control over his whole being. He was what my friend Tuck would have called a cold-hot man: the most dangerous type of individual, according to him. I could well believe the stories that I had heard about Mercadier—his cruelty to those enemies that fell into his power; his disdain for mercy. I thought about

Brother Dominic, the monk of the Holy Trinity Abbey in Vendôme, and knew in my heart that I was looking at his killer.

I said nothing but made to turn away. However, Mercadier was speaking again, in that cold, stony voice: "I held Normandy for him when he was in prison, you know. When almost everyone else had forsaken him, and sided with John—including you, I believe, and that traitorous creature over there." Mercadier nodded at Sir Nicholas de Scras, who was now demonstrating a high lateral block to the crowd of men-at-arms. "When everyone else had forsaken the King, I remained loyal. When the rest of his fine *gentlemen*"—Mercadier pronounced the word with deep contempt—"had changed their allegiance as easily as a pair of soiled hose and sided with his renegade fool of a brother, I remained steadfast. My men bled and died on this very soil for the King while he was in the power of his enemies. I took this for him." He made a short chopping gesture with his left hand toward his scarred face. "And I held his land against the full might of Philip of France, as best I could. Later I took Loches and Bigaroque and Issoudun for him, and killed half my men in doing so—and yet he made *you* a knight. He ranked *you* over me! He gave you Clermont-sur-Andelle—a fine manor that he knew I had long coveted—and a knighthood! You, who are as base-born as I; you, who are no more than the scrapings of a Nottingham gutter, were given a gentleman's rank . . ."

My right hand had gone to my hilt, and I think I would have taken my blade to him, had the scarred man's dull, poisonous flow not been suddenly interrupted by Sir Nicholas de Scras's familiar cheery voice: "Sir Alan Dale, my friend, how wonderful to see you! When did you get here? And Captain Mercadier, greetings—what an honor to be observed at my labors by such distinguished men of the sword."

I turned to look at Sir Nicholas and managed a tight smile, and when I turned back to Mercadier to say something—I know not what, probably something fatuous about my grandfather the Seigneur—in reply to his insults about my origins, I saw that he had turned his back on the both of us and was walking briskly away across the courtyard.

"What an ill-bred, loutish churl," said Sir Nicholas, as he stared after Mercadier's broad retreating back.

"He is only a little worse born than I," I said.

"Well, you at least have decent manners and a proper sense of honor," Sir Nicholas said casually. And I smiled gratefully at him.

The erstwhile Hospitaler and I took a cup of wine together at the seller's stand, and my friend gave me the mood of the castle. The men-at-arms had been worked hard in recent weeks but remained eager for the fight. They loved Richard for his mad ambitions and reckless disregard for his own safety, and were prepared to fight to the death for their lord and King. Richard had recently returned from a raid at the port of St. Valéry. He had found English ships there trading with the French, and had seized their cargos, burned the vessels to the waterline and hanged the crews. The men had thoroughly approved of the King's actions, and almost all of them had profited from a day or two of unrestrained looting in the captured French town.

"You saw the King this morning, Alan—how was his temper?" asked Sir Nicholas. "Is he ready to press the fight against the French once again?"

I answered my friend honestly. "He's more than ready. In fact, I must confess, he seemed rather too enthusiastic, almost hectic; not as calm as I have seen him previously."

Sir Nicholas nodded thoughtfully. "He appears so to me, also," he said. "But then he has so much that he wishes to achieve this season, and too little time in which to do it."

And there we left it.

That evening, I played my vielle for my King. It was not a happy occasion. I was not well attuned to the mood of the hall, and perhaps wishing to impress the assembled barons with my sophistication, I played some new compositions. They were perhaps too mournful, colored no doubt by my months of melancholy soul-sickness, and I struck the wrong note with that brisk, healthy gathering. The King did not care for them at all, they did not suit his current mood of frenzied optimism, and worse, Mercadier sat next to him during the performance and whispered in his ear. At one point, the poignant climax to a tale of doomed love, Richard actually laughed out loud at something Mercadier had said. I barely managed to finish the piece before withdrawing from the hall with a bow and an excuse, and as much grace as I could scrape together. The next morning we rode off to war.

24

WE SALLIED OUT OF CHÂTEAU-GAILLARD JOYOUSLY and in great force; Richard himself and a hundred knights and two hundred mounted men-at-arms under a forest of spears and brightly colored banners. The King was accompanied by the grizzled Earl of Striguil and his knights, but not by the Earl of Locksley, who had been ordered to hold Château-Gaillard in place of his royal master. I had been given the honor of leading a contingent of Locksley men in green, fifty strong, as well as my own fourteen men-at-arms, who all sported fresh red surcoats with my snarling boar device on their chests.

Before we left, Robin had taken me aside. "John and I are staying here," he said. "We must hold Château-Gaillard in case it all goes wrong and Richard has to retreat; but in truth we could do with the rest. I'm giving you a company of men, who are a little more rested than the others. And I want you to know that I have full confidence in you. Don't feel you have anything to prove to anyone. Don't throw the lives of *any* of my men away—particularly not this one." And he clapped me hard on the shoulder.

Mercadier, I was glad to see, was not to accompany the King; the mercenary captain had been dispatched with his own force of paid men before dawn on a mission of some kind in the direction of Beauvais, deep into enemy territory, while we followed in his tracks making northeast for the border castle of Gournay.

The countryside we rode through had been much ravaged by three years of war—by our men and Philip's—and there was barely a farm beast alive or a cottage unburned that we passed on our march that day. We traveled light and fast—all the men well mounted and the column unslowed by baggage or a siege train. By early evening we had traveled the twenty-five miles to Gournay and were greeted at the gate by none other than Richard's brother Prince John, Count of Mortain and Earl of Gloucester.

My old enemy was a humbled man these days; he saluted his royal brother respectfully, without a trace of his former haughtiness, and bore him away, with William the Marshal, to his private chamber to discuss a plan he had concocted for the imminent assault on Philip's domains. Prince John did not acknowledge me in any way, although I caught him staring at me when he thought I was not looking, and I was content to busy myself with finding adequate quarters in that crowded castle for the men and our horses. Thomas and I dined poorly on a thin cabbage soup from the castle kitchens, which we supplemented with bread, a soft Norman cheese, and a brisk red wine, from our rations.

The next morning word reached us that we were to saddle up and prepare to advance into enemy territory. As Thomas and I were chivvying the sleepy men from their warm bedrolls, William the Marshal came striding across the courtyard to speak to me.

"It's Milly," the Earl of Striguil said. "We're going to take Milly-sur-Thérain. Do you know it?"

I shook my head.

"It's a small castle a dozen miles east of here—John has had intelligence that it's not well defended and he has asked that he be allowed to lead the expedition to capture it. It was his idea, and Richard has agreed."

"The King isn't coming with us?" I asked, astonished.

"He's got other fish to fry," said the Marshal. "Mercadier is a few miles south of here threatening the stronghold of Beauvais, and Richard wants to remain here so that he can coordinate both operations."

"So Prince John is to be in command?" My face must have been a picture, for the Marshal laughed out loud.

"Don't worry, young Alan, I'm coming along too. I'll see to it that he doesn't a make a total hash of it."

"Still . . . ," I said doubtfully.

"All will be well, Alan, trust me," said William. "It's an insignificant castle, poorly defended, and we will snap it up like a trout rising to a mayfly."

Insignificant Milly may have been, but poorly defended it was not. We had the walls surrounded by noon, with Prince John's tent pitched to the north of the castle, and I took a bite of bread and ham with Thomas while we looked at the fortress from a copse a hundred or so paces from the western side. Thick walls, fifteen feet tall, a deep earth ditch before them, and scores of defenders, far from intimidated—indeed defiant—massed on the battlements. We had no siege engines, alas, for Richard's "castle-breakers" would have made short work of these walls—but to bring them up would have meant a delay of several days, and might have brought Philip's main field army down on our heads in overwhelming force. Besides, Richard wanted a quick victory here, the castle captured, its constable made prisoner—and his brother John had promised it to him.

"Locksley's men will undertake the first assault," Prince John had croaked a half-hour earlier when the captains had met for a brief conference in his tent. He had barely looked at me while issuing these orders, but I could see a gleam of something unpleasant in his eyes as he spoke the words: was it a spark of revenge? I knew that he had not forgotten my supposed perfidy while Richard was imprisoned. The company that made the initial attack would face the heaviest casualties. It was a great honor to be the first men into the breach, but it was also the most dangerous task of the operation.

"Perhaps, Your Highness, if my knights were to make a diversionary attack on the gatehouse, it might increase the chances of success for the Locksley assault," said William the Marshal. A veteran of a score of sieges, he knew full well how risky the assault would be. And while he may have been trying to spare my men, his suggestion was also sound from a military point of view. Two attacks going in simultaneously would divide the castle's forces and consequently have a greater chance of success.

"No, Marshal," John had said with a little smile. "My brother has told me of your perpetual eagerness for a fight, and I commend you for it, but I must insist the Locksley men go in alone: it will be a chance for them to prove their mettle. Unless there is some difficulty? Your men do have the stomach for it, do they not, Sir Alan?"

There was nothing I could do but nod gravely and agree, while cursing silently that our men would assault the castle—alone.

Now Thomas and I lay on our bellies, side by side, in this damp wood, with sixty-odd men laid flat behind us. We were as yet undetected, we hoped, by the defenders and I was fairly sure that with a good deal of courage and determination we could take the castle. But my troops were unhappy at being asked to storm the walls alone—Prince John's sneering words had spread like lightning among the ranks—and I could only hope that they would prove equal to the difficult task at hand. I had tried to appear confident as I crawled around the various groups of men, indicating where on the battlements they should make their individual ladder assaults, and trying to put heart into them. In a few moments we would go. And I did not want to. I would have happily spent the rest of the day, the rest of my life, in that sodden copse, and let pride, Robin, Prince John and the whole world go hang. Inside my head, a voice was asking: why had I come to Normandy if I did not wish to fight? And I knew deep in my soul that I was frightened. It had been three years since I had felt this sensation: the cold, watery bowels, the sudden itch on leg or arm, the startling clarity of everything before my eyes. I was going into battle again; I was facing yet another dance with Death. And there was no way I could escape it and keep my honor. I touched my chest, and felt the ridge of scar tissue on the left-hand side even through my mail suit. I closed my eyes, dropped my forehead into the moist leaf litter in front of me, and uttered a prayer to St. Michael.

When I looked up again, to my right, through the trees I saw a flutter of bright cloth: the Marshal, God bless him, was parading his knights in front of the main gate, just out of crossbow range. I recalled his gruff, half-whispered words after the meeting at Prince John's tent. "He may forbid me to aid you in the assault, Alan, but he may not tell me where and when I can inspect my own men. We will make a bit of noise and a brave show in front of the gates, and that shall be your signal to attack. God go with you."

Thirty knights were wheeling their horses, clumsily arranging them in a battle formation, and then appearing to change their minds at the last minute; the trappers on the horses, constantly in motion, were a bewildering range of colors: reds and blues, white, gold and black. The iron links of their mail shone silver in the sunlight, their steel helms, too, reflecting blindingly. The horsemen shouted to each other and brandished their lances, pennants fluttering. A few waved unsheathed swords and called to their friends. Some shouted insults at the garrison of Milly or bellowed their personal war cries.

It was time.

I took a deep breath and forced myself up on all fours. I looked behind me at the white, fearful-expectant faces in the gloom of the wood. "Well," I said in a low voice, just carrying to the furthest man, "we've done this before and been victorious. Let us show these Frenchmen how the Locksley men can fight. Archers to your posts. Laddermen to the front! Quick and quiet, boys. Off we go."

And off we went.

We sprinted out of the wood and made for the deep ditch in front of the western wall of the castle as quietly as we could—which is to say not very quietly at all. A man to my right appeared to twist his ankle and fell to the ground with a loud yell before we had got twenty yards. Another, seeing him, stopped to help the injured man. But we were off and running and, at first, it seemed as if we had managed to take the castle by surprise.

Then there were shouts from the battlements and a single crossbow fired. In answer, I heard the first fluting of the arrows as they flashed above our heads. I had left ten of Robin's best archers behind in the tree line to pick off the defenders as we charged. And as I looked up at the looming castle walls that rushed toward us, I saw an arrow lance into the head of a shouting defender and jerk him backward. Then we were in the ditch below the walls, and planting the feet of the ladders in the brown watery mud.

"Up, up!" I was shouting and climbing at the same time, my palms slippery on the rough wooden rungs of the ladder, my shield slung on my back, Fidelity gripped clumsily in my right hand. A head popped over the parapet in front of me and I lunged forward with my sword. I was too far away to badly injure the man but, as I had hoped, he pulled back and gave me a few precious moments to scramble up the remaining rungs. My enemy reappeared: a screaming red mouth, a conical steel helmet, and a short swinging axe. I ducked, and felt a blow skittering across the top of my own helmet, and lunged again, slicing the spear-tip of Fidelity into his face. And I was over the wall. A quick glance to my left told me that the Marshal's diversionary tactic had worked well, for the defenders had massed above the main gate and only now were they realizing the danger from our assault on the western wall. The man at my feet, a bloody flap of skin from his cheek swinging free, grabbed at my legs and I stamped hard on his throat with my mailed feet, crushing the larynx and leaving him choking. Beside me, left and right, the ladders were thumping against the stone walls, but enemies were coming at me along the walkway from both sides too. I went right, fumbling my shield from its straps across my back; the nearest man-at-arms swung his sword, I blocked and aimed a counterthrust, spitting him in the belly. The enemy man-at-arms behind me shouted something and struck at me with a mace, but I managed to catch the heavy blow on my shield and, turning, I swept his legs from under him with my sword. The blood was singing in my veins, I felt the ancient glow of battle from my fingertips to my toes. Another man loosed a crossbow bolt at me, and I received it safely in the center of my shield, took two steps toward him and sank the edge of my blade into the corner between his neck and his shoulder. And turned to look for my comrades, who should have been spilling over the walls behind me.

I was alone.

There were two dead men, in red Westbury surcoats, on the walkway behind the wall, and I could see the head of Alfred, Thomas's mentor, poking cautiously above the twin rungs of a ladder. He was being assailed by two Milly men-at-arms at the same time—and as I watched, the left-hand man split his head with a massive sword cut and he dropped away. I risked a quick glance over the wall. Two ladders remained propped against the walls, one packed with men seemingly struggling upward, the other only half-filled. I saw that one man was frozen halfway up. His face terrified, unable to climb the last few feet to his certain death, and behind him men were blocked from ascending by his fear. I saw a scattering of our dead and wounded in the ditch, and among them the body of Thomas, his steel helmet broken and bloodied.

A shout of pain and grief erupted from my lungs, but I had no time to mourn: my enemies were coming for me, dozens of them. And I was alone. I knew I would be united with Thomas very, very soon. The first man reached me and I dispatched him with a fast, hacking blow that opened his waist; I held off another with my shield and turned to smash the hilt of my sword into his face. I felled another with a slice to the back of the neck. There were bodies, wounded and dead, all about me. But more were coming on. The walkway held room for only two men on each side, else I would have been dead in moments; as it was, I struck and struggled against the men who rushed forward on both sides with shining blades swinging. An axe blow sliced the top corner off my shield, something clanged off my helmet and my legs wavered, but I straightened and killed the next man on pure instinct—a hard lunge through the belly. I could feel the crenellations of the wall in the small of my back. I blocked another blow, swung and cut at thin air. Something battered against my lower leg. And then I heard a voice below me shouting: "Out the way, out the way, you cowardly villains," and a volley of shouts and curses. And from the corner of my eye I saw the top of a ladder bouncing wildly. I blocked another sword strike, and hacked at a man's head, but I caught a blow that came out of nowhere on my right arm near the shoulder—thank God for good mail. I swung feebly at a tall man in a black surcoat, missing him by a foot or more and feeling the strength draining from my sword arm, but the blow was enough to cause him to take a cautious step back.

And then William the Marshal himself tumbled breathlessly over the wall and barged his way into the fight.

That grizzled old warhorse, armed with sword and mace, dropped two men in as many moments, engaged the tall knight in black in a brief duel and smashed him unconscious with a backhand mace blow to the side of his helmet. I had recovered somewhat and managed to force back two men-at-arms to my right with a couple of wild swinging cuts. And between us, the Marshal and I managed to create enough space for another two knights to come bundling over the wall—one of them being Sir Nicholas de Scras. And from that moment onward the castle of Milly was ours. Sir Nicholas mowed into his opponents on the left of the walkway, chopping and shoving, grunting, slicing and snarling his way inexorably forward. More of our men joined him. Once the Marshal's knights had broken the initial resistance on the western wall, the Locksley men swarmed up the ladders at last and poured into the castle. I took no further part in the battle, collapsing exhausted on the walkway, my ears ringing and my leg and sword arm throbbing from the blows I had taken. I was also quite breathless; while I had assumed I was fit, young as I was, I had in fact taken my fitness for granted—I was not nearly in good enough wind for prolonged sword combat. Some of the Locksley men, I noticed, could not meet my eye as they passed me and charged down into the courtyard of the castle seeking out defenders to slaughter; others seemed indifferent to their shame. They were not my men, I reminded myself, but Robin's, and they had a lesser duty to me than they would have had to their own lord. To ask a man or a group of men to risk their lives is no small thing. But I could not help feeling a sense of sadness that, as I had been away from them for so long, the bonds between us had been so loosened. Three years ago there'd have been no fearful hesitation during an escalade, no matter how dangerous, none at all.

The Marshal also evidently believed that he had done his share of the work that day for he sat down a few yards from me, resting his behind comfortably on the unconscious body of the tall black-clad knight. When I had thanked him for his timely intervention—and given thanks for his complete disregard for Prince John's orders—he brushed away my words and said: "Well, Sir Alan, I am nearly fifty years old, and so I believe I am entitled to take a little rest during a battle—what is your excuse?"

With those jesting words he shamed me into rising and following the Locksley men down into the castle of Milly.

Thomas was not dead—praise God and all the saints in Heaven. He had received a nasty sword cut to the head, but his helmet had taken the force of the blow and while he was a little dazed for a day or so, and his cut scalp had bled copiously, within a week he was his old cheerful self.

Prince John was eloquent when he praised William the Marshal's actions that day—and not a word was said about the Earl of Striguil's blatant disregard of his orders to leave us to assault the castle alone. Victory forgives all, it would seem. John hanged all the men-at-arms he had captured, which to me seemed unnecessarily cruel—though not, of course, the knights. These downcast warriors were chivvied into a storeroom and locked in while our men-at-arms sat outside and gleefully reckoned their probable ransoms in loud, mocking voices, meant to be heard.

The Locksley men had taken a dozen casualties in the assault, but only six dead, which included two Westbury men and Alfred. It crossed my mind to seek out the man who had apparently twisted his ankle in the attack and so avoided making the assault, but I did not have the stomach for it. If I found that he had been shamming, I would have had to hang him as an example to the others, and I could not face the task. That was pure weakness on my part, I admit, but I was heartsick that the men had performed so badly. And they knew it.

I sent them back to Château-Gaillard the next day with a wagon containing a dazed Thomas, and told them to inform Robin how the battle had taken place, and to describe truthfully their part in it. I kept the remaining ten Westbury men with me, for while we too had been dismissed by Prince John—a detachment of the Marshal's men were to garrison Milly—and told to return to the saucy castle, I wanted to make a private pilgrimage with my own men before returning to Robin.

We took a detour on the way home from Milly, and wandered a little to the north of our original line of march. And two days after the assault, I found myself, with ten good Westbury men around me, sitting my horse in almost exactly the same spot slightly back from the tree line, that I had occupied with Thomas and Hanno three years previously. I was gazing out between the branches at the manor of Clermont-sur-Andelle—the rich manor that had once been promised to me by the Lionheart. Or rather I was gazing at the place where the rich manor of Clermont had once been.

It had been totally devastated. In truth, we had been able to smell the place on the slight breeze from half a mile away. It was the familiar stink of rural destruction: sour wet smoke and rotting carcasses, with notes of dung and despair. We trotted down across the water meadow where the two black-headed knights had flown their brave falcon to the bridge over the River Andelle, and not a living thing did we see. A holocaust had engulfed the whole settlement here, and recently, at a guess, no more than a few days ago. The hall and its surrounding palisade had been burned almost to the ground—the mill had been fired and it looked as if the fine flour in the air had exploded, too, a common enough risk, and all that remained was the massive millstone squatting like a blackened round table amid the piles of ash and charred wood. Even the church had been burned down; and the broad fertile fields of green barley and wheat had been trampled by many horsemen. The destruction was complete, absolute—as if ruin was the real objective and not gathering booty, or foraging for food. It was as if a malevolent being were punishing this manor and its wretched inhabitants for some nameless crime.

The people were all gone—perhaps driven to take refuge in a local monastery, or even to swell the throngs of beggars in the stews of Paris, though I noticed a dozen fresh graves in the churchyard, and concluded that a few villagers must have lingered long enough to bury their dead before they departed. All the livestock had disappeared, too, perhaps taken by the villagers, perhaps driven off by the marauders.

The marauders: I knew who had done this. It was Mercadier's work. I knew that they had passed through this area a few days previously. Was it a strike at me? Was Mercadier trying to punish me for being given this manor by Richard? It seemed slightly odd behavior, even for a ruthless warlord like Mercadier, a little moon-crazed, to be honest. I had not been receiving the benefits of these lands before they had been despoiled, and I would not have any chance of garnering any profit from them now. But I had not been damaged by his actions; I would not miss revenues I had never received.

I sat in my saddle looking down at the half-burnt carcass of an elderly nag that lay half in and half out of the charred remains of the stable block. What could Mercadier mean by this excess of destruction? Was he saying that I should never possess this land? Certainly, even if Philip's borders were pushed back and I were to take on this manor, as the King intended, I would have to spend a good deal of silver to restore its fortunes; rebuilding the church alone could cost half what I received in a year from Westbury. And if the laboring people did not return, I would have to find villeins from somewhere to work the land; perhaps even parcel some of it out to freeholders. It did not seem worth the trouble. Yes, Mercadier's actions seemed perplexing to me. What was he trying to achieve? Was he merely saying, by this destruction of a manor that might one day have been mine, that he hated me? It seemed so.

25

I RETURNED TO CHÂTEAU-GAILLARD TO FIND MERCADIER a hero, crowned with fresh laurels and riding even higher in our King's favor. While I had been assaulting the insignificant castle of Milly, the mercenary had boldly attacked the mighty stronghold of Beauvais—the lair of Bishop Philip, a loyal Frenchman and sworn enemy of our King. And the grim-faced captain had even managed to capture the feisty Bishop of Beauvais, outside the walls in full armor, and bring him bound and furious to Château-Gaillard, where he had been promptly imprisoned in the deepest cellar. Capturing Richard's enemy had been a stroke of good fortune; capturing him fully armed and helmeted for war meant that Richard could keep this high churchman imprisoned. And there was a satisfying symmetry to this coup, from Richard's point of view. The Bishop had been responsible for the rumor half a dozen years before that Richard had ordered the assassination of the King of Jerusalem, a lie that had given the Holy Roman Emperor an excuse to keep the Lionheart in chains in Germany. Now it was the rumor-mongering Bishop of Beauvais who languished in chains.

King Richard gave a lavish feast in Mercadier's honor, which I was obliged to attend, although mercifully I was not asked to perform my music. I caught my enemy's eye as he sat at the right hand of the monarch, basking in his favor, and he grinned smugly at me. I smiled back, and politely inclined my head. And thought: *I shall kill you one day—perhaps not today, perhaps not this year—but one day I shall surely give myself the pleasure of watching the spark of life being extinguished in your eyes.*

In the weeks that followed, I spent a good deal of time working with my ten remaining Westbury men, training with them and taking them on mounted patrols around the neighborhood of Château-Gaillard. King Philip's men held the powerful castle of Gaillon only five miles to the southwest of Château-Gaillard and so the patrols had some purpose, not only in providing intelligence about enemy troop movements, but also in providing regular skirmishing practice for my men when we encountered enemy patrols. We had no orders to stay and fight and die, so we did not do battle *à l' outrance*, as the saying goes, when we encountered the enemy; we would try to ambush them occasionally, and they us, but if we were overmatched we exchanged a few cuts and cheerfully fled for our lives.

Two of my Westbury men particularly distinguished themselves that summer in Normandy: a tall, quick-witted lad called Christopher, whom we all called "Kit"—who single-handedly killed a French knight with his lance in a mêlée, and Edwin, known as "Ox-head"—a thick-bodied youth, immensely strong, with a large poll, as his name suggested, and a wide easy smile. Ox-head was a natural peacemaker in the troop but was a fearsome man in a fight, using his strength to batter down his opponents. But the natural leader, after me, was Thomas: it was he who forged these men over the course of the summer into a small but deadly fighting force.

We were, of course, differentiated from Robin's men by our red surcoats, but we also kept ourselves apart from the bigger force of men in green, while maintaining cordial relations with them as best we could. Their hesitation at Milly had not been forgotten by my men, and it was much resented, although I had forbidden them to speak of it. And while Robin's men outnumbered us ten to one, we began to feel that we were a superior force: tight-knit, hard-fighting, disciplined and well trained—for I made sure that we exercised in arms together every day, rain or shine, in the courtyard of Château-Gaillard. I was proud of them.

That summer the war went Richard's way almost entirely: he captured Dangu, a small castle only four miles from Gisors—during which, it must be said, Robin's men fought heroically under their silver-eyed lord—and we all had a sense that the frontier between Normandy and the French King's possessions was being pushed back toward its rightful location. At one point, Richard's furthest scouts were able to make a quick raid on the outskirts of Paris—although, in truth, like rabbits they merely robbed a few vegetable gardens and scampered away when King Philip sent a sizable force of knights to confront them. But we were winning the war in the north, and we all knew it.

Richard was also making great strides in his diplomatic struggle, as well. He had forged a lasting peace with his old enemy in the south, Raymond, Count of Toulouse, whose father and grandfather, encouraged by the French, had plagued the House of Aquitaine in their most southerly dominions. In July, we had the honor at Château-Gaillard of a visit from Baldwin, Count of Flanders. He was a handsome man; tall, fair of face, with a soldier's carriage and a straight, honest gaze. In the presence of Count Robert of Meulan, William of Caïeux and Hugh of Gournay, all of whom had recently abandoned the French King and come over to Richard's side, the Count of Flanders signed a formal treaty with our King stating that neither would make peace with Philip without the other's consent. In exchange, the Count received a "gift" from King Richard of five thousand marks.

The French King now faced enemies to his north and west, and it was not long before Baldwin of Flanders made good his pledges to Richard and invaded Artois, besieging the French-held castle of Arras. Philip's vigorous response surprised almost everybody. The French King replied with massive force, first striking west, retaking Dangu, and pushing back Richard's forces in Normandy, then surging north to relieve Arras. We had all perhaps been too confident of victory—Richard was in the south in the County of Berry with the bulk of the army when Philip struck and one hot morning in August I found myself looking east from the battlements of Château-Gaillard to see a huge French army below me—hundreds of knights, thousands of men; I could even see a fleur-de-lys fluttering from a knot of horsemen to the rear of the force.

However, Philip had no intention of besieging the saucy castle; he was just trying, once again, to intimidate us, to keep us penned in Château-Gaillard while he planned his attack against Baldwin. And he succeeded: with Richard and Mercadier in the south, we had not the manpower to engage his army, and Robin, who was Constable of the castle in the King's absence, ordered us to stay put behind its walls. "You do not exchange a position of strength for one of weakness," he told me one night over a cup of wine in his chamber at the top of the north tower in the inner bailey. "Philip cannot stay outside our walls for long, and we cannot sally out and attack him without courting disaster. Besides, our orders are to hold this castle. Richard is storming through Berry and the Auvergne—I've had word that half a dozen castles in the south have fallen to him. And Baldwin is at Arras, in the north, which will fall to him soon enough, if it is not relieved. Philip cannot stay here."

So we did nothing. As Robin had predicted, Philip soon departed and, in a series of swift marches, covered the hundred or so miles northeast to Arras, relieved the beleaguered garrison and pushed Baldwin's troops back almost as far as Flanders. But in his blind fury, and driven by an ardent wish to punish Baldwin for his disloyalty, Philip fell into the Flemish trap. The French advanced, but Baldwin's troops retreated ahead of him, burning the crops, driving livestock before them, and destroying the bridges after they had been crossed—and behind Philip's army, too. It was no doubt a cunning maneuver on Baldwin's part, yet I could not but remember the destruction at Clermont-sur-Andelle and wonder what the ruined peasants of Flanders would eat this coming winter with their crops and livestock gone. Still, it was no business of mine, and Philip's men, deprived of food and forced to forage from a barren landscape, began slowly to starve. The French king was being humiliated, and we rejoiced at the news.

Now facing disaster, Philip tried to make a separate truce with Baldwin, which would have allowed him to extricate his men from Flanders and unleash them on Normandy, but that steadfast prince of the Lowlands showed his rectitude: the noble lord remained true to his agreement with Richard and resolutely refused to parley with the French heralds.

It was a summer of war, a summer of victory, but like all good things it had to come to an end. Richard's men had been covering themselves with glory in Berry, and Baldwin's had fought the French to a standstill in Flanders, but when the King of England and that honest Flemish Count met in Rouen in September, it was to discuss the terms of the truce they would jointly make with Philip. The war was not over; Philip had merely been hemmed in, his borders shrunk in the north, the west and the south, but it was the time of year for all combatants to take a breath, and rest their limbs in the cold months of autumn and winter.

"Next year," said Richard jovially, "next year, Blondel, we shall take Gisors, and once that is back in our hands, the whole of the Vexin shall be mine. Next year, God willing, I shall regain my entire patrimony from that French thief."

I had been entertaining the King and his senior barons in the audience room at Château-Gaillard, and when the rest had retired the King had asked me to stay behind and play something solely for him. There was but one choice: "My Joy Summons Me"—a piece that I had played under the walls of Ochsenfurt in Bavaria and, by his response to it, from a high cell in one of the towers of the city, I had located my captive King when he was in the hands of his mortal enemy Duke Leopold of Austria.

I had expected the King to join me in singing some of the verses—after all, he had written the alternate ones—but while I played my vielle and sang, he stayed mute, watching me with his eyes half-closed, a smile on his lips. When I had finished, he repeated one of the verses, the third one that I had written, quietly in his normal speaking voice:

"A lord has one obligation
Greater than love itself
Which is to reward most generously
The knight who serves him well . . ."

We sat in silence for a moment and then my King said: "Well, Blondel, you have served me well—I cannot deny that. You served me well in the German lands, and at Nottingham, and at Verneuil, too—and the Marshal tells me that you were the first man over the wall at Milly. Tell me truly, have I been a generous lord to you?"

I did not hesitate for a moment. "Yes, Sire," I said.

"Your master, my lord of Locksley, does not seem to think I am a generous lord. He complains that the lands I have given him are in French hands, and says that he will never live to enjoy them. What say you?"

I thought about Clermont-sur-Andelle, now destroyed. "We all live by the fortunes of war, Sire, and the will of God. I think He does not mean me to enjoy Clermont."

"That is a good answer, Blondel," said my King, and he laughed. "When this war is over you shall have more and better lands to compensate you for Clermont—or if you choose, I shall give you the necessary silver to repair the ravages done to it."

I bowed my head. "That is most generous, Sire," I said. And I meant it. But the King was still speaking: "Robert of Locksley, however, does not feel that I have been openhanded. Now that the truce has been signed, he has requested that I allow him to leave my side and go off on some sort of treasure hunt—I do not fully grasp the details, but it seems he wishes to go to the Duke of Burgundy's lands in pursuit of some fantastical object of miraculous provenance and exceedingly great value. And I am not minded to refuse him."

The Grail, I thought, with no little shock. *Robin is seeking the Grail.* But the King was still in mid-flow. "Locksley too has served me well and I must grant him this request. However, it does mean that I cannot spare you. I cannot have all my knights departing before the ink is dry on the treaty. Some must remain to garrison the castles or, truce or no truce, Philip will be beating down all the doors in Normandy. I know that you had wished to return to England to marry your sweetheart—a commendable desire, I am sure; my mother the Queen has met the lady concerned and tells me that she is a most beauteous, mild and charming creature"—*not when her anger is roused*, I thought privately, but said nothing—"and I understand that she is an orphan, and a ward of the Countess of Locksley. Therefore, I propose that, with your agreement, when we have pushed Philip out of these lands, I should give the lady in marriage to you—with a suitable dowry, of course, of, say, a hundred pounds in silver!"

The King searched my face, and I could see that he was enjoying the look of surprise and joy he saw on it. A hundred pounds in silver—it was a great fortune, without a doubt; I could rebuild Clermont, if I wished, or purchase a far bigger, richer manor in England. But there was more.

"I want you here at Château-Gaillard," said the King, "holding the place for me as the Constable. I shall be coming and going, but you will have the responsibility in the next few months for my fair castle on the rock. Will you do that for me, Blondel?"

I would be the Constable of the greatest castle in Normandy, a position of vast honor and responsibility—and all that the King desired in exchange was that I postpone my wedding for a while. I bowed once again, and said: "You are truly a most generous lord."

I found Robin in his chamber in the north tower reading from a leather-bound book, seated at a table piled high with parchments and scrolls. I knocked and entered and Robin barely glanced up from his book but waved a hand vaguely at a tray on a sideboard with a flagon of wine on it and several cups. I poured myself a drink and one for Robin too and waited patiently while he finished the page he was reading.

"What did he offer you?" my lord said, laying down the book. I was slightly taken aback by Robin's bluntness.

"A hundred pounds in silver and the post of Constable of this castle."

"Constable, that's good. Did he say when he would give you the silver?"

"He offered to give Goody to me in marriage—and to let me have the money as a dowry. When we have retaken all Normandy, he will personally bless our union."

Robin grinned. "That's our Richard. He would always rather promise money to be paid at some future date than hand over the cash here and now. But well done, Alan!"

I said nothing for a few moments. Then: "So you are going to Burgundy?"

"Yes, I'm going to see this fellow"—he tapped the book in front of him—"Robert de Boron, a knight who serves the Seigneur de Montfaucon. Reuben knows him, apparently—our friend has excellent connections down there—and has arranged a meeting in Avignon, which is close by."

"What's the book about?"

"It's about Joseph of Arimathea, that blessed man who entombed the crucified body of Our Savior Jesus Christ."

I gave Robin a look, and he stared straight back at me, his expression grave and humble. I knew that look: Robin was trying to appear sincere. I could not help myself: I laughed. Robin joined me, chuckling and shaking his head.

"You know why I'm going," he said, "don't you?"

"You want the Grail."

He nodded.

"In God's name, why?"

"I can't fully explain. I've been thinking about it almost constantly since you first mentioned it to me. I could tell you that it is the most fabulous treasure in the world, an object worth a county at least, and that's why I want it. I could say that I long to possess the vessel that Christ drank from and which held his sacred blood—but I think you would laugh at me again. I could say that owning it would make me the most powerful man in Christendom; and that taking it away from a gang of renegade Templars would give me enormous satisfaction. I could say that I have had enough of Richard's endless petty wars and I need a new and better task to fulfill me. And all of that would be partially true. But the honest answer is, I want it, I want it with all my heart—and I will have it." Robin's eyes were shining with a passion I'd not seen in years.

"You realize that it is probably just an old bowl?"

"That may well be. Still, I must have it."

"So what are your plans?"

"I'm heading south—tomorrow, actually. I am going to Avignon to meet this Robert de Boron. He writes with authority on the Grail, and I am sure he must know more than he has written. After that, I will go on to stay with Reuben in Montpellier, then through the County of Toulouse toward the Pyrenees. I'm not sure where the trail will lead. We will see what I can discover. The scraps of evidence that I have managed to gather"—he waved a hand at the piles of parchment on the table—"all seem to indicate that the legends began down there. And the Master was originally from those parts, too, if I recall rightly."

"You make it sound like a pilgrimage," I said.

"And perhaps it is," said Robin.

"So you leave tomorrow?"

"Yes, I'm taking Little John with me, and twenty men as a bodyguard—but the rest I'm leaving with you. Can you manage them? I gather there was some . . . difficulty at Milly."

I frowned. The Locksley men's hesitation in that escalade was still a sore memory.

"I'll manage," I said gruffly.

"May I give you a piece of advice? Don't try to get them to like you.

Keep them busy. Ride them hard. If any man challenges your authority, flog him half to death. If he challenges you a second time—hang him."

I nodded again, but did not meet his eye. I still felt a little weak-kneed at the thought of hanging a man out of hand, the way my poor father had been hanged.

"You'll be fine. There is one thing I am worried about . . ." Robin trailed off and I looked up at him, meeting his silver eyes with a touch of anxiety.

"I am worried that you might die . . . ," said my lord.

"What?"

"I'm concerned that, with a long truce declared, you might well die—of boredom."

And we laughed.

We had laughed together at Robin's jest and yet, as is so often the case with drolleries, there was some scrap of truth in it. Life is dull for a soldier in peacetime, and at times over the next few months I envied Robin and his questing in the southern lands. I took my lord's advice about his men too, and rode them hard: patrols daily and regular arms training in the courtyard of the middle bailey, organized by Thomas. I even hanged a man—a thief who stole from his mates and whom nobody liked much anyway. I could not watch the execution, but I heard the man jeered into his grave by his fellow soldiers. I also kept the men busy at work on the surrounding lands.

As Constable of Château-Gaillard I was responsible for the manor of Andeli, which had once belonged to Archbishop Walter of Coutances. But the lands thereabouts had been much ravaged by the rough tides of war sweeping over them the past three years. And so I set my men to building bridges—occasionally borrowing a few skilled craftsmen from the walls of the castle itself, which was nearing completion—and to repairing barns and cottages that had been burned or ruined by the enemy, or in some cases by Mercadier's foraging *routiers*. This work had several benefits: firstly it kept the soldiers busy and fit during that rain-swept autumn and winter, although we did stop work for a week in December when the land was blanketed by the first falls of snow; secondly our improvements increased the value of the manor, and so pleased King Richard. Lastly it made me feel more comfortable in myself, as I felt I was making some amends to the destruction that my fellow warriors had wrought on the land, and that God was looking down on my actions with approval. I was busy myself, and while I missed Goody and took pains to write to her regularly, having charge of a great castle meant that I had no leisure to mourn the postponement of our marriage. After a tolerably hard winter, when spring finally came I had the men out in the fields with the local villeins, helping to sow the seed for the new season's crops.

The King came and went with a small group of his closest household knights—and on each visit he brought with him a fevered sense of urgency, as if there were never enough hours to accomplish all that he had a mind to do; he did not come as often as I would have liked, for he had much business in Rouen but also found time to journey further south and visit his lands in Maine and Anjou. But whenever he visited, I found my heart lifted by his good cheer and boundless energy.

I saw almost nothing of Mercadier, who was based permanently in the south, except for one brief visit in March, when we observed chilly civilities at dinner and avoided each other as much as possible. William the Marshal and his men came to Château-Gaillard twice, and I had a suspicion that he was checking to see that all was well. But if he was overseeing me, he must have been satisfied that I was undertaking my role competently and there was no immediate cause for alarm.

The truce was largely observed all the way through until the early summer of the Year of Our Lord eleven hundred and ninety-eight—but if there was no actual warfare there was no letup in the political battle. The Marshal told me that the King had persuaded the Count of Boulogne to join his side, which meant that we were even more strengthened in the north; and wily old Geoffrey of the Perche finally came back into the fold, among other barons that held land on Philip's borders.

But the French King was playing the same diplomatic game: he made an alliance with Philip of Swabia, a German magnate, in which they both swore an oath to aid each other in war against Richard, and, in Aquitaine, he managed by means of a vast bribe to seduce Viscount Aimar of Limoges, Richard's unruly vassal, to his side.

This news, delivered to me by the Marshal, filled me with concern for Robin, who would have passed through the turncoat's lands. Now that Aimar had revealed himself as an enemy of our King, I was concerned that Robin might be captured and held for ransom. But a week later I received a much travel-stained letter from the Earl of Locksley himself, informing me that he had met Robert de Boron and talked long into the night with him and that he was safely in Montpellier, in the County of Toulouse, Richard's new southern ally, and staying at Reuben's sumptuous house in the center of that ancient and most civilized city.

Robin was careful in his letter not to openly mention the Grail—he called it "the bowl," a reference to our last conversation before his departure from Château-Gaillard—but he said that he had learned much about the origins of "the bowl" and had encouraging news about its whereabouts, and also the whereabouts of "a masterful old friend of ours from our time in Paris."

When I read these words, I felt a sudden chill, like a cold draft of air. I had not troubled myself with thoughts of the Master for many months. He had seemed phantom-like; a dream figure beyond the grasp of my waking mind. But Robin's words kindled something inside me and I found myself clutching the parchment letter and suddenly trembling with a rage too long suppressed. My heart was thumping in my chest; my palms were damp. Thomas was with me at the time, we were going over a list of the castle's stores together, but when he asked what ailed me, I could not tell him and merely said it must be the beginning of a summer ague.

When I retired to my chamber that night, I allowed my mind at long last to consider the continued existence of the "man you cannot refuse." And I knew one thing for certain, as surely as I knew that

Christ was my Savior. I knew that, foolish indulgence or not, I wanted to have vengeance on the Master. I wanted him dead—for the sake of Hanno, and my poor hanged father Henry; for the kindly priest Jean of Verneuil, for pungent Master Fulk, even for the fat, old, music-mad Cardinal Heribert of Vendôme.

I wanted to watch the Master suffer and die.

26

KING RICHARD AND HIS HOUSEHOLD KNIGHTS returned to Château-Gaillard in August, as the Locksley and Westbury men were helping the local peasants to bring in the wheat harvest, and he came bearing a letter from Goody. After I had greeted the King in a suitable fashion and installed him and his followers in his quarters in the keep, I took the letter to my own lodgings—I had taken over Robin's chamber in the north tower of the inner bailey—and greedily devoured the precious missive.

While my betrothed was now a full-grown woman of twenty years in the full bloom of her looks, her handwriting, I fear, was still that of a young girl; and her command of Latin was at best rudimentary. But the warmth of the love and the urgency of her ardor that seemed to spill from these parchment pages made these trifling failings recede into insignificance. She missed me—she wrote—she longed to be married and to hold me in her arms; she ached to give herself fully to me and to bear my children. When would I come back to her? Surely I had served the King long enough and the time had come for me to return to her side. She noted the extreme honor that the King did her by offering to give her away, and she fully acknowledged the wonderful generosity of his dowry, but all of that was less important to her mind than the fact that we must be married—and soon. The letter finished with these words: "Come to me, my love, come and take me to our marriage bed. The wretched creature has not been seen nor heard of in these parts for a year or more, and I will not let fear of her malediction ruin our lives and our happiness. I would rather live a single year as your loving wife than a lifetime without you. Come to me, my darling, and make me whole."

Her letter aroused a chorus of fierce emotions in my heart and, if I am honest, my loins, and I promised myself that I would not let another twelvemonth go by without taking my beautiful Goody to wife.

A week later Robin returned to the castle, face burned by southern suns, his frame lean from hard travel, his demeanor wearily cheerful. He had come most recently, he told me, from Paris, where under cover of the truce he had been visiting friends and taking a measure of the French capital for Richard.

"War is upon us, Alan," he said, "this truce will not last another month." He was wolfing down a plate of cold pork and barley bread in my comfortable chambers in the north tower, which, I noted gloomily, I would now have to relinquish to him. "Paris is full of armed men, French knights, militiamen, foreign crossbowmen, mercenaries—King Philip has no intention, it is clear, of sticking to the agreement to suspend hostilities until next year. Philip is fully armed and ready for battle; the question is, where will he strike?"

That question was answered within the week. We had news that our staunch ally Baldwin of Flanders had attacked in the north again, and had swept down into Artois and was besieging St. Omer. King Richard delivered the news to his senior knights and barons at the daily council—and by the over-pleased tone he used to convey the information, I knew that it was part of a deep plan that he had hatched privately with Baldwin. Their strategy was reasonably simple to divine: Baldwin would come down from Flanders and Philip was then supposed to rush north to confront him, at which point Richard would attack from the west and trap Philip between his army and

Baldwin's and crush it utterly. But, once again, Philip showed that he was no fool—he could smell a trap as well as the next man. When Baldwin came down from the north, Philip ignored his advance, in effect, sacrificing the beautiful town of St. Omer to fire and rapine. Instead he sent his mighty army west, toward us, pouring his full strength over the border at Gisors and on into Normandy.

Philip was on our doorstep again.

Uncharacteristically, Richard was taken by surprise by the speed of the French advance. His troops were scattered across the duchy, and when King Philip came roaring into his domain, heading due west directly for Château-Gaillard, the Lionheart could do nothing but retreat before him. For ten days we fought a desperate rearguard action, skirmishing hard against the French knights as they burned and pillaged through the lands that my men and I had spent the last year working so hard to repair. Robin had resumed command of the Locksley men, and while I was his senior lieutenant, I now rode out mainly with my ten-strong, red-clad Westbury troop. It was heartbreaking to see the destruction caused by the French as they ravaged the lands between Gisors and Château-Gaillard—orchards torched, churches looted, livestock slaughtered and left to rot—but we took our revenge when and where we could.

One warm September morning our troop came across a band of French knights pillaging an isolated farmstead near Suzay. Kit, the scout, came galloping back to the column and told me in breathless terms that there were a half-dozen French knights burning and looting with abandon not far ahead. I gave thanks to God for the grueling training for war that I had insisted on during the long dull months of the truce. There was no need for detailed instructions: "Lances, then side arms," I said. "Stay together, we will not linger; we go in fast, surprise them, kill as many as we can and get out. If they flee, do *not* chase them—it could be a trap. Does everybody understand?"

It was no trap: we barreled into the enemy at the gallop, our lances leveled, and two knights and two mounted men-at-arms died in moments, skewered in the first rushing assault. I took the first knight, a red-faced oaf, directly in his slack belly with my lance, the numbing shock transmitting sharply through my right arm as the steel lance head smashed through his mail links and splintered his spine. I killed a second man after a brief exchange of cuts with Fidelity, a savage backhand chop to the neck. We surprised and outnumbered them, and they died easily. I think they were fuddled with drink, for they all seemed to react rather slowly to our initial screaming charge. One mounted man-at-arms at the back of the group, perhaps more sober than the rest, hauled his horse around and galloped away immediately when he saw us, and we let that coward go; another man loosed a crossbow at us, missed and then sought to escape on foot, but Oxhead rode him down within a dozen paces and dropped him with a neat axe blow to the back of the skull. None of our men was harmed. We wasted only a few moments gathering up their plunder and rounding up two of the warhorses—the other mounts having made successful bids for freedom—and leaving the bodies where they lay, we headed off again southwest toward Château-Gaillard, our faces aglow at this small victory against the invaders.

The next day we rode out again with the King himself—but not as ragtag skirmishers, this time with all the armed strength we could muster. With him were Robin, the Marshal and half a dozen other barons, who had all concentrated at Château-Gaillard when it became clear that Philip's main thrust was against us in Normandy, and that the Flemish assault from Baldwin in the north was being ignored. The first thing the King said to us, as we mustered in the dawn in the middle bailey of the castle—fifty grim-faced, fully armored knights and twice that number of mounted men-at-arms—was: "We have held him thus far; now we push him back. Mercadier is coming up fast from the south. It's time to show Philip our true mettle."

We rode out of Château-Gaillard and formed up immediately in the attack formation, four ranks of horsemen in the vanguard, two of knights, and behind them two ranks of sergeants, including my Westbury lads. Then we set out along the main road east toward Gamaches, firmly resolved to force back Philip's men all the way to the border or die in the attempt. On each wing were a score or so of lighter horsemen, Locksley men for the most part, whose duties included scouting, but also sweeping the scattered enemy ahead of our main column, and ensuring that none were left behind to harry our flanks and rear. Behind us came a great mass of infantry, a couple of light siege engines and the baggage train. We had not traveled three miles before we came upon a sizable body of enemy horsemen, perhaps thirty knights and men-at-arms, cantering diagonally across our path on a field of stubble. I was in the front rank, next to Robin, and perhaps four or five places along from the King. Richard, naturally, didn't hesitate for a moment: "There they go! At them," he shouted, lowered his lance and urged his horse forward. I clapped my spurs to Shaitan's sides and the whole front rank of twenty-five knights thundered forward as one man.

I heard the panicked shouts of the enemy knights as they saw us coming and tried to turn their warhorses to face our attack, but their forward horsemen created chaos by stopping abruptly, then turning their beasts, while the ones behind, unaware that they were under attack, barged into the haunches of the horses in front of them. They were in utter confusion even before our galloping line smashed into them. I shouted: "Westbury!" and attempted to sink my lance into the side of a knight who was half-turned away from me and struggling to control his madly kicking horse. I missed and received a hard clout on the back of my helmet from the knight's axe as I thundered past. My lance speared into the trapper-covered rump of a horse beyond my intended victim, sank deep in the poor animal's flesh, and was snatched out of my hands. A French knight materialized in front of me and took a swing with his long sword, but I received the blow on my shield, turned Shaitan with my knees and fumbled at my waist for Goody's mace. My enemy turned his horse too and came at me for another pass, his blade lifted high. I ducked his swipe and cracked his upper arm with a short hard blow from the mace as we pounded past each other. He howled and fell back in the saddle, as I circled him again, and I saw that the limb was clearly broken, but before I could finish him my attention was wrenched away: another Frenchman was coming at me from my right side only yards away, jabbing forward with his lance, and shouting: "St. Denis, St. Denis!" The tip of his spear narrowly missed my belly and passed between the high front of my saddle and my groin. I leaned forward and trapped the ash shaft there, let the mace fall and dangle from the leather strap that attached it to my wrist, seized the lance with my right hand and hauled it from the astounded man's grasp. The man, his horse now only a foot or so from mine, grasped at the handle of his scabbarded sword. I flipped the lance off my lap and away, grabbed the dangling mace and swung hard and low with the same movement, smashing its heavy ridged metallic head into his kneecap. His agonized scream was only cut short by a rider galloping past me and decapitating him with a single sweep of the sword: I caught a glimpse of Robin's snarling battle-face under his helmet, just for an instant as he passed. And then it was over.

The French knights who had survived were running for it, and we were laughing, panting and calling out jests to old friends: the King seemed to be illuminated with animal vigor and energy, at least that is how I remember it. He truly seemed to be lit by an inner fire, like a fine beeswax candle in a horn lantern, that made his white teeth shine, his bright blue eyes sparkle and his red-gold hair glow like sunshine.

We rested for a quarter of an hour, checked our horses for wounds—Shaitan was unharmed, thank the Lord, and he seemed to be vastly enjoying the excitement of the day. We shared flasks of wine or water, mopped our brows and mounted up again. The second rank of knights now took the lead and we pressed onward.

I fought once more that day—charging a group of men-at-arms who were looting a church, and killing one with Fidelity, then riding another down and crushing him under Shaitan's hooves—but we were all aware, from the clouds of dust kicked up by hundreds of hooves, that a great battle was taking place a few miles ahead. Mercadier had come up from the south and had attacked the King of France and his household knights directly—he had only with difficulty been driven off. We hurried to join up with the scar-faced mercenary and his murderous ruffians, and did so some two miles later, but it was clear that the French were by now in full retreat. I felt a little queasy at the sight of King Richard embracing Mercadier—who had captured a score or so of noble prisoners by his exertions that day—when they met a mile or so outside Gamaches, and I busied myself with the welfare of the Westbury men, tutting over their scrapes and bruises—none had been killed, mercifully, or badly wounded—and congratulating them for the courage they had shown.

And we had indeed done well; the scouts had reported that Philip had been forced to retreat far to the south, probably as far as his castle at Mantes, a good fifteen miles away. His powerful thrust into Normandy had been halted and bloodily repulsed; he had been out-fought, his army mauled and sent packing—but our task was by no means finished. Richard might have expelled Philip from his lands, but our sovereign now meant to return the compliment and take the fight deep into French-controlled territory. We bivouacked in and around Gamaches that night, the King naturally staying in the castle with his senior barons and knights, but I made myself scarce and slept among my men. I could not stomach another royal feast in which Mercadier would be praised to the skies as the hero of the hour. Worse, I might be asked to compose a victory song in praise of his actions. I told myself that, if that were to happen, I would rather refuse and offend the King, but I did not want to put my resolve to the test. And so I spent the evening with a barrel of wine that Ox-head had "captured," carousing, singing and telling bawdy tales with the Westbury men and Thomas in a thicket of ash, half a mile from the castle. It was a loud, raucous and enjoyable night, the little of it I can remember.

Hungover but happy, we set off again the next day: the King was determined that this would be the campaign, this would be the season, in which God would give us Gisors. That mighty fortress, key to the border, was perhaps the most powerful castle in Normandy after Château-Gaillard—surrounded as it was by a ring of four lesser castles. Gisors was the prize, Richard always insisted. To take back Gisors was, in effect, to win the war. Accordingly, we headed eastward into the lands of the enemy, our hearts beating strongly, our heads as high as our hopes.

However, the Westbury men and I took little part in the fighting over the next few days, as Richard's army, with a grim, mechanical skill, took possession one by one of the outlying fortresses of Dangu, Courcelles, Boury and Sérifontaine that stood guard around Gisors. Dangu had been in and out of our hands several times in the past years, and there was a certain resignation in the face of the elderly French knight who surrendered it to us without a fight, after seeing Richard with overwhelming force camped before him. Courcelles defied us, but a very swift, bloody surging attack by Mercadier's men overran its walls, and then that was ours, too. Boury, we took by bribery; the Constable, a young, ambitious man, agreeing to open its gates to William the Marshal in exchange for a grant of lands in western Normandy and England. Four miles to the north of Gisors, the Earl of Leicester's men broke down the front gates of Sérifontaine, and within a week the great prize itself was halfway surrounded, its defensive ring of smaller forts all in our hands.

The King based his court at Dangu, and there he paused for a day or so, resting the horses. His troops were a little scattered, some occupying the newly captured castles around Gisors, others, who had been summoned from the far corners of Normandy, still in Château-Gaillard. News arrived that his powerful siege train with its massive "castle-breakers" had unfortunately become mired somewhere outside Rouen—but few of us, wrapped as we were in the glow of victory, believed that this was important. We were winning; we might all be tired, but our successes made our steps light. Nevertheless, after the exertions of the past week, we all felt we needed to regroup and rest—all of us, that is, save Richard.

The Earl of Locksley's men, who were some of the freshest troops, had been given the task of patrolling aggressively beyond the River Epte, the traditional border between France and Normandy, and we sent out large parties of men forty or fifty strong to raid the farms and scout the land. And, more often than not, the King would join these tiring, dusty patrols, as if he were a young knight or squire of tender years and not the greatest of all the Christian monarchs and comfortably past his fortieth year.

It so happened that we were riding through a thick wood, a mile or so to the east of Boury—Robin, myself, Little John, Thomas and a score of Locksley men-at-arms and my ten Westbury fellows, together with Richard and a dozen of his younger household knights—when the King held up a hand and stopped us all. We were in thick woodland, unable to see beyond fifty yards in any direction, but the King said: "Listen!" And we all dutifully strained our ears.

I could make out nothing at first, and then I caught it—a faint metallic jingling noise like a man idly playing with a large bag of silver. "Blondel, you've got young eyes, go forward on foot," said the King, "quietly now—go a hundred paces, see what can be seen, and report back."

I slipped off Shaitan and handed the reins to Thomas, who was beside me looking grim and grown-up on his brown palfrey, a long lance in his right hand. I walked forward as quietly as I could, keeping behind the thicker trunks as the woodland petered out into scattered trees, and finally gave way to a wide fallow field.

And beheld an army.

I saw a long line of horsemen, mailed, armed and shod for war—hundreds of French knights in bright surcoats, the trappers of their destriers matching their riders' attire. They were coming from the southeast, from Mantes, at a guess. The chinking noise had grown louder; it was the tinny sound of several hundred buckles, stirrups, spurs and assorted accoutrements clashing against iron mail. I was looking at the flower of French chivalry, coming north to challenge Richard's bold intrusion, and push him back into his own lands. In the center of the line, among a score or more of bright flags, in red and silver and green, I saw the white and gold fleur-de-lys of King Philip himself.

I made a rough count of the numbers of armored knights and hazarded three hundred, but behind them came long lines of sergeants and mounted crossbowmen, and last of all blocks of marching infantry wielding spears. It was a horde—perhaps six or seven hundred strong. We could not possibly hope to face them in battle and triumph.

I made my way back to the King and said: "It is Philip, Sire, and three hundred of his knights, coming up fast and heading toward Courcelles; if we are quiet, I believe we can make it to Boury and evade them, and we can send word to Courcelles to shut up their gates."

"What are you talking about, Blondel?" said the King, frowning at me as if he genuinely could not comprehend my speech. "The enemy is before us; you say that thief Philip himself is there; and you want me to run away like a craven? What in God's name is the matter with you?"

"Sire, there are three hundred knights yonder, and as many men-at-arms; we are fewer than fifty men here—we cannot fight them," I said, but I knew the King tolerably well by then and the flesh all over my body was contracting, pimpling in excitement, fear and a little joy equally mixed, a coldness in my stomach, my cheeks flushed—it was madness, wonderful, magical, royal madness—for I knew exactly what the Lionheart must say.

"Nonsense, Blondel, we have plenty of men for the task; we will attack at once and show these French fellows the true meaning of prowess." He turned to the youngest of his household knights, a nervous-looking youth, three or four years younger than I. "Sir Geoffrey, be so good as to ride to Boury; the Marshal is there. Tell him that I shall be attacking the enemy directly and would consider it a great favor if he would stir himself, sally out and join the fun."

I caught Robin's gray eye and he merely gave me a half-smile and a slight shrug of his shoulders. When the King commands, we his loyal men must obey.

"Well, come on then," said Richard; he was grinning all over his face, a wolfish predatory expression that I had seen him wear many times before on the eve of battle. Richard was about to do what he had been born to do; what he loved to do more than anything else in the world: a glorious headlong charge into an unsuspecting enemy, followed by a great and terrible slaughter—hopefully a great and terrible slaughter of the French knights. Oddly, I found myself grinning like a moon-crazed maniac, too.

We bounded out of the woodland like a pack of starving wild beasts scenting their prey, fewer than fifty horsemen attacking an enemy ten times our number. To put it like that is to make it sound a desperate, foolish endeavor, a reckless gamble, but that does not do justice to our bold, but not completely brain-addled, leader. The enemy was spread out on the line of march, perhaps six or seven hundred men straggling over half a mile or more. We came boiling out of that wood in a tight, fierce knot and smashed into the center of the enemy line, with precious little warning, bringing our furious blades to surprised and frightened men and cutting straight through the files of knights and squires, shattering them—it was as if an iron-bound mallet were swung against a long dry stick. King Richard led the charge, a dozen pounding heartbeats of pure exhilaration, and we crashed into the enemy ranks, screaming fit to burst our lungs, and the line of French horsemen disintegrated before us. My lance pierced a thin-faced squire just above the hip, the blade crunching through his young body and clean out the other side. I left the long ash shaft waggling in the air, the boy dying, white-faced with shock, and drew Fidelity. I saw that our charge had brought us right through the enemy line of march, sowing bloody disaster in our train, and we were now free and clear on the other side of the column. The enemy force had been cut cleanly in two by our assault. To the south were the mounted men-at-arms, and the plodding infantry, some being mercenaries and some mere militia, barely trained men recruited from the poorest stews of French towns that had been singed by the fires of war. They seemed terrified, stunned into immobility by our shattering eruption from concealment, although a few groups of more experienced men began to arrange themselves with a painful slowness into clumsy defensive formations. To the north, the tale was very different: there stood the cream of French chivalry, in all their gaudy, dangerous splendor. These heavily armored aristocratic horsemen had immediately halted their march, turned to face us, and were forming up in their disciplined ranks with alarming speed. I saw that our scattered men, who had smashed so bravely through the middle of the French column, were soon to be charged in turn. Richard was shouting: "At them, at them! Before they recover!" and gesturing with his sword at the French knights to the north of us, hundreds of them, who even now were ordering their neat lines, rank upon rank, knee to knee, lowering their lances, their horses taking their first steps toward us.

Robin was shouting: "A Locksley, a Locksley!" And I realized that if we did not disrupt the French cavalry charge before it began, the sheer weight of their numbers would overwhelm us and we would all be crushed to bloody pulp. To my left, the King was bellowing to his closest knights, urging them to form up for the attack, his sword pointed to the heavens, the sunlight flashing on his steel and gold-chased helm; he was laughing once again, madly, happily, his face suffused with reckless joy. The royal blade swung down, pointing like a spear at the advancing enemy ranks; he punched back his spurs and his stallion took off like a startled stag, hurtling his master straight toward the wall of enemies. I slapped my own heels into Shaitan's flanks and, pointing Fidelity in a similar manner, charged in my sovereign's wake toward the oncoming ranks of the French. I saw King Richard, alone, smash into the body of the enemy line, causing instant confusion to the neat rows of horsemen, his sword arm flailing, the blood flying with every sweep of his blade. In three heartbeats, I was among them too, beside my King, protecting him, swinging wildly with Fidelity and trying to force back the press of enemies on his left flank. I felt a massive hammer-blow against my shield, but the enemy lance slid away and then I was deep in their midst, hacking at enemy faces, chopping at mailed limbs. I caught a glimpse of Richard battering at the crumpled tubular helmet of a knight, relentlessly, again and again; his household knights had caught up with us by then, and were forcing their way into the gap Richard had made. I saw one of his companions chop efficiently through a darting lance that might well have skewered the royal back. But I had no time for gawping: suddenly I found myself alone and surrounded by yelling foemen. I fended off a lance strike to my chest with my shield, and dispatched the attacking knight with a lateral sword blow to the face, severing his jaw. I hacked the right hand from another man, whose horse barged into Shaitan, leaving the Frenchman screaming with a blood-pissing stump. Shaitan lashed out his hind legs, cracking his iron horseshoes into the nose of a beast behind him, which reared and spilled its French rider. Something smashed across my backbone, winding me, but I turned and lunged desperately at this new attacker, a savage-faced knight in sky-blue wielding a long sword. Mostly by good fortune, my sword entered a gap in his ventail, piercing his neck through and through, and with a spray of crimson, I ripped the blade free, and he wheeled away dying. Two horsemen parted before me and I caught another sight of King Richard battling two enemy knights at the same time, chopping left and right, left and right, the mailed sleeve of his sword arm red up to the shoulder, then one enemy was down, and one of Richard's household knights hacked the head from the other man.

We were so few, a handful of bold knights in a sea of French foes, and yet they feared us and seemed to hang back, melting away before our ferocity. I saw that Little John had joined the mêlée and was taking heads and lopping limbs from the saddle of his huge horse with great sweeps of his axe, and now the Locksley men in their dark green cloaks were fighting all about me like the heroes of old. Robin was beside me too, and I saw that we had miraculously come through the first ranks of attacking knights and were into a space behind them. The Earl shouted: "There, Alan, there—the King! It is Philip!" and pointed with his gory sword. Fifty yards away, at the head of a slight rise, I could see another wall of knights, perhaps eighty men, bright in their surcoats, lances at the ready and mounted on snorting, pawing, battle-roused destriers, and above their heads the weakly fluttering white and gold of the French royal standard.

"Come on," my lord shouted. "Come on!" And he threw back his head and howled: "A Locksley!" I bawled "Westbury! Westbury!" and together we charged up the incline toward that waiting line of shining death. We were not alone; I could sense rather than see the clustering of green-cloaked Locksley horsemen and some of my own red-decked men around Robin and myself; and the sound of royal bellowing from behind my right shoulder told me that Richard had fought his way through, had seen our prize and was coming with his surviving household knights to help us take it. I managed to snatch a glance at the King's face as he raced toward Robin and myself: beneath the spattered blood and sweat of battle, framed by the gleaming metal of his helm and his golden beard, I saw that he was still smiling, a wide, easy smile of glorious satisfaction.

The French knights came down the hill to meet us; in a magnificently controlled charge, their front rank as straight as an arrow, they sliced into our men, emptying a dozen saddles in a single moment. Out of the corner of my eye, I saw a green-clad man-at-arms hurled from his mount by an elegant lance strike. On the other side a Westbury man went down screaming. But I was too busy to take much notice of other men; a lance came at my face out of nowhere and almost tore my cheek open, but I managed to get my shield up just in the very nick of time and deflect the spear, the blade scraping over my domed helmet. And once again I was in the middle of a hellish mêlée, enemies all around, blows raining down from every quarter. I hacked and cut and swore, I lunged and killed, and my battered red shield took half a dozen blows that would have ended me. We were surely lost. We had attempted too much. Our reckless arrogance had been our downfall. I could see none of my friends. I found myself dueling with a knight, a big man full of desperate rage; I blocked a welter of massive overhand blows from his sword, and then saw an opening, and took it. I killed his horse with a single downward slice into its arched neck, and the poor beast dropped as if poleaxed. I left the man trapped and roaring on the churned earth of the field, his right leg pinned under the weight of the dead beast.

I drew back from the fray, circling Shaitan away from the enemy lines. We had so few men still in the saddle, and there was no sign of Robin. Green-clad bodies littered the weedy fallow field; forlorn horses nuzzling their dead owners. I saw, a dozen yards away, King Richard, also momentarily disengaged from the battle; he was leaning over his saddle, panting, a young knight on foot was speaking to him with a concerned expression. King Philip was still surrounded by a knot of a score or so knights; not a gleaming, multicolored wall as before, more ragged, and smaller, their numbers fewer too, and milling about uneasily as the King's closest personal knights watched the fight below them, restrained from joining it by their master. But they were still a formidable force.

For all our valor, we had failed to break through to the heart of the enemy position, and very soon the French King, safe behind his household knights, would rally his surviving men, summon his militia and his mercenaries to him, gather his full overwhelming strength and come down from that hill and destroy our remaining scattered, wounded men on their exhausted horses. Soon, all would be lost. Or so I believed then. Of course, Richard had known better. For at that very moment, William the Marshal, the knight *"sans peur et sans reproche,"* threw his fresh men into battle.

The Marshal had brought no more than forty knights with him, and yet they were some of the hardest fighting-men in our army. First, he attacked the southern portion of what had been the French line of march, slicing through a mass of militiamen on foot, a hundred spearmen at least, dispersing them like a pack of wolves descending on a flock of sheep. The militia broke apart and fled for their lives, but the Marshal's men did not waste their time killing the fugitives; the knights quickly reformed again like the superb troops they were, making neat, close lines, many riders with unbroken lances, others holding their bright swords aloft, and on they came, trotting up the hill toward us.

King Richard had recovered himself, perhaps at the brave sight of the Marshal's charge, and he was shouting to his knights, dispersed all over the field, urging them to come to him and reform. Then he saw me, and shouted: "To me, Sir Alan, to me. One more time, one more time and we shall have them. One last charge for victory!"

I turned my head and saw Thomas at my side; I was a little surprised for I had seen nothing of him in the battle and had feared that he might be among the fallen—but my squire was whole except for a long, shallow cut just below the ear and, miracle of miracles, he was offering me a fresh lance. Beyond him I saw Ox-head and Kit, both apparently unwounded, and still looking eager for the fight, and another two Westbury men. I grinned at them all, wordless. And so the six of us trotted over to join the King.

There was no time to waste: William the Marshal was coming up fast, and the King had gathered some twenty knights and sergeants around him. "One more charge!" the King kept repeating; he was laughing wildly again, white teeth gleaming in the gore-flecked gold of his beard, supremely happy in that moment. "We've got him, we've got the wretched thief!" And then he bellowed: "For God and my right!" and we charged up that incline together, all of us, King Richard, Robin, Little John, Thomas, a dozen living Locksley and Westbury men, a handful of household knights—with William the Marshal's fresh troop of forty knights drumming the earth hard on our heels. We charged up that slope, filthy, bloody, our bodies wrenched by fatigue, we threw ourselves heedlessly once more into the milling, pristine ranks of the enemy.

And they fled.

27

WE CHASED THEM; HOW WE CHASED them, and the slower ones we killed. They were slaughtered in their saddles or ridden down, but if they had the sense to surrender, and managed to communicate this desire to our knights through the mayhem and gore-madness of battle, we made them captive. However, God in his wisdom did not see fit to deliver the French King unto us that day. The Almighty did, however, deign to humble that haughty monarch more than a little.

When our ragged band of exhausted men charged that loose group of French household knights gathered around the fleur-de-lys, I thought for a moment that we might even break through and reach the King himself. I killed two knights in that last blood-crazed, howling assault, and I truly believe we might well have made Philip a captive that day, such was our lust for victory—and that would have ended the war at a stroke—but the French King decided that his life and freedom were worth more than his honor, and he ran away, like the cowardly dog that he was. I knew nothing of this at the time, having received something of a shock. I had found myself exchanging vicious sword blows in that last desperate charge with a young blond knight with a long handsome face, although it was disfigured by a battle-grimace and a curious red, shiny mark on the left-hand side of his face, the mark of a healed burn. He cut hard at me and I blocked him; I returned the blow, but uncertainly, and then we both drew back at almost exactly the same time, reining our destriers in. "Greetings, cousin," I said, breathing hard.

"Alan," came the equally breathless reply. And then Roland d'Alle smiled tightly and said: "God go with you!" and he turned his horse and galloped toward the royal standard and the remaining French knights, who were already beginning to turn their horses away to accompany their King to safety. I watched him go; glad he was alive, and very happy that we had not tried with any more vigor to slaughter each other.

The French King and his surviving knights retreated northward, but this was no orderly withdrawal, it was a full-scale rout with the wild despairing cries of "*Sauve qui peut*" ringing in the warm September air. They galloped away with all speed, and our fresher men, the Marshal's men, were right behind, chivvying them like a herd of panicked deer.

The enemy made straight for the castle of Gisors, some hundreds of men galloping madly on the narrow road north toward the River Epte, desperate to escape the wrath of Richard's seemingly invincible warriors. But I did not ride with them. Shaitan had received a serious wound, a bad sword cut to his haunch; such was my noble beast's bravery that I had not known when or where it had been inflicted. Only in the course of the pursuit, after a mile or so, did my courageous black friend begin to stumble and limp, and soon we halted at the top of a slight rise by a stand of alders, not far from the river. As I dismounted to look at Shaitan's glossy rump, now sheeted with blood, I had a perfect view of the massive castle of Gisors and the narrow bridge before it that crossed the River Epte. I was content to take no further part in the battle. We had won; Richard, with his uncanny ability to judge the balance of these things, had destroyed an army by applying the right amount of pressure at the right place and time: a few score men had defeated and put to terrified flight an army of many hundreds. I was proud to have been part of it, but as I watched the bright dabs of color as the French knights streamed northward, I offered up a prayer to St. Michael for my cousin Roland's safe escape; and gave humble thanks to God for my own survival.

I was tenderly mopping the blood from Shaitan's trembling haunch, and wondering what had become of Thomas in that last terrible assault, whether he lived or not, and God forgive me, whether he might bring up a spare horse for me, when my eye was drawn to the bridge over the Epte. From the west, along the line of the river, I could see the pluming dust and swift-moving shapes of mounted troops approaching, the leader carrying a black flag with flashes of gold on the somber flapping fabric. Mercadier was on the field and joining in the rout, harrying the broken French with enthusiasm. But on the bridge itself there seemed to be a blockage: a great press of men and horses, forty or fifty of each, jammed, almost immobile between its narrow wooden sides. I knew that bridge, I had reconnoitered it with the Westbury men not six months ago, and I knew it to be old, crumbling and only a single wagon-width at its narrowest part. I could well imagine the terror of the Frenchmen, crammed together in that constricted pass, their horses maddened by the press of bodies, kicking out, biting, blundering into the railing, with yet more knights trying to force themselves into the crush. That old bridge could not possibly support the jostling weight of fifty or sixty huge, frantic destriers and their heavily armored riders . . .

I heard the noise, even from my position a mile away, when that old bridge over the Epte collapsed. A deep crack and rumble, and above that, the tiny screams of men and terrified neighing of stricken horses as they tumbled into the slow brown river beneath them; churning it a creamy blood-streaked yellow with their death frenzy. Mercadier's men, and the knights of William the Marshal, were coming up fast, and I could just make out Richard with them, his red-and-gold standard, and a half-dozen of his household knights, but I noticed that three score Frenchmen were trapped on the wrong side of the bridge, our side, surrendering, handing over swords, lifting their arms and demanding the mercy that their rank permitted.

The river by now was a thrashing carnival of drowning men, fighting each other for survival, hampered by their hysterical mounts. A few, including King Philip himself, I learned later, managed to scramble to the further shore and were hauled out onto the bank by their friends. But Mercadier's crossbowmen had come up by this point and they began a withering shower of quarrels that fatally skewered many a man who had narrowly escaped drowning in his heavy armor—perhaps by scrambling over the living bodies of his comrades, pushing them below the surface—and had thought himself safely crawled up upon the far bank.

We were at the gates of Gisors, albeit with a deep, wide and now bridgeless river between it and us, but we had not the strength to take that stronghold. Our horses were blown, for the most part, or wounded like poor Shaitan, the King's knights dispersed and exhausted. The great siege engines, the castle-breakers, were some twenty miles away, and Philip, the coward, was mewed up tight in his fortress and able to defy us with his fifty remaining men. But if that was a slightly bitter note, the day had been an overwhelmingly sweet one: we were victorious, we had taken on a giant and slain him. Or perhaps more accurately, we had confronted a creature that roared as if it were a mighty lion and had trounced him, and chased him like a mouse into his hole.

We gathered up our dead and wounded and retreated to the ring of forts around Gisors: Dangu, Courcelles, Sérifontaine and Boury. We had captured almost a hundred French noblemen and knights that day—Mercadier had taken thirty himself. And I cursed my unthinking naïveté in not securing even one enemy captive, a rich one that would have made my fortune. My part in the battle had been a series of reckless, desperate, almost suicidal attacks, with no time for the protocols of war, and when poor Shaitan had been wounded and unable to bear me any further, I had no way of joining in the orgy of prisoner-taking before the fallen bridge. Robin, with the Locksley men's help, had managed to take the surrender of a dozen men of various ranks. And when I met him in the courtyard of Dangu Castle, shortly after dusk, he had a deeply satisfied grin carved across his lean, handsome face.

"Eight knights, three barons and a count," he said to me triumphantly by way of greeting, his silver eyes shining in the light of the castle torches. "They have all given me their parole. And the count is uncommonly rich—a cousin of King Philip's, no less. What a marvelous day's catch!"

"Congratulations!" I said, trying to be happy for him.

He looked closely at me: "No luck, Alan?"

"Shaitan was injured, and I had to break off the pursuit," I admitted. I was feeling deflated; stricken once again with my familiar post-battle melancholy.

"How awful for you; I am so sorry." Robin's expression was the soul of compassion itself; Our Lord Jesus Christ—our Savior himself—could not have bettered it.

"Well, we won the battle," I said, struggling to sound cheerful. "And we are both still hale and mostly whole." I had discovered after the battle that I had a shallow cut below my cheekbone, and absolutely no recollection of how I had come by that wound.

"Yes, there is that, I suppose," Robin said doubtfully. "Alan—I know you must be bitterly disappointed, but there will be other opportunities to take prisoners, I'm sure of it. Now, if you will excuse me, I must see to the men." And he gripped my shoulder for a moment and turned away.

I nodded and walked away to roust out Thomas, who was sleeping in one of the store sheds. I was thinking of what there might be for our supper when the quiet of the night was interrupted by a terrible howl of pain, followed by a gust of boozy laughter. It was coming from a side of the castle courtyard near the stables, an area that I had been deliberately ignoring, filled as it was with a drunken squad of Mercadier's *routiers*.

That terrible scream caused me to swing around and observe what was occurring in that particular dark corner of Hell, and I thank the Good Lord that I did.

About thirty of Mercadier's men—their scarred captain was absent—were grouped around a dozen of the poorer French knights, bound hand and foot, who had been taken captive that day. Some of the knights were weeping, others praying, some just sat stoically, grim-faced and silent. There was a large wooden box about three feet high in the center of the group, which the men had been using as a kind of table for their dice games earlier that evening. And I saw that there was a man stretched across it—a French knight, I guessed, though he had been stripped of his armor and most of his clothes. His back was to the box, his body arched over it, his eyes pointing heavenward: what was left of them. As I looked, a *routier* was lifting a pair of iron pincers holding a large red-hot coal from the brazier away from his face. The knight was whimpering from the pain, and I could see a stream of viscous fluid running down his cheek, and it was clear to me that he had been blinded in both eyes only moments before.

As I looked on, I saw the other *routiers* guffawing with laughter as they cut the poor man loose and shoved him into a corner against the wall, one *routier* hurling a wine-soaked cloth after him to allow him to bind up his burned face. Then another French knight, this one fighting like a madman, was wrestled by a dozen of Mercadier's cutthroats down onto the table. He was secured in a few efficient moments and, as the man jerked his body against the ropes frantically and whipped his head left and right, I saw with a horrible, sickening sense of despair that it was Roland d'Alle.

He caught my eye, stopped his wild thrashing and fixed his terrified gaze on mine in mute appeal, but I was already striding over to the mercenaries, my hand on my sword hilt.

"Hold hard," I said. "What are you doing here?"

"What does it look like . . . Sir Knight?" said the man by the brazier, and I realized that I recognized him from that long ago day when he and his mates had held Brother Dominic in their grasp, and Hanno had shot their red-haired friend stone dead with the crossbow bolt. I would have given my right arm, at that moment, to have Hanno, shaven-headed, fully armed and growling by my side.

"These men are prisoners of war," I said. "They are knights who have surrendered and given their word that they will not escape, and who will be ransomed by their families in the fullness of time."

"We know who they are . . . Sir Knight," said the man by the brazier, leering at me. I noticed that the lump of charcoal held in the iron pincers in his fist had been extinguished. He saw where I was looking, dropped the black lump into the brazier and selected another, this one glowing the color of a ripe cherry. He moved toward Roland and I was transported back nearly a decade to a stinking cell in Winchester where an enemy of mine had threatened me with a similar torment.

"No, wait," I said. "I forbid you. You cannot do this!"

"And why not, Sir Knight?" said a cold voice, chilling as the grave, that came from behind my right shoulder.

I turned to look upon Mercadier. His scar was a furrow of black that cut across his swarthy face; his eyes stagnant pools of malice.

"Why can I not do this?" he repeated.

"It is inhuman—it is immoral. It runs against all the laws of God and chivalry."

"Chivalry?" said Mercadier. "There is no true chivalry in war, that is a mere fancy, invented by milksop poets such as yourself for the amusement of bored ladies. There is only victory or defeat; the living or the dead; friend or foe."

"These men are prisoners; they have surrendered and so must be treated honorably. They can do us no harm."

"They are the enemy," he said in his quiet, stone-like tone. "Too often we have taken men in battle, accepted their surrender, handed over their living bodies for silver and then had to fight them again the next year. That will not happen with these knights. We will ransom them, yes. But they will never fight again against King Richard."

"Does the King know about this . . . this outrage?" I was beginning to feel desperate.

Now Mercadier laughed, a slow, evil grating sound. "Do you think the King does not know what I do for him?" he said. "Everything I do, Sir Knight, I do with his royal blessing."

The man with the hot coal moved forward toward Roland. My cousin closed his eyes, and lay there, his brow beaded with sweat but immobile, accepting his fate.

"Stop," I shouted. "Stop, right now. I will buy this man from you—unharmed! I will ransom him from you. Name your price, Mercadier."

"You, Sir Knight? You will ransom this Frenchman?" For the first time, Mercadier showed emotion, if greed can be called an emotion. "Now that is an interesting idea: what price shall I name then?"

I said nothing. Roland had opened his eyes and was looking at me. I kept my gaze fixed on him, willing him to take courage, silently promising him that I would not let him suffer this awful mutilation.

"You can have him for a hundred pounds in silver," said Mercadier blandly.

"What!" I was genuinely astounded by the price. "A hundred pounds? You are jesting. He is a young knight, not a duke. His ransom should be no more than ten."

I was not haggling for the sake of it; ten pounds was a year's revenue from Westbury, and the most I could raise in Normandy, even if I went to the Jews of Rouen.

"You refuse? Very well, Jean, carry on—blind him."

"Wait," I shouted, "wait!" I thought about the King's offer of a dowry of a hundred pounds—it was a huge sum of money, and if I promised it to Mercadier, it would mean that I might never be able to rebuild Clermont or buy another, better fief.

"I will pay it," I said. "Release the prisoner."

"You want him very badly, it seems. But I think a man who will pay a hundred pounds for one enemy knight will willingly pay two hundred. The new price is two hundred."

For a fleeting moment, I thought about drawing my sword and slicing my blade into his ugly face; but I knew I would not live to boast of my actions: Mercadier had thirty men there, I was alone. But I honestly could not pay the sum he asked. I did not have two hundred pounds and I had no way of raising it. I looked at Roland, and my despair must have been apparent. But he was smiling at me ruefully, and shaking his head. "I thank you for your efforts, Sir Alan," he murmured. "But apparently it is God's will that I must suffer this."

"I cannot pay it; I truly cannot!" I said, speaking to the friend, the cousin whose sight I could not afford to save.

"But I can," said a voice, a strong, commanding voice, the voice of an outlaw, or an earl. "I shall pay this trifling ransom. You have made an offer of two hundred pounds, and I accept it. There will be no further negotiations. Cut the Frenchman free."

Mercadier looked over at Robin, who had appeared at my shoulder. He frowned at my lord, confused and angry. "Very well, my lord. I will release him to you—when I have been paid the full amount—in silver."

Robin turned his head and shouted across the courtyard: "John, be so good as to bring me two of the chests from Paris. Quick as you like." A few moments later, Little John and two Locksley men came lumbering over with a pair of heavy wooden boxes, which they dumped on the ground at Robin's feet.

"Open them, would you, John; their contents are for our zealous friend here, Captain Mercadier."

I think I was as astonished as the mercenary to see what the boxes held: each chest was packed with small, lumpy white canvas bags marked with a bold red cross. It was a symbol I had seen before. Each bag was the same size as the one Robin had given me after fleecing the merchants of Tours and, as I knew very well, they contained five pounds in silver pennies. If each chest held twenty bags, and they looked as if they did, I was staring at two hundred pounds in silver: to be exact, two hundred pounds of silver that had come from the vaults of a Templar preceptory.

Roland gulped at his wine cup, emptying it and silently holding the vessel out to be refilled; and who could blame him? My cousin, Robin and I were sitting at a table on the ground floor of the Dangu keep, in an area that the Locksley men had made their own. A few of Robin's men-at-arms looked at the young French knight curiously—word of the vast sum that Robin had expended on him had spread speedily through their ranks.

From the courtyard outside came the sound of screams—although we had rescued Roland, the blinding continued. Mercadier was making sure that these French knights would never fight again. Each time a scream echoed around the courtyard, Roland flinched. I did too—I thought of Mercadier's parting words as we walked away with our shivering captive and shuddered: "Would you like any more of them, my lord?" the scarred mercenary had asked with elaborate courtesy. "I have another ten of these French rascals, if you have the silver to spend on saving them."

Another agonizing scream tortured the night; another brave man's sight was burned away.

"The Seigneur d'Alle will return the money to you, my lord," Roland said, looking earnestly at Robin. "Though it will take a while, even for him, to raise that amount of coin, he will pay it. But, as God is my witness, I can never repay what you—both of you—did for me tonight."

"That is very good of you," said Robin. "But there is absolutely no hurry; after all, you are one of the family, in a manner of speaking."

I looked at Robin, his face kindly in the candlelight, and I felt a strange mélange of emotions. This man, who so often appalled me with his ruthless money-grubbing, with his unstoppable lust for silver, had saved my cousin with an act of stunning, reckless generosity. And I knew that it was entirely in character. He had lightly mentioned the word "family" when referring to Roland, but I realized then how seriously he took that word. I was inside his circle, that charmed circle of friends, family and servitors, for whom Robin would give his all, and so Roland, my cousin, must be saved—whatever the cost. Robin's relentless money-chasing, his silver-greed, his methods of enriching himself, were always at the expense of people *outside* that circle. They were his prey.

The Templars were outside that circle: they were prey. For I had worked out by then how Robin must have obtained those chests of silver, the gleaming bounty that he gave away so lightly. He must have copied the letter of credit that I had received from the Templars, or found some clever man in Paris, perhaps a former disgruntled Templar clerk who understood the codes, to do it for him; he had then changed the sum denoted and presented the copied letter at the Paris Temple. I could imagine his cold smile when the forged paper was honored by the Templar clerks, and his satisfaction as several chests of their silver, in bags marked with a red cross, were delivered up to him.

A part of me admired the scheme, and I found that I could fully understand Robin's motives. To his mind, the Templars had deprived him of the lucrative frankincense trade in Outremer, and when Richard had disappointed him, he had taken his compensation directly from the knights. Another part of me was incandescently angry: I was the man who had been issued with the promissory note by the Templars in Paris. The theft would be discovered at some point; perhaps not for a while, if the clerks were none too rigorous, but at some time in the future Robin's crime would be detected, and I would be blamed. It might be that the Templars would seek to revenge themselves on me. And who would protect me against the wrath of the mighty Poor Fellow-Soldiers of Christ and of the Temple of Solomon? Who else but Robin?

I took a sip of wine and smiled reassuringly at my cousin, who was still badly shaken. But I was thinking that Robin had, indeed, been rather clever. He had revenged himself on his enemies the Templars; and he had drawn me even further into his tight circle. It occurred to me that, after Robin's massive fraud, there was no way that I could join that band of holy warriors now, even if I had wanted to. But then there was Roland: Robin had saved my cousin from a horrible fate, and it had cost him dearly. Would I have stolen from the Templars to save Roland? Yes, the truth was that I would. In that terrible moment when Mercadier ordered his blinding, I would have done almost anything to save him. And so I could not reproach Robin for his crime. I did not even find myself surprised by his actions. That was my master, my friend: a cunning thief, an outlaw still in his heart of hearts, and a truly generous lord.

King Philip called for a truce again that autumn, and Richard, perhaps surprisingly, agreed to it. Before we had had time to bring our full strength against Gisors, news came in that a large company of French knights was loose in Normandy to the south of the Seine, burning and pillaging manors to the south and west of Château-Gaillard. They had penetrated as far as Évreux, we heard, and burned the town to the ground. And Richard was obliged to send many of his best men south to push them out of his lands. We also retaliated to the wanton destruction of Évreux with an attack in the north: Mercadier raided Abbeville during a trade fair there and slaughtered hundreds of unarmed merchants from all the lands of northern Europe, very few of whom were enemies of King Richard. Both the French and we, by this time, were quite regularly blinding our prisoners; and I made a silent vow to myself that I would not allow my person to be captured—I would rather die in battle, I told myself, than live the life of a helpless blind beggar. Such is youth: today I know that life, almost any life, even that of a despised blind man, is better than death.

So when Philip asked for a truce, Richard agreed. The cruel fighting that bloody year had thinned the ranks of his knights, and the King needed time to recruit more. Also, the completion of the fortifications of Château-Gaillard meant that the swarming workmen were now at liberty to begin work repairing and improving the other castles that

Richard had taken that summer. But a period of peace was urgently needed to allow the necessary work to be done.

Richard had demanded possession of Gisors as part of the truce negotiations, but Philip had sensibly refused to surrender the key to the border. However, our sovereign did make other significant gains as part of the new accord. As the King said to me, shortly before Christmas that year: "King Philip has given up almost everything in Normandy, except Gisors, and next year, Alan, we shall take that too."

I recalled that he had said something similar the year before, but held my tongue. Our position had improved a good deal since then: on the border we held Dangu, Courcelles, Boury and Sérifontaine; we had recovered large stretches of lands to the north of Gisors, west of the River Epte, and the broad fields of grain north of the Avre were ours once again—even poor ruined Clermont-sur-Andelle was back in our hands, although I had not attempted to return there and rebuild the manor, and I had not troubled to ask Richard to confirm me in its possession. Maybe this time, I thought to myself, maybe this time King Richard was right, perhaps next year we would hold our Christmas feast in the great keep of Gisors, and this long war would truly be over.

On a freezing January morning, the two Kings met to discuss the truce in quite extraordinary circumstances. Philip, protesting that he did not trust Richard not to attack his person, insisted that Richard remain on one of our trading galleys in the middle of the Seine for the meeting, which took place a few miles to the south of Château-Gaillard. Meanwhile, Philip and his knights remained a-horse on the bank of the river, able, should their trembling terror of our lionhearted king overwhelm them, to rush away at a moment's notice. It was an insult, we all agreed; King Richard had always rigorously observed the codes of honor in war, and he was not a man to break his sacred word. Nonetheless, despite this grave affront, a solemn truce was agreed for five years—although I don't think a man present believed it would last for even half that time.

We celebrated yet another cessation of hostilities with a lavish dinner in the big round audience room in the keep of Château-Gaillard—a great number of the King's senior knights and barons were there—and, naturally, when we had eaten and drunk to repletion, the talk turned to the war. "How should we pass our time during this irksome truce?" That was the question on every man's lips.

My master Robert, Earl of Locksley, had the answer. He stood up from his place at the high table, a place of honor that only Richard's closest barons enjoyed, and raised a silver goblet: "Sire, if I may say a few words," he said in his battle-voice, and his tone caused a hush to fall around the room. "We have done mighty deeds this past year," Robin said, "and we have lost many dear companions . . ." There was a murmur of assent around the circular room. "But now we have a truce, for however long it lasts, and our righteous war has been suspended for a time. We have sworn before Almighty God that we shall not trouble King Philip—even though his liegemen still hold many lands and castles that belong by right to our noble King Richard."

"Hear, hear," roared a royal voice from not very far away.

"So what is to be done? Shall we sit in idleness, wrapped in costly furs, supping good wine by our hearth-fires and toasting our toes?"

"Sounds like an excellent idea to me!" said William the Marshal, with a tipsy grin. There was a burst of laughter.

"You would not be able to sit idle by your warm hearth for long, Marshal, even if I had you chained there," called out the King, to more laughter.

"My friends, we are men of the sword, we are knights sworn to King Richard's service, not sleepy, muddle-brained, old drunkards—well, most of us are," said Robin, inclining his head toward the Marshal. More laughter, and the Marshal scowled grotesquely like a mystery-player and shook his fist in mock anger at the Earl of Locksley.

"My friends," Robin continued, his voice deepening and his face becoming serious. "We are knights sworn to Richard's service, and yet there is one unruly baron who yet defies his rightful King; there is one who has rebelled against his lawful lord and with whom we have made no treaty, one who is not protected by this truce. Can we call ourselves the King's loyal men and not punish those who insult him?

I say that we must hunt down this rebellious dog and destroy him!" Muttering rumbled about the tables like wine barrels on cobblestones; the company had become uneasy—a good many men at the feast had at one time or another rebelled against Richard.

"I speak, of course, of the traitor Viscount Aimar of Limoges," said Robin, to a general sigh of relief. "He is a wealthy man, with a hoard of silver and jewels, and his sunlit southern lands are wide and rich." More appreciative murmurs. "And I say that, come the spring, we must go south and teach this proud rascal that our King will not be mocked! In the spring, let us go down to the Limousin, punish this haughty Viscount Aimar, and take our swords to this plump nest of rebels!"

A few cheers, but most knights confined themselves with nodding in benevolent agreement, and beginning to discuss with their fellows the delightful prospect of looting the rich territory of the Limousin.

The next day, in the mid-afternoon twilight of the short winter day, the King called me to his private chamber: he wanted me to play a little music for him, he said, to cheer a dreary season. But the real reason he summoned me, I soon discovered, was that he wanted me to play the informer.

"What was all that nonsense about Viscount Aimar?" he asked me. "Why does Locksley so urgently want me to go down and have at him?"

"He has rebelled against you, Sire," I said.

"I know that," the King said impatiently. "He's a fool and Philip has sent him silver and knights and turned his head with extravagant promises. But other men in Aquitaine have rebelled too. Adémar of Angoulême, for example: he's made an alliance with Philip, too, and he's a much bigger fish than Aimar. Why does Robin want me to go after the Viscount of Limoges?"

I stood there flat-footed, not knowing what to say to my King. I knew, of course, exactly why Robin wished the army to go south and attack Aimar. And, while he had not actually sworn me to secrecy, it was understood that one did not discuss Robin's private affairs with anyone, king or commoner. I mumbled something about my lord being a loyal man, who hated all of Richard's enemies equally.

The King looked hurt; his bright blue eyes clouded with sorrow: "My good Blondel," he said, "we have fought together, side by side, on many a bloody field, over many long years; we made the Great Pilgrimage together to Outremer and battled the Saracen hordes; you came to Germany when I was in despair and languishing in darkness, and you found me and brought me back into the light. Do not speak falsehoods to me now. Why does the Earl of Locksley wish me to humble Aimar of Limoges?"

I could not bear it; I felt that I was being pulled in two, my loyalty to my lord and to my King tugging my soul in different directions. And so I answered him.

"There is a treasure," I said. "There is a great and wonderful treasure that Aimar of Limoges, or rather that one of his relatives, has in his possession. And my lord the Earl of Locksley burns to possess it."

"Not that same treasure that he went off on a goose chase in Burgundy to discover last year?" said the King.

"The same."

"What do you know of this treasure?" he said, looking at me keenly. "Have you ever seen it? Is it truly valuable?"

"I have not seen it," I said, ignoring the first part of his question. "But I believe that it is truly valuable—perhaps the most valuable object in Christendom and certainly something that many men—counts, kings, even the Pope himself—would give a fortune to have in their possession."

"I think I should like to see this treasure," said the King.

28

THAT SPRING RICHARD'S KNIGHTS AND MERCADIER'S *routiers* ravaged the Limousin without mercy; and Robin and I played our parts, too. We burned farmsteads, stole livestock and destroyed crops, although I would not allow my men to despoil churches—it was Lent, the season in which all Christian warriors are expected to observe the Truce of God and lay down their arms, but we served King Richard, and he was not a man to allow the strictures of the Church to stand in his way. So, may God forgive us, we fought all through that March even though it was Lent, harrying Viscount Aimar and his knights from manor to manor. We ate meat and eggs, too, when we could get them, but we left places of worship unmolested. It was a sop, a gesture, but my men were not unhappy at that curb: in battle we all need God's protection, and it would not do to anger Him by stealing from His house. However, I felt the dark shadow of guilt on my soul during that southern spring of blood and fire: I believed Richard and his barons' enthusiasm for the harrying of the Limousin, and the relentless pursuit of Count Aimar and his men, might have had a good deal to do with my talk of the fabulous "treasure" in his possession. These rich lands were ruined, and many poor peasants were put out of their hovels, their meager wealth snatched, their children brought to starvation, because Robin and I had moved the King to make it so. Such is war; but I felt the burden of it as a heavy weight on my conscience.

I do not know how Robin came into the knowledge that the Master and the remaining Knights of Our Lady had taken refuge with Viscount Aimar, but Robin had many friends in Paris, and all over France, who had been searching for news of the Master for nearly five years now, and so perhaps a better question would have been why had we not uncovered his whereabouts sooner. From the little that Robin had gleaned, it seemed that the Master and his men had been in hiding on the far side of the Pyrenees, in lands that the original members of the Order would have campaigned over in their glory days fighting the Moors. Doubtless, the Master still had allies there. But recently, Robin's informants had told him, he had grown in confidence and forsaken the wild lands beyond mountains and had taken up a more comfortable position with his cousin Viscount Aimar—exactly as Bishop de Sully had predicted. And one thing was certain: wherever the Master went, the treasure we sought, the Grail, would go, too.

Whenever Robin spoke of the Grail, which was not often, I noticed that he became strangely animated; and I confess I was puzzled by this. Robin, as I have often mentioned, was not a godly man. Or perhaps I should say he was not a man who respected the Church or subscribed to its teachings, and yet this Grail, this object that was said to have once contained Our Lord's sacred blood, seemed to have seized his imagination. I think he pretended to himself that it was the vessel's worldly value that drew him; for it surely would have fetched a mountain of gold if it were shown to be the genuine article. But I think there was more to it than his usual lust for money; in my private heart, I think that Robin was searching for an object that could demonstrate for him the truth—or otherwise—of the Christian faith. For him, the Grail was the embodiment of God—and I dreaded the likely discovery that this thing, which was claimed to have once held the holy blood of Jesus Christ and to possess miraculous powers of life and death, was merely an ancient, dusty bowl.

At this time, I was determined to be indifferent to the Grail—I could not afford to allow myself to believe in its wonders and then to have my hopes dashed. It must be, I told myself firmly, it must be no more than an old bowl, as Bishop de Sully had suggested, merely an object to be used in a bit of mummery to relieve credulous folk of their money. I was aided in this discipline of the mind, this denial of the possibility of the Grail's authenticity, by the fact that it was, for me, irrevocably stained with death and surrounded by a dark aura of sadness: for the sake of this object my father had been hounded from Paris; in its name both he and Hanno had been murdered before my eyes.

But where the Grail was, there would the Master be. And I nursed my hatred of him to my bosom. If Robin wished to pursue this Grail, and to persuade King Richard to come south with his army, I was happy to follow him, for this path would lead me to the Master and my long-delayed revenge. And I felt in my bones then, in the last weeks of March, in the Year of the Incarnation eleven hundred and ninety-nine, that my vengeance was imminent: for we had Viscount Aimar and his few surviving men cornered, trapped at last in the tiny castle of Châlus-Chabrol, some fifteen miles southwest of Limoges.

While Richard's men surrounded the castle—a simple affair at the top of a steep round hill, with a curtain wall and one round tower for a keep—we Locksley folk made our main camp to the west of the fortress on the flatter lands on the other side of the river. The castle foolishly defied us—for there cannot have been more than a handful of defenders, forty at most. But the defenders did include at least one man-at-arms in a white surcoat with a blue cross in a black-bordered shield on the chest. He was not a fellow I recognized, but my spirits rose when I saw him on the third day of the siege, leaning over the curtain wall to take a shot with a crossbow at a squad of Robin's green-clad cavalry, which happened to be riding past. He missed the shot; it flew a dozen yards wide. But I was cheered by the glimpse of the device on his chest: if the Knights of Our Lady were here, that meant Robin's information was true, and I grimly looked forward to renewing my acquaintance with the Master and Sir Eustace de la Falaise, when the castle inevitably fell.

Richard was at that time perhaps the most experienced man in Christendom in the art of siege warfare: he was not going to be troubled for long by an insignificant fortification such as Châlus. Indeed, his engineers had already been at work for three days, laboring under the cover of a stout canvas-and-wood shelter, digging in shifts, night and day, and burrowing under the very walls of the castle.

The miners would soon complete a broad tunnel right under the outer fortifications. It would be prevented from collapsing under the weight of the walls above by wooden pillars and planks, which formed the walls and roof of the excavation. When the engineers had determined that the tunnel was directly under the curtain wall, its dark cavity would be packed with bundles of brushwood, old logs and many barrels of pig fat, which would be set alight. The fierce blaze would burn right through the wooden planks that supported its ceiling, and, once the inferno had consumed them, the tunnel would collapse under the weight from above—with God's blessing, also bringing the stone wall of the castle tumbling down, and thus opening a breach in the defenses.

Our knights would then charge up the steep slope and pour through the breach, and the merciless slaughter of the garrison would begin. They were fools to defy us; it was merely a matter of time before we would be inside Château Châlus-Chabrol, and under the accepted rules of warfare, because they had defied us, their lives were forfeit. Had they surrendered immediately, Richard might well have shown his customary mercy and pardoned them all.

While I was reasonably certain that the Master was inside the castle, my first glimpse of him was something of a shock. I was with Robin and a dozen of his archers, completing a discreet patrol at dusk on foot around the bottom of the hill on which the castle stood. For all its meager number of defenders, the castle still managed to post half a dozen sentries, who could be glimpsed at all hours of the day or night—no more than a helmeted head showing briefly on the battlements, a black ball against the skyline. Our archers would occasionally take a potshot at these men, but Robin eventually ordered them to stop; we were short of arrows, and they must be husbanded for the assault. Besides, as the enemy rarely showed their heads for long, so far no sentry had been harmed. As we strolled along the track at the bottom of the hill, I looked up at the steep grassy slope and the wall at the top of it. I could make out the tall dark shape of the round tower on the far side of the castle, and to my right, outside the walls and halfway up the slope, I could see the broad squat structure that housed the entrance to the mine, and a line of Richard's engineers burdened down with bundles of thick staves and barrels, hurrying in and out of the housing. My eye was caught by movement on the wall immediately above us: two figures, one a monk, the other a young man with bright red hair cradling a crossbow. The monk was pointing at the line of scurrying engineers, seemingly urging the crossbowman to shoot at them. The man-at-arms lifted his bow and loosed. The quarrel went wide, but I did not care where it struck: I was staring in shock at the monk. Without a doubt it was the Master; even from a hundred yards away, at dusk and looking up at such a great height, I could recognize his dark hair, cut in the tonsure, and his gaunt features. He looked strangely innocent; I could easily imagine him speaking in quiet, kindly tones to the crossbowman and urging him not to lose heart but to reload and try again.

"Do you see him, Alan?" said Robin.

"I do," I said, gazing up at the slim, dark figure we had sought for so long.

The leader of the squad of archers, a steady man named Peter, who had fought bravely with me at Verneuil, said quietly: "My lord, I believe I can hit him; may I try one?" But Robin was staring hard at the monk with a fixed, almost manic intensity. The light was poor for shooting, all the world made up only of layer upon layer of gray, and I expected Robin to refuse the archer's request. "Give me your bow," he said, extending a hand behind him to Peter.

Robin rarely carried his own bow these days; it was after all a yeoman's weapon and he was an earl and a senior adviser to the King. But he took the proffered bow and nocked the arrow with all his old ease and skill.

At that moment the King himself came riding along the path with two of his younger knights. He reined in without a word when he saw Robin with the drawn bow in his hands. My lord pulled the cord easily back to his ear, and loosed the arrow in one smooth movement, and the shaft leaped from the string, up, up, straight and true, flashing toward the monk on the wall; and it would have spitted him, too, except that, at the last instant, the redheaded crossbowman gave a cry and swung a large round object up between the monk's body and the hurtling shaft. The iron point of the arrow pinged off the makeshift shield and away—I could see now that it was a large iron frying pan that had saved the Master's life—and behind me came a loud royal shout: "Bravo, well done that man!"

The King, clearly in a good humor, was applauding the swift reflexes of the crossbowman, or perhaps his ingenuity in improvising an efficient shield-substitute from a kitchen implement. "That's the kind of spirit I like to see in a soldier!" He was chuckling merrily to himself, the prospect of the coming battle as ever animating his spirits.

"Beware, Sire," said Robin, "that fellow is making ready to shoot again!"

Robin was right: the Master was pointing at the King, and the redhead was leaning over the parapet, his crossbow aimed in our direction. The distance was too great for accurate shooting, but every man in that group had his shield up, held with the top rim just below his eyeline—every man, that is, except King Richard. The King sat his horse, totally unconcerned, and I saw with a jolt of alarm that he was only wearing light armor, short-sleeved with very fine iron links, the kind that we used to wear in the heat of Outremer. His stout shield, with its golden lions on a blood-red field, was slung carelessly on his back.

"Sire!" said Robin urgently.

"Be at peace, Locksley," said the King. "That bold fellow at the very least deserves a clear shot at me."

The quarrel came on as an evil black streak and, with a cold splash of fear in my stomach, I saw it strike the King on his left shoulder, penetrating deeply despite the light armor; rocking his body in the saddle from the impact.

For three heartbeats nobody moved: we were as still as rocks. I heard a faint cheer from the battlements above, then we all surged forward at once, surrounding the King, some holding up their shields to protect him against any further missiles from the castle walls, others helping him gently down from the saddle of his tall horse.

"God's legs, that was an unlucky blow," muttered the King, his face white, teeth gritted against the pain. "Get me to my tent, Locksley—quickly now, and quietly. Cover my face with your cloak; it would not do to alarm the men."

Three days later the engineers ignited the mine under the walls of Châlus-Chabrol. Thick black smoke boiled out of the tunnel that led into the hillside, in a huge dark plume, and an hour or so later, long jagged cracks appeared in the walls above. By mid-afternoon, with a great rippling crash, a wide section of wall collapsed, leaving a gap in the defenses like a missing tooth in an old man's mouth.

We were massed below the walls, out of crossbow range, the hundred or so Locksley men and my eight Westbury lads—we had lost one poor fellow on the field at Gisors, and another who died of wounds after the battle. Robin had begged for the honor of making the first assault on the castle, and Richard from his camp-bed had agreed. Behind us were the black flags of Mercadier's men—some two hundred of the most foul-hearted, vicious, evil-looking scoundrels in France, and led by a scar-faced villain who topped them all for cruelty. They were there to support our attack, King Richard had ordered, but this was a war hammer to crack a hazelnut—there were only about forty defenders, and the Locksley men, even if they were to suffer heavy casualties in the assault, would still easily overwhelm them. More than likely Mercadier's men, rather than genuinely wishing to support us, merely wanted to be in at the kill to have first pick of the loot. But then Robin's motives in volunteering his men for the attack were not exactly pure either: by the private gleam in his gray eyes, I knew he was thinking of the Grail.

"How does the King?" I asked him as we stood side by side, looking up the slope at the gap in the wall, which was still shrouded with billowing clouds of rock dust.

"Not well, Alan, not well, indeed." Robin was one of the few barons who had been allowed to visit him in his tent: the King wished to keep his injury a secret from the troops for fear of their losing heart. It had not worked; despite his seclusion, every man in the army knew that the King had been badly wounded, and the sense of raw, vindictive anger among the ranks against the defenders of the castle beat like a feverish pulse.

"He tried to pull the quarrel out himself," Robin continued, speaking quietly in a toneless voice in the hope that he would not be overheard by the nearby men. "But he made a mess of it and the shaft snapped off in his hand. Then he called a surgeon, that fat little butcher Enguerrand, who hacked him about something awful—it was dark by then, and Enguerrand was, of course, drunk—but after digging about in his shoulder for most of an hour he managed to get the quarrel head out and bandage him up. But it's not healing cleanly; the rot has begun and the smell of corruption in that tent is foul enough to make you gag."

"The King has been sorely wounded before," I said, "and has eventually recovered to full health."

"Several times, yes, he has, so let us all hope . . ." Robin's words were cut off by a trumpet blast. "Time to go, Alan; see you inside the castle—and be a good fellow and take the Master alive, if you can; beat him, maim him, cut him up as much as you like, but alive, if you please: I want to have a talk with him before we send him to Hell."

Robin strode out in front of the troops. He turned to face them, raised his sword in the air: "In the name of God and our King—for Richard! For England! Forward!" And the Locksley men cheered and, led by Robin's nimble feet, with a deep, angry roaring, they charged up that slope.

It may sound absurd, but almost the hardest part of that assault for me was the run up that very steep, grassy hill, and the scramble up the rocky staircase to the breach. Although my wounded chest was long healed, my wind was still not as sound as I would have liked and I found myself breathless, red-faced and panting when I eventually reached the breach in the wall. The Westbury men and I were not in the vanguard, thank the Lord; and we ran hard, but my lungs felt as if they were on fire, and by the time we reached the gap in the fortifications, a flood of angry Locksley men had swept it clear of enemies. As I stepped over the broken rubble of the wall and down into the tiny courtyard, still breathing heavily, Thomas was at my side, carrying a crossbow he had acquired from somewhere, and a loose cloud of Westbury men were all around me. The first thing I saw was that almost all the fight had gone out of the garrison. Enemy men-at-arms were lying dead in bloody heaps, and others were attempting to surrender or being cut down by furious Locksley men; on the far side of the courtyard a lone knight, Viscount Aimar himself, I believe, battled against a mob of green-clad men. He killed one of our fellows with an elegant backhand, and then was himself overrun by a mass of stabbing, hacking, yelling fiends. To my right, at the foot of the round tower, a scrum of men were fighting outside a small door that led into the castle's last redoubt. I saw flashing white surcoats adorned with a blue cross, and for the first time that day the battle-lust surged through my veins. I rushed forward, shouldered a Locksley man out of the way and engaged the nearest Knight of Our Lady. He snarled at me and cut; I blocked, feinted, ducked a blow and swept him off his feet with a sword strike to the ankles, and the Westbury men swarmed over him, stabbing down with awful efficiency. The other knight was very fast on his feet; he was already inside the tower and was desperately trying to swing the heavy wooden door shut in my face.

But I was faster.

I took a quick step toward him, punched the cross-guard of Fidelity into his face, crunching teeth and knocking him to the floor, then I stabbed down hard, plunging my blade through his heaving belly. And I was inside the door, in the tower, climbing and glaring upward, the blood rushing hot in my veins. A stone, spiral staircase turning to the right, a dim form above me. I stepped back just in time as a spear clattered on the stone steps in front of me. Then I started to climb again. My sword arm, my right arm, was impeded by the central core of the spiral stairway, but this was not so for the knight above me; he smashed a blow down on me, aiming for my head, and I caught it on my shield, feeling the manic force of the strike right down through my spine. I was knocked back two steps, and looked upward to see the mad, gleaming black eyes of Sir Eustace de la Falaise staring down at me through the gloom. He had a sword in his right hand, an axe in his left, and he smiled happily as he took a step down toward me, and unleashed a ravaging storm of blows from both hands.

Sword and axe, sword and axe, right and left—the strikes battered my helmet and shield and my hunched mailed shoulders with a terrible ferocity. I could barely use my sword either to defend or attack, the design of the stairwell, with the rising steps rotating sunwise, making it impossible for me to swing my blade. I took as much of the punishment as I could on my shield, but that article was soon battered into a shapeless mass of splintering wood and flapping leather. I fended off Sir Eustace with jabs of my sword-point, giving ground, step by step, being forced back down, down and around to the ground floor. Sir Eustace shouted: "Die, die, you peasant scum," and hammered down his left hand, his axe hand. I felt the blade crunch into the muscle of my shoulder, splitting the iron mail links and just penetrating the flesh. I staggered back another step, but managed to catch my enemy's next sword strike on the remains of my shield.

Somebody was under my stumbling feet, and I glanced down swiftly to see Thomas coming up and forward under my shield arm, his knees on the steps; from the level of my thighs, he poked the crossbow upward, aimed, loosed, and the quarrel shot forward and punched deep into the side of the ranting, spitting knight above me, just as he was raising his sword to strike again. He gave a shout of outrage and looked down at the quarrel sticking from his waist. Another crossbow twanged from below me, from the jostling mass of Westbury men who had followed me into the tower. The bolt clattered harmlessly off the round wall behind Sir Eustace's snarling, bestial face, but it caused the knight to scream in frustrated rage and to hurl his axe at my head, end over end, with shocking force. I ducked in the nick of time, the axe blade crashing onto the round top of my helm and bouncing away. And he ran. Sir Eustace bounded up the stone stairs away from me like a mountain goat; disappearing instantly from view, his slapping steps diminishing and finally ending with the clear sound, high above, of a slammed wooden door.

Even so, we climbed the stairs cautiously. Myself in the lead, with a fresh red Westbury shield furnished by Thomas on my left arm, and my squire advancing behind my left shoulder, his crossbow spanned and ready once again.

At the top of the stairs we paused in front of the door. I looked at Thomas. "If it is possible, I want to kill him myself, do you understand?" I said, nodding down at the deadly loaded crossbow in his steady hands.

"For Hanno?" asked Thomas.

"Yes, for Hanno—and all the others."

The door yielded to one hard stamp of my right foot, and I was in a large, round, dim chamber, the only light coming from arrow slits in the stone walls. And there was the Master, on the far side of the room, his hands calmly folded inside the opposite sleeves of his robe, in the position in which I had first seen him. Hiding his thumbs.

A flicker of movement to my left—but hardly unexpected. I relaxed my knees and bobbed down and a sword blade flashed over my lowered head and struck sparks against the stone wall behind me, but I was already moving away, circling the room. I saw that Sir Eustace de la Falaise had the sword in his right hand; he had drawn the lance-dagger, the strange weapon that had ended Hanno and so many other good men, and was holding it in his left.

The crossbow quarrel was deeply embedded above his right hip, and his white surcoat on that side bore a large and growing red stain. I smiled at him, and I swear at that moment I felt no fear at all. God had placed him in my path so that I might have my vengeance. He smiled back at me with his amiable idiot's grin, and mad little black eyes, swung the sword again, hard, and I took the blow full on my new red shield. Almost at the same time, less than a heartbeat later, he lunged forward with the lance-dagger, lightning fast, aiming for the center of my chest. But I had anticipated the move and twisted my torso side-on in time to allow the strange blade to strike nothing more precious than air. Then I struck: a full, sweeping downward blow with my sword that would have split his skull if it had landed. But the man had been a Templar, a true Templar with all the martial skill of that famous Order, and wounded or not, he was still formidable. His sword whipped up and deflected my strike harmlessly away and to his left, and we both stepped back at the same time and began warily to circle each other again.

The room was filling with my men, but Thomas kept them against the walls, leaving Sir Eustace and I room to fight our duel. The Master had not moved from his stance by the arrow-slit window on the far side of the round chamber. One glance at his serene, handsome face, his blue eyes watching us, seemingly filled with compassion for all mankind, and I felt a wave of nauseous disgust. He looked like a bishop, a grave man of God, someone who should be revered. I knew better: he was filth, murdering filth, hiding behind a godly robe and a pious manner.

I wanted to hear him scream for mercy.

Sir Eustace attacked again, using exactly the same maneuver: a swing of the sword and a snake-quick thrust with the lance-dagger. And once again I blocked the sword with my shield, and dodged the dagger thrust. Then I came at him—hard, fast and with all the bottled anger in my grieving soul. I swept Fidelity laterally at his neck, from the left and then the right, punched at the quarrel shaft protruding from his waist with my shield, driving it deeper into him, causing him to shout in pain and leap away—and then I took two quick steps in and smashed Fidelity hard and down into the outside of his mailed left knee. My blade did not penetrate but he howled, dropped to a kneeling position on the floor. I smashed the outer rim of my shield down onto his right wrist, and his sword clattered away. Immediately, he came surging up at me in a stumbling lunge, trying to grapple my shoulder with his empty right hand and plunge the lance-dagger into my belly with his left. I dodged to my right, out of his path, swung Fidelity and sliced down with all my might as he passed me, hacking through the mail and deep into his shoulder. He shouted once more, a short hard cry of shocked rage. His arm hung limp, useless, a deep purple gash of flesh exposed for an instant, a flash of round white bone. And then the blood fountained up; the lance-dagger dropped from his unfeeling fingers and skittered across the stone floor to land against my mailed foot. He turned to face me, and stood silent, massive-eyed, swaying, weaponless, his whole body drenched with his own spurting gore. I tucked Fidelity under my shield arm, bent down quickly and scooped up the lance-dagger in my right hand, hefted it, looked deeply into his black eyes, then stepped in and punched the blade into his chest, aiming for a spot an inch or so to the left of his sternum. He died there on his feet, staring back at me in disbelief for a single moment, before crashing to the floor.

I turned to the Master and saw that he was now on his knees. I grasped Fidelity once more. The man's eyes were tightly shut, his head bowed in prayer, his hands still tucked together in the sleeves of his gown.

I was aware of a sigh, a gust of breath from half a dozen throats, followed by an admiring murmur from the assembled Westbury men, and sensed that others too were entering the room. There was a crush of bodies by the door, and I heard Thomas saying in a quiet steady voice: "Leave them be, this is Sir Alan's task and his alone; stay back, boys, if you please, stand back."

But my eyes were fixed upon the Master, and over the low hum of the watching folk behind me, I heard him repeat the familiar Latin words: *"Ave Maria, gratia plena, Dominus tecum, benedicta tu in mulieribus, et benedictus fructus ventris tui Iesus. Sancta Maria mater Dei, ora pro nobis peccatoribus, nunc, et in hora mortis nostrae . . ."*

Hail Mary, full of grace, the Lord is with thee, blessed art thou among women, and blessed is the fruit of thy womb, Jesus. Holy Mary, Mother of God, pray for us sinners, now, and at the hour of our death.

I looked down at him, Fidelity slack in my right hand. I must tell you, my friends, for all that I knew he was truly evil, it is no easy thing to kill a monk who is on his knees praying, no easy thing at all. I conjured up an image of Hanno in my mind, his laughing face, the shaven head and terrible teeth; I thought of the adventures we'd had together in far-off lands, his stories, his love of fat women and good ale, and still I hesitated to strike my enemy down.

I thought of my father—and finally lifted Fidelity, high above my head, my wrists cocked, ready to strike the final blow. Brother Michel opened his bright blue eyes and looked up at my face—and deep into my soul. His left hand emerged from the sleeve of his robe: it bore a small silver crucifix; plain, brilliant, the miniature figure of Our Lord exquisitely rendered. He held it out toward me. He held it so that his ugly split thumb divided either side of the lower part of the cross, twin perfect digits, with well-trimmed white nails poking out to the left and right of Our Lord's tiny, silver feet, as if supporting him, as if easing his suffering in the hour of his death.

"You cannot kill me, Alan," he said in a soft, calm, infinitely reasonable voice, raising the crucifix toward me. "You do know that, don't you? I serve the Mother of God and her only son Our Lord Jesus Christ. I am a man of God. You could no more kill me than you could take your own life. To kill me is to deny God! I command you, by the power of the Almighty, by the power of Our Lady Mary, to lay down your sword."

The world shook itself, and blurred sickeningly before my eyes.

The muscles of my arms and back, the meaty fibers that supported Fidelity in its attack position above my head, were frozen; I could never have moved, even if my life had depended on it. Suddenly I was transported to Nottingham Castle five years earlier—and Sir Ralph Murdac, my hated enemy, saying: "If you kill me, you will never know the secret of your father's death."

I knew that secret now; I knew that it was this man, the "man you cannot refuse," presently unarmed and, in turn, on his knees before me, holding out that sliver of precious silver in his left hand—I knew it was he who had ordered my father's shameful death. Yet through some strange alchemy, or because of an invisible strength in his words or emanating from his soul, I could not strike him down.

The Master rose to his feet. He jerked the tiny silver crucifix at me, and I took an involuntary step backward. Fidelity was still poised above my head, forgotten. The Master looked deep inside me, his clear blue eyes filled with all the sadness and pity of the world. "I shall pray for your soul, my son," he said. And he began to walk lightly, easily toward the door of that high, round room.

I could not move: I was locked tight, with Fidelity held impotently, absurdly, above my head as the Master—the man I hated more than the Devil, the monster who had killed my friend and my father—walked serenely toward the door. Not a man moved to stop him. The Westbury men, even my steady, reliable Thomas, moved out of his path, parting before him like a red curtain as if moved by an unseen force: this truly was magic, this was a powerful enchantment of a magnitude that put all of poor, crazed Nur's shabby countryside tricks to shame.

The Master walked unmolested to the door. Under its lintel, however, he stopped dead. I could see nothing but the back of his tonsured head. He was motionless, as frozen as I, or any other mortal man in that room.

"Back in there, I think," said a calm, familiar voice.

And the Master took a step backward, into the round room. His thin face had paled, I could see even from my poor angle of view, and a shining steel blade extended horizontally from under his chin into the darkness of the stairwell.

"Keep going, Brother—if you want to live," said the voice. The Master took two more steps back into the room. And Robin emerged from the darkness of the stairwell, his unwavering sword held to the Master's throat.

"Well done, Sir Alan," said my lord. "I thought you'd kill him out of hand. It is so gratifying to see self-restraint practiced by the young men of today. Well done, indeed." Then louder: "Sam, Gerry, bind this slippery bastard securely and take him down to the camp; he's our prisoner."

And two burly Locksley men bustled through the doorway, and brushed roughly past the dazed, spellbound Westbury men to carry out Robin's orders. I looked at my lord, his silver eyes sparkling with unholy merriment, then I lowered Fidelity with more than a little effort, shook my head to clear it, and managed a feeble smile of welcome.

"Where is it? Where is it, you maggoty little turd?" Robin's face was a mask of cold fury, and only inches from the Master's. We were in Robin's large green campaign tent, on the flat land below the castle. It was two days after we had stormed Château Châlus-Chabrol, and while the men had celebrated the victory in the usual raucous, bibulous manner, there was an air of bleached gray gloom over the whole camp like a dank mist. The King was sinking fast: his shoulder was swollen, greeny-black and stinking, and the poison was spreading down his arm, Robin had reported. Richard had summoned his priests to hear his last confession, and written to his mother Eleanor of Aquitaine, and we heard that she was hurrying south to see her beloved son one last time on this Earth.

I felt as if my heart was breaking, breathless, sick and dim of sight as if the sun was guttering and fading: my King, one of the finest men I had ever known, was slipping away, killed by a silly, insignificant wound—one that on another day he might have shrugged off with a golden laugh and a flash of his strong teeth. It had been no more than a lucky shot with a crossbow, a shot that should have missed at that distance, which might easily have been stopped with a small movement of his shield. It was a useless death, a paltry, ignoble, meaningless end for such a man, for such a king—how could the greatest hero of Christendom be laid low by an unknown peasant's chance shot? And yet he had been—and Richard was as forthright when facing death as he was in life. I finally managed to see him, face-to-face, on the sixth day after he had taken his wound. For all that he had wanted to keep the hurt a secret, he had failed, and hundreds of men from the lowest beggars to the haughtiest barons wished to speak to him one last time before he went to the Great Beyond. He had time for them all.

To me, when I was finally admitted to his tent, he said in a low scratchy voice: "We had some rare times together, Blondel, my friend—some laughter, some song, some joy and a little shared glory . . ." I could not prevent my eyes from blurring with tears. He was clad only in a dirty chemise, propped up on sweat-stained silk pillows in a low pallet in his pavilion, his face waxy-white, eyes brilliant against the pallor, his once-bright hair now lank and flat. "And I thank you for all you have done for me these many years; I hope you will remember me fondly when I am gone."

I choked back a sob, and said: "You must not say such things, Sire. You will survive, you will surely find the strength to overcome this illness and . . ."

"I am dying, Alan. Let there be truth between us at the last. We have both seen much of death and of dying men, have we not? Let us not deceive ourselves."

I was weeping openly by this time. The King took my hand in his unnaturally hot, bony grasp, and his glittering blue eyes fell upon a velvet bundle at my feet. "You are to practice your music a little more often, Blondel," he said mock-sternly. "I command it. I have noticed of late that you have been neglecting the vielle; it can be as powerful as the sword in the right hands, you know. You do too much soldiering and not enough singing, in my opinion."

I smiled at him, through the mist of tears, and offered to play for him for a while. He agreed, but after a verse or two I saw that his eyes had closed and he was asleep, and his household knights behind him were frowning at me and gesturing frantically and silently that I should leave him in peace. And so I tiptoed away. I never saw my King alive again, and even now, many years later, the memory of his well-loved, fine-drawn sleeping face squeezes my throat and makes it hard for me to take a breath.

While the King was dying, Robin occupied himself interrogating the Master: we had rifled his baggage, and gone through the piles of loot, and searched the whole of the castle from the top of the tower to the deepest latrine, and found nothing. Either the Grail was indeed a magical object that could make itself invisible, or it was not in the castle. At first the Master had refused to speak of it at all; then after he had been roughly handled by Little John, who had threatened to roast his balls like chestnuts over a campfire, the Master had admitted that he had once had possession of the Grail, but insisted that he no longer knew where it was.

I dreaded what would come next; I knew Robin would not shrink from the vilest torture to get what he desired. But I did not want to see any man, even one as deserving as the Master, undergo the sort of torments that I knew Robin and Little John could inflict.

Robin strode out of his tent, calling a little too loudly for a brazier, firewood and irons, and I took my chance to speak with the prisoner. He was still bound, with his arms behind him, but his legs had been freed. As he sat there on the ground, his back against a bulky clothes chest, with his skinny white legs protruding from his drab monk's robe and extended in front of him, it was difficult to remember that this was a man who casually ordered killings, a master of gangs of ruthless French woodland thieves, the head of a secret organization of would-be Templar knights, and someone who called himself the "man you cannot refuse."

I knelt down beside him and looked into his pale, pockmarked face. Slowly, he raised his innocent blue eyes until he was staring into mine. "They are even now fetching the instruments," I said. He nodded sadly but said nothing.

"You must die, of course," I said, "for what you have done to my family and my friends"—he nodded again, an acknowledgment of his doom—"but I can make it quick. And, if you wish, I could use this."

From the leather sheath at my waist, I plucked the lance-dagger, now cleaned and oiled, that I had recovered from Sir Eustace de la Falaise's corpse. His eyes fixed upon it and I thought I detected a glow of veneration. He truly believed, I thought, that this was the blade that had pierced Christ's body. "All you have to do is tell me where the Grail is, and swear on your immortal soul that you do not lie, and I will use this on you, swiftly, and you will feel no pain and go to your reward without the red-hot horrors that my lord of Locksley and his men would inflict upon you. Tell me, Brother Michel, where is the Grail? Tell me quickly before they return."

"I liked your father," he said. "Truly I did. And it grieved me that he had to take the blame. But he had to, you know, he was the only one who could."

I was a little thrown by this change of subject but not so thrown that I could not retort: "You may have liked him but you ordered his death without a qualm, did you not? You had Murdac hang him like a felon, didn't you?"

"I had a dream, a vision. Our Lady came to me while I slept. She told me that I must take the Grail from that fat, slothful, self-indulgent bishop, a man not worthy of its grace, and use its power to magnify her name. And she came to me again a year later in the plague tents, when I lay dying in that stinking cot, surrounded by all the suffering men and women of Paris; she came to me then, too, and kissed me on the brow, and wiped away my tears, and gave me new life. She told me that I must drink from the Grail—just water, ordinary water made sacred and healing by the grace of the Grail, that wondrous symbol of her holy Christ-giving womb. I rose from my plague cot and left that place of sickness, and I drank from the Grail that very night and that pure draft put the breath and strength back into my feeble, dying body. She told me what I must do to repay her for that second chance, that second life. I saw so clearly what she wanted: a company of knights dedicated to her name, protecting that holy vessel and using its power to spread the love of the Queen of Heaven across the whole world. The cathedral, too, she asked me for that: the greatest church in Christendom devoted to her name. She has been most shamefully neglected: the Mother of Our Lord Jesus Christ, the blessed womb, the font from which God's love springs—I knew then that it was my duty to devote my whole life to her everlasting glory."

"By killing and robbing innocent men and women—that is spreading her love, is it?"

"Their deaths meant nothing: she told me so herself; all those who fell in her cause would be received into Heaven by her intercession. Those souls who died—including your father, my old friend Henri—have been saved! They are with the Mother of God in Heaven."

I felt sick. Was he mad, I wondered. And how can one tell with folk who believe themselves touched by God? Or, in his case, the Mother of God. I had taken part in the Great Pilgrimage with thousands of other ordinary folk, and we had crossed Europe to bring war and death to the Holy Land in the name of Christ. Was this any different? Was he truly inspired by the Blessed Virgin Mary? Was she the source of his strange power that had very nearly allowed him to walk calmly from under my sword only a few days ago?

"Cut my bonds, Alan," said the Master. "Allow me to go free to serve the Queen of Heaven and her Son. Cut them now: nobody will know but you and I. And you will assure yourself of a place in Heaven by your actions."

His bright blue eyes compelled me, and my will dissolved; I could feel it melting away like snow on a boot top propped by a hearth; then with a dreamy jolt, I found I was outside my own body, like a ghost, looking across at a young blond knight stretching his left hand forward to grasp the cruel ropes that bound this innocent man of God, this good and holy monk . . .

No, no, a thousand times, no. With a wrench, I broke our locked gaze, came to my senses and snatched my left hand away as if from a flame. I reminded myself that this slight monk had commanded savage gangs of lawless bandits to do his bidding; he had controlled scores of knights and sent them out to kill at his behest. I had felt the full force of his mind and had nearly been overcome. I had a glimpse of Robin's mocking face, and I knew that he would find the feebleness of my will entirely risible. He alone, among a dozen Westbury men, had been impervious to the Master's powers in the round room above the tower: was it his cynicism, his godlessness, that had protected him?

I lifted the lance-dagger in my right hand, taking refuge in its implied threat. I was about to make one more appeal to the man before me when I heard movement behind and turned to see roughly dressed, well-armed men pushing Robin's sentries out of their way and swaggering into the tent: it was Mercadier and half a dozen of his *routiers.*

"We have orders from the King," said Mercadier. "That monk is to be fetched to the royal tent, immediately. Put that ridiculous blade away and stand aside . . . Sir Knight."

I stood and sheathed the lance-dagger. "He is my prisoner," I said. "You cannot merely steal him from under my nose in broad daylight."

"The King needs him! We have information from another wretch that this monk has in his possession a magical bowl, a relic of some sort, that can cure a man no matter how severe his hurt. So I say once again, Sir Knight, for the last time: stand aside by order of the King!"

I looked down at the Master. His eyes were closed; I heard him whisper: "Thank you, Lady, for your mercy!"

I made a final effort: "He does not have the magical bowl you seek. I have been trying to persuade him to reveal its hiding place . . ."

"We shall persuade him more effectively than you, I think," said Mercadier, with a cold smile.

I put my hand on my sword hilt. But Mercadier spoke again: "Think carefully, Sir Knight, before you lose your head! You once took a captive monk from me by force—do you remember? Do you think I would flinch from doing the same to you in order for a chance to save the King's life?"

On either side of Mercadier, two crossbowmen were aiming their weapons at my chest. I took a breath, shrugged and released my hilt. "Guard him closely," I said, moving out of the way of Mercadier's men, who went forward swiftly to seize the Master. "I shall certainly want him back from you when you are done with him."

I expected Robin to be angry with me for allowing the mercenary to steal our prisoner but he merely smiled and said: "Persuasion is an ugly business, and that scarred brute is more practiced at it than I am; better that he should do it."

But it galled me to have had to surrender the Master to my enemy, and I said as much. "There was nothing you could have done," said Robin. "Mercadier had a warrant from the King to seize him; he would have killed you had you resisted him. Besides, all is not lost. When Mercadier is finished, we will reclaim him; and perhaps the Grail, too."

The King died the next day. Quietly, holding his mother's hand, having made his last confession, the Lionheart took his leave of this earthly life. The first I heard of it was a deep hollow baying, like a pack of hounds at feeding time, the cries of many hundreds of grief-stricken men, and word spread throughout the camp in a ripple of sorrow growing louder and louder. Knights wailed and tore their hair; I saw grizzled men-at-arms who would cheerfully murder a child or loot a church weeping like girls. And quietly, almost imperceptibly, that very same day the royal army began to melt away.

I drank a cup of wine in the Marshal's tent that evening, with Robin, some of the Marshal's knights, and Sir Nicholas de Scras. I was stunned, unable quite to compass what had happened—the King was truly dead and yet the world still existed. I would never see his face again, nor joke with him, nor sing for him, nor ride into battle at his side, and feel the exhilaration of his reckless enthusiasm for war. It seemed unreal, and yet I saw everything with an unusual clarity. The Earl of Striguil's lined face had aged another ten years that day: he looked like an old, old man, his hair now entirely gray, black pouches of tiredness below his eyes. For a long while in that gloom-filled tent, nobody spoke.

Then Robin spoke for us all: "Well then, what now?"

"Now," said the Marshal, lifting his heavy head, "now, we all have a choice. We do homage to Arthur, Duke of Brittany, Richard's little nephew . . ."

"That brat? He is but twelve years old," protested one of the knights. "The English barons will never follow him."

"I said we had a choice," the Marshal rumbled. "We may swear allegiance to Arthur of Brittany . . . or to Prince John. Richard named him as his heir, almost with his last breath—and Queen Eleanor witnessed it and approves. He is her son, too, after all."

There was a long, long silence.

"So it is John," said Robin with a deep sigh.

"I fear it must be John," replied the Marshal.

At some point during the pale orgy of grief and uncertainty that followed King Richard's death, the Master talked one of his captors into releasing his bonds, and he slipped away from the camp unseen. Mercadier's men cared little about their prisoner's escape—he was but a monk, after all, not a magnate who might provide a rich ransom. And each individual *routier* was busy considering what he might do, now that the army was disintegrating and the prospects of payment had died with the King. Some rode out of the camp and immediately took up the wild life of bandits, squeezing the last few drops of nourishment from a ravaged landscape; others gathered their weapons, women and loot, formed disciplined bands and marched north to seek employment in Flanders or the German lands. Mercadier himself, black-faced with an icy rage, located the redheaded crossbowman who had loosed the deadly quarrel against the King and had him publicly flayed alive, although the wretched man insisted, screaming, that he had had an audience with the King before he died and had been granted a full pardon for his crime.

In all this confusion, the Master disappeared. And by the time the thought had pierced through the bitter fog of my grief, and it occurred to me that I should attempt to reclaim him, as Robin had put it, he was long gone.

Oddly, I did not rage and curse at Mercadier, or myself, after his disappearance: he was bound for Hell, I knew, and God would punish him in due course, or so I earnestly hoped. With Richard gone, I found it difficult to care for anything, anything at all; all strength seemed to have seeped from my limbs; I could barely stir myself to eat, drink and empty my bowels.

Eventually, after days of sorrowful idleness, I pulled myself together, slowly gathered up the Westbury men, as Robin gathered up his Locksley folk, and we packed our traps and folded our tents, and mustered on horseback in the dawn. Then, dolefully, we took the road north; north toward England, home and family. North to Goody.

I married my beloved—Godifa, daughter of Thangbrand—at the door of the little church in Westbury on the first day of July in the year of Our Lord Eleven Hundred and Ninety-Nine. Robin gave her away to me, while Marie-Anne, Countess of Locksley, and her women looked on and wept for joy. There would be no rich dowry from the King—that generous offer had died with him—but Robin provided Goody with a half-dozen lumpy linen bags, each displaying a bright red Templar cross. And we celebrated the marriage with a solemn Mass inside the village church afterward, conducted not by Arnold the local priest but by Marie-Anne's chaplain and our old friend Father Tuck, and with a feast the like of which Westbury had never seen.

After the meal, Little John and Thomas stripped to the waist, greased their torsos with goose fat and took on all comers in a roped-off wrestling enclosure. And after having defeated a dozen local men, and encouraged by a great deal of mead, they fought each other in a friendly bout that Little John narrowly won, and only then because he lost his temper and dislocated Thomas's right shoulder. Bernard de Sézanne, Queen Eleanor of Aquitaine's famous *trouvère* and my erstwhile music master, arrived and sang and laughed and sang again, and then became so drunk that he had to be carried to bed; William the Marshal and a dozen of his knights attended also, including my friend Sir Nicholas de Scras, and they consented to give a display of skill at arms that had the villagers of Westbury gasping with awe. And, afterward, fired with martial ardor, half a dozen of the local lads came to me and asked if they might have the honor of serving me as men-at-arms.

It was a happy, happy day. And when I took Goody's hand in the porch of the church, and Tuck blessed us and wrapped a band of silk around our joining, I knew beyond a shadow of a doubt that, not only did I love her with my whole heart, my body and my soul, but that I would love her for the rest of my days. And so I have.

And later, breathless in the warm dark of the great bed in my chamber, after we had made love for the first time, and I was still tingling at the touch of her lips and breasts and warm loins, and wondering at the magic in her being, I knew that God had smiled on me, and I was truly blessed.

And as I drifted into sleep, I heard a tap-tapping of a thin branch against the wooden window shutter, and drowsing, sinking into delightful sleep, I heard that insistent but light rattling form a rhythm, a dry whispering beat that my sleepy mind only dimly recognized: one-two, one-two, one-two-three, one-two.

Epilogue

My hands ache from scribbling these words, and it seems to me that this must be a good place to end this tale of my young self, and Robin, and my beloved sovereign the lionhearted Richard, and finally to lay down my quill. Writing of the King's death has brought back all the sorrow of that time in a bitter flood. I truly loved him, my King, my hero, and when I think on his death, I feel the prick of hot tears once more in my old, dry eyes. I sometimes wonder what Richard might have achieved if he had deigned to sport his shield that black day outside Château Châlus-Chabrol. Would he have finally taken Gisors and driven the French King from Normandy? Would he have begat sons to rule after he was dead and denied the throne to his brother John? We shall never know. But I comfort myself with the thought that, like Hanno, King Richard shall never grow old and tired and frail, as I have—and that, like Hanno, he died a warrior's death, with brave words on his lips and defiance in his heart. I think that perhaps only a fighting man can understand that satisfaction. Hanno and Richard lived and died as men—and their memory will ever be honored among those warriors who shared their perils.

I have shown these pages to my grandson Alan and he told me after supper one day that he liked them very much. But he was also a little confused and full of questions: "What of your vengeance, Grandpa?" he asked, wrinkling his young brow. "Did you not have your revenge on the Master as you did on Sir Eustace de la Falaise?"

"I did," I replied, "but not at this time."

"And what of that ill-born dog Mercadier? Surely you did not suffer him to live and prosper in peace?"

"Oh, he certainly died," I said. "He did not prosper, and he died quite soon after the King."

"But how did he die, Grandpa? What were the circumstances of his death? Did you kill him in battle? Did you fight him in a duel? Did you kill the Master, too? The 'man you cannot refuse'? And the Grail—what became of that? Did you ever find it? Was it really the blessed vessel that once held Our Savior's blood?"

"Hush now, my boy," I said. "Too many questions for this time of night. All that passed after Richard's death is a story for another day." And I dismissed him to his bed. But his questions stayed with me: my dead memories called to me silently from the dark corners of the hall, and in my half-waking dreams at dawn they danced through my mind. So perhaps my aching hand will, with rest, recover its suppleness in a few days, and perhaps I will pick up my quill once more and write one last tale of Robin and myself, of our friends and enemies, of Nur and Prince John, of Mercadier and the Master—and our quest for that most wondrous, tantalizing, blood-tainted object, the Holy Grail.

Historical Note

At my parents' house the other day, I was sorting through some childhood possessions when I came across a slim, hardback book, written by Lawrence Du Garde Peach, illustrated by John Kenney and published in 1965 by Wills & Hepworth Ltd of Loughborough. On the cover is a tall, commanding medieval knight in a full suit of mail with a white crusader's surcoat over the top. His domed helmet is adorned with a golden crown; a red shield is slung across his broad back; his left hand rests casually on the pommel of the scabbarded sword at his waist; he gazes into the distance at an unfolding but unseen battle. On the cover of the book are the words: *Richard the Lion Heart*—A Ladybird Book—An Adventure from History. Holding it in my hand, I experienced a great flood of half-forgotten happy memories. This little book, which I must have read some forty years ago, is, I believe, responsible for my lifelong interest in Richard the Lionheart. In language suitable for a six-year-old child, it encapsulated his aristocratic arrogance, his love of battle and his generosity of spirit; and while I have done a good deal of grown-up reading about the subject since then, my mental image of Richard remains that of the imperious knight on the cover of that slim volume.

Most people are familiar, from novels, films and plays, with the highlights of Richard's career—the warrior king who led the Third Crusade, and was then captured, imprisoned and held for ransom on his way home—but storytellers seldom focus on the last five years of his life. I think this is because, to modern eyes, the half-decade before his death in April 1199 was rather a confused period—it was a time of intermittent warfare against Philip of France, with few clear victories or defeats and very little glory. Bands of knights and mercenaries ravaged the lands from Boulogne to Bordeaux, thousands of peasants perished from hunger, towns were burned, castles were captured, retaken, destroyed, rebuilt—and there were frequent truces between the warring sides while everyone wielding a sword and wearing armor took a breath and planned their next move. And that is partly why I wanted to write about this chapter of history—I felt that few other novelists had explored it and I wanted to get across a sense of the destructiveness of medieval war, and the appalling impact it had on the landscape and on people's livelihoods—as well as on the minds of the combatants. But I also discovered why this period of the Lionheart's life is seldom written about: it is rather difficult to shape into a recognizably heroic narrative structure—it ends without any significant military triumphs and with King Richard's almost random death at the hands of a nobody in a minor battle at an obscure castle. Such is real life; even great heroes sometimes die pointlessly.

At the time, or shortly afterward, many of the chroniclers of the Lionheart's exploits were also slightly bemused and deflated by his anticlimactic demise and various attempts were made to give the facts of his death more meaning. To the medieval mind, the lives of great men must have a pattern; they must demonstrate God's purpose in some way, as chaotic chance was surely the work of the Devil. Accordingly, some historians of the day happily used their imagination when describing Richard's end: they claimed that the Lionheart had been seeking a valuable treasure at Château Châlus-Chabrol, which had been discovered by the Viscount of Limoges, and which Richard wished to lay his hands on. This turned the hero's death into a parable about greed—the mighty lion slain by an insignificant ant as a punishment for avarice.

However, I was quite delighted to discover this fantastic tale of a hidden treasure when I was researching King Richard's death—even though it was unlikely to have any basis in fact: it made my job a little easier. I had been wanting to include the story of the Holy Grail—a hugely influential contemporary legend made popular by the *trouvère* Chretien de Troyes and others—as an element in my Robin Hood stories for some time, and this seemed like the perfect opportunity. And so, in my novel, my fictional heroes Robin and Alan persuade Richard to come south to punish Viscount Aimar with the lure of a wondrous treasure, the Holy Grail. The Grail storyline continues in the next book in this series—indeed, it is the main theme—and I will say more about that fabulous object then. But the point of this note is to help the reader understand which parts of my books are based on historical fact, and which parts are not. So, there was no Holy Grail at Château Châlus-Chabrol when Richard died there on 6 April 1199, and probably no hidden treasure either—but there are many other parts of my story that might sound equally incredible but which do happen to be true.

The episode with Alan at Verneuil at the beginning of the book is based on a real battle. The Castle of Verneuil was being besieged by King Philip with a huge army and, on Richard's arrival in Normandy in May 1194, he sent a small contingent of men to break through the French lines and stiffen the resolve of the defenders. This they did, bravely holding off their attackers until King Philip and more than half his force suddenly departed to take revenge for the massacre of the civilians by Prince John at Évreux. Verneuil was saved, and when Richard arrived with his army a day or so later, he captured the King of France's siege train from his fleeing enemies. Richard was so delighted by the successful defense of Verneuil that he kissed all the surviving defenders and rewarded them generously. History does not record what the King thought of the mocking chalk drawing on the front of the castle gate of a mace-bearing Philip—although that weapon was probably in his hands, not "springing from his loins," which is an exercise of literary license by me designed to make the insulting cartoon more comprehensible to modern eyes. Jokes don't travel well over the centuries.

After Verneuil, on his way south to pacify Aquitaine, King Richard's army terrified the citizens of Tours—who had been involved in disloyal negotiations with the French—into handing over a "gift" of two thousand marks to appease the royal anger; but Robin's involvement in the arrangement of this bribe is, of course, my own invention. The taking of Loches was a notable victory for Richard—the castle was widely seen as impregnable, but the Lionheart captured it in a single day (13 June 1194) in one fierce and prolonged assault. Outside Vendôme, a couple of weeks later, Richard prepared for a pitched battle with Philip, but after one skirmish the French retreated toward Chateâudun; the Lionheart's cavalry, in hot pursuit, caught up with the rearguard and captured their entire wagon train. The haul of booty was enormous, including much of Philip's treasure and the royal archives, which provided the names of those of Richard's knightly subjects who had made plans to defect to the enemy.

The Truce of Tillières (23 July 1194) was the first of several accords that were signed during the period before Richard's death. It was intended to last until 1 November 1195, and like all truces was based on the status quo—which meant that Alan's fictional manor of Clermont-sur-Andelle would remain in the hands of its French usurpers. This brief window of peace made Alan's visit to Paris possible, and the city was indeed in the midst of a building boom in the summer and autumn of 1194, as I have described. King Philip was busy surrounding Paris with a great defensive wall, which was at that time only half-completed, but which was meant to protect his capital from the depredations of Richard's marauders. Bishop Maurice de Sully—a powerful but beloved prelate who had nothing to do with the Holy Grail or my fictional Master's gangs of bandits, and who died at the Abbey of St. Victor in 1196—was building the magnificent Notre-Dame cathedral for the glory of God and the Virgin Mary. The cathedral, which was not completed until the middle of the thirteenth century, still summons pilgrims from the far corners of Christendom.

The Knights Templar were also busily engaged in the construction of a formidable new base to the northeast of the city. Incidentally, Sir Gilbert Horal, 12th Grand Master of the Knights Templar, did indeed fight against the Moors of Spain, and his personal device was a blue cross, but he never formed a separate sub-order of Templar knights dedicated to the Queen of Heaven. He was, though, as Sir Aymeric de St. Maur (a real Anglo-Norman Templar) comments, genuinely in favor of making peace with the Muslims in the Holy Land.

Paris, then as now, was a magnet for students from all over Europe—and the war between Richard and Philip did not prevent clever Englishmen from flocking there to take part in the intellectual flowering of the city. My fictional character, the malodorous Master Fulk, is partly based on a famous English teacher called Adam du Petit-Pont who lived and taught his students on the smaller bridge over the Seine to the south of the Île de la Cité.

The plot twist at the end of the second part of the book, when Alan apparently gets stabbed in the heart and lives, is, I'm reliably informed, quite possible medically. One person in ten thousand—so 700,000 people alive in the world at the moment—is believed to have the condition called *situs inversus viscerum*, in which their heart and other organs are on the wrong side of the body. However, to be fair, in medieval times Alan would have been extraordinarily lucky to survive that strike as it might well have severed one or many crucial blood vessels in that part of his chest, and, failing that, the risk of fatal infection would have been high: mercifully, Reuben, with his near-miraculous medical skills, was at hand to save his life.

Paris was not the only hive of building activity in northern France: Château-Gaillard, the saucy castle, was another extraordinarily energetic feat of construction that took place during this period. It was completed in just two years (1196–1198) and may have cost as much as £20,000—a staggering sum for the time. In comparison, Dover Castle, which was built between 1179 and 1191—taking more than a decade to build—cost £7,000. King Richard clearly loved his "fair" castle in Normandy, referring to it as his "one-year-old daughter" on one occasion and remarking that he could defend its walls if they were made of butter.

My descriptions of his campaigns against the occupied part of the duchy are reasonably accurate, although much simplified: Prince John presided over the capture of Milly, and William the Marshal was the first man over the wall after the initial attack faltered. That aging warrior knocked out the constable of the castle and then sat on his unconscious body to rest his weary limbs. Or, perhaps, to make sure that no one else claimed him as a valuable prisoner of war.

The battle of Gisors (27 September 1198) took place much as I have described it, except that William the Marshal's charge is my own invention. In fact, some scholars think the Earl of Striguil was not present at the battle at all. Richard, while out scouting with a small group of knights, came across a large French army, some three hundred knights and a similar number of men-at-arms and militia spread out in the line of march, which was advancing northwest toward Courcelles. The Lionheart, with characteristic decisiveness, immediately attacked the French, despite being massively outnumbered, and put them to flight. Richard is said to have used "God and my right!" (*Dieu et mon droit*), a public denial of his fealty to King Philip, as his battle cry at Gisors, which subsequently became the motto of the British Monarchy. The collapse of the bridge over the River Epte was a notable feature of the battle, and Philip was mocked by his enemies afterward for being "forced to take a drink from the river." Many prisoners were taken after the battle—Mercadier himself took thirty knights prisoner—and such was the hatred between the two sides at this point in the war that a good many atrocities were committed on the POWs, including blinding. The historian John Gillingham writes in his definitive book on the subject, *Richard I*: "It may be that Howden's [a contemporary chronicler] comments on the war of 1198, that it was waged more fiercely than ever, with Philip blinding prisoners and

Richard, unwillingly, retaliating in kind, applies to the aftermath of the French King's dip in the river Epte."

I have no direct evidence that Mercadier did actually blind any of his knightly prisoners after Gisors, but it might have been in keeping with his character—or rather the way his character was perceived by the chroniclers of the day, who usually depict him as a merciless villain. The frying-pan-wielding crossbowman who fatally wounded the King at Châlus-Chabrol, named variously as Bertrand de Gurdon, Peter Basil and Dudo in different accounts of the siege, was said to have been brought to Richard's deathbed after the castle had fallen. And the Lionheart, knowing he was doomed, repented of his sins and forgave the crossbowman and ordered that he be set free. However, once outside the royal pavilion, Mercadier had the unfortunate man taken up by his men, flayed alive and then hanged.

In my portrayal of the mercenary captain, I may, like the chroniclers of old, be doing him a disservice—and if so, I apologize to his ghost, and to his descendants: he was certainly an effective soldier, much feared by the enemies of his lord, and a man who carried out the brutal tactics of the day with a ruthless efficiency. It is always a mistake to judge the actions of people in the past by the moral standards of the present: in the twenty-first century, Mercadier would doubtless be viewed as a war criminal—but then so too would Richard the Lionheart.

Angus Donald
Kent, February 2012

Acknowledgments

There are a large number of people who deserve my gratitude for helping to bring this book into the light, but sadly I do not have time or space to name them all. However, the people mentioned below have been of particular help in ensuring that this copy of *Warlord* is now safely in your hands. Firstly I'd like to mention my brilliantly efficient agents at Sheil Land Associates, Ian Drury and Gaia Banks, who have been so supportive during the making of this book. I'd also like to thank the talented editorial team at Sphere—Daniel Mallory, Thalia Proctor, and Anne O'Brien—and the many others in the Little, Brown family who have been so kind, helpful, and enthusiastic: Carleen Peters, Sally Wray, Rhiannon Smith, Sarah Shrubb, Darren Turpin, and Felice Howden.

I owe a very large debt of thanks to the historian Professor John Gillingham for his magnificent *Richard I*, which I used as the main source for the historical parts of *Warlord*; and, for the second part of my story, which is set in Paris, I am very grateful to John W. Baldwin for his book *Paris, 1200* and also to the wonderfully named Urban Tigner Holmes, Junior, for *Daily Living in the Twelfth Century: Based on the Observations of Alexander Neckam in London and Paris*. Professor David Crouch was very helpful on the subject of Mercadier, and his riveting work *William Marshal: Knighthood, War and Chivalry, 1147–1219* has also been of enormous value to me over the years. Finally, Professor Joseph Goering's *The Virgin and the Grail: Origins of a Legend* is by far the best book I've ever read on that subject, and I must confess that I lifted the Chretien de Troyes passage that Master Fulk reads aloud to Alan from its pages. (The passage that Goering himself quotes is a slight adaptation from an original translation by David Staines, included in his book *The Complete Romances of Chretien de Troyes*.)

My friend and former colleague Dr. Martyn Lobley was most obliging when consulted on certain medical matters—particularly in helping me to confirm that Alan could have survived his chest wound at the end of the second part of the book. He also pointed out that this plot device had already appeared in Ian Fleming's *Dr. No.* I don't think I've read that book and I can't remember the film all that well, but the idea was out there before I used it and it may be that I subconsciously lifted the idea from Bond—if so, I'm sorry, Mr. Fleming, it was too good a wheeze to pass up.

While we are mentioning physical oddities—the idea for the split thumbs on Trois Pouces came from my time as a youthful beach-bum in Greece. I used to hang out at a small café in Crete in the mid-1980s and the kindly man who ran the place had this same condition. He used to give me credit when I was broke and always made sure, on the rare occasions that I went off to work picking tomatoes or cucumbers in the local greenhouses, that I had a hot drink and a thick piece of bread and jam inside me beforehand. Last time I visited the café, on a holiday with my wife a few years ago, I heard that he had died. So I'm lifting a cup of milky coffee to you, Costas. Thank you for the inspiration for Trois Pouces—and all those *marmalades*.